MW00888071

Belvedere

Aubrey Mayes

"To thine own self be true"— *William Shakespeare*
"That goes for everybody."— *Me*

Trigger Warnings Listed at Facebook.com/BelvedereTheSeries under Our Story.

Chapter 1

Estelle Presswood gave a satisfied sigh as she clicked her pen closed and took a moment to read over the paperwork she was about to hand in. Sitting cross-legged on the floor, her bright brown eyes surveyed the library's office, recounting the six large cardboard boxes that had replaced the piles of over two hundred books given to her that morning to sort and catalog. Feeling confident in her work, she stacked up the immensely heavy boxes of book donations, put the forms in the top box and hailed her supervisor's attention as she clocked out for the night.

"Hey, Paul! Everything's all set for the fundraiser. They should be here in the morning to pick everything up for transport to tomorrow's book sale at the main branch."

"Excellent! What would we do without you, Estelle?"

"Aww, thanks, Paul," she replied, buttoning her coat.

He watched her for a moment, taking in her fair, freckled complexion, her curved hips and her short, chocolate brown hair, and then said, "I was going to grab some dinner at Phil's Diner, wanna come along?"

Estelle brushed her dark bangs aside, trying to find the millionth way to tell him she wasn't interested. "That's okay— I was hoping to catch up with my book tonight. Thanks, th—"

"Catch up? You spend all your spare time reading. How about drinks this weekend?"

"Paul, we've been through this before," she said slowly, stepping closer to the door. "I don't like mixing my career with my personal life."

"What about Carolyn?" he asked, becoming instantly petulant.

Estelle struggled to keep her irritation hidden, and replied with an icy, "You're right, Paul. I did not stop talking to my best friend of a decade because we were transferred to the same library. Now please, try to understand that my relationship with you will always be professional."

He stood motionless in the office looking affronted, but she slung her purse over her shoulder and walked out with her head high. She waited in the cold air outside the library for Carolyn to emerge, and as she walked up to Estelle, Carolyn said, "You really should report that guy again."

"We'll see. One more time and I'll go straight to the board."

"Finally got him facing a camera?"

"Sure did. Hopefully now it won't matter whose nephew he is."

"Good! What are you up to tonight?" Carolyn asked, pulling her blonde hair into a ponytail as they walked to her car.

"Just the usual."

"Come on, Estelle. Why not come to dinner with me? I hate that you go there."

"Really? I had no idea. Three months of you telling me that everyday gave me absolutely NO indication—"

"Hysterical."

"Relax. They have the best espresso in the city, and I love my spot at the bar. It's not too warm or cold, I can focus on my book and still have the option of people watching in the mirrors." Granted, she never looked up from her book long enough to people watch— but she kept that thought to herself.

"AND it's owned and run by Don Libera himself. You're giving money directly to the Mafia."

"So are our tax dollars, but you don't see me blowing off the IRS."

Carolyn sighed, once again defeated with reality— there wasn't a public office in the city that wasn't swayed by Libera. "I know you're right. I just don't like it."

"You don't like the unpredictable," Estelle prodded.

"That I don't. Just... be careful, all right?"

"I always am. But once again, I'd like to remind you that nothing's happened at Libera's while I've been there. Or ever, for that matter. It's always the same old, same old. Try not to worry so much."

After Carolyn's departure, Estelle started out on the half-block trek towards her beloved nighttime routine. Thankful the cold walk was short, she came up on the familiar glass-front façade under the glowing sign reading

LIBERA'S FINE ITALIAN FOOD* WINE* COCKTAILS* ESPRESSO.

She looked through the window and took a quick inventory of the people inside to make sure Paul didn't "accidentally" decide to go to the same place she visited every night after work. She instead saw a fair smattering of customers— a pleasant cocktail of usual faces with a handful of newcomers looking nervously delighted in the food before them, as well as the typical wait staff and bartender. And there, as always, in the back, corner booth was Don Benedict Libera.

Libera was tall with dark hair that was streaked with gray, and he was remarkably fit for a man in his early fifties. He was wearing a gray Prada suit, and his dark eyes would light up as he laughed, but they were known to become equally as cold when business called for it. He sat in the corner, which not only gave him a clear visual of the majority of the dining room, it also extended his peripheral vision in the mirrored walls. He was entertaining a few associates over cocktails and cheesecake— all of whom were laughing respectfully with their Patron.

As she walked through the jingling door, she looked up at her usual, beloved seat at the end of the bar, but instead of a comforting empty space, saw the back of a dark, expensive looking suit, and shiny, dark, expensive looking hair. She sighed softly, trying to decide on a different bar chair to occupy for the evening before hearing a warm, polite voice say, "Excuse me, Miss. I believe I'm in your seat."

She looked around and recognized the man talking to her, but only by sight— and reputation. His name was Simone Belvedere, and he was Don Libera's top lieutenant. He was known for an exceptional ability to negotiate coupled with a short temper and an equally good shot. This was all rumor and speculation, of course, as nothing had ever been proven.

"That's all right," she said, feeling as though his reputation was supposed to make her find him fearsome and intimidating, rather than polite, handsome and immaculately dressed.

"I'd hate to interfere with your routine. I just lost track of time," he said, pulling the chair out for her and motioning towards it.

"I hadn't realized you'd noticed me," she heard herself say, feeling immediately trite.

"Anyone would notice such a beautiful woman across the bar from them every night. You beat me there every night for a week, so I switched to the other side." Simone looked down, trying to hide his self-conscious gaze.

Estelle smiled, charmed both by his remembering her and his embarrassment at admitting such. With a flirtatious smirk she said, "So really, I've been in your seat."

He laughed gently and motioned again for her to take the coveted chair. "Never."

As she sat down, Simone looked up and saw Libera gesturing for his attention.

"Excuse me—" he said, pausing inquisitively.

"Estelle."

"Excuse me, Estelle," he said with a small nod and a half-smile that she found more intoxicating than anything behind the bar.

She smiled to herself as he walked away and caught the bartender's eye. He adjusted his trendy, rectangular glasses and asked, "Double espresso with cream?"

'Thank you, Stephen."

"You know," he started quietly with a quick glance around, "I've been here for two years and have NEVER seen that before."

"What's that?" she asked, intrigued.

He ran a hand over his dark, curly hair and said, "Belvedere. In the whole time I've been here, never ONCE has he approached a girl. Just sits there and reads."

"We apparently have that in common," she said, feeling both confident for being different and noticed, and surprised that he hadn't been picking up women at the bar. *It's like shooting gold digging fish in a couture barrel*, she thought.

As Stephen pulled her espresso shots over an ounce of cream, she looked down and, with a gasp of delighted surprise, saw that Simone had left his book at the bar.

"I haven't read this in years!" It was her favorite book, and without hesitation, she gave into her curiosity and picked up 'A Midsummer Night's Dream,' opening it to where the page was turned down.

> *"Over hill, over dale,*
> *Thorough bush, thorough brier,*
> *Over park, over pale,*
> *Thorough flood, thorough fire,*
> *I do wander everywhere,*
> *Swifter than the moon's sphere;*
> *And I serve the fairy queen,*
> *To dew her orbs upon the green.*
> *The cowslips tall her pensioners be:*
> *In their gold coats spots you see;*
> *Those be rubies, fairy favours…"*

"Thanks!" she said, taking a sip from the cup he placed in front of her. "It's perfect!"

Stephen smiled as he walked away to refill a draft beer halfway down the bar.

> *"In those freckles live their savours:*
> *I must go seek some dewdrops here*
> *And hang a pearl in every cowslip's ear.*
> *Farewell, thou lob of spirits; I'll be gone:*
> *Our queen and all our elves come here anon."*

"Nothing compliments the bitter notes of espresso like Shakespeare."

Estelle looked up to see Simone intrigued at how brazenly unafraid she was of him. She closed the book and gave an enticing laugh before saying, "Very well said, Mr. Belvedere."

His eyes narrowed for a split second, as if trying to decide if she were making fun of him. "I know 'Midsummer' is a bit of a cliché, but it's my favorite," he said softly.

"Mine, too!"

"Is that so?" he asked, grinning at her genuine excitement. Estelle took a moment to appreciate his attractiveness before saying, "Would you care to join me?"

Simone looked visibly shocked for an instant. There were usually two kinds of women in Libera's— those afraid of him, and those wanting to buy his scotch and assuming a one-night stand would buy them expensive gifts in return. He smiled and, sounding calmer than he felt, said, "I'd love to."

He nodded to Stephen for his usual scotch and gave a false but convincing half-smile of confidence to Libera, who was grinning and watching with blunt interest in the mirror behind the bar.

"So, Estelle—?"

"Presswood," she supplied.

"Estelle Presswood," he said. "You come here after work?"

"I do. I'm a librarian for the branch down the street."

"That sounds amazing. I spent a lot of time in classics there as a child."

"Oh?"

"I did. I've always preferred classic literature to modern fiction— or people for that matter."

"I feel the same way!"

Drinking in her nearly palpable interest, he said, "So you enjoy your job then?"

"Oh my, yes. Being surrounded by books is how I expect regular people feel when surrounded by their families at Christmas."

As he laughed appreciatively, she thought, *god, this is a handsome man. And he is so sweet— never would have imagined...*

"Excuse me, Mr. Belvedere," Stephen began slowly, "Another?"

"No, thank you. I will, however, join this charming woman in another espresso if she'll oblige."

"I'd love to."

Stephen hurried away, doing his best to disguise his shocked look as just "busy."

They continued to talk for nearly two hours and a third, but decaf, espresso. As she took the last sip, she was surprised to see the mildly foreboding figure of Benedict Libera walking towards them.

"Hello, Miss," he said, shaking her hand. "It looks like my boy here has pulled you away from your book tonight."

She didn't fully understand why, but she felt like Simone should somehow feel insulted. "He certainly did. And I hope," she said, standing and opening her purse to leave a twenty-dollar bill on the bar, "that he will again, very soon."

Simone cocked his head with polite surprise at her candidness with his Patron. "Th-thank you, Estelle, I'd like that, also."

"Good night, Mr. Belvedere. And to you, Mr. Libera," she finished, as she turned and left. Simone watched her leave, entranced by her lack of apprehension with himself and Libera, and marveling at how much enjoyment he had gotten from a social conversation—which was something that he generally avoided.

"What the hell just happened?" Libera asked, with an incredulous look on his face and a condescending punch to Simone's arm.

Simone laughed politely and said, "I honestly have no idea, but I sincerely hope it happens again."

Libera laughed and struck Simone's arm again with the air of someone halfway between father and older brother. "I bet you do, Simone. It's about time you—" he stopped talking as Stephen set down two rocks glasses, each filled halfway with high-end scotch and exactly three ice cubes. "You know I hate to bring you back down to work, but something's arisen that I need you to take care of first thing tomorrow."

Simone took a polite sip with his Patron before saying, "Of course, sir."

He noticed a gleam in Libera's eye that implied he very much enjoyed bringing Simone an important job after a few hours of distraction. "What can I do for you?"

Libera smiled arrogantly at Simone's outward devotion and said, "Ben Tomlinson."

"The guy that owns the used car lot?"

"The very same."

"What do you—?"

"He approached me today, very interested in the offer I made him last week, but he's still unconvinced. I need you to complete the transaction."

"Of course. How much time?"

"Three days, and then we send Landini to check on things. Go—get some sleep. See him first thing tomorrow. I want you here to report back by noon."

"Of course. Good night, sir."

Libera nodded, giving Simone's arm a pat, silently dismissing him for the evening.

Chapter 2

The next morning, Simone walked into Tomlinson's Used Auto Sales, just across the furthest parking lot for Libera's most popular casino, Athena. He leaned on the reception desk and gave the receptionist an arrogant half-smile, saying, "I have a meeting with Ben Tomlinson."

"Of course, Mr. Belvedere. Go right in."

"Thank you."

He tapped his hand twice, palm flat, against the desk and went into the office just to the right of the entrance. Knocking twice on the door, he said, "Hello, Ben."

Ben Tomlinson was a short, balding man, just over forty. He was wearing a navy, department store suit and stood, motioning for the chair across his desk. "Mr. Belvedere, it's good to see you."

"And you," Simone said, unbuttoning his Armani jacket and taking the indicated seat. "Mr. Libera tells me that you're interested in selling your lot to us."

"I am," Tomlinson replied, eyes only looking halfway convinced of his own words.

"If you have any reservations, I'd be happy to work with you."

"This lot's by far my biggest earner, and losing that would force business to move elsewhere, and this isn't exactly an industry that sees a lot of brand loyalty. If the percentage of customers I receive based purely on location are forced to shop elsewhere, it would most likely be with a competitor down the street, rather than my other locations across town."

"A perfectly understandable concern," Simone said, accepting the cigarette Tomlinson was offering and lighting it. "However, you would be gaining a royalty fee from the business done in the casino, which I'm sure would make up for a large part of those losses. I actually have the preliminary papers with me, if you'd be interested in seeing them. Of course, you are in no way obligated—"

"No, I'd very much like to take a look at them. Thank you."

Simone nodded his head and took a set of tri-folded papers from the breast pocket of his jacket, before tapping his cigarette against the crystal ash tray on Tomlinson's desk.

After several moments of silently watching Tomlinson reading the document, Simone said, "As you can see, your stipend would be the equivalent of your average month's sales."

"But that would lower the profit line in the long run, assuming that my most profitable months stayed steady."

"Perhaps. It would, however, eliminate the risk that your average and top months would fall, ensuring that you were making a clean profit every month."

Tomlinson's interest was palpably clear in his eyes as he looked up at Simone. "That it would."

"We would also be willing to hire any staff that you couldn't relocate, as well as offering severance packages to those uninterested in the jobs available thanks to the growth this expansion would bring to the casino. On top of that, your property would be adding around a hundred more jobs to the area, and that's in addition to the twelve we'd employ from you, assuming they all came to work for us."

"How preliminary is this document?"

Simone half-smiled. "You sound interested."

"I sincerely am. My biggest concerns are clearly already alleviated, and I admit, taking the risk out of part of my profit stream is immensely appealing."

"You don't need to have your lawyer look over the document?"

Tomlinson laughed. "You mean the bottom dollar lawyer I found in the phone book? No, I can wholeheartedly assume that your lawyer was more than capable of taking care of this."

Simone inclined his head in gratitude and let the end of his cigarette burn itself out in the crystal. "Do you need any of the contract's terms clarified?"

"I don't."

"And you do understand that signing this document is providing the immediate sale of the property, giving you ninety days to relocate before Mr. Libera's contractor takes control of the property, with no option to withdraw?"

"I do."

Simone took a pen from the pocket that previously held the documents and handed it to Tomlinson, who signed them and said, "Please pass along my thanks to Don Libera."

"I shall."

"And thank you, Mr. Belvedere, for taking the time out to clarify everything."

With one last half-smile, Simone said, "Not at all, Mr. Tomlinson. We're glad to be doing business with you."

Chapter 3

As Joel, Simone's companion and immediate subordinate, parked Simone's polished Mercedes outside of Libera's restaurant, Simone double checked that everything in the contract was taken care of and stowed the papers safely back in his jacket.

"I can't believe he signed it today," Joel said, looking across the top of the car as they both stood and buttoned their suit jackets.

"To be honest, neither can I. Who signs away their property without having their lawyer look at it first?"

Joel just laughed and shook his head, before waving to Simone as they parted ways. Joel walked around to the front of the building, entering into the restaurant, and Simone knocked twice on Libera's back office door before walking inside, as always.

Libera looked up at Simone, and then back down at his watch. "You've been gone an hour and a half."

Simone said nothing, but half-smiled and took the papers from his jacket pocket, dropping them onto Libera's desk. Libera smirked and said, "That's my boy." He opened up the contract and initialed next to the signatures, before saying, "Have a seat."

"I have an odd feeling that he may try to renege, but it doesn't matter. He's already signed it, there's nothing he can do now."

"What makes you say that?"

"He was nervous when I came in, but then calmed down when he started looking at the numbers. Once the novelty of the profit wears off, I'm worried he'll go back to being nervous and try to back out."

"Well, as you said, there's nothing he can do now. He knew what he was doing?"

"Explicitly."

"Good. How long until we can take it over?"

"Ninety days. I doubt he'd take that long, though. The way his numbers look, next month would be the prime window to close up."

"Even the full ninety keeps us on schedule with the build, though."

"It does."

"Good work, Simone."

"Thank you, sir. I take it I now need to start setting plans for the build in motion?"

"Absolutely. The quicker we can get this done, the quicker we'll see the turnaround."

"I'll take care of it."

Libera smiled at Simone for a moment and said, "I know you will."

Chapter 4

"I'm so glad the library sale happens every year," Carolyn said, as she and Estelle sat down for lunch at Phil's Diner. "A paid day off, PLUS we know that Paul's busy at the sale across town!"

"I'll drink to that!" Estelle said, raising her water. "How was your night last night?"

"Not bad. Ordered some Chinese and watched Hairspray again. What about you?"

"Just the same as always..." Estelle said, trying to hide her inner excitement by taking another drink of water.

"YOU met someone!"

"No, it's—"

"You NEVER blush— you must REALLY like this guy!" She leaned in and dramatically whispered, "It's not Paul, is it?"

"Oh god, no. He's— no— I don't want to jinx it."

"Come on— did you meet him at Libera's?"

"I did."

"Oh my god, who is he?"

"I told you, I don't want to jinx it."

"You have to tell me something."

Estelle sat for a second and bit her bottom lip as she smiled and replayed the previous evening in her head. "Well, he's absolutely gorgeous. Dresses REALLY well."

"Oh, come on, Estelle, we both know he has to be more than just attractive for you to be into him."

"He's intelligent. Sophisticated. Doesn't just act like he wants a one-night thing. We talked for two hours about the book he was reading when I came in."

"So, when's the wedding?" Carolyn asked, titling her head to the side.

"Please, I just met the man."

"What book was he reading?"

Estelle bit her lip again before saying, "*A Midsummer Night's Dream*."

"Yep. You're marrying him."

Chapter 5

Simone was sitting in the bar at Libera's, directly across from Estelle's usual reading spot. His normally undisturbed focus was struggling to remain on the pages in his hands, rather than the door he'd been subconsciously glancing at, wondering if Estelle would be back for her usual espresso, or if she would be scared off now that she'd had time to think about their conversation and fully realize who she'd been talking to.

A strong hand on his shoulder pulled him out of these thoughts, however, and he looked up to see Libera standing next to him.

"Yes, sir?"

"You called it."

Simone thought for a moment and said, "Tomlinson?"

Nodding, Libera said, "He's here. Wants his fee increased to cover the transition and the relocation costs."

Simone gave a humorless laugh and said, "That'll happen."

"My thoughts exactly. I'll cover half of the relocation, and I'm willing to increase his fee by five percent. No more."

"Yes, sir. Where is he?"

"Outside. I'll have Paolo send him in to you."

Simone nodded and stood, catching Stephen's eye.

"Usual, Mr. Belvedere?"

"No, thanks, though. Listen," he started, taking a fifty dollar bill out of his pocket and putting it into the bartender's hand. "I'm about to start a meeting, hopefully won't take very long. If she comes in, bring a scotch over to the table I'm at?"

"Yes, sir, thank you," Stephen said, smiling gently and pocketing the bill.

Simone tapped his palm twice on the bar top and went over to an empty table, tapping his thumb impatiently as he waited for Tomlinson. It wasn't long, however, before Tomlinson approached him, holding up a hand in a nervous wave.

"Please, have a seat," Simone said, being careful to keep his voice hospitable.

Tomlinson took the indicated seat, setting down the pocket notebook he was carrying. "I'm sorry if I interrupted—"

"Not at all. What can I do for you?"

"I'm concerned about the interim and relocation costs."

"I see. Did we miss something when we ran the numbers for you?"

"No, of course not," Tomlinson said quickly, afraid of offending the organization. "I just failed to consider it before signing."

"I see," Simone said, tilting his head to the side, considering the man before him. "What is it that you need?"

Before Tomlinson could answer, Simone looked up and half-smiled as Stephen set a glass of scotch in front of him. "One second," Simone said, putting a light hand on Stephen's arm.

"Yes, sir?"

Simone pulled the napkin from under his glass and the pen from his jacket pocket, and quickly scribbled out a note, folding it and putting it into Stephen's hand. Stephen said nothing, but smiled and nodded, before returning to the bar.

"My apologies," Simone said, looking back at Tomlinson. "What is it that you need?"

Tomlinson tore half a page from his notebook and hastily wrote down an offer, sliding it across the table. Simone picked up the paper fragment and, without changing his expression, laughed inwardly at the ten percent written and stowed it in his jacket, shaking his head.

"Mr. Libera was very clear about the terms of the agreement he gave to me," Simone said, leaning forward. "And he won't even consider what you've presented. But here's what I can do. I understand that the relocation is costing you, and I understand how inconvenient that can be. May I?"

He nodded towards Tomlinson's notebook, and once Tomlinson had nodded, Simone began writing, but then looked up as Stephen returned, handing him the napkin he had just sent. He opened the note and felt an unfamiliar flutter in his chest as he read, not Estelle's words, but Shakespeare's. "My apologies again," he said, looking up at Tomlinson, who waved his hand.

"You're a busy man, Mr. Belvedere. I appreciate you taking the time to see me at all."

Simone nodded politely as he finished writing and said, "What if I take this to him, and see if he can be persuaded?" He passed the notebook back to Tomlinson, who tilted his head, intrigued by the proposition.

"And Mr. Libera would agree to that?"

"Potentially," Simone said carefully. "I can take it to him tonight, and someone can bring you an answer tomorrow morning."

"Thank you, Mr. Belvedere. I'd greatly appreciate that."

"My pleasure," Simone said, half-smiling.

Tomlinson tore the page with the new figure out of his notebook and handed it to Simone, who stood and reached out his hand. "We'll talk soon," he said, as Tomlinson accepted the handshake and nodded, before turning and walking out of the restaurant.

Simone made his way to Libera's corner booth, and set the piece of paper down in front of his Patron. Libera laughed and gave an approving punch to Simone's arm, before motioning for him to be seated.

"A third of relocation and three percent?"

"Yes, sir."

"Tomlinson's easily pleased," Libera said, picking up the scotch bottle in front of him and pouring a few ounces for Simone.

"Or easily intimidated," Simone mused, lifting the glass to his lips. "Maybe send Al in the morning with the addendum, make sure he knows we're done playing his way?"

"Works for me." Libera took a sip from his own glass and looked at Simone for a moment before saying, "She waiting for you?"

Simone half-smiled and looked down into his glass. "She is."

"Go. I'll let you know when Al gets here."

"Thank you, sir."

Libera nodded and watched as Simone stood and buttoned his jacket, taking a reassuring breath.

"Don't be so nervous," Libera said, leaning back against the booth. "She's already hooked."

"I wish it were that simple, sir."

Simone started to walk away, but stopped as he felt his Patron's hand on his arm. "It is that simple, Simone."

Chapter 6

The library sale having given her the day off, Estelle perfectly timed the trip from her apartment and walked into Libera's hoping, for the first time, that her seat was occupied. She was disappointed, however, to see that the only people at the bar were the bartender and a pair of barely college-age girls nursing their pink cocktails, so she set her things down in the next seat and sat in her favorite place, pulling *1984* out of her bag. She looked up to try to catch the bartender's eye for her drink, but Stephen had already gone to see to another customer.

She opened the worn-out book to where she had left off and immediately lost herself in the story in an attempt to tune out the giggles of the tipsy students across from her. A few pages in, Stephen tapped the bar with his fingers to get her attention without startling her and set down a freshly pulled espresso. "Thanks for remembering!" she said, pulling it towards her.

"I also have this for you," he said, setting down a cocktail napkin that had been folded in half.

"What is—?"

Stephen chuckled and said, "I didn't read it. I was just asked to deliver it."

Estelle pulled the corner of her bottom lip under her teeth to try to hide her smile as she read the simple message.

"I'll be free soon. May I join you?"

She looked up at Stephen, who made a nonchalant nod to the left of the girls across from her. She followed his nod with her eyes and saw Simone at a table with a man she didn't recognize. They were having an inaudible discussion, and after a moment, the unknown man wrote down a figure and passed it to Simone, who put the paper slip into the breast pocket of his jacket and shook his head in simple disagreement.

She took a sip of her espresso and smiled up at Stephen, who handed her the pen from his shirt pocket. She thought for a second and wrote,

"No more yielding, but a dream."

Estelle folded the napkin in half and handed it back to Stephen, and her eyes followed him in the mirror behind the bar, carefully watching until she saw the corner of Simone's mouth twitch as he read it and resumed his conversation. Feeling confident in her move, she decided to go back to her book and espresso, and, a discrete glance in the mirror at a time, she began to take in more of Simone's features.

Everything about him seemed to be so careful and deliberate. His slicked backed hair was dark, like the soft, black wool of his Armani suit. His deep brown eyes were impossible to read, but the cavalier half-smile that came with conquering the negotiator was unmistakable. His manners were impeccable, and he took care to offend no one, including the wait-staff. He rose and shook hands with the man he'd been conferring with, and then went to join his Patron at the corner table, who, upon reading the newest figure, tapped Simone's arm in approval and poured a drink.

Feeling it was best to avoid glancing at the corner table, she resumed her book, and after another chapter, she felt a remarkably gentle hand on her arm.

"Sorry to keep you waiting," Simone said.

She set her book upside-down on the bar and confidently simpered up at him. "I don't mind waiting."

Stephen brought over a scotch and set it down in front of Simone.

"Thank you, Stephen. Another espresso, Estelle?"

"Oh, you don't have to—"

"By all means, for keeping you waiting."

"Thank you, Mr. Belvedere," she said with a flirtatious air.

"Of course." Looking at the cover of her book, he lifted his drink to his lips and said, "I see you enjoy light and cheerful reading."

"Oh, yes. Nothing like a few totalitarian spies to perk your night up."

As he laughed and took another sip of his drink, she was mesmerized at how easy it was to talk to him. He was so different from all the things she had heard buzzing around the city.

"I'd ask if this is your first time reading it," Simone pointed out, "but it looks like the cover'll fall off soon."

"You know, I actually had that happen once," she started, resting against her elbows on the bar. "Not with this though— that was a Salinger."

He laughed again, relaxing. "Mine was HG Wells."

"Time Machine?"

He shook his head. "Invisible Man. Much better."

"Oh, that one is fantastic. A lot of people coming into the library dismiss it because it's so widely known, but it's definitely a classic for a reason. I think classics are always the right way to go."

"Absolutely." Simone watched as she thanked Stephen and took a sip from the still-hot espresso he had just brought over. His thoughts began to get the better of him, rapidly invading his mind in the few seconds it took her to flip her book over and dog-ear the page, putting it back into her bag. *Should I really be doing this? She is so intelligent. So different. So beautiful. I could never be enough for her...*

"Still working on *Midsummer*?" she asked, pulling him out of his thoughts.

"I always make sure that book's never finished. I am enjoying Shelley at the moment, as well, though."

"*Frankenstein?*"

"Of course."

"I've been meaning to get around to that one. How is it?"

"Very interesting. Dark, of course, but very interesting."

Before she could reply, one of Simone's associates came over and touched Simone's arm. He leaned back to hear the whispered words, before nodding and placing his nearly empty glass on the bar. "Thank you, Marco." He turned to look at Estelle and said, "I'm sorry, it looks like I'm needed again."

"Not at all. It was good to see you again, Mr. Belvedere." She reached for a handshake, and was delightfully taken aback when he lifted her hand and gently kissed it.

"I hope to see you again soon."

With another half-smile, he turned and headed over to Libera's table. Estelle smiled as she stood to put on her coat, lost in blissful thought. *Yes. Classics are always the right way to go.*

Chapter 7

Glad to be off for the weekend, Estelle walked into Libera's for her Friday night glass of wine. As she pulled out her favorite chair, Stephen came up to her. "Moscato?"

"You're the best!"

"I think I have something that can change your mind about that," Stephen said, smirking as he reached under the bar and set a glossy, new paperback book in front of her. "He asked me to give you this."

Estelle exhaled sharply as she picked up the copy of *Frankenstein* that Simone had left for her and ran her fingers over the slick cover before opening it, dropping a folded note onto the polished bar top. "And that's how it's done..." Stephen said, impressed with Simone's approach as he went to retrieve Estelle's wine.

She opened the note, pulse quickening from excitement.

> *Estelle,*
> *I'm sorry I missed you tonight. I hope you enjoy the book, and I hope that we can discuss it over dinner tomorrow night. I'll be here at 7— hoping you will as well.*
>
> *Simone*

She refolded the note and placed it in the middle of the book, awaiting its new duty of bookmark. *Looks like I've got some catching up to do,* she thought.

The next night was Estelle's first trip to Libera's on a Saturday. It was busier than she was used to, and several heads turned as she made her way to the bar in her favorite plum dress, that was cut just low enough to draw attention to her floating diamond pendant. "So, do you live here?" Estelle asked Stephen as she approached the bar.

"Nah, just filling in for someone else— her kid's sick."

"I'm sorry to hear that."

"It's all good," Stephen said. "He's got a table towards the back for you."

She followed the bartender to the back corner, opposite Libera's permanently occupied table. It was far enough away from Libera and the bar to have a small sense of privacy, but close enough to other tables as to not be completely isolated. *He's thought of everything,* she thought as Stephen pulled the chair facing away from the dining room out for her. "Moscato?"

"Sounds wonderful. Thank you."

"My pleasure. He's just finishing up with something, but it shouldn't take long."

"No worries at all," she said, wondering if taking her book out would be inappropriate. "Do you know about how long—?"

"I'm sure you can get a few pages in," Stephen said, smirking.

"You know me so well," she said, pulling her book out of her handbag.

As Stephen predicted, she was about five pages in when she felt Simone place his hand on her shoulder. "I'd apologize for keeping you waiting, but it looks like you're getting to the good part." As he sat down across from her, back to the corner of the room, he said genuinely, "You look wonderful."

"Thank you!" she said, blushing. "And thank you so much for the book! It was so sweet of you."

"I couldn't resist. I take it you're enjoying it?"

"Absolutely! I'm nearly halfway through it!"

"As am I."

"You read a lot, then?" she asked.

"Just about any time that I'm not working. I like keeping several books going at a time in different places, because I don't carry them with me."

"That's why I never buy a small purse. If it doesn't fit a book, it doesn't come home."

She smiled at his gentle laugh as the server brought their menus over. "Thank you, Mandy."

"My pleasure, Mr. Belvedere. I'll be at the bar when you need me."

"You know I've never actually eaten here before?" Estelle said, picking up her menu.

"In all the time you've been coming here?"

"Never! I needed a place out of the rain on a walk home from work a few months ago, so I came in for an espresso, and I've been back most weeknights since."

"I've noticed."

She took a sip of wine and said, "So why have I not run into you before this week?"

"I like to keep to myself. Keeps my mind free to notice other things. Shall I call Mandy back?"

Taking note of the change of subject, she nodded and decided it was best to avoid discussing his work. Ninety minutes and two courses later, they had discussed her work and several books, and Estelle couldn't believe that the man across from her was the same man she'd heard the rumors about. He was polite, gentle, and complimentary—

and had read more books than anyone else she had ever met. She hated to see the night end so soon, so she said, "I have a wonderful local wine collection. If you'd like to walk me home, I'm sure I can find something you'd like."

His expression was infuriatingly unreadable, but after a brief moment of consideration he said, "I'd love to."

As they rose and walked towards the door, she noticed that the customers took little notice of them, but the small group at Libera's table hushed as they passed by, grinning like schoolboys on the playground.

As they exited the restaurant, Simone laughed nervously and said, "Tomorrow morning's going to be interesting."

"They looked as though they'd never seen two people leave the place together."

"Oh, they have. Just not when I'm one of them."

"Oh?"

"No, I don't do this much."

"Well, Mr. Belvedere, you're very good at it."

He gave a nervous laugh and said, "I assure you, it's the company." Taking out a cigarette, he asked, "Will it bother you?"

"Not in the slightest," Estelle said truthfully.

She smiled and pushed her hair behind her ear. They continued talking about their shared book for the rest of the ten-minute journey, and only stopped when Estelle said, "This is me," as they approached her apartment building.

They entered the elevator, and as she hit the button for the tenth floor, she was surprised to notice that he seemed nervous. *How is such an intelligent, attractive man so nervous? I wonder why…*

"Here we are," she said as she unlocked her door and turned on the light. "It's not much, but it has an amazing view!"

"It certainly does," Simone said, taking in the breathtaking view of the bright lights of the skyline against the black sky.

"Red or white?" Estelle asked, walking over to her wine rack.

"What do you prefer?" he inquired.

"Well, I always love the Moscato from this local vineyard, but I have a nice European Pinot Noir as well. It's nice if you're not in the mood for anything too sweet."

"Dry sounds perfect."

She smiled, opened the bottle, and poured them each a glass. "Make yourself at home," she said, handing him his glass and sitting on the pale blue sofa that looked out towards the skyline, rather than at the television across the room.

He unbuttoned his suit jacket and took the seat next to her. Looking around at her full shelves, he said, "You have quite the extensive collection."

"I'll never have enough," she said, looking at Simone, who was still taking in her personal library. "I've had a wonderful time with you tonight," she said softly, slipping her shoes off and leaning her head on the couch.

"As have I."

As she hoped, Simone began to relax and they were back to the comfortable conversation of Libera's. They continued to talk through the rest of the bottle of wine and, before long, Simone realized how close they had moved together. She was sitting facing him, knees bent under her, mere centimeters away from him. She was close enough that he could smell her Chanel perfume, and he found himself taking in the bright brown of her irises more than her words.

"Are you all right?" she asked when he didn't respond to her question.

"Of course. I'm sorry. I got…caught up… I suppose."

She leaned forward and said, "I'm glad I'm not the only one."

This can't be happening, Simone thought. *I can't let this happen.* She leaned her head forward, so her forehead rested lightly on his. He could feel that she was breathing as quickly as he was— and there was nothing he longed for more than to feel her lips on his. They stayed that way for several minutes, brow to brow, passionate energy building between them. He closed his eyes, trying to find the rational decision that was slipping further and further away. He felt his hand move up into her hair as if of its own accord, and as she brought her torso forward ever so slightly, he felt his concealed shoulder-rig holster brush against his chest. Instantly, every reason he had for keeping his distance came sprinting back to him. He moved his head so that his right temple was against her left. Still with his hand in her hair, he said, "I'm sorry, I can't do this."

"I'm sorry— I pushed too fast—"

"No!" he said quickly, pulling back. "No— you were… I'm just…" He took a moment to compose his thoughts. "My life is just so— uncertain. I have no right to put any of that on anyone."

She gave him a sad, but comforting smile. "I understand."

There was a heavy pause— neither finding the right words to put the other— or themselves— at ease. Simone put his elbow against the arm of the couch, staring intently into the last of the wine in his glass. Finally, Estelle smiled, nodded towards the polished chrome peeking out of Simone's jacket and said, "You can take that off if you want to."

"I'm all right."

"You look uncomfortable."

"People tend to get…uneasy… when I move it."

"I think I'll be okay."

He considered her for a moment; not out of distrust, but out of disbelief. Quietly, he said, "You're really not afraid of me?"

"Should I be?"

He looked away, staring out at the skyline. "Everyone else seems to be."

"I'm not everyone else."

Looking back at her, he said, "No. You're not."

His eyes narrowed for a moment, worried that he was leading her on, but not wanting to bring the evening to a close— especially on such an uncomfortable note. Reaching into his jacket and outside of his comfort zone, he pulled out his extensively customized weapon and laid it gently on the coffee table, before removing his jacket and holster.

"Feel better?" she asked.

"I do, thanks," he replied, despite the nerves starting to creep back into his voice.

Estelle nodded towards the coffee table. "Taurus?"

He sat looking at her for a stunned moment, before laughing loudly. "Yes— the 99. How… how the hell did you know that?"

She leaned back with a triumphant smile and said, "It's what they used in the '96 Romeo and Juliet."

He tilted his head, half-smile returning. "You know I have associates that have to ask what it is…I didn't realize it was in the film— I haven't seen it since it was released."

"Would you like to see it again? I can put it on if you'd like. Just as friends, of course."

He smiled at the compassion in her tone and replied, "I'd like that very much."

Chapter 8

The next morning, an exhausted Simone made his way into the office at the back of Libera's.

"Morning, Simone," Libera said. "Late night?"

"A bit. What do you have for me today?"

Libera gave Simone a mischievous smirk. "So, just business as usual? Nothing interesting to talk about?"

Simone gave a polite smile, hiding his irritation. "There's nothing to tell, sir. Nothing happened."

"You're not talking about that girl you left with last night?" a lower level associate named Paolo Bassi asked, walking into the room along with Libera's accountant, Dante Gallo, who was followed by Simone's enforcer, Joel Fontaine.

Irritation rising, Simone replied, "Yes, Paolo. I am." He turned back to look at Libera, who had taken his seat with Gallo and Joel. "She's just a good friend."

"Damn good friend, by the looks of her," Paolo said, tapping Simone's arm with a laugh. "Seriously, Belvedere, nothing happened?"

"I believe that's what I said, yes," Simone said, irritation finally bleeding out into the open.

"What? Didn't have the cash this week, Belvedere? Besides, it looked like she was practically giving it away—"

Everyone, including Libera, jumped to their feet as Simone threw Paolo up against the wall, hand tight around Paolo's throat.

"I'm sorry— what was that?" Simone hissed, less than an inch away from his subordinate's intimidated face.

"S-sor-sorry— no-nothing—" Paolo stammered, gasping for air.

"Try to show some fucking respect."

With a jerk, he let go of the already bruising throat, and Paolo slid an inch down the wall, bracing himself with his forearm. "Jesus Christ, Belvedere..." he muttered, catching his breath and pushing the furthest reach of Simone's patience. He grabbed Paolo by his collar and in one blow broke the young associate's nose and pushed him back up against the wall.

"What did I JUST SAY?" Simone yelled, before feeling a strong hand on his shoulder.

"That's enough." Libera's voice was final, and Simone let go of Paolo, refastening the emerald cufflink that had come undone.

"My apologies, Don Libera."

"I take it some of us have learned something important here, today," Libera said, dark amusement glistening in his eyes. "Paolo?"

"Yes, sir... 'pologies, Mr. Belvedere," Paolo said quickly, trying to gain control of his bleeding nose.

Simone said nothing, but glowered at him for a moment before looking to Libera and saying, "What can I do for you?"

"Phil Maxwell has expressed interest in the offer we made him last year, to take over his diner when he was tired of running it. I need you to accompany Gallo to negotiate the terms of the agreement."

"Of course, sir." He rose to leave, prompting Gallo to do the same.

"One minute, Simone. Will you boys excuse us?"

Gallo led Joel and Paolo out of Libera's office, closing the door behind them. "Sit."

Simone obeyed. "Sir, I am sincerely—"

"This isn't about Paolo. Little punk has had it coming for a while. No respect... No. This is about you. Here." Libera tossed Simone a handkerchief for the hand bleeding from the impact with Paolo's nose.

"Me, sir?" Simone asked, putting pressure on his knuckles.

"What's the matter with you?"

"I don't understand."

"I've known you longer and better than anyone. Yes?"

"That's right sir."

"I've kept my distance when it comes to your personal life, correct?"

"You do, yes."

"May I be blunt?"

"Of course, sir."

"She's not your mother, Simone."

Simone's eyes narrowed, but he said, "I don't know what you—"

"Don't play coy with me. Some people just aren't cut out for the business. Your mother didn't know what she was getting into with your father."

"I'm not sure he did, either," Simone said bitterly.

"That's very possible. But this girl— what's her name, again?"

Reluctant to continue the conversation, Simone sighed and said, "Estelle."

"Right. Estelle seems to know who you are. Probably better than you do. Don't underestimate her."

Simone stared out the window for a moment before saying, "I should get to Maxwell."

"Simone."

He begrudgingly looked back over at Libera and said, "I appreciate what you're saying, but with all due respect, sir, I know what I'm doing."

Libera nodded and said, "Just, think it over, all right?"

"Of course, sir."

Chapter 9

Two months had gone by since Estelle and Simone's first dinner together, and in the subsequent weeks they had begun having dinner together every few days, in addition to Estelle's continued routine at Libera's and the daily text messages they had begun to send each other. After another long day of shelving books and rebuking Paul's advances, Estelle was glad to see a message from Simone, asking her to dinner. Typing quickly, she replied,

> *I'd love to. How does Chinese at my place sound?*
>> *Perfect. 8:00 ok?*
> *Absolutely.*
>> *Wonderful. See you soon.*

When the buzzer sounded just before eight, she went downstairs, surprised to see that the Chinese food had arrived before Simone. She signed the slip for her credit card and went to open the door to head back upstairs, but as the delivery driver pulled away, she heard a car door close and looked up to see Simone crossing the street as his sleek, black Mercedes Benz Coupe pulled away.

"Perfect timing!" she said, smiling as he walked up.

"Thanks. I wanted to wait until he left to come up. Here, let me take that," he said, taking the Chinese bag as she unlocked the entryway door and held it open.

As they entered the elevator, she said, "Sorry— why did you wait?"

"I didn't want— I just thought it would be best to not make my presence known."

"And why is that?"

"I mean, I'm— you're not— I didn't want—" *Christ,* Simone thought. *I sound like an idiot.*

She unlocked her apartment and held the door open for him to set the food down on the coffee table. After closing and relocking the door, she said, "Why would you think I don't want to be seen with you?"

He thought for a moment, still tightly clutching onto the secret he was holding about Libera's office, unsure of how to answer her.

"What aren't you telling me?"

He sighed, unbuttoned his jacket and sat down. "Remember   the night we had dinner at Libera's, and as we left I said that the next morning would be interesting?"

"Of course, I do," she said, taking a seat next to him.

"Well, the next morning, the word going around that charming group we walked past was that you were…" he looked away and started on his food, trying to find a gentler word than the ones that were coming to him.

Estelle swallowed the bite she had just taken. "A hooker?"

"Well… yes… I'm sorry, Estelle."

"Why? I mean, I assume you told them I wasn't?"

"Oh, they were aware of that pretty quickly."

"Then what's the— hold on. How exactly were they made aware of this?"

Simone's eyes narrowed at her question, as though her words were actually physically painful. "That's not important… what is important—"

"Don't try to be cute with me, Simone Belvedere," she said, crossing her arms. The use of his full name caught him off guard, and he wasn't sure why he found it so titillating— and so disarming.

"Okay. I *may* have broken the guy's nose…"

She stared blankly at him for a moment before saying, "MAY have? Or DID?"

"May have…" he said, with his signature half-smile.

"You did NOT!" she said, starting to laugh. "Why would you do that?"

"There are just things that shouldn't be said to certain people. I don't pretend to be humble about my position."

"Nor would I expect you to. Not that I actually fully know what that is…"

"Few people do…" he said, without thinking.

"So, tell me. Complete honesty."

"Estelle—"

"Simone?"

What if she can't handle it? His fears were immediately followed by the memory of Libera's words— *Don't underestimate her.*

"I'm not going to judge you, Simone. I just want to know you better."

"You realize that I'd be breaking about six different rules, right?"

"Okay. I don't want you to get in trouble—"

He laughed. "I didn't say it would be a problem, I just said I'm not supposed to do it."

"Only if you want to."

He closed his eyes for a moment to consider what was going on. *I put this all away so long ago… what if I just can't connect with her like this?* Opening his eyes, he saw her patient, affirming gaze, and immediately knew that this was the time to open up to her.

Taking out his phone and working through the mixture of thrill and tranquility coming over him, he said, "If we're going to do this, I'm going to need a drink." He dialed and after a moment said, "Hi, Joel. Can you meet me at Estelle's in ten minutes with a bottle of Bowmore? Yeah... No, a new bottle from the bar... Thanks."

In response to her inquiring look, he set his phone on the table and said, "Joel works directly for me, and he has my car. Since he's coming from Libera's, it was just easier for him to bring it instead of me going to get it..."

"Makes sense," she said, smiling at the embarrassed underlining to his explanation. "Why does he have your car at Libera's? I thought he was always with you."

"Because I didn't want him sitting in it downstairs."

"Of course, what was I thinking?" Estelle said, deadpan.

As they continued eating, Simone's phone beeped, alerting him to Joel's presence.

"There's a spare key on the end table, if you want to take it," Estelle said.

"Thanks. I'll just be a minute."

After he closed the door behind him, she went to the kitchen and took out a highball glass for Simone and grabbed herself a long-stemmed glass and a new bottle of Moscato.

"Ice?" she asked, as he reentered the apartment several minutes later.

"Not tonight," he replied. "Thanks, though. I put your key back on the end table."

"Or you could keep it," she said, sitting on the floor at the coffee table and pouring herself a glass of wine.

"What?"

"That way you don't have to wait for me to come down when you get here. It eliminates the problem."

"You— are you sure?"

He joined her on the floor, and broke the seal on the new bottle of premium liquor. She took a sip from her glass and said, "I am."

"Why don't we talk about what I do," he started, pouring his scotch, "and then you can make that decision."

"If you insist."

"Maybe we should start with what you already know?" he suggested.

"All I know is what I've heard..."

"And what is that?"

"Are you sure? It's just gossip."

"Of course. It's always entertaining to hear what people are saying about me."

"Mostly that you're the only one that works directly under Libera, that you're easily pissed off, and that you've proven several times that you're an exceptionally good shot."

Simone laughed and said, "Well, it's not all wrong. I am directly under Libera, but it's not as simple as just a bunch of people reporting to someone. Libera comes to me almost exclusively when he needs negotiations. Everyone else comes to me when they need to go to Libera. Most of the time, the chain stops with me. Everybody thinks they need the top, when they don't."

He stopped and drained his glass before continuing, "And I am a damn good shot, but that experience came from years of training at a range, which is probably what started the rumors in the first place. As for being easily pissed off, I'm really not. It's just the times I do lose my temper that make it around, rather than the rest of the time that I don't. I don't act without just cause."

"And what exactly is just cause?"

"Why don't we work up to that one and come back to it?" he said, pouring a few more ounces into his glass. "Also, for the record, I want you to know that I don't normally drink this much. It just eases my... conversational... anxiety."

"I can't believe you have conversational anxiety," Estelle said, refilling her own glass.

"Just socially. I'm fine when I'm somewhere with a clear cut, financial purpose. Things like that are easily anticipated and understood."

"You say that so humbly," Estelle said, laughing.

Simone's half-smile appeared as he raised his glass to his lips. "Again, I don't pretend to be humble about my position— or my abilities."

"Which are?"

"Well... only once, in sixteen years, have I ever failed to complete the task Libera handed to me. And even that was just three years ago."

"Sixteen years?"

"That's right."

"So, you've been working for Libera—"

"Since I was sixteen. Yes."

"Why so young?"

I can't turn back now. He poured and took another shot. "Because that's when my father died."

"Oh. I'm so sorry."

"Don't be."

- 28 -

"If you're all right with me asking," she started, "how did he—"

"Libera."

"You're not serious?"

"I am very serious."

"Why did he…? I mean… Why do you work for the man that—"

"My mother, Angela, left when I was ten. She lives in Italy now."

"She just left you?"

"When she left, I found out that my father had been amusing himself by beating the hell out of her on a semi-daily basis. I found this out when he needed someone else to knock around to take up his free time."

Estelle set her glass down on the table and moved closer to Simone, who finished another drink and ran his fingers through his hair.

"When I was fifteen, he sent me out to collect a debt for Libera, and it was just something that came easily to me. I've always been good at negotiating business stuff… It very rarely gets out of hand with me… A year later, word was getting around that it wasn't Vinny collecting for Libera— it was me. Once he found out that people were talking about it, he started to get scared that Libera wouldn't like it, and decided that knocking me down a flight of stairs would somehow help the situation."

He stopped to take another shot. It was clear he had never told anyone this before, and that he never thought he'd ever share it at all. She put her hand into his, and whispered, "What happened?"

He looked into her eyes and said, "He took out his gun and told me that I had 'always been trouble', and that he regretted ever raping my mother, because it led to me."

"Oh, Simone…"

"About three seconds later, there was one shot fired, and Libera came around the corner and said, 'You okay, Simone?' I just nodded, and then next thing I knew he had brought me on as an associate. Paid me enough to get by, taught me what I didn't already know, and I worked up the ranks fairly quickly."

He downed another drink before putting his elbow on the coffee table for his hand to support his head, slowly rubbing his eyes. "I've been directly under Libera for about five years."

Estelle moved another inch closer and laid her head onto Simone's shoulder, and comforted, he rested his head on top of hers— his cheek against her soft hair. He went on, saying, "When I was twenty-five, my mother came back to the States to visit her sister. She came looking for me, to tell me that she was sorry for leaving. I told her that I knew what happened, and that I understood why she needed to leave.

"But I asked her why she didn't take me with her, and she said that I looked too much like my father, and that she assumed he had been honing me for the business life; which he had. She told me that she couldn't deal with being in that world anymore, and that was the only way she knew to get out, and that taking me with her would be taking him with her, and that I wasn't worth her self-respect. And that was it." After he poured and emptied another drink, Estelle picked up the bottle, refilled his glass and downed it herself before setting the bottle on the other end of the table.

"So, you didn't actually decide to work for Libera?"

"I take full responsibility for everything I have done. I could have taken the risk and run away. But yes. It just... kind of... happened."

"Do you wish it hadn't?"

"It is what it is. I'm good at what I do. I'm not exceptionally proud of it, but people don't just walk out on men like Libera, especially people that know as much as me. I do everything I can to keep the boys reined in, and I never escalate a business deal to violence without myself or one of my guys being in immediate physical danger. That's what I meant by 'just cause'..."

"How many—"

"I don't know. I don't keep track. It's the only way I can live with myself."

Estelle finished the wine in her glass and poured another. "One more?" she asked, pointing to the scotch bottle now only housing a third of what it had originally.

He shook his head and gave her a weak smile. "No, I have to be somewhat functional tomorrow." He closed his eyes and said, "Estelle, please don't..."

She put a silencing finger to his lips. "Never. Just us."

Her finger lingered on his lips for a moment, and as she lowered her hand away, Estelle wondered if she had imagined the delicate, barely visible kiss he gave as she lightly brushed his bottom lip. Trying to keep his resolve, he nodded in appreciation of her words. "That's why I can't... why I don't want to get involved with anyone. It's not my place to put the burden of this business on anyone else. It's too..." he trailed off and looked out the window at the skyline against the jet-black sky.

"You have to do what's best for you, Simone."

She laid her head back on his shoulder, and they sat in silence for another hour, looking out over the sleeping city. Once he left, adding a new key to his keyring, she laid down in her bed and wept, heart breaking for Simone's broken heart that she wanted desperately to make whole.

Chapter 10

"Did the mystery man come over again?" Carolyn asked, resting against the break room counter and stirring raw sugar into her coffee.

"He did."

"Third time in a week, isn't it?"

"Yes, but only because that's how many times we missed each other at the restaurant."

"AND?"

"AND... I should have ordered one of those bagels this morning."

Carolyn broke off a piece of her bagel and gave it to Estelle. "There. Now you have a bagel. What happened last night?"

"He came over, we talked...We had some wine... I gave him a key... a couple weeks ago..."

Carolyn burned her tongue inhaling in her coffee in surprise. "You gave him a key? Like, to your actual apartment?"

"No, my fake apartment. In Narnia."

"And you're still not telling me who he is?"

"Who's who?" Paul asked, walking into the break room.

"No one," Carolyn said. "Come on, new books aren't going to put themselves out."

Paul rolled his eyes as they hurried off for the storage room to escape their supervisor's intrusion. The moment they had entered the storage room, Carolyn put her hand on Estelle's arm and said, "Now, can you tell me?"

Estelle sighed. She knew she couldn't postpone answering Carolyn's questions any longer, and she was dying to tell her friend how she was feeling. "Okay. But look, this has to stay between us. And he's just a friend. Trust me, he's seriously not interested in being boyfriend material. We're just friends. And you're probably not going to like him."

She was glad that she was pushing a cart of books and had to keep her eyes on the path in front of her, rather than look at her friend.

"Fine. Who are you JUST friends with? Wait— is it someone I know?"

"Well, you know of him..."

"Oh my god— who is it?" Carolyn asked, racking her brain to figure out who she could possibly know of at Libera's.

"His last name is... Belvedere."

"Belvedere?"

"Yes, Carolyn. Belvedere."

"Belvedere... SIMONE Belvedere? Estelle—"

"I don't know why you're so surprised. You know I have espresso at Libera's most nights after work."

"So, you're telling me… that the sophisticated, sexy guy that you've been 'just friends' with for three months—"

"We ARE just friends, Carolyn."

"He has a key to your apartment!"

"And he uses it to have a glass of wine and discuss what we've been reading."

"A man in the mob has a key to your apartment? Oh! But is this just any man in the mob? No! Benedict Libera's ONLY LIEUTENANT has the KEY to your APARTMENT?"

"Carolyn, keep your voice down! We are in a library after all. I told you, this has to stay between us!"

"I know! This is just so unlike you!"

Estelle smiled as she continued to arrange the New Arrivals, but couldn't figure out why her friend's words stung. Was it so absurd for her to be falling in love? Or was she viewed as so mundane that she couldn't possibly impress or handle a relationship with a man in the Mafia? *In this city, you'd be hard pressed to find a man OUT of organized crime, at least at some level.*

"You have to take me to Libera's," Carolyn said, out of nowhere.

"What? Why on earth would you even WANT to go there? I thought you were SO against giving them business."

"I am. It's your business I'm interested in," Carolyn replied with a giggle. "After all, he texts you about six times a work day. AND you see him every night after work."

"I see Simone at the restaurant and he asks about my day and we talk about what we're reading. And then he gets called away by Libera and I go back to my book. As I always have."

"Except now you have a well-dressed man talking about your book."

"He is a good dresser, isn't he?" Estelle said, indulging herself. "The designer suits, the vintage pocket watch— what?"

"You are so in love with this guy."

"What are you talking about? We're just—"

"Friends. I know." Carolyn rolled her eyes as she walked away, thinking. *Books and wine. Because no librarian would be interested in a man like that…*

Estelle took out her phone and looked again at the messages from this morning. She didn't dare share them with Carolyn yet, and she sighed in relief knowing that Simone didn't realize she actually *was* falling in love with him. *Why is perfection always out of reach? He'll never want a relationship.*

Maybe, with time, he'd begin to see that she could handle his life— his work— as long as she had him next to her. She couldn't walk away.

Chapter 11

Why hasn't she responded to my text? Simone asked himself. It was just after six in the evening— a full eight hours since he had sent the message he'd been working up the courage to send for a month. *I'm supposed to see her in three hours. Maybe I should go early to make sure everything is all right.*

Simone moaned in pain as his Patron sharply slapped his face.

"SIMONE!" Don Libera barked. "You listening to me? You going to take care of the Tomlinson account or are you going to sit there staring at an empty chair? That son of a bitch wants to threaten me, he'll learn he's got something else coming."

Simone jumped lightly and answered "Of course, sir. I'm sor-sorry. It'll be taken care of today."

As he walked away, pride hurting as much as his bruising cheek, he took the phone from his jacket pocket and reread his earlier message for the hundredth time.

1/3 Hello, Estelle. I think it's time we stop pretending that we aren't attracted to each other. I know we both feel it- and I know we both want each other. I

2/3 know that you fully understand that so long as I am in this business, a romantic relationship just isn't realistic. But I do propose that we find time to

3/3 be together- like I know we both want. No commitments. Just finally giving in.

He worried that she saw through his attempt to keep things unattached, but there was no way that he could tell her how he felt— not with as dangerous as his life had become. He worked for the most powerful man in the city, and did it well. *Sure, there was the one deal that went wrong three years ago...* Simone remembered vividly when Libera received the news that spurred him to abruptly and accidentally break Simone's hand, but nothing else had been outside of his control. He made certain that it remained that way.

Later that night, thankful that he had been able to let Landini decide what would become of Mr. Tomlinson, he lit a cigarette as Joel drove towards Estelle's apartment.

"Still acting like you're not sleeping with her?"

With a laugh Simone replied, "Honestly, Joel, she's just a good friend."

Joel laughed and shook his head, but Simone was still worrying that he had crossed the line. That was the only reason he could find as to why she had ignored his message. Still deep in silent thought, he left the vehicle and dropped the end of his cigarette as Joel parked across the street— fulfilling his purpose of protection. As Simone waited for the elevator, he finally decided that she probably just hadn't made up her mind and wanted to discuss it further. After a quick breath of relief at this thought, he approached her door, and took out the last of his spearmints as though it could mask the smell of tobacco.

As she undressed, she heard the soft, newly familiar click of the front door being unlocked and the happy "Hello, Estelle," that he called out to her.

He's early, she thought. She stepped into the shower and smiled to herself— remembering the text message she had read several hours before, and making her final decision right then and there in the hot steam of the shower. This would be a means to her end, just as much as to his.

"I'm in here!" she called back, hearing Simone's steps hesitate before making his way through the open door of the bathroom. Continuing to wet her hair, her voice as smooth as her recently shaved legs, she said, "I got your message."

"O-Oh?" he started. "I was worried that you had been offended, and th-"

"Of course not, dear. I just assumed you would prefer me to accept your offer in person." She was somewhat surprised at her own excitement for the situation. She knew that this was the scene she'd been cultivating in her mind, but she hadn't quite realized how tantalizing the prospect would be in the moment.

"You-you're accepting my offer?"

"Of course. I wouldn't leave you hanging all day if the answer wasn't...what you wanted." As she spoke the last few words, she placed her foot on the far edge of the tub, taking care to point her pedicured toes, allowing hot water from the shower to careen down her tight calf.

"You wouldn't?"

"Of course."

She noticed her use of his often-repeated words, and even over the shower she could hear his breathing quicken.

"To be clear," he began, "You do understand that this is not a romantic proposition, and that I have no intention of making any..."

"Commitments?" she supplied. "I actually wanted to ask you the same question. I'd hate for this to undermine our friendship."

"I completely agree." Though he remained calm and pleasant, she could hear the quiet enthusiasm that intrigued her so deeply. He went on to ask, "I assume you have a few questions of your own?"

"Well, I have to know that everything we do is... safe."

He smiled at her question, half amused, and replied, "By safe, do you mean…"

"Oh! I just meant—"

"I know. I'm teasing you."

Dammit, she thought to herself. Why was she so amused by this? This man was actually dangerous. He was assumed guilty of crimes the police nor the public could never prove, and his gallant humor taken from the prospect of her questioning safety…of any kind…

"You are safe. In all ways. With me."

Not wanting to betray her emotions, she steamrolled on. "Well, I also wondered about the other people you've been with. I'd like to know what I need to live up to."

She switched legs and pushed the shower curtain open another inch to show off more of her leg. His demeanor and tone never strayed from his polite, happy nature. "If we go through with this, you'll be the first…"

"Really?" Her question was gentle, but her mind was running circuits around this revelation. *I know he's not the lumberjack that the world seems to find sexy right now, but his demeanor and sense of humor— his confidence and influence, and my god— the suits… Men just don't care about themselves like him anymore. I'd have thought that plenty of gold diggers would want to trade attention for…*

As if reading her mind, he said, "I never found anyone that interested me like…"

She was glad he left her out of the last sentence. She didn't know how, but she knew, by that, he would be keeping himself emotionally detached, and she could keep loving him from afar. "If this is the first time, then, do you want to be the one calling the shots?"

She thought, given his nature, that he would want to be in charge of this encounter— just as she could tell he needed to be in charge of his business encounters. Her gamble was correct— he very much knew that he wanted her— and wanted her on his terms. His voice a little lower, but still with manners intact, he asked, "When would you like to…"

His voice trailed off as he looked for a word good enough for what he was trying to convey. She smiled at his attempt to keep a professional tone to the conversation, in case she wanted to postpone to give it more thought, but she knew he was far out of his conversational comfort zone.

She pulled the shower curtain open— this time from the head of the shower back, taking care to keep the water running through her pixied hair, and turning her wet body to face him. She saw that he was standing halfway between the sink and the bathtub, not wanting to intrude upon her space until asked— like the gentleman they both knew he was. He was standing as he always did— head barely bowed, with his hands in his black, well-tailored suit pockets and light reflecting from the vintage pocket watch chain that was always in his vest. He was noticeably shocked to be presented with her body so suddenly, but she noticed the mischievous half-smile that came along with pleasing business proposals when he knew he'd won.

"What time is it?" she asked with a small smile. As she hoped, he took out his pocket watch and replied, caught off guard, "Tw-twenty after eight."

"Thanks. You can set that on the sink if you'd like." His half-smile returned as he gently placed his beloved watch on the sink and closed the door. As he shut the door, she reached forward and pulled his tie out from its hiding place below his vest. *How long I've wanted to do this,* she thought. His mouth opened imperceptibly in surprise, eyes following the hand silently giving him permission to move forward by loosening his tie. She gave the tie a slow pull towards her, and leaned forward with her shoulders until he was barely an inch away from her. Even now, she noticed his usual post-Libera's smell of tobacco and scotch, and found it, as usual, intoxicating.

Confidence building, he placed his right hand on the warm, wet tile under the shower head, leaned forward, and kissed her neck. As he did, she noticed that his dark hair, suit jacket and crisp, white collar were becoming damp from the shower. She brought her head backwards, arching her back, and she saw his lips part, revealing the tip of his tongue being held in place with his teeth, head tilt to the side in appreciation of the wet figure before him.

As she brought her head forward, she kissed along his jaw and pulled the tie from below his collar, dropping it to the floor. He slid his left hand onto her waist as she started to unbutton his vest, and in what seemed like an instant his jacket and vest were laying on the floor next to his shoes. He moved his hand from her waist only when he realized his leather belt was starting to get wet from the still running shower. As he started to remove his belt his confidence began to pull back, but upon seeing the look of genuine interest in her eyes, he locked eyes with her and felt his pulse quicken as he pulled the belt off and dropped it to the floor. He took a step forward and replaced his left hand back onto her waist, his right hand bracing against the wall across from him as his lips finally met hers— the force of the kisses rising with his confidence.

She was fascinated by his touch and his kisses, and by how similar they were to the rest of him. His touch was surprisingly gentle, with bursts of dominance when he became surer of his actions. His kisses pulled her into his trance further, cycling from brief and chaste to long, slow, breathy pulls of her bottom lip with his teeth. As she again felt the thrill of one of those pulls, she, delighted in her own daring, slid her hands down the back of his wet, unbuttoned shirt and around to unfasten his pants. She began kissing her way down his neck onto his wet chest, continuing down until she was kneeling before him. She looked up and saw the tantalizing half-smile, and as she stared into his eyes, she took her time to remove the rest of his clothes— feeling a rush of excitement from the pleasant sting of his fingernails on her shoulder. She broke eye contact and brushed her cheek on his thigh, kissing lightly. He took her hands into his and stood her back up, feeling the slow movement of her wet breasts travelling up his skin with her.

To escape the dropping temperature of the water, he turned the shower off and pulled one of the pink towels from the hook on the wall, leading her to the center of the bathroom where he had stood, mild mannered as ever half an hour before. He turned her so her back was pressed against his chest, and as he began to slowly dry her hair, she could, for the first time, feel his intense hardness against her skin. He moved the soft towel down to her shoulders, and with his right hand continued to dry down to her breasts, his left hand feeling its way up her neck and into her hair. Again shivering from the pressure of his fingernails, this time in her hair and on the back of her neck, she realized how attractive his confidence was to them both. As the towel reached her waist, he turned her around and, with one end of the towel in each hand, pulled her closer into him, kisses rising again with his faith in himself.

He led her this way down to her bedroom at the end of the hall, and as they approached the door, he stopped kissing her and looked hard into her eyes with a look of determination she had caught only fleeting glimpses of before as he departed Libera's. After a few long seconds of feeling her breathing quickly against his chest, he reached behind him and opened the door. As she reached up to turn on the light, she felt his hand jump to her wrist and saw his eyes narrow for an instant before he was kissing her again. He closed the door and took a few small steps towards her, until his chest was against hers and her back was pressed against the door. It was several full, passionate minutes before she realized his hand was still snug around her wrist, and a second more before she realized just how much she liked it there. She had never realized how strong his hands were, and was taken aback by how much his tailored jackets disguised the strength in his arms.

Entranced by the command that had come over him, she leaned her head against the door and took immense pleasure in listening to the sounds he made as his lips moved down her neck. Letting go of his unspoken fears, he traced his lips down her neck and felt a surge of exhilaration as he tasted the silken skin between her breasts. From the glow of the streetlight coming in through the window, he looked up with that same determined stare and knelt down to his knees, pulling her, eyes still closed with intense excitement, down with him.

As his knees met the floor, he turned them around and gently but pointedly laid her down— her bare back against the soft pile of the carpet. Estelle looked up at Simone and saw tenacious passion in his deep, dark eyes, and watched as he slid his hands from her shoulders down to each wrist. With a gasp of ecstasy, she let him pull her wrists up towards her head, and then out level with her hips, his gentle grip holding them against the floor.

He leaned forward and kissed her neck again, with a subtle bite every so often at the soft skin. He was amazed at how delighted she was at his touch, and he could feel how incredibly excited he, himself, was— though he had been careful to limit her feeling as much yet, fearing she would think less of him for being so eager so soon. His lips and teeth continued down her neck to her breast, pushed higher from the angle at which he held her arms. She could feel his warm breath on her nipple, and she gave a quiet whimper, wanting to feel his lips and teeth there instead. After a small laugh in appreciation of her whimpers, he obliged, and as his tongue circled around her erect nipple, his hand began to trace a lingering path down her curved silhouette.

Chapter 12

Five very short hours after leaving Estelle's apartment, Simone made his way into Libera's office. When he came in, Libera was nowhere to be seen, but Landini was sitting on the sofa in the corner of the office, wearing gray cargo pants, an All-American Rejects T-shirt, his favorite Cubs hat to keep his dark, wavy hair out of his eyes, and black Doc Martens.

"Morning, Belv."

"Hey, Al, how's it going?"

"Not bad."

"Please tell me there's coffee already made."

"There is. That's where Don went." He looked up from his phone and looked Simone over before saying, "How was she?"

"I'm sorry, what?" Simone asked, backtracking several steps from his coveted path to caffeine.

"You're ten minutes late for the first time in your life, you look like you haven't slept and you didn't hand my ass to me for asking that question, so I'll ask it again." He smirked and said, "How was she?"

Simone put his hands into his pockets, but half-smiled and gave a soft laugh before saying, "I'm going to go get coffee."

"You can't avoid me forever, Belv."

"Later," Simone said quietly, hearing Libera's footsteps approaching.

Landini nodded and went back to smirking at his phone as Simone waved a quick greeting to Libera as he passed, finally making his way back into the kitchen of the restaurant to pour what would be his first of several cups of coffee that day. As he slowly stirred in a packet of sugar, he started remembering how wonderful it felt to be so close to Estelle and how complete he felt when he was around her— and wondered if she was having the same thoughts as she awoke that morning.

Chapter 13

After a work day that flew past in a whirl of daydreaming about the previous night, Estelle went to clock out from the library as Carolyn came up beside her and asked, "Can I borrow your black Kate Spade bag?"

"Sure! How come?"

"Jay asked me to the symphony tonight, and I don't have anything that goes with the dress I want to wear."

"That's so sweet! Coming around on him a little?"

"I'm still not sure. I just don't understand how he can be so good in bed and so boring out in public."

Estelle laughed and said, "If that's the worst of your problems, I think you're all right. I thought you didn't want anything serious anyway?"

"I don't, and he's definitely still on the rebound— at least I hope that's why he won't shut up about her..."

"You could always break it off," Estelle said, opening the door for her friend.

"OR— I could sleep with him again and THEN break it off."

"That does sound like more fun than my plan. If you drive me home you can grab the bag now."

"Thanks! No Belvedere tonight?"

"No, he texted me earlier, said he was busy tonight," Estelle said, smiling down at her phone, rereading his complimentary message about the night before.

"What's that look mean?"

"I don't have a look."

"Right..." Carolyn said, smirking and unlocking the car.

When they got upstairs, Estelle turned the light on and set her things down on the couch.

"It's in my bedroom closet if you want to grab it. I'm going to have some Moscato, want some?"

"Definitely!" Carolyn called back, already on her way to find the purse.

Estelle pulled the cork out of the already open bottle from the refrigerator and poured what was left into two glasses. She had just sat down on the couch when Carolyn walked back into the living room with a mischievous grin.

"Well, what have I got here?" Carolyn said, holding up an empty foil packet that Estelle had forgotten about on her nightstand. "So... Still just friends, eh?"

"Yes, as a matter of fact, we are still just friends. That—" she stopped, pointing to Carolyn's hand, "has nothing to do with it."

"Okay. What about the two others that were next to it?"

Estelle tried to hide her grin with her wine glass. "So, we're just really GOOD friends now..."

"What does this mean?" Carolyn asked, tossing the wrapper onto the coffee table and taking her wine glass.

"It doesn't mean anything. He's still not boyfriend material. He's just..." she trailed off, trying to find the right word but actually getting lost in the memories of her heated night with Simone.

"Damn, that man must be good in bed," Carolyn said, correctly interpreting Estelle's abandoned train of thought. Estelle said nothing, but smirked as she took another sip of wine.

Chapter 14

Across town, Simone was sitting at the bar of Libera's restaurant, and was just finishing up with the paperwork Libera had given him when he felt Landini's hand on his shoulder. "Hey," he said, looking up for a moment before initialing the last page he'd been reading and closing the folder.

"Hey. You done for the night?"

"I am."

"Wanna go for a drink?"

Simone half-smiled and said, "Sure. So long as you aren't planning on asking about last night."

"Oh, come on. I didn't think I'd ever have the chance to have this conversation."

"Me, too," Simone said truthfully. He looked at Landini's arrogant gaze for a moment before conceding. "Fine."

Landini tapped Simone's shoulder and nodded towards the door. He followed Simone out to his Mercedes, and as he waited for the doors to be unlocked, he asked, "What's her name, again?"

"Estelle," Simone said, smiling gently as he put the key in the lock.

As they both got into the vehicle, Landini asked, "How long have you guys been dating?"

"We're not."

Landini looked over at Simone in exasperation, not saying anything. As Simone pulled out of the parking lot, he said, "Don't look at me like that. We're not. We're just friends."

"No, you and I are just friends. Closest you've ever come to seeing me naked is when you pulled that bullet out of my leg."

Simone chuckled and said, "And I appreciate that."

"So, did you actually—"

Simone nodded as he lit a cigarette, quickly returning his hand to the wheel. "We did."

"And was that the first time?"

"For me, or for us?"

Landini half-smiled and said, "Both."

Nodding again, Simone exhaled, saying, "Yes, on both counts."

"I've always wondered, was that decision based on lack of opportunity, or did puberty just hit REALLY late?"

Simone laughed as he pulled into the parking lot of their usual bar. "Never seemed necessary."

Once they were seated at their usual corner table, Landini ordered their drinks and as the server walked away, he said, "So what makes her different?"

"What do you mean?"

"I mean, if you were drinking all the scotch women are sending you at Libera's every night, you'd be an alcoholic by now. And yet you've never once taken the bait. So, what makes her different?"

"She's different," he said, nodding his thanks as the server set his scotch in front of him. "I've never met anyone like her."

"What does she do?"

"You mean for work?"

Landini nodded, taking a sip from his gin and tonic. Simone started to glide his thumb along the rim of his glass and said, "She's a librarian."

"So, you didn't stand a chance," Landini replied, laughing.

Simone took another sip of his drink in an attempt to hide his self-conscious smile, but Landini leaned forward against his forearms and said, "You love her."

"No, I don't."

"Give me a fucking break, man. I can see every time you talk to her that you love her."

"It doesn't matter," Simone said, frowning as he downed his drink. "I'm not cut out for anything more, and she even said herself that she didn't want what happened last night to undermine our friendship."

"I'm not going to have the relationship availability argument with you again," Landini said, getting the server's attention for another round. "But what I do want to know is why you think that having sex with her is going to make it psychologically easier to not be her boyfriend."

"I didn't say that it did," Simone replied, having had the same realization himself the night before as he made love to Estelle for the second time.

"Then what the hell are you doing?"

Simone shrugged, momentarily holding his hand up before picking up his glass. "I just couldn't not be with her, even if that's the most I can have."

Landini gave Simone a sad look for a moment, and then resolutely changed his demeanor, recognizing the onset of hurt in his friend's eyes. He half-smiled and said, "So how was it?"

Simone gave another embarrassed grin and said, "I technically have no frame of reference."

"Maybe not. But you've read about it in a million books, and I refuse to believe you've been celibate for over thirty years without watching porn."

"I don't," Simone said, causing Landini to laugh in disbelief.

"Who you think you're kidding?"

"I don't. Reading it, on the other hand…"

"Pun intended?"

Simone laughed and said, "Convenient coincidence."

"So, was it at least better than that?"

"Incomparably."

"Who came onto who?"

"I had texted her earlier in the day, asking if she wanted to. Then when I got to her apartment she made her answer…very clear."

"So, she started it?"

Simone nodded. "Which was probably best. I have absolutely no idea what I'd have done if she'd have wanted me to make the first move."

"How'd she do it?"

"What do you mean?"

"I mean, was she waiting for you in the bedroom, did she jump you as soon as you walked in?"

Grinning in spite of himself, Simone said, "I had actually gotten there early, so she was still in the shower."

"What did you do?"

"She told me I could come in so we could talk, so I did."

"And?" Landini asked, waving his hand towards Simone, asking for more information.

"AND… she said that she was interested, we talked about it for a bit…making sure we were on the same page… then she, uh… she pulled the shower curtain open…"

Half-smiling again, Landini said, "And I'm guessing it took about three point five seconds before you were in the shower with her?"

"It took a little longer than that… kind of wish I'd have thought to take my jacket off before kissing her, though."

"Probably would have been a good idea. That's about a twenty-five-hundred-dollar kiss, isn't it?"

"Try thirty-six," Simone said, raising his glass to his lips. "And completely worth it… Luckily, I didn't leave until close to four, so the rest of my clothes had dried out before I needed them again."

Landini raised his eyebrows and said, "Close to four?"

Simone nodded, looking down again. Landini leaned back and said, "So how many times did you—"

"Three."

"Damn."

"Being fair, the first one only counted as about half…" Simone looked away again, not sure how his last sentence escaped him.

"S'alright," Landini said, tapping his arm. "I think everybody's first time's like that."

Simone laughed and said, "Yeah, I was worried at first, but once we were half an hour or so into the second time I figured I was okay."

They both started to laugh and Simone nodded to the server, confirming the next round of drinks. Once she was gone again, Landini rested his chin on his hand again and said, "So was she... satisfied... with everything?"

"I think so..."

"You're not sure?"

"I mean... it seemed like it...and sounded like it..."

"But?"

Simone shrugged a little and said, "Again, I have no frame of reference. How do I know it was actually happening and not just her stroking my ego?"

"You're asking me?" Landini asked, chuckling. Once Simone had laughed, Landini went on, "Seriously, though. Especially in a situation like this— if she's hell-bent on just staying friends, what good does it do to fake it?"

"You're asking me?" Simone echoed.

"What were you doing when she may or may not have...?"

"What do you think we've been talking about so far?"

Landini lowered his voice and leaned closer. "I mean, was this a mutual activity? Or were you going down on her? Using your hand?"

"The latter. Definitely not sure enough of myself to even attempt the middle one."

"Well, first of all, get the fuck over yourself. You're not going to get good at it by thinking about it."

"How would you know?"

Landini leaned back as he covered his eyes, laughing. "Point taken. But I'm not wrong. Second of all, did she seem into it before that? Being nervous may have just translated to not seeming into it—"

"No, it was just more...enthusiastic... than I was expecting."

"As in vocally, or physically?"

"Both."

"I see. So, a woman is in bed with you, and looking and sounding like she's having a good time, so clearly it's because you suck."

"Exactly," Simone said, laughing at himself.

"Because god forbid you actually be good in bed."

"I'm not saying I felt like I was bad at it— and trust me— I am beyond ecstatic that she had a good time. I just didn't expect her to... be so into it..."

"Or maybe you didn't expect her to be so into you?"

"She's not THAT into me."

"Right. Talking to you every night, texting you every day, and fucking you three times in the same night REALLY says she wants to slow things down."

Simone just shrugged and picked up his new glass. "Fine," Landini said, leaning forward. "Let me ask you this. How often do you buy her things?"

"I don't. I mean, I gave her a book once. But it takes me ten minutes just to convince her to let me buy her dinner once a week."

"As I suspected, we're ruling out gold digger, and given that I've watched the two of you talking—"

"You've watched us talking?"

"Of course, I have. It's fucking adorable. Regardless, I've seen the way she looks at you, and she's actually interested in what you have to say. Trust me, Estelle's into you. And you do realize that all this 'just friends' talk is probably just as much bullshit coming from her as it is from you?"

"Yeah, because life is that simple."

"Maybe it is, Belv."

Chapter 15

It was a rain-sodden Wednesday, and just over a month since Estelle had accepted Simone's offer. Since that first night, they had found four other nights together— four long, passionate nights, always culminating in Simone lighting a cigarette before dismissing his enforcer for the night and driving himself home. She was momentarily surprised to discover Joel's presence outside her apartment building that first night, given Simone's previous feelings about it, but understanding the reality of the business, she knew the necessity of his presence when Simone was away from Libera's.

Every night they parted she found it increasingly tormenting to say good night. With his firm determination to remain unattached as long as he was working for Libera, she knew she wouldn't dare ask him to stay the night without him knowing she loved him, and she was already a little concerned that he suspected her feelings. During her continued visits to Libera's each night after leaving the library, Estelle began to notice Simone watching her read with an unreadable expression on his face. Tonight was no exception, but she knew what she had to do.

As she stared at her book that night, Simone realized that she was fighting back tears. He was surprised to see that she was reading her favorite *A Midsummer Night's Dream*, and couldn't comprehend what in the story moved her so, until he saw that her eyes weren't moving along the page. His Patron, who had been mildly interested in their encounters at the restaurant, also took notice of this. "How long are you going to string that girl along, my friend?"

Surprised by the Don's knowledge of his affair, Simone stammered "I... I'm not stringing her along."

"I see. You're saying the business is too dangerous for a wife? Listen, Simone," he continued as he gave Simone's shoulder a condescending pat. "These women— they know what this business is about. They know how it works. It's always the men that take them out of it."

Libera discreetly pointed towards Estelle. "That's a good woman you have there. God knows why women pick men like us, but I've seen the look that woman has on her face right now— and it always ends with the woman walking out this door and not coming back. They can't hide it forever."

Simone had no words to respond. He loathed the condescension with which Libera spoke, and how he kept referring to Estelle as 'that woman', but he couldn't deny the truth in his Patron's words. Simone could see her love flicker in her eyes as she watched his orgasms, and when she would let go of his hand as she said 'good night', and he could see it now, in the tears she was holding back. He nodded to Stephen, and as his scotch was being poured over ice, Simone was frantically trying to both wrap his mind around his perfect woman genuinely loving him, and trying to find a way to convince her to continue on as they had. Drink in hand, he walked over to Estelle and stood beside her as he always did, this time hoping he wouldn't have to find words he didn't have. "Hello, Estelle."

"Hello, Simone," she replied, as usual, but she couldn't find the smile she always had for him. She couldn't even meet his eyes until he gently spoke, "Estelle."

It was not a question. She knew he saw her inward struggle, and all she could say was, "I can't."

"Estelle, please."

"I thought I could handle the life you have," she lied, hoping to mask her heartbreak, "but I can't. You need to find someone that won't be afraid."

"I thought you trusted me?" he found himself saying.

He knew she was lying, but Simone still needed to hear the answer to his question. He was slightly appalled to see his eavesdropping Patron in the mirrored wall shaking his head with a silent laugh, but in the next second, Libera meant nothing to him. The business meant nothing to him. Simone, for the first time, was hit with the full force of the realization that she was, in fact, going to 'walk out that door'. And out of his life, completely. He tried, but couldn't find the words he needed to convince her to remain his mistress, and his secret love. Words had never failed him before Estelle. It was a rare memory to find a time when he couldn't convince someone to do what he wanted— what he needed— one way or another.

Estelle finally replied, "I do…trust you. I don't know why I do— I mean, of all of the men in this city, you're probably the last one I should trust. Why do I trust you so completely?" she finished, searching his eyes for the answer.

"Estelle, why are you lying about being afraid?" he asked abruptly. But before she could answer, he said, rather too quickly, "Don't go."

She stared at him for a moment, surprised at his words. She had expected him to accept her words and move onto the next woman that was sure to come. All she could do was ask a soft "Why?"

After a mere second, he stepped closer— he had never been this close to her in public. His hand flirted with her cheek— fingertips in her hair as his thumb caressed the soft skin near her ear, the gentility beneath the passion of his gesture catching her off guard. He looked into her eyes with the determined look she'd come to know so well, and he knew all that mattered was keeping his love in his life. His voice started to barely shake as he spoke— his emotion betraying his confidence.

"Because I love you."

His thumb brushed her cheek and then swept down to her bottom lip as he continued "a-and I know…that you love me."

He leaned forward and brought his lips to hers, both of them oblivious to the shocked laugh of Libera; blind to the stunned looks from the staff, who had rarely seen an ounce of emotion from Simone. They were aware only of the first honest kiss between them, and the unexpected future they finally had.

Chapter 16

A mild spring had given way to a sweltering summer, and on a Friday night at the start of July, Estelle and Simone lay once again in the soft glow of the streetlights coming in through the window, thankful for the air-conditioned oasis of Estelle's bedroom. Her head was resting comfortably on Simone's chest, both of his arms around her.

"What's wrong?" he asked, after hearing a soft, sad sigh.

"I told my parents about us, I hope that's all right."

"Of course, it is," he said, tilting his head. "I take it they didn't take it well?"

"Dad was just happy that I'm happy," she started. "But Mom…"

Simone nodded. "I'm used to people not liking me on principle, really. It's okay."

"But you're so sweet…and kind… And she'll never get to see any of that…"

"But you see that," Simone said, kissing her. "That's all that matters to me."

"I hate that you have to leave," she said, lightly kissing his chest.

He smiled and kissed her hair. "So do I."

Propping herself up on her elbow, she leaned forward, gave him a long, slow kiss and said, "So stay."

"I can't. Saturday mornings are my early meetings with Gallo, and I don't have anything here."

"We could always go to your place."

"I have thought of that," Simone said, turning towards her. "But Libera has a key to my place, and very little regard for privacy."

"Maybe you should start keeping some things here," Estelle said, having already anticipated his response.

He leaned forward and kissed her. "I'll tell you what. Libera very rarely needs me early on Sundays, if at all. Why don't I pick you up tomorrow when I'm done and we'll stop by my place and pick up a couple things so I can stay on Saturday nights?"

"That sounds amazing." She leaned forward and kissed him again. "Just don't leave yet?"

He pulled her closer and said, "Of course."

She sighed as she settled back into him, gently rubbing his chest. "What are these from?" she asked, fingering the half dozen subtle scars that freckled the skin just under his collarbone.

"Hmm?" he asked, barely staying awake. "Oh, those. I was up at Athena about six years ago."

"Libera's Casino?"

"Yeah. This was before we moved Mustang from Athena to Olympus. They'd been having some trouble in Mustang with a guy not paying his tab, and Libera sent me to take care of it. Mack and Bronte met me out front, and we went in together. When we got there, the guy was all coked out and grabbed one of the girls, held her at knifepoint and said that he was only going to let her go if we dropped his tab."

"Oh my god!"

"But ... he was too high and accidentally cut her before we could even try to reason with him. I put my gun away and took a step forward, trying to get him to let me help her, and he dropped her and went for me. Bronte got her help fast, though, and she said she didn't even scar. Libera paid for her house as an apology."

"So, the girls at Mustang aren't just strippers, are they?"

Simone laughed. "What do you think?"

"That's what I figured... always wondered."

"They are all there of their own volition, welcome to leave at any time, and with temporary benefits. They are also paid more than nearly anyone else in the casino, save for Mack and a couple other people— some of the girls several times over, and they have better health screenings and coverage than most CEOs."

"No judgement," Estelle said. "Just curious. It's got to be good money."

"Oh— you have no idea... That was also the only incident like that Mustang's had. He didn't do any real damage to me— just needed stitches in a few places, and he was SO coked out he wound up having a heart attack before anyone else could do anything."

"That's terrible!"

"I agree," Simone conceded, "but it could have been a lot worse."

Estelle closed her eyes and brushed the top of her head against his chin. "Do things like that happen to you now?"

He hugged her tighter and said, "Not anymore. If Libera thinks there's a problem— or that there will be a problem— he sends Landini. Or Pagani."

"I worry about you."

"I know. And I'm sorry."

"Hey," she said, propping herself up and looking into his eyes. "Never."

He leaned forward and kissed her, pulling her back close to him. The kisses started building again, as they had earlier that evening, but after a few minutes, Estelle pulled back.

"What's wrong?" he asked, concerned that he was misreading her unspoken signals.

"Can I ask you something?"

"Of course."

She looked down, still debating as to whether or not she actually wanted to ask the question that had been bothering her.

"What is it?"

"Where do you go from here?"

"What do you mean?"

"I mean..." she paused, worried her question was inappropriate. "When Libera doesn't want to be... or can't be..."

"Oh."

"I'm sorry. It's not my place."

"What are you talking about? I think it's a perfectly logical question to have— one that I've asked myself several times. And one Libera has asked me about, to be honest."

"Really?"

"Really. And I'll tell you exactly what I told him. I don't want to be Don. At all. Ever."

Estelle felt relieved and intrigued at the same time. "You don't?"

"Oh, no. Jesus. I don't ever want to have to be the one making those decisions... giving those orders... No— I've thought for a while that Bronte would be the one to take over. But that's pure speculation," he added quickly. "I've never seen or heard anything that says that I'm right."

"But you usually are?"

"My logic is generally correct, yes."

She laughed and leaned back in for more kisses, but pulled back again a few minutes later. "Wait— he asked you?"

"A couple years ago. He asked me if I was interested in moving up in the future, and I told him flat out that I wasn't."

"How'd he take it?"

"I could tell he was disappointed, but he respected my decision. He said that it's usually the ones that don't want the job that are the best at it. And then never said anything else about it."

"You're sure you don't want it?"

"Oh, I'm sure."

"You know I'll support you no matter what, right?"

"I do." He laid there, looking into her eyes in the soft lighting from the window, and said, "Do you know how much I love you?"

She answered him with a kiss, and this time had no questions to pull her back.

Chapter 17

The next day, Estelle spent some time making room in various parts of her apartment so Simone could bring over whatever he needed to. Once she received the message alerting her to his presence later that afternoon, she went downstairs to find Joel and Simone waiting in front of her building. Joining Simone in the back seat of his car, he leaned to kiss her before lighting a cigarette. "Hi, Joel," she said. "It's good to see you again."

He smiled, not used to people acknowledging him when he was with his boss. "You, too, Miss Estelle."

Simone said, "We have to run by Libera's and drop Joel off, then we'll head out."

"Sounds good," she said, relieved that Joel wasn't coming along on her first trip to Simone's house.

Once Joel was getting into his own car in the parking lot of Libera's, Simone and Estelle moved to the front seats. As he started the car, Simone put out the end of his cigarette and immediately lit another. Never having actually seen him drive before, Estelle watched him as he pulled out of the parking lot, driving a few blocks on the downtown street to get onto the highway. "You look nervous," she said, putting a hand on his shoulder.

He smiled and shook his head, inhaling from his cigarette deeply to postpone speaking. After a few miles he said, "Part of it is that I can't always tell what you're thinking. You're not like anyone else I've ever known, and that's one of the things I love about you. You don't just say what you think I want to hear, and you don't treat me differently than you would anyone else. You're not intimidated."

"No, I'm definitely not," Estelle said with a small laugh.

"You know, before I met you I never got nervous. Didn't matter who I was talking to, or what I was doing, I never got nervous. Unless Libera was pissed off, of course. But now…" he trailed off.

"Why do you think that is?" she asked, noticing that he was already pulling into an exit lane.

"Before, no matter what I did, the outcome never mattered to the rest of the game. But now," he paused, focusing on turning the car onto a slower street. "Now if I screw this up, I lose everything."

She found herself just thinking the word *never,* and then realized that there would never be anyone else that she wanted talking to her this way. Estelle said nothing, but began to nestle her fingers in the ends of his hair. Smiling at her touch, he turned down a side street and said, "We're almost there."

Surprised at where they were, she said, "You're not as far away from the city as I expected."

"I like to be close by. Libera lives a street over."

"Really?"

"He does. And the house I grew up in is just ten minutes away."

"I had no idea."

"I knew the area well, so I didn't want to change neighborhoods. Plus, Libera bought the house," he finished, half-smile returning.

"He did?"

"Yeah. About five years ago when I moved up." He pulled into his driveway and took the key from the ignition. "Sure you want to do this?"

"Why wouldn't I?"

"I don't know…"

He sat looking at his keys for a moment and said, "I guess I just keep wondering when you'll realize you're too good for me."

"Hey."

She leaned across the console and put her fingers on his jaw to gently turn him so he was looking at her. "I love you. Flaws and all."

"My job is much more than a flaw."

She shook her head. "Whatever our souls are made of, his and mine are the same."

He closed his eyes and kissed the palm of the hand still touching his cheek. "Wuthering Heights."

Estelle gave a teary smile and said, "See?"

Simone nodded his head towards his house. "Come on," he said pulling himself together. They emerged from the Mercedes and walked up to the gated front yard. An immaculately landscaped path led the way to a comfortable looking porch attached to the stone façade of a two-story home. There were two wooden chairs next to a small wooden table with an ash tray and a permanent ring from a highball glass.

"Your house is much more… Midwestern… than I expected!" Estelle said.

"Why is that?" he asked, laughing and opening the screen door as he located the correct key.

"Do I need to remind you of the E-Class Mercedes-Benz or will the designer suits be enough?"

His half-smile appeared as he unlocked the front door and held it open for her to enter. "Just wait."

He turned on the lights as she entered, and she couldn't believe the difference between the exterior of the house and the room she had walked into. "Oh my god."

"That more like it?"

"This is incredible."

Simone's house was, indeed, like the rest of him. The door opened up onto a large living area, bookshelves lining the bottom half of every wall, with the exception of a two-foot minibar across the room and a turntable with several dozen records taking up two of the middle shelves. A soft, black couch faced an electric fire place beneath a built-in flat screen television. Halfway between the couch and the door was a round, black table, ready to seat four, with a poker set stacked neatly in the middle and a file with papers sitting off to the side. The walls were a modern gray trimmed with white, and the dark, hardwood floors made the room look welcoming and warm. Coming around the corner of the entry wall, Estelle could see that the living room continued all the way to the kitchen, separated only by a large, black quartz-topped island accompanied by three black stools.

"Looks like Libera hasn't been by today," Simone said, opening the file on the table.

"Does he usually?"

"Not really. He had some things to take care of away from the restaurant and needed that," he finished, pointing to the file. "He's probably just going to pick it up tomorrow. Drink?"

"Yes, please."

He walked into the kitchen and pulled a bottle of Moscato out of the shiny, black refrigerator. "Picked this up last night."

"That was so sweet of you," she said, walking over and leaning on the island. He opened the bottle and poured them each a glass. "Thanks," she said, taking a sip. "Not just for the wine, but for bringing me here."

"I've wanted to have you over for a while, but I didn't want to move quicker than you'd like."

"You think of everything, don't you?"

"I try," he said, taking a sip from his own glass of the sweet wine.

"You know," Estelle started, setting her glass down. "There's something I've been wanting to do, as well."

"Oh?"

"Oh yes." She put her arms around his neck and kissed him, pulling once on his bottom lip with her teeth. "And I think now's a good time for it."

He put his own glass on the counter and said, "And what would that be?"

"Just wait."

He smiled again as she resumed kissing him, pushing him up against the island, facing away from the living room. She slowly unbuttoned his jacket and slid her arms around his waist and up his back. As she started kissing his neck and along his jaw, his hands made their way into the back pockets of her jeans, and he felt his holster press up against his chest. Breathing quickly in response to her kisses, he said, "I should take off my—"

"No need," she said with a mischievous grin. "I won't be up here for long."

She went back to kissing him, this time unfastening his Tom Ford belt.

Comprehending her intentions, he asked a breathy, "Are you sure?"

"Oh, god yes."

She continued kissing down his neck and chest, until she was kneeling in front of him. As she unfastened his pants, he said, "You know you don't have to do this, right?"

Taking him into her hands and making coy eye contact, she said, "I know that. Do you want me to stop?"

A moment later she was unable to speak, and his only words were a raspy and surprised, "Christ, don't stop."

He braced himself against the counter behind him with his left hand— his right hand wrapped loosely in her hair. The sounds she was making were clearly telling him how greatly she was enjoying what she was doing, and he found that just as stimulating as the quick motions of her tongue. A mere ten minutes later, he realized how close he already was to climax, and as Estelle also began to realize this, she put her free hand around his calf, ready to help him keep his balance, and as his breathing began to quicken, signaling his approaching release, they heard a loud, "Simone! Where ya at?"

"Shit!" Simone whispered, hearing Libera's steps approaching faster than he could make himself presentable.

"There you are!"

Libera walked into the living room, only able to see the back of Simone's tailored jacket. "I forgot to come by earlier, and I saw your car out front—" he had begun to take another step forward when Simone interrupted him, turning only his torso and head, holding up a hand.

"Stop! I mean, with all due respect, sir— please, just— just stay there."

Estelle had just finished refastening Simone's belt when Libera said, "The hell is wrong with you, talking to me like that?"

Not wanting Simone's words to be viewed as disrespectful, Estelle forced his hand from her shoulder and stood up, attempting to fix her hair that had been disheveled by Simone's hand. "Hi, Mr. Libera."

Libera started laughing and said, "Oh, Jesus, I, uh, I didn't see you there."

"Probably best," Estelle said, picking up her glass of wine and quickly draining it.

"I am so sorry, kids. I'm just going to take this," he said, turning quickly and picking up the file from the table, "and go. I'll see you Monday, Simone."

Simone gave an embarrassed, "Of course, sir," before finishing his own glass of wine.

Once they heard the door close and lock, Estelle leaned forward onto the island and hid her face in her hands. "I'm sorry! I didn't know what else to do!"

Simone gave a nervous laugh and leaned to rest his forehead on hers. "Are you kidding? You saved my ass. I'm sorry—"

"For what?"

"For not thinking this would happen, and for your reputation taking the hit for me."

"I don't see it as damaging to my reputation. It's not like we were behind the bar at the restaurant— we were alone in your house, and I'm at perfect liberty to do whatever I like with you in the privacy of one of our homes."

"You're not embarrassed?"

"Oh, I'm mortified. But not any more than if you had me on my back anywhere else in the house when he came in."

"Christ, your confidence is sexy."

She flashed a self-assured smile and said, "I know."

Half-smiling, he said, "Why don't we get what we need from upstairs and then head back to your place, and we can finish what we started?"

"Lead the way!"

They walked past a door underneath the stairs, and Simone said, "That leads down to the gym in the basement."

"You work out a lot, then?"

"Depends on your definition of a lot," he said, laughing. "About an hour and a half most mornings, sometimes again after work if I'm stressed out."

"You must get stressed out a lot," she said, simpering up at him.

He flashed another arrogant smile before taking her hand and leading her up the stairs. He unlocked the first door and turned on the light, saying, "So, this is my office."

It was a minimally furnished room, with a closed laptop on a mahogany desk, several locked filing cabinets and a safe. He walked over to the closet and opened a second safe, before returning and setting a Beretta Tomcat on the laptop. He unplugged the power cord and said, "If I'm bringing anything that bothers you, tell me and I'll leave it."

"My dad was a marine and still is an NRA member. Your guns don't bother me."

"Good. I was worried about that."

"How many are there?"

"Between here, my car and Libera's there's nine. All purchased and carried legally."

"And that's not overkill?"

Half-smiling, he said, "Probably a bit. There's the Taurus that I always carry, and this one that travels with me." He pointed to the laptop as he closed the safe and closet door. "I have two more of the same Taurus, one stays in the safe and one under the front seat of my car. I also have a matching Tomcat that stays in the console."

"You don't branch out much, do you?"

"No need. I know what I like, and I know what I work best with."

"That was only five."

"There's a shotgun in the trunk of my car and under the bar at Libera's, as well as in the safe here. I also have a Colt M1911 that my friend Al gave me for Christmas a few years ago. It's nickel plated with pearl grips, and I keep it in a locked showcase box in the living room. Until today, it was the most beautiful thing that's been inside this house."

He picked up the laptop and Beretta before kissing her cheek and leaving the room. *Damn, he's good,* she thought, following him down the hall to the last room.

She walked into Simone's master suite, and was surprised at how chic it was, compared to minimalistic office.

"This is beautiful."

"Thank you," he said, putting what he was carrying on his dresser. "Not too masculine?"

"Oh god, no. That's not to say— I don't mean that it's overly feminine, either— I just meant that it suits the space well..."

He laughed and said, "I appreciate the effort, but I assure you, my masculinity is undamaged by accidental insinuations about style choices."

She smiled and sat down on the foot of the black-clad bed, looking around at the artwork that hung against the light gray walls. They were all photographs of old, ornate libraries from around the world, except for the print of Van Gogh's *Café at Night* that hung above the emerald, velvet-upholstered headboard. She laid backwards, looking up at the painting. "Wow— the headboard really brings out the green in that painting. I never noticed it that much before."

"It does."

He turned to look at her, and leaned against the doorway of his closet. *All that's missing here is you.* Secreting his thoughts away, he walked into his closet and started looking for a travel bag.

"Oh my."

She had joined him in the closet, and was in awe of the hyper-organized wonder before her. "I think my kitchen would fit in here."

"Not quite," he fibbed.

"So, exactly how many suits are in here?"

He laughed. "Jesus, I don't even know anymore."

"Gucci, Prada, Tom Ford, Armani... You've got more labels in here than Fashion Week."

"Sometimes I think my tailor knows me better than Libera does."

"No kidding!"

As he pulled a few things from the dresser, she looked around, feeling a little out of place in her jeans and tank top.

His eyes narrowed a little as he came back into the closet, sensing how she was feeling.

"You okay?"

"Do I fit in here?"

Putting his arms around her, he said, "Of course you do. My other interests have no bearing on that."

"Since when are fifty designer suits interests?"

"That's all they are. I have very expensive taste, yes, but everything here doesn't define me any more than what you are wearing defines you."

She leaned her head on his chest and asked, "How do you always know what to say?"

He smiled and said, "Besides, maybe someday, you'll be able to show that you have equally as expensive taste."

"And what makes you say that?" she asked, raising a coy eyebrow.

"The designer purses were my first clue. The giant pile of Vogues by your bed was another, not to mention that fact that you could recognize every designer in here, without looking at the labels."

"Why, I don't know what you mean, Mr. Belvedere!" she said playfully, before stopping and turning around, finally registering exactly what he had said. "What did you mean by that "maybe someday"?"

Wanting to hide the embarrassed look on his face, he turned, going back to what he had been doing. "I just meant maybe someday."

She came up behind him and put her arms around his waist. "You're cute when you're being evasive."

As he turned around and kissed her, he said, "I know."

He pulled two suits from the rack, still in their plastic travel bags, as well as two silk ties and laid them on the bed. "Do you mind grabbing the green cufflinks as you walk by?"

She looked on top of the dresser and quietly gasped. "These aren't real emeralds?"

He looked at her, bemused for a moment. "They are."

"So, by extension, that means that these are all real diamonds, aren't they?"

"Technically, the blue ones are sapphires," he said, walking into the attached bathroom and bringing back a razor and several assorted bottles.

She handed him the cufflinks, and as he put them in the bag, she said, "You know, one of the first things I noticed about you was how well you take care of yourself."

"Oh?"

"There's just something so sexy about the way you dress, how you carry yourself. I love that you aren't shy about it."

"I just know what I like," he said, cheeks flushing.

"As do I." She kissed him and sat back down on the bed. "Anything else I can do to help?"

"Yes, actually. Can you move that bag for me?" After she moved the bag he had been filling to the end of the bed, he knelt forward and kissed her. "Thanks."

She giggled as he stood to put the computer and a long, black velvet box that she assumed housed a watch into the bag. He unloaded the Tomcat before placing it on top of the computer and said, "I think that does it."

They left the bedroom and walked past a second, smaller bathroom, heading towards the stairs. Passing another closed door, she asked, "So what's that room for?"

Half-smiling, he said, "I hoped you'd ask me that."

He opened the door and turned on the light, intently watching her reaction.

"Oh. My. God."

The last bedroom had only a small table and a soft, emerald armchair in the corner, surrounded by floor to ceiling bookshelves. "Needless to say, this is where I spend most of the time that I'm here."

"This is one of the most beautiful things I've ever seen!" she exclaimed, taking in the warm, welcoming room.

"Thank you. I've put a lot of myself into it."

"I can tell!" She ran her fingers along a row of books and said, "Okay, get me out, or we'll be here all night." After a gentle laugh, he led the way down the hall to relock the office, so they could make their way back downstairs and out to the car.

"Should we order dinner tonight?" she asked as he drove back onto the highway.

"I have to drop my car at Libera's— want me to just pick up something there?"

"That sounds amazing! Thanks!"

He smiled and lit a cigarette.

"Can I ask you another question about your work, and I swear it'll be the last one?"

"You can ask me as many questions as you need to, and I'll answer as much as I'm able."

"If you don't want to answer, you don't have to."

"You want to know where my money comes from."

"How did you know that?"

He smiled. "Process of elimination. It's the only other thing I could think of that you'd want to know. Add that in with the fact that you have to have known how much everything in my closet alone must have cost. I'm actually surprised that you didn't ask me sooner."

"You are?"

"Absolutely. It seems like the most natural question to have."

"I'd wondered before, but didn't know if I was supposed to ask or not."

"With anyone else, I probably wouldn't. However, I'm mostly paid by Mack and Bronte, and I'm actually one of the few people in the organization listed on an actual payroll."

"And they're the guys from the casinos?"

"Correct. I'm listed as a business consultant. I pay taxes and everything. That, along with me not having a prison record, helps keep Libera in good standing with the IRS."

"Libera doesn't pay you?"

"Only occasionally, when I close something big. And even then, it's usually in goods, not cash. There's no need for him to with Mack and Bronte paying me. It's all Libera's money, anyway."

"That actually makes a lot of sense."

"You look relieved."

"I guess I don't even know what I assumed."

He laughed. "It's best not to assume when Libera's involved. I think we found that one out tonight…"

Chapter 18

When he pulled up in front of her building, he said, "I'll be back as soon as I can."

"Want me to take your bags up? That way you're not fighting with those and food at the same time?"

He considered the contents of one of the bags for a moment before saying, "You don't have to—"

"Look, we can 'leave the gun, take the cannoli' as much as you want, but I'm going to eat you if I don't get some food soon."

He covered his eyes and erupted in laughter. "Christ, how long have you been waiting to say that?"

"It actually just occurred to me," she said, smiling at his laughter and taking his bags out of the back seat. She walked around to the driver window and leaned down to kiss him. "The one I've been waiting for is "It's not personal, Sonny.""

Simone nodded his head and finished, "It's strictly business."

She stepped back as he pulled away, still laughing at what she was sure would be the dumbest joke she'd ever make in front of him.

As he pulled into the lot at Libera's, he saw his Patron's car in its usual spot. *This ought to be fun*, he thought, knowing it was best to make his presence known. As he walked into the restaurant and over to Libera's table, Libera looked up, surprised to see him. He stood up and, still looking amused, shook Simone's hand. "I thought you were occupied this evening."

"I am. Came by to drop the car off and pick up some food."

"Have time for a drink?" Libera asked, nodding towards his empty table.

"Of course, sir."

Libera waved to the nearest server, who returned a few moments later with two glasses of scotch. "Hey, Marshall," Simone said, causing the new waiter to jump as he retracted his steps.

"Yes, Mr. Belvedere?"

"Can you have Stephen put in mine and Estelle's usual order to go for me?" he asked, putting a fifty into the waiter's hand.

"Yes, sir."

"Thanks."

"I love watching the new kids talk to you," Libera said, laughing. "They act like you'll take them out back if they mess your order up."

Simone half-smiled and said, "A few good tips usually loosen them up a little."

"Speaking of loosening up," Libera started, gleefully watching Simone shift uncomfortably. "I apologize for interrupting earlier."

"It's really, REALLY nothing we need to discuss. Ever."

Libera laughed and took a sip of his drink. "I completely agree. However—" he set his glass down and leaned closer to an increasingly anxious Simone, "We've never talked about her. How is... everything?"

Simone took a sip from his glass, torn between giving an honest or respectable answer. He decided to say nothing and just half-smiled, taking another sip from his glass. Libera laughed and said, "You know it's good when they can't talk about it."

Curious to see where Libera was going, Simone continued his silence, but finished his drink and stared, half-smiling, into his glass. As he predicted, Libera went on to say, "You think she's the one?"

Simone looked up and leaned in. "Don, I've never been more sure of anything."

"I think so, too. Is she okay with what you do?"

"You already know the answer to that, sir."

"I do?"

"I think you knew before I did. It was that morning in your office, when you told me not to underestimate her."

"I take it you took my advice?"

"I did."

"I thought so. Tell her about your parents?"

"Minimally. I left out the part about my mother trying to contact me recently."

"I figured as much. It's not often one of my driest boys buys an entire bottle of $350 scotch."

"Was I wrong to tell her?" Simone asked, wanting more to gauge Libera's reaction than gain confidence in his decision.

"Definitely not. You have to be honest with her about some things, and it's best to do it before you marry her."

"S-sorry, what?"

"I can see it in your eyes. You can bluff the best of them, Simone, but I can tell when it comes to her. She completes you, and I can see that you know that."

"It's too soon," Simone said, having had the same realization himself earlier that evening.

"That may be. But you'll see. Before the year is out, I'd put money on it. Just don't give her any unnecessary names."

"I wouldn't dream of it, sir," Simone said truthfully, standing as Marshall brought his order over. He put another fifty into Marshall's hand, and a twenty on the table for the drinks. "Thank you, Don Libera."

"My pleasure, Simone."

As he left, he considered Libera's prediction and tried to find a rational answer, but all he could think of was the princess cut diamond he had seen when purchasing Estelle's birthday gift.

Chapter 19

That night, as Estelle got out of the shower, she walked into her bedroom to find Simone wearing only navy lounge pants and leaning against her headboard, scrolling through numbers on the laptop he had packed earlier. "You're still wearing Ralph Lauren, aren't you?"

Half-smiling without looking up, he said, "Did you expect any different?"

"Of course not." She walked into her closet and put on the sheer, black nightgown she'd purchased for Simone's first night staying over, along with the matching lace that went under it. She stood in the doorway of the closet, one arm up against the doorframe, the other at her side, fingers toying with the short hem against her thigh. "Have a lot of work left?"

He shook his head, still oblivious to the seductive figure before him. "Nothing that can't wait until morning."

"Simone?" she cooed, trying to get his attention.

"Sorry," he said, closing the computer and finally looking up. "So very sorry," he finished, rising to his knees and holding a hand out to her as he took in her appearance.

"You like?" she said, taking his hand and standing in front of him, her lips an inch away from his.

He pulled at her bottom lip with his teeth and said, "Very much."

She put her arms around his neck and kissed him, but after a moment he pulled back and said, "Something's missing, though."

"Oh? What would that be?"

He pulled the black velvet box that she had seen earlier out of his pants pocket. "How about this?"

"What's this?"

He kissed her ear lobe and whispered, "Open it."

She opened the velvet box and put a hand to her mouth to muffle her gasp. The inner lining of the box had been embroidered with the words *'Those be rubies, fairy favours','* and resting on the bottom half of the box was an emerald cut ruby pendant on a delicate silver chain, along with matching earrings.

"Oh, Simone. They're beautiful! What is this for?"

"Your birthday's in a few days, and I thought it would be a good opportunity to indulge you a little."

"This is too much!"

He tilted her chin up so she was looking at him. "Never." He kissed her cheek and said, "That was the line I was reading when you walked in that night, and I've never been the same since."

She kissed him and asked, "Put it on me?"

He took the necklace from the box and put it gently around her neck, kissing just above it. "It's perfect," she said, turning and putting her arms around his neck again.

"I'm glad." He walked the box over to her dresser and turned the light out. "You're perfect," he said, before kissing her and lifting her into his arms. Laying her down underneath him, he whispered again, "You're perfect."

Chapter 20

When Estelle turned off her alarm at seven the next morning, she stood, intending to make a pot of coffee, but felt a gentle hand take hold of hers and pull her towards the bed. "My alarm's set for 8," Simone said, putting his arm around her and pulling her close.

She smiled and turned so her face was nestled against his neck. "You have to be anywhere today?"

"As far as I know I am all yours today."

"Good."

She kissed his neck, and then started to kiss her way down his chest. "I was so disappointed that I never got to finish what I started before he walked in yesterday," she said, pulling herself on top of him and sitting on her knees, one leg on either side of him.

"You weren't the only one," he said, sliding his hands down her arms.

She looked up at him, roused by the cavalier smile on his unshaven face, and continued kissing down his chest and running her tongue over the black-outlined feather tattooed towards the bottom of his ribcage.

"I love this," she said, pausing and passing her fingers over it. "How long have you had it?"

He smiled and said, "Seven years. I'd wanted it for a long time, though. Old Egyptian mythology…"

"It suits you well."

She kept kissing down further, until she had resumed what she had been doing the evening before in his kitchen, her free hand holding onto his hip. Biting his lower lip, he entwined his left hand gently in her hair, right hand resting on his chest, losing himself in her movements and sounds.

Chapter 21

After a tense dinner with Libera in early November, Joel drove Simone and Estelle to her apartment, all three of them sitting in pained silence. Every couple minutes, Joel would glance back at the two of them in the rear-view mirror, eyes moving quickly between them before focusing back on the road. Estelle sat staring out the window at the mist, rubbing her front teeth against her bottom lip and tapping her right thumb continuously on her knee. Simone's elbow was against the bottom of the window— his thumb pressed into his jaw and fingers resting casually against his lips. His eyes were narrowed as he looked out through the windshield, chancing occasional sideways glances at Estelle.

The silence remained unbroken until Estelle said, "Thanks, Joel," before getting out of the car and stepping up onto the curb to locate her keys within her handbag. Simone paid Joel for the night and hesitated for a breath before opening his door.

"Good luck, Boss," Joel said, attempting to conceal a small smile at the expense of the couple. Simone gave a short laugh through his nose, saying, "Thanks, Joel," as he patted his companion's shoulder before exiting the car.

They had barely entered Estelle's apartment when Simone softly said, "Would you like to tell me what's wrong?"

Estelle dropped her purse and keys loudly on the table by the door before walking around to the couch and unfastening her strappy heels. "What the hell is his problem?" she said, a little louder than necessary.

He walked over to the window, and as he opened it he asked, "Who, Libera? That's just—"

"No!" Estelle said, louder, still. "Don't you dare just tell me that's just how he is."

Simone looked blindsided for a moment before he lit a cigarette, cocked his head to the side and said, "What did you expect?"

He immediately closed his eyes and dropped his head, realizing his remark, though honest, was poorly chosen.

"What did I expect?" Estelle spat. "What did I EXPECT? Maybe for you to be treated with some level of respect? Surely he owes you some kind of—"

"Owes me?" Simone started, clearly stung. "Of course he owes me. You think he's going to treat me differently than anyone else in public?"

"And not making you look like a dependent—"

"I do not depend on him," Simone hissed.

The anger in his tone had never been directed towards Estelle, but she sat back against the couch for a minute, caught off guard and unsure of who his anger was with.

"I didn't mean..." she mumbled, trailing off.

He looked around quickly, realizing her uncertainty. "No! Estelle, I—"

"No," she said flatly, standing up. "It wasn't my place."

She turned to go change out of her expensive satin into something soft and infinitely more comfortable.

"What the hell do you mean, 'Not your place'?" he said louder than he intended, putting out his cigarette and closing the window.

She gave him a sad look and said "Look, I should have just let it go. I thought tonight was just a relaxed, social event and it was clearly just a way for him to reinforce his— and your— place."

"Of course it was!" Simone retorted, still incensed. "He's an arrogant, condescending dick that retains his control by taking it away from someone else. That's what the business is—"

"You think I don't know? You think I don't realize how this world works?" Estelle yelled back. "You think I don't know the shit you put up with, the things you do for him?"

"Lower your voice." Simone said, suddenly direct. "You   want someone to—?"

"No. I don't." Estelle interrupted, lowering her volume but retaining the same level of vitriol. "But do you know what I do want, Simone? For you to stop acting like I don't know what the hell is going on, and for you to just get a piece of the respect you deserve. You've been working for him for seventeen years and he still treats you like a child!"

"The hell do you want me to do about it, Estelle?" Simone said, volume rising again.

Whatever you have to, Estelle thought. Her thoughts seemed to translate through the angry look she was giving Simone, because, rather than keeping with his previously angry responses, he just sat down and started to laugh.

"Jesus Christ, did I underestimate you."

"What the hell does that mean?" she asked, feeling patronized.

"Not tonight— when we met. Yet here we are, and you'd have me put a contract out on a major Midwest boss less than a year later."

"I never meant—"

"What did you mean, then?"

Finally flustered with the argument and not knowing how she felt about what her look implied, she just quietly said, "I don't know. I guess I did."

Simone looked up at her and said, "I shouldn't have lost my temper."

"You had every right. I'm sorry I started the argument."

"No, I understand. And I agree with you about his attitude. But baby, that really is just how it has to be. I've been through too much with Libera to walk away. I owe him at least that."

"I understand how you feel. But I don't think that treating you like an adult would cost him his entire territory."

"He treats me as he always has, and that's unlikely to change. He can be a good leader, and an even better friend when he wants to be. Unfortunately, no one else is ever around to see it..."

"I know. He just got to me tonight. I'm sorry." Estelle turned and began to walk quickly down the hall to her bedroom.

"No, don't be— Estelle?" Simone said, not wanting to end the conversation without finding a way to apologize for how he had spoken to her. He tried to coax her back to the conversation, but could only get out "Estelle, please—" before she had closed the bedroom door.

He turned and looked out the window, thinking, *Am I supposed to follow her?* Deciding to give her some space, he reopened the window and lit another cigarette.

Estelle sat down on her bed and stared for a few minutes at the wall, trying to organize her thoughts. She didn't want him to see her cry, but only because she, herself, didn't fully understand how she was feeling. After another few moments of holding back, she finally let go and let her tears fall, trying to work through them as they came. After several more minutes, Simone, having finished his last cigarette for the night, opened the door and stood frozen for a moment before slowly sitting down next to her.

"Estelle?" he asked cautiously. "I'm sorry, Estelle, I hadn't realized I'd upset you so—"

"No," she replied through her tears. "I think I'm just overwhelmed. I've been so worried about you lately, with all the expansion talk... and I was angry about the way Libera talked to you— and now I'm worried that you just think I'm a crying... worrying... mess that can't handle it."

"I think a night like tonight was enough to overwhelm anyone, and I think that you're exceptionally brave to have even considered a relationship with a man like me, and even braver for sitting down to dinner with either Libera or myself— let alone both of us. Few people— in or out of the business— would be willing to do that. We just have to find a way to dilute his attitude a little when you're around, which I'm sure can be done..." He put his arm around her waist and pulled her close, so she was resting her head on his shoulder. "And your worrying shows me how much you love me, and you'll never know how much that means to me. But I promise you, everything is under control."

Estelle looked up at him, her crying slowing, but with no words to give, so Simone continued, "And above anything, you have calmed my biggest fear I've had for a long while— a fear I had even before our relationship began."

Estelle just looked at him in surprise. "Oh, yes. You," he stopped to kiss her forehead, "have shown me that you're not only unafraid of my work, you understand it, and you aren't repulsed by it, like so many people outside of the business are. And you, my love, don't look at me as anything less or more than human."

They sat in silence for a long while, Simone's arm tightly around her. Estelle had never felt closer to Simone. She loved that his confidence at work was balanced by self-doubt in his ability to connect with someone— and she loved how freeing her love and acceptance were to those doubts.

Simone looked into her eyes as she wiped away her tears, wishing he could find more words to soothe her, but after a moment, she leaned forward and gently kissed him. As he returned her kiss, he felt her shoulders lean into him, and he wrapped the fingers of his right hand in her hair, just behind her ear. Each kiss seemed to build upon the foundation of the last, and Estelle was several buttons in before he realized that she was unbuttoning his shirt. As his shirt hit the floor, Estelle rose and stood directly in front of Simone, who was still sitting on the edge of the bed. She leaned down, kissing his lips and feeling his hands pull the thin straps of her dress off of her shoulders. His lips began a slow path down her neck and chest, his hands taking her dress slowly down with him until it rested at her hips.

Standing back up, she looked deep into Simone's eyes and gave him a sly smile as she unhooked the fastenings on the red satin that had been veiled under her Dior. She helped it fall slowly to the floor before slinking the dress the rest of the way off, and as the satin dress floated down her smooth skin, she realized that this would be the first full experience they had together in more than the streetlights coming in through the windows. Her right hand slid up her hip, and she could see Simone's desire rise as she held her breast momentarily in her hand.

As she let her hands continue their exploration, her eyes were busy taking in as much of Simone as was visible— his dark eyes and intoxicating half-smile, down to the barely visible scars on his chest. Her eyes flitted over the feather tattoo at his ribcage and the larger scar on his hip that he still refused to talk about, just above the right pocket of his pants. His left hand was pushing his dark hair out of his face, while the other was slowly unfastening his belt.

No one has ever looked at me this way. Simone watched her eyes follow along their intake of his features, but instead of the feeling of exposure he always feared, he felt his emotional boundaries drop away, and finally let himself feel closer to Estelle.

Keeping his hands off of her had become a task in and of itself, and as he became aware of how quickly he was breathing, she leaned forward for more passionate kisses, and felt Simone hook his thumbs under the hips of the last piece of red lace she was still wearing, slowly pulling down until it fell past her knees and onto the floor. She could tell by the way he leaned his head into every kiss and the slow, drawn-out motions of his tongue against hers that he was past the point of just wanting to be with her— every fiber of his being needed to make love to her, and his desire for her was only matched by her desire for him. Unable to continue the slow build up, she put one knee on each side of him and slowly leaned into his chest. He pressed his hands onto her back, holding her close to him as he laid them backwards onto the bed, kissing her more passionately than ever before.

Neither lover had a thought of anything beyond the other as Simone turned so she was underneath him. His lips were kissing every part of her they could find, and Estelle's hands were quickly removing the rest of his clothes. Simone's lips returned to Estelle's before making their way down her neck to her breasts, but instead of continuing their circle up as she expected, she felt his lips on the soft skin under her breast, and then felt his tongue tracing a path down her side until his lips slowed at the peak of her hip. She could feel his breathing pick up again as his kisses reached her thigh, and then gave a sharp gasp as his tongue reached its destination.

His moans were telling her that he'd been longing to do this, but he could never find the sexual confidence to attempt it. She had sensed before that he wanted to taste and indulge her in this way, and for several months she had been longing for it, but she hadn't wanted to push him too quickly out of his boundaries.

Simone, reveling both in the enjoyment of what he was doing and the volume of Estelle's reaction, continued the patterns his tongue was tracing, occasionally tasting deep inside her at increasingly futile attempts to teasingly postpone her climax. Estelle's hand became happily entangled in Simone's hair as he continued to bring her closer and closer to her building orgasm, and twenty passion fueled minutes later, her hips began to sway under his strong jaw and she could feel his half-smile against the thigh that was propped up on his shoulder. She could feel her orgasm approaching, and kept trying to find words that could somehow convey the magnitude of Simone's skill, until finally his lips and tongue pushed her over the edge into oblivious euphoria.

One hand grasping his hair and the other clenching the pillow above her head, Estelle rode the intense waves that was undoubtedly the strongest climax she had ever reached before gently nudging him— silently asking him to pull back the intensity. Not wanting to lose momentum, Simone kissed his way back up to her neck until Estelle delicately pulled him by his hair into a passionate kiss.

Breathing heavily through a night of many firsts, Simone had no need to ask if Estelle was ready for him. There were no hesitations, no fears, and no self-doubts. Her inarticulate clamor was pulling him further into their daze, and as she uttered the breathy confirmation that was his name, he felt her smooth calf glide against his back. Without conscious thought, Simone pushed himself into her and issued a loud, gruff moan at the rapturous sensation of her tight warmth molding around him.

The minutes swept past as he continued to thrust inside her, leaning forward for their lips to meet as she held his hip tight against her with one hand— her other hand clasped tightly to the back of his head. Simone put his left arm under her head, his right forearm supporting his upper body. She realized he was getting closer when he began to move his hips in a deep circular motion, gently increasing speed as he brought his arms into a close embrace around her. Estelle had never felt him so hard— so intense— inside her, and she wrapped her legs tighter around him, until every motion pushed him as far in as was possible.

"Jesus... fucking... Christ..." he said loudly, still subconsciously increasing speed.

Estelle nuzzled her cheek against his, taking in every hot, breathy word loud in her ear. He had never been as vocal as he was tonight, and she longed to feel— and hear— his intense release. "Simone, please, come for me."

Her fingernails dug into his shoulders as he felt himself approaching his peak. Simone's carnal sounds became louder and he locked eyes with Estelle, his orgasm rippling through every extremity.

As their breathing began to normalize, he closed his eyes and brought his lips to hers. Even her shoulders seemed to melt into the kisses, which still lingered in the moments after Simone shifted his weight off of her. Turning onto his side, he pulled Estelle into a close embrace, her head contently under his chin.

"Estelle?"

"Hmm?"

"I love you."

She smiled and nuzzled her cheek against his chest. "I love you, too, Simone."

After half an hour of listening to her breathing happily against his chest, Simone became aware that Estelle had fallen asleep. Not wanting to wake her, he slowly lifted her head onto her pillow and pulled on the pants that lay discarded on the floor next to her expensive dress. Running a hand through his hair, he sighed softly and walked into the living room to take a cigarette out of his jacket pocket. He walked over to his usual window, and opened it enough to let the smoke escape into night air. He lit the cigarette and inhaled deeply, looking out over the city, and feeling more genuinely human than he previously had ever known.

Estelle awoke around eight thirty the next morning to find Simone's arm wrapped lovingly around her waist, pulling her back into his chest.

"You're awake," he said, kissing the back of her neck.

"You're very observant, Mr. Belvedere," Estelle said, smiling as she turned to face her lover.

Simone smiled back and kissed her. As she brushed his hair out of his eyes, she asked, "How long have you been awake?"

"Not long. My phone rang around eight. I came back to bed about fifteen minutes ago."

"Did you need to get some more sleep?"

"I'm all right," Simone said, kissing her forehead. "I actually have to go take care of something, but I would love to see you for dinner tonight."

"I'd love that, too."

Simone kissed her again before rising from the bed and heading into the bathroom for a shower. Estelle sat up in bed, resting her head on her knees for a moment, trying to work up the motivation to start a slow Sunday morning. She laid back against her pillows with her hand where Simone had been asleep next to her, reliving the memories of the romantic night before. *Everything was perfect. Absolutely everything— oh god.*

Estelle rose quickly and walked into the living room in search of her cell phone. After finding it under Simone's jacket and double checking that he was in the shower, she began to type a harried barrage of text messages.

Carolyn, are you up?
I'm sorry to text so early— are you busy?
Can we meet for an early lunch?
I REALLY need to talk to you.

She sat waiting for the ten minutes it took for Simone to finish his hurried shower before Carolyn responded.

I haven't had my coffee yet. How have you already had a crisis?

Who said it was a crisis?

The twenty-seven texts waking me up told me.

...Sorry about that.

Don't be. I can be over in half an hour.

We have to wait until Simone leaves. Should be soon.

...You sure everything's ok?

Can you just meet me soon?

All right. Want to go to Phil's for eggs or order something at your place? Might be quieter.

Good point. Want to meet me here?

                Sure will. Just text me when he leaves and I'll head over.

"Someone's popular this morning," Simone said, fastening his diamond cufflinks as he walked into the room.

"Just Carolyn," Estelle said, watching him deftly maneuvering his tie before buttoning his vest.

"You were right about keeping a few things here, by the way," he added, with his customary half-smile. He walked over to where she was sitting on the couch and put his hands on the back of it behind each of her shoulders. "You've been right about a lot of things."

Estelle smiled and put her arms around his neck. "I like being right," she said with a coy simper, before leaning up to kiss him.

"I'm sorry I have to leave so quickly this morning," Simone said, pressing his forehead against hers.

"I know," she replied, closing her eyes.

Simone stood back up and returned to the bedroom for his new jacket before coming back to gather his pocket watch, money clip and cigarettes. His eyes narrowed as he watched Estelle staring out the window. "Everything all right?"

She shook her head to pull herself out of her thoughts. "Sorry," she said quickly. "Just a little tired, still."

Estelle smiled up at Simone who, pocketing his keys, smiled back gently and said, "It was quite the night last night." He leaned down and gave Estelle another slow, gentle kiss. "I'll see you tonight?"

"Of course."

Chapter 22

"So, what's the emergency?" Carolyn asked, taking off her sweater and sitting down on Estelle's couch.

"You don't waste any time, do you?"

"You kidding? How many messages did you send me?"

"Sorry— I was still... surprised."

"It's all okay— just tell me what happened."

"I had the best sex of my life last night."

Carolyn blinked for a moment before saying, "And that's... bad?"

"No— yes— I don't know."

"I want to help you, but I'm going to need a little more information."

"All right. So, last night, we had dinner with Libera."

"You have my deepest sympathy. Go on."

"It was ridiculous. He was just so much of..."

"Himself?" Carolyn supplied.

"Pretty much. He can be a nice guy when he wants to be... I just hate the way he talks to Simone..."

Estelle immediately regretted her choice of words.

"What do you mean?"

"Not important— the point is, it makes me crazy. We got home and I was all pissed off, and we had this huge fight."

"Well, it was bound to happen eventually."

"I know. And looking back at it, it wasn't that bad. Actually, once we both calmed down, he was really sweet. I feel like we're closer now."

"But that's a good thing— sometimes it just takes something like that to move forward."

"Well, we were sitting on the edge of the bed, and he was holding me, trying to make me feel better, and then I kissed him, and things just kept moving further and further..."

"This still doesn't sound like a problem."

"The PROBLEM," Estelle said, internal butterflies erupting at being faced with actually vocalizing what she had realized, "is that it just KEPT going, without either of us remembering to..."

"Oh. OH!" Carolyn, finally catching on, leaned closer to Estelle, who nodded.

"Yeah."

"You didn't use—"

Estelle shook her head.

"And you're not on—"

"Not even a little."

"And he—"

"OOOH yeah." Estelle paused, having a pleasant shiver from the memory of Simone's climax.

"Okay— focus!" Carolyn said, clapping her hands.

"Sorry!" Estelle said, shaking her head and concentrating on the problem at hand. "I don't know what to do. Do I tell him?"

"I'm sure he knows. If not already, he'll realize it at some point today."

"Do I bring it up?"

"Hmmm. Well, you can, but you should probably realize that it might just be freaking him out for no reason. I mean, the odds of conception are technically very small, especially if this is the only time this has happened. This IS the only time this has happened?"

"Absolutely. We've always used protection."

"ALWAYS? Not even the old just—"

"Always," Estelle said, waving her hands to stop Carolyn from talking. "Always."

"I think it'll all be okay. It was just the one time. It happens to a lot of people, and nothing comes from it. I know that Simone isn't like most guys, but I still think that telling him that you're worried about it would just freak him out."

"That's true. He probably won't assume anything's wrong unless I bring it up. I'm probably just freaking out over nothing, anyway," Estelle reasoned.

"Everything will work out. No matter what happens, everything will be fine. I promise."

Chapter 23

By mid-December, it had become one busy week at the library after another. The local university was in the middle of finals, parents were attempting to keep their children's attention over a break from school with books rather than video games, and a popular series had just released a new film, driving up demand for the book that inspired it, and therefore bringing in people that couldn't even seem to find the display by the door with twenty copies of the god-forsaken book, let alone find it on the shelf.

"Effing vampires," Carolyn said under her breath, walking away from another nineteen-year-old that couldn't find the display. She turned and headed over to the desk to complain to Estelle, but found Paul in her place. Puzzled, she began to weave through the aisles of books and realized it had been a good two hours since she had seen Estelle.

After fifteen minutes of maneuvering through dozens of shelves on various floors, she found Estelle sitting on a step-stool in the home repair section next to a still full cart of books waiting to resume their homes on the shelves. She had her elbows on her knees, propping up her head as she looked out the window, and it took a moment for her to become aware of Carolyn's presence.

"Oh, Carolyn! I'm so sorry! I was tired and sat down for a moment and lost track of my thoughts!"

"It's okay! I'm just worried about you. You don't seem like yourself today."

"I'm definitely not myself today," Estelle said, looking back towards the window.

"Are you sick? Or is it something with Simone?" Carolyn asked carefully.

"Something like that," Estelle said, still not looking at her friend.

"Why don't you head home? We close in less than an hour, and there's enough of us to finish the night out."

"Yeah, I should probably do that. But can you come over when you get off?"

"Absolutely! Is everything okay?"

"I think so. I just need to talk it through with someone."

"I'll be over right after work."

"Thank you," Estelle said, hugging her friend.

As Carolyn headed back to the desk to tell their supervisor of Estelle's early departure, Estelle took out her phone and began to dial Simone's number. After five seemingly endless rings she heard, "Hello, Estelle."

"Hey, Simone. I was going to stay in tonight and spend some time with Carolyn. Do you mind if I take a raincheck on dinner?"

"Of course, not. Is everything all right?"

"It is. We just need a long girl-talk."

"That sounds like a wonderful night for you. I was worried I was taking you away from her too much."

"Of course not."

"Would you like to have dinner at Libera's tomorrow night? It'll be a year tomorrow from the day we met."

"Oh my goodness! You are so sweet for remembering! I'd love to!"

"Wonderful! I'll see you tomorrow night at six?"

"Absolutely."

"All my love," Simone finished.

"And mine," Estelle said, hanging up the phone with a sigh of contentment mingled heavily with anxiety.

Over at Libera's, Simone smiled at his phone before replacing it in his jacket pocket. He sipped at his scotch, patiently awaiting his Patron to finish his lengthy discussion on the week's numbers from the casinos. As the conversation concluded, Libera caught Simone's gaze and sauntered over to the bar, grasping Simone's hand as he did so.

"All is well, I take it?" Simone asked.

"Never better," Libera replied casually. "You look like you got some good news yourself."

"In fact, I did," Simone said, trying to disguise his enthusiasm. "She'll be here tomorrow night at six."

"And you're sure about what you're doing?"

"Absolutely."

"That's my boy," Libera replied happily, tapping Simone's arm with each word. "I'll close the place down around four to make sure everything's ready. Everyone on board?"

"They are. I was even able to get her friend in on it, though she just thinks it's an anniversary party. She'll get Estelle here on time."

"Wonderful!" Libera said. "Wonderful."

Chapter 24

Estelle originally planned on trying to fit in some sleep before Carolyn came over, but couldn't quiet her nerves enough to do so. She decided, therefore, to settle on ordering a couple small pizzas and waiting for her friend to arrive.

An hour and a half later, Carolyn knocked at Estelle's door, holding the pizzas. "We got here at the same time, so I signed for you."

"Thanks!" Estelle said happily. As she sat down at her couch and opened her pizza box, Carolyn took two wine glasses from the mini bar and began to open a bottle of Moscato. As she sat the glasses down on the coffee table, Estelle said quickly, "Oh, none for me, thanks."

"You ignored your books today, and now you don't want your favorite wine? Tell me what's wrong."

Estelle sat looking at her pizza and said, "Carolyn, I'm pregnant."

"Oh my god," Carolyn said, waving a hand in apology and continuing, "No— that's not what I meant! I meant— oh my god..." Carolyn continued to stammer for another moment before saying, "When did you find out?"

"This morning. That's why I was late to work. I'd been feeling sick for about a week, so I went to the doctor. I'm around six weeks."

"Does Simone know?"

"No, I can't decide how I think he'll take it, so I want to tell him in person."

"The man may be stone cold at work, but if there is one thing I am certain of, it's that Simone loves you more than I've seen any man love anyone."

Estelle rolled her eyes at Carolyn's continued perpetuation of Simone's rumored demeanor. "I know he does. But he was so hesitant to take on the commitment of the title 'boyfriend.' How is he going to take adding the title of 'father'?"

"How do YOU feel about it, Estelle? That's priority number one."

"I'm thrilled," Estelle chirped, heart fluttering with excitement. "I mean, I know it's scary, and it's not going to be easy. But I'm going to be a mother, and it just feels right for me— for us. I've known for a while that Simone is the only one for me— and I know that someday, if he were ever ready to hear it, I'd happily tell him that. And I know Simone. He's not going to run just because he's scared."

"When are you going to tell him?"

"Tomorrow at dinner, I think."

"TOMORROW!" Carolyn blurted out. "I mean, isn't tomorrow your anniversary?"

"It is," Estelle went on, nonplussed. "But I can't wait. I know if I do I'll blurb out something stupid, and—"

"You're right. Tomorrow it is. I'll walk over with you if you want."

"That would be amazing!" Estelle went on slowly, saying, "And I'm sure… your godchild appreciates it, too."

Carolyn's eyes filled with appreciative tears as they hugged.

"So," Carolyn said as she let go of the hug. "Six weeks? So that would be about the time—"

"Of that one time. Yep."

Chapter 25

"Here they come, boss," Joel called to Simone.

"You sure about this?" Libera asked again.

"Of course. Thank you, again, for your assistance."

"My sincere pleasure, my friend."

Simone looked around, checking to ensure everything was perfect. Mack and Gallo were happily chatting with Landini halfway down the bar. Champagne glasses were being filled at one of the candlelit tables, a few of Libera's and Simone's friends and colleagues loitered around the appetizer bar, and Simone leaned against the bar where they met— this time home to a dozen of Estelle's favorite pink roses.

"Carolyn, what is going on?" Estelle asked as Carolyn prodded her friend through the jingling door, turning her to look at the romantic scene laid out before her.

"Hello, Estelle," Simone murmured, taking her by the hand and leading her to the rose-laden bar-top.

"Oh my goodness, Simone! This is wonderful!" Estelle said, looking around through a happy mist in her eyes.

"I couldn't have done it without Don Libera's help. And Carolyn's," Simone added with a polite nod to Estelle's friend.

Carolyn made a dramatic curtsey in acknowledgement, patted Estelle's arm and said, "I think I'm hungry."

"This way," Libera began, leading her to the appetizers. "We've got the best..."

His voice trailed away as Estelle put her arms around Simone's neck and sank into the gentle kiss he gave her. She smiled up at him and cooed, "I love you, Simone."

Libera raised his glass and, once the room had silenced, said, "I would like to say that I have known Simone for a very long time, and it gives me great joy to see him— and Miss Estelle— so happy together."

As everyone clapped and drank to the couple's happiness, Simone took a deep breath before responding to the room. To their general surprise, he smiled and said, "Thank you, Don Libera. I know that I am not well known as a man that shares his thoughts, but tonight, I have to. Estelle, you are unlike any person I have ever met or known, and you have shown me that true love and pure acceptance exist, and for that, I am forever grateful."

"Simone," Estelle said, approaching him, "I love YOU. All of you."

"I know you do. And that's why—"

Estelle and Carolyn both gasped as Simone knelt before his love. Carolyn, forgetting herself for a moment, steadied herself on Libera's arm, and Estelle locked eyes with Simone— all of her lingering doubts and fears from the previous day floating away.

"I want you to know, Estelle, that I love you, and I want to be the one there for you, appreciating you, protecting you, and above all, loving you, for the rest of our lives. Estelle, will you marry me?"

He took a small paper box from his pocket, and as he held it up she saw that it was a sparkling diamond ring nestled in a small paper box made from pages of Shakespeare. Estelle began to cry happy tears into her hands for a moment before kneeling down on both knees so that her eyes were level with his. She knew now, before she answered— before he was locked into a commitment, was the moment. She leaned forward and whispered in his ear.

"Simone, I'm pregnant."

He turned his head quickly, as it had been leaning to the side to hear her whisper, and put both hands on her shoulders. Forgetting the room was still listening, he said loudly, with his unreadable expression, "Are you sure?"

Libera and a few others looked nervous, but Estelle just kept his gaze and said, "Yes, I am."

Simone looked into her eyes for a long moment before standing up and helping Estelle to her feet, and his face broke into a smile of pure exhilaration that she had never seen before. "You're really sure?" he asked again, as if it were too wonderful to be believed.

"Yes! I'm sure!" she said with a laugh.

He threw his head back in a boyish laugh and hugged her so quickly that he lifted her feet off of the floor. Still with her in his arms he said quickly, "Wait! You never said—"

"Of course, I will!"

He kissed her again, and as he placed the two-carat diamond on her finger, Libera gave Carolyn a puzzled look as everyone began to clap and said, "So was that a 'yes' twice?"

"Not exactly," Carolyn said with a sly smile.

"Oh!" Estelle said to Simone, "I have something for you!"

She took his hand in hers and led him to the bar chair with her purse. She pulled out a small black and white photo and handed it to Simone. "We're about six weeks along."

With comprehension dawning around the room, Simone looked at the image for a moment and then took Estelle into his arms in the gentlest embrace she had ever known, bringing his lips to hers in a slow, chaste kiss. Arms still around her waist, Simone looked into the distance for a moment. "Six weeks— that would have been around the night we had dinner here with him, wouldn't it?"

"I'm fairly certain that was the night. That was the only time we didn't..." her voice trailed off as he nodded.

"I wondered," he started, "if I should have said something about what happened, but I thought it was just a fluke, that wouldn't... I didn't realize it had happened until after I had already left your apartment, and didn't want you to worry, and I didn't want you to feel like I thought that's all that mattered about it, either."

"Oh, I know. I thought the same thing. Just ask Carolyn."

The door of Libera's jingled open again, and Simone looked up with a surprised smile and went to greet the new arrivals. Estelle looked up and stood shocked into place at the sight of her parents. "I'm so glad you could make it," Simone said politely, recognizing them from photos in Estelle's apartment and shaking their hands.

Estelle's mother looked taken aback by his polite nature, but her father smiled and said, "Glad to finally meet you, Mr. Belvedere."

"Simone, please," Simone requested as he led them over to Estelle.

"Hi!" Estelle said, coming to her senses and hugging her parents. "What are you doing here? I thought—"

"This is not a gesture of approval, Estelle," Mrs. Presswood began, "but if he has the decency to invite us—"

"What your mother is trying to say," Mr. Presswood interrupted, "Is that we understand how much you love each other and didn't want to miss the entire evening. Though judging by that," he pointed at her new ring, "We already missed something."

"I'm just so glad you're here!" Estelle said, hugging her father again.

"I'm not sure we've met," Libera's smooth voice began. "Benedict Libera. Welcome."

He gently shook the hand of a scandalized Mrs. Presswood before shaking hands with Estelle's father.

"John Presswood. This is Estelle's mother, Karen."

"Glad to meet you both." Libera turned to Simone and, with a mischievous sparkle in his eye, asked, "So, have you told them?"

"Not quite yet, sir," Simone replied cautiously.

"Told us what?" Mrs. Presswood snipped.

Estelle went to her purse and took out the other copy of the black and white sonogram and handed it to her father. "You're going to be grandparents."

Her mother stood stiffly and gazed at the picture, but her father pulled her into a big hug and said "My dear! This is wonderful!"

He shook Simone's hand with both of his own, but was interrupted by an icy "And how do you feel about this Mr. Belvedere?"

She was clearly testing Simone's resolve, and Estelle, feelings hurt, said, "Mother—"

"No, it's a perfectly natural question to have," Simone replied gently. With a calm, determined gaze he said, "I couldn't be happier at this new adventure, and you have my word that Estelle and our child will be well provided for and protected."

Her mother continued her icy stare for a moment before saying, "I suppose that's all a mother can ask for."

She gave him a brief, but rigid handshake before changing her demeanor completely, taking a glass of champagne, along with Estelle's reluctant arm, and leading her to a table to further discuss Estelle's pregnancy and engagement.

Chapter 26

It was just after eleven when Estelle and Simone were hugging Carolyn good night after the party. As Carolyn walked away, Simone took Estelle's hand and brought it gently to his lips. She smiled and said, "I know it's a weeknight, but I would love for you to stay with me tonight."

"I'd like that very much. Let me see if Libera needs me again tonight or—"

"No, my friend," Libera said, overhearing the conversation as he walked up to offer his congratulations again before Estelle's departure. "This lady needs you tonight more than I do. Business will keep," he finished, patting Simone's arm with an arrogant smile.

"Thank you, sir."

"My pleasure," Libera said, before kissing Estelle's cheek. "You make sure my boy treats you right."

"He always does," Estelle replied, giving Simone a tired, but loving, smile. She turned and put her arms briefly around Libera, saying, "Thank you, Mr. Libera, for everything."

Libera smiled, drinking in her gratitude. "My pleasure, Miss Estelle. You get some rest."

"I can hardly wait," she said, holding on to Simone's arm as she gave up and slipped out of her shoes.

Libera had turned to head back inside his establishment when he said, "Forget something?"

They both turned to look at who Libera's words were directed to and saw an irritated Carolyn say, "I think I left my keys somewhere in there."

"I'll help you find them," Libera said, leading the way.

"We should get you home," Simone said, pulling her close and leading her to his car.

It was Simone, and not Joel that drove them to Estelle's apartment for the night, and as they entered the lobby of her building together, Estelle realized how very safe she felt with Simone, and how happy she was that they were starting a new chapter of life together. She smiled at how comfortable Simone was while unlocking her apartment, turning on the lamp by the door and setting his keys and pocket watch on the end table. They sat down on the couch together, exhausted, but still reveling.

As he began to remove his tie, Simone looked up at Estelle and said, "You made me a very happy man tonight."

Estelle moved closer and nuzzled up to his arm, which he lifted to allow her to snuggle into his chest. "I'm so glad you were happy about the baby."

"Why wouldn't I be?" he asked gently.

"I could feel, deep down, that you would be. I was just afraid that you'd feel too—"

"Tied down?" Simone supplied.

"Well, yes," Estelle whispered.

"I can understand that."

"You can?"

"Of course. I haven't exactly been free-giving with my commitments. But you, love, haven't told me how you feel about it."

"I feel wonderful," Estelle said, happily yawning.

Simone looked deep into her eyes and again asked, "You're REALLY pregnant?"

She gave a soft laugh and nudged his nose with hers. "I really am."

She moved back so she was next to him, and pulled the sonogram from his unbuttoned jacket pocket. She put the picture in his left hand and then placed his right just below her navel. "This is your baby, Simone."

It was several minutes before either of them spoke. Simone sat looking between the picture and his hand, working through the cocktail of excitement and nervousness that was setting in. Estelle sat laid back, sleepily watching him.

"You're allowed to be happy, Simone," she said gently.

"Am I?" he asked, suddenly serious. "I spend my life carrying out the words of someone else. The things I've done—"

"Are things we both know you don't regret," Estelle said sternly. "Look at me, Simone Belvedere."

He looked up, surprised at the authority that had come over her. "You," she continued, "Do what you have do to in order to survive in a business that literally chose you, and you are damn good at it. I will not have you questioning your entire life because of me."

He continued to look into her eyes, fighting back the half-smile and arousal he could feel coming on as Estelle continued, "I love you because of who you are, and changing any part of that would mean changing the man I love."

He leaned forward, entwined his fingers in her hair and passionately kissed her. After a moment he stopped and put his forehead against hers before saying, "I love you, Estelle. Your courage, your spitfire, every—" he kissed her between each of the last few words—" single— thing— about— you."

He could feel her fingernails through his collar, and knew better than to hesitate, but as he removed his jacket and laid her back on the couch, a new worry began to nag at him and he stopped, laying his head on her arm. Estelle laughed and ran her fingers through his hair. He looked up at her giggles and she said, "You being on top of me won't hurt the baby, Simone."

He smiled softly and said, "You always know."

She gave him a mischievous smile and said, "But if you're worried…"

Without another word she sat up and kissed him while slowly pushing against him, until he was sitting upright— his back against the back of the couch. She put one knee on either side of him and leaned forward into another passionate kiss.

Simone was very pleasantly taken by surprise at her newfound authority, and he loved the way she swayed her hips slowly as she kissed him, teasing the erection that was fighting against his tightly tailored slacks. He was entranced by the way she smiled as she kissed him, as though she'd been hoping for this opportunity for some time. He put his hands on her thighs and slid them up her hips, under her shirt, and onto her soft back.

Estelle gave a slight shiver from the enjoyment of his lips on her neck and his hands feeling their way around her hips before sliding around to begin unbuttoning her shirt. Her arms were barely out of her sleeves before he was unhooking her bra, and before the black lace hit the floor she could feel his soft lips surrounding her nipple. He could tell by her sounds that she was more sensitive than usual, and immensely enjoyed listening to the level of pleasure she was having at his tongue's quick motions.

He slid his hands back around her waist, letting them wander along her back and hips as he realized how far up her skirt had ridden from the movement of her hips against him. As she threw his vest to the floor and began unbuttoning his shirt, Simone's right hand began to travel up her thigh and under her skirt. She still had three buttons to go when she gasped loudly, clasping the back of his head with one hand— the other hand pressed firmly against his chest.

His lips again found hers as he relished the addicting sensation of her wet warmth surrounding two of his fingers. Her hips began to sway against his hand as she finished with the last of his shirt buttons and ran her hands up his chest, letting them come to rest on each side of his jaw as she teasingly traced his lips with her tongue.

She stopped kissing him just long enough to watch his breathing quicken as she unbuttoned his slacks and slid them down just far enough to free his intense erection. Laughing silently to himself,

Simone dismissed his fleeting impulse to pull the foil pouch from his pocket, but the inner laugh was quickly replaced with a loud, outward gasp as he felt her hand close around his shaft and pull him under her skirt, gently forcing his fingers just over an inch higher, her hips steadily rocking towards him.

Time flew by as they continued on their passionate climb, and Simone couldn't tell if minutes or hours had passed. He had never before seen her like this. They had shared many steamy nights together, and her orgasm was far from foreign to him, but he had never felt her this close to orgasm with more than his hand or tongue. He continued the circles his fingers had been tracing, increasing speed to match the increasing speed of her hips. She began to tighten around him as his pace increased, and he was finding it harder and harder to keep his focus on his hand, rather than his rapidly approaching release.

Suddenly, Simone felt his head being pulled back by his hair, and she put her forehead against his, pressing her fingernails into his shoulder as the rocking of her hips ceased, replaced by the quick spasms of her orgasm. Between her loud moans in his ear and the rapid movement of her climax, he could feel himself getting steadily closer to his own peak. He put his hands on her waist as he began to move faster inside her, until all he could do was let out a loud, three syllable "Fuck!" and become consumed by the orgasm he was releasing inside of her.

He brought his hands up and pulled her into a close hug. Estelle nibbled at his ear for a moment, before laying her head on his shoulder, neither speaking for nearly a quarter of an hour.

"Simone?"

"Hmm?"

"Can we have a simple wedding down at the courthouse? Just something small, that doesn't require us to invite half the state?"

Simone closed his eyes as he rested his cheek softly against her head, and smiled.

"I'd love that. It sounds perfect for us."

Several minutes later, he looked up and gently kissed her. "Maybe we should get you to bed, baby," he suggested, smiling at the happy exhaustion in her eyes.

"Hmmm. That sounds nice."

"Why don't you call in tomorrow and get some rest?"

Through her exhaustion, she said, "Because I'm already so far behind." But as she stood up, she was struck with a sudden thought that shook her awake. "You don't mind me working once we're married and the baby comes, do you?"

"Of course, I don't!" Simone said with a genuine laugh. "You need to be surrounded by your books, and I'd never dream of asking you to give that up— nor would I want you to. If you would be happier staying home with the baby, I will absolutely make sure that you both are very well taken care of. But I would never consider making that decision for you. I just want to make sure you're happy, and if working makes you happy, that is absolutely the best decision, and I will be behind you completely," he finished, removing the shoes and pants that didn't quite make it off while they were making love.

She smiled at him and crossed to the bathroom to start getting ready for bed, and as she was brushing her teeth, he came in and kissed her shoulder, smiling as he watched her eyes following her new diamond in the mirror. "The ring suits you well," he said, giving her a satisfied smile.

As she dried her hands she said, "I think so, too," and kissed his cheek before walking into her bedroom.

She changed into her favorite soft, leopard spotted pajama pants and pink camisole, climbed into bed, and quickly settled into her pillow. Simone came in and stood for a moment looking at the contented woman laying before him, before changing, turning out the light and lying down next to her.

"Estelle?" Simone asked quietly.

"Hmmm?"

"Thank you."

Estelle opened her eyes and propped herself up on her elbow. "For what, love?"

"For choosing me. For loving me. For being strong willed and independent. For marrying me and carrying our baby. You—" he hesitated, embarrassed about opening up so much in one evening.

"What is it?" Estelle asked gently.

"You make me feel safe."

Estelle looked at Simone in the dark for a moment, astounded at his words.

"I do?"

"Of course. Your trust in me, and your faith in me— I know I've talked a lot today about protecting you, but you need to know that you make me feel more protected here in your arms than I've ever felt in my life."

"Simone," she said softly, laying her head on his chest. "That's what I'm here for."

He pulled her close and kissed her forehead. "Good night, Estelle."

"Good night, love."

She laid there snuggled up to him, thinking about his words and how lucky she felt to have found Simone. And in that moment, she realized just how safe and secure they felt with the other. Not just physically— she knew that Simone was more than capable of taking care of himself. No, she knew the feeling of security she gave him went much deeper. He didn't have to hide the grittiness of his work, nor the sincerity of his feelings. He could completely be himself around her, and, smiling at the secure feeling they shared, she fell asleep in his arms, both of them feeling loved and safe, and looking forward to their life together.

Chapter 27

Estelle awoke the next morning to Simone getting dressed near the foot of the bed. Smiling at the familiar sounds, she rolled onto her back and said, "Good morning, Simone."

"Good morning, beautiful. Did I wake you?"

"Don't know. What time is it?"

"Not quite 7:30."

"I'd be getting up soon anyhow. Do you have to go so soon? I could make us breakfast."

"I wish I could, but I have to pick something up from Libera's office before my meeting later. If I'm lucky he went home last night instead of sleeping it off in the office."

"Not in the mood for Don Hangover this morning?" Estelle joked, sitting up against her headboard.

Simone's half-smile appeared as he loaded his custom Taurus and placed it into its awaiting sheath. Buttoning his jacket over it, he said, "It's not that. Well, it's not ALL that. He just gets all chatty and it slows the morning down." He walked over to the bed and leaned down to kiss her. "Dinner tonight?"

"Absolutely."

"I'll text you later once I know what time I'll be free."

"Be careful, okay?"

"Always am." He kissed her again and turned to leave, heading into the living room to take out the cigarettes and cash from the jacket he had been wearing the night before. As he picked up the jacket, the sonogram Estelle had given him fell to the floor. He knelt down to retrieve it, and remained there for a moment, looking again at the image, feeling purely intimidated for the first time in nearly two decades. "I swear I'll give you a better life growing up than what I had."

Standing, he opened the money clip that had just gone into his jacket and put the picture on the top, so it would be carefully concealed in the center when the clip was closed. He picked up his keys and locked the door behind him, not seeing a teary Estelle watching from the bedroom doorway.

The drive to the restaurant was a short one, and Simone parked next to Libera's Cadillac, inwardly grumbling about having to delay his meeting on account of his Patron. He walked into the unlocked door of the back office, expecting Libera to be at his desk. Simone was not, however, expecting to see his boss still on the pull-out sofa— and he was especially not expecting to see the woman on top of him, with her head thrown back and her hands pressed hard into his bare chest. With a short gasp of surprise at Simone's sudden presence, she quickly curled up against him, both lovers still breathing quickly.

"Christ— I am— I'm sorry, sir."

He turned around, unsure as to what he was supposed to do next.

"Well, I guess this makes us even," Libera said, laughing nervously and putting a comforting hand on his embarrassed lover's back, her face now hidden against his chest.

"I'll come back later."

Simone turned and left, locking the door behind him. He immediately got into his car, called to move his morning meeting to the afternoon, and drove back to Estelle's apartment.

When he came in, Estelle was sitting on the couch and looked up from her oatmeal, surprised to see him back so soon. "Everything all right?" she asked at the still harried look on his face.

He sat down next to her, leaned his head back and put his hand over his eyes as he dissolved into laughter.

"What's going on?" she asked, chuckling at his uncontrolled amusement.

As he regained his composure, he moved his hand to the back of the couch and said, "Now, you cannot tell ANYONE what I'm about to tell you."

"Naturally."

"Libera was definitely in his office."

"So, you just left?"

He started laughing again. "He wasn't alone."

"NO!" Estelle exclaimed, putting down her oatmeal in shocked amusement. "That couldn't have been—"

"Oh— there's more."

"What?" Estelle moved closer, caught up in the scandal.

"You are never going to BELIEVE who he was with."

"Oh my god! Who—?" Estelle's phone bleeped with a new text message.

"You should probably check that," Simone said, half-smile implying he knew who was texting her.

"It's just Carolyn," she said, reading the message. "It just says 'He told you, didn't he?'"

His laughter restarted and, comprehending what was going on, Estelle said, "NO SHE DID NOT!"

Simone just continued laughing, unable to say anything as her phone started ringing. Estelle stared at it for a moment before picking up.

"Hi, Carolyn," she said with a tap to Simone's leg in a futile attempt to get him to quiet. "What's— no, he's just sitting here laughing like a teenage girl, what the hell is— I'm sorry, what did you just say?"

Simone stood, still laughing and went to the kitchen to pour himself a cup of coffee.

"Yeah, we'll be here," she finished, hanging up. "That's decaf, just so you know."

He shrugged. "That's what sugar's for, right?"

"She's coming over. She wants to talk to you," Estelle said, joining Simone in the kitchen.

"I'll bet she does," Simone said, starting to laugh again as he took a drink of his overly-sweet coffee. "How pissed is she?"

"SO pissed," Estelle said, nodding her head.

"Well maybe next time they can just do it at her place, rather than the restaurant."

"I can say with some certainty that there will NOT be a next time."

"I should hope not. I can't believe there was a first time."

There was a knock at the door a few minutes later, and as Estelle walked to open it she said, "You be nice."

"I'm always nice. She's the one that needs to be nice."

Estelle rolled her eyes in agreement before opening the door, and Carolyn walked in, wearing a look of humiliated contempt and the dress from the previous night's party.

"How drunk were you?" Estelle asked as Carolyn set her purse down, avoiding making eye contact.

"Not as much as I'd like to believe," Carolyn said. "He was pretty wasted, though. Not sure what that says about me…"

Simone came in and sat down on the couch. "Good morning. Nice to see you again."

"Ha ha ha!" Carolyn retorted. "How quickly did you tell her?"

"Come on. You think I'd talk about my boss like that?" Simone asked, suppressing more laughter as he took another sip from his coffee.

"Shut up."

He laughed and said, "No really, you told her before I even had a chance to."

"Like you weren't going to tell her."

"Well, now I don't have to," Simone said, only somewhat trying to hide his amusement at Carolyn's anger with him.

"So, can we expect a double wedding?" Estelle asked, tilting her head.

"Bite me," Carolyn said, sitting down and covering her face in her hands. "What the hell was I thinking?"

"I'm guessing that you weren't," Simone said honestly.

"I'm sorry, what?" Carolyn asked, infuriated.

"I mean no offense by that. See, I like to believe that the women randomly sleeping with him just turned their brains off for a little while, so it seemed like a good idea at the time."

"I like that theory," she said, looking at Estelle. "It wasn't me, it was the brain switch."

"And, what? This morning was just residual brain switch?" Estelle asked, causing Simone to start laughing again.

"Yeah, we'll go with that. Oh," she started, looking at Simone. "He assumed I was coming over here and asked me to send you over when I leave."

"Thanks. I should probably—"

"One second, speedy," Carolyn said, standing up and walking towards Simone. "What did he mean when he said that this made you even?"

Ignoring Estelle's giggles, Simone, slightly embarrassed, said, "Well, this has technically happened before, just the other way around. And I still think that was worse than this was," he finished, standing to refill his coffee.

"You walked in on me riding your boss. What the hell is worse than that?"

Before Simone could answer, Estelle said, "Try having your boyfriend's boss walk in only seeing him, and having to stand up."

"Oh my god!" Carolyn said, finally easing up.

"Told you," Simone said, raising his coffee mug.

"The hell do I do now?" Carolyn asked, looking to Estelle. It was Simone, however, that answered.

"The same thing all the others do. Ask for the surveillance footage to be erased and try to forget it ever happened."

Estelle covered her mouth to keep from laughing as Carolyn hung her head and said, "Thanks, Simone. BIG help."

"You're right. I'm sorry, Carolyn. But it isn't that bad. It just seems like it now."

She looked up, surprised. "Thank you."

"Told you he's not a jerk," Estelle said, putting an arm around him.

After a quick half-smile, he ran his hand through his hair and said, "All right. I should probably go tell Libera the same thing."

He kissed Estelle, then turned to Carolyn and said, "Sorry about all this."

"Oh, please. It was my bad decision, not yours."

Chapter 28

"What the actual hell?" Estelle asked herself, after being yelled at by a forty-five-year-old woman for being out of copies of the book everyone was demanding. She walked away, pressing on her temples in an attempt to relieve the pressure in her head.

"You okay?" Carolyn asked, coming back from her break.

"Today sucks."

"I agree. So how did last night go after you left?"

"Wonderful."

"Wonderful or WONDERful?"

"Both!" Estelle chirped, remembering her conversation with Simone and the events that led up to it.

"Then why do you look so down?"

"Oh, it's just a crappy day. Customers are in a mood, I'm way behind on shelving, and all I want to do is take a giant nap."

"Not to mention the most romantic day of your life is a tough act to follow?"

"That, too," Estelle said, pulling her bottom lip under her teeth.

"Want me to help you with shelving after my help desk hour?"

"No, that's okay. It'll let me hide from the clientele."

Carolyn laughed and said, "True. But seriously, let me know if you need help."

"I will. Thank you," Estelle said, hugging her friend. "For everything."

After Carolyn patted Estelle's back and walked away, Estelle went back to her shelving and had barely placed the last book on the shelf when she heard the closing announcement over the speaker. Eternally grateful that it wasn't her night to lock the door— and that she had the whole weekend off— she pushed the last of her empty shelving carts into the sorting room and said goodnight to Carolyn before setting out for Libera's. As she did, her phone rang.

"Hello, Estelle. Any chance you would be up for a night in tonight? Maybe we can go to your place and order dinner?"

"Oh, I'd love that!" Estelle said genuinely, thrilled at the thought of just being home with Simone in comfortable clothes.

"Great. I'll see you as soon as possible. All my love."

"And mine."

She hung up the phone and set out towards her building, but she hadn't walked half a block before Joel pulled up beside her.

"Boss said to pick you up," Joel said cheerfully.

"But why aren't you with him? I thought he needed you to—"

"He can take care of himself. Besides, he's already at your place."

"Oh! I didn't mean— well thank you, Joel," she said as she got into the passenger seat.

"No problem."

"Is everything okay?" she asked tentatively.

"Yeah. Today was just a little rough on him."

"That makes two of us," Estelle said, sighing.

Joel laughed. "Rough at a library?"

"Today I got yelled at by a woman nearly as old as my own mother for being out of a book written for teenagers and was personally accused of hiding them for the 'important people'."

"Who are the important people?"

"I DON'T EVEN KNOW!" Estelle replied, voice rising at the thought of the customer.

"Hey, Miss Estelle, I'm sorry I—"

Estelle quickly replied, "Oh, Joel! No! I just got all worked up about her again. And please," she added as they pulled up next to her building. "Just call me Estelle."

"Will do, Estelle. I'll be across the street for an hour if either of you need me."

"Thank you, Joel."

She got out of the car and headed up in the elevator feeling silly for comparing a rough day at the library to a rough day in Simone's world— a feeling that was intensified when she opened her door and saw Simone, who was leaning against the window opposite the door, finishing a cigarette with a fresh glass of scotch condensating on the window sill.

"What the hell happened to you?" Estelle asked, heart racing as she slammed the door closed.

Simone's lip was still swollen, the left side of his face was covered in bruises, and there were specks of blood on his white shirt.

"Nothing."

He picked up his glass in an effort to postpone making eye contact with her, and took as long as possible to put his lighter back into his jacket, which was draped casually on a nearby chair. She didn't fully understand why, but his attempt to keep her calm only infuriated her.

"Simone Belvedere!" she hissed.

He looked up, shocked to see her losing her temper. "I come in and find you— like THIS— and you expect me to believe that NOTHING happened?"

"Estelle, calm—"

"I will NOT…" she went on. "You—"

"Okay!" he said with a cautious smile. "I'm sorry."

He sat down on the couch and motioned for her to sit next to him, but, still indignant, she remained where she was and crossed her arms, waiting for him to start talking.

"Apparently," he began slowly, "a certain individual decided that he didn't need to uphold his end of a written contract." He paused to take a sip from his glass, wincing. "He honestly thought he could just fight his way out."

"And?" Estelle asked impatiently.

"A-and," he continued, "I laughed. I didn't think he was actually serious. He was, though."

"And you actually agreed to fight with him over a contract?" Estelle asked, incredulous at the juvenile idea.

"Of course not. He just threw a couple punches in before we realized he was serious."

"And then?"

"And then…it…wasn't a problem anymore," Simone said slowly. "Joel's got a quick hand, let me tell you…" his voice trailed off, realizing he'd said too much.

Estelle wondered for a moment whose blood was on Simone's shirt, and then was overcome with relief that Simone was comparatively unharmed. Unable to read the expression on her face, Simone said, "I'm sorry, Estelle, I shouldn't have said— it's too—"

"Take your shirt off."

"O-okay… Sorry, what?"

"You should let me get that stain out before it sets."

He cocked his head for a moment, taken aback by the understanding in her voice.

"Simone, I know how your job works and I am far from shocked at what may or may not have happened today."

Half-smiling, he began unbuttoning his shirt to give to Estelle. She walked over, took the shirt from his hands, kissed the unbruised cheek and gave him a serious look. "I know that you only do what's necessary. You don't have to worry about me judging you."

She kissed his cheek again and walked into the kitchen, filling the sink with water to soak the high-end fabric.

"Do you have to worry about—" she stopped herself, not knowing how to finish the sentence. He walked into the kitchen and put his arms around her waist.

"Mai."

She looked up at him blankly, and he smiled. "It's Italian for 'never.'"

"He must have had friends," she said, worry glistening in her eyes.

"He did. And they are all loyal to Libera. Trust me."

He looked down at her teary eyes, hating the worry he had caused. "Estelle, I'm sorry—"

"Never," she said, echoing his words with a teary smile as she ruffled through a drawer for her favorite Thai delivery menu.

"I'd ask how your day was, but you look like it was about as great as mine."

"Pretty much," she agreed, finding the menu that had been jumbled in the messy drawer.

"Want to talk about it?"

"No, I'd much rather forget about it."

"Move in with me?"

"What?" She looked up from the menu she'd been reading over and set her phone down on the kitchen counter.

"Move in with me?" he asked again, smiling at her and sitting down on the couch.

"Before we're married?"

He laughed. "I had no idea you were so conventional."

"That's not what I meant, and you know it," she said, sitting down across from him.

"I know, baby. And yes, before we're married."

"We haven't even set a wedding date yet— what if we decide to be crazy and elope tomorrow?"

He leaned forward and barely brushed his lips against hers. "Then I guess we're eating at my place tonight."

She turned and leaned up against him, resting her head under his. "I don't want to take away the last of your bachelor days. Don't you want the time to be free and do whatever it is you do when you're by yourself?"

"I can read with you there," he said, half-smiling. "Seriously, I don't consider our marriage to be taking away any freedom, therefore, I don't feel I need to postpone waking up next to you every day."

She burrowed her face into his chest and started to cry. "Hey," he said, pulling his arms tighter around her. "Hey, what's the matter?"

"Nothing, I'm s-sorry," she stammered through her tears.

"It's all right, what's wrong?"

"I just… I feel like you have to make all these changes, and it's all so fast. I feel like I've turned your life upside down."

He kissed the top of her head and smiled. "Yes, you have. But Estelle, I promise you, I wouldn't have it any other way."

"Are you sure?"

"Why does everyone keep asking me that? I'm Simone fucking Belvedere. I do nothing unless I'm sure."

Her tears started to mingle with laughter.

"That's better," he said, kissing her again. "How about we spend this weekend at my place, and we can have Libera's contractor come out to see where we can add some more bookshelves, and we can decide if it's the office or the library that goes. I figured it would be the library, so the baby would be closer to the bedroom, but I didn't want to make the decision without you there."

She gently kissed him and stood to retrieve her phone and the menu from the kitchen, before coming back and sitting cross-legged next to him. "Want me to order the usual?" Simone asked. She scrunched her nose and shook her head. "That sounds terrible."

He looked at her for a moment and said, "I never thought I'd hear that. You said they're the only ones that make it hot enough."

"Ugh," she said, putting her arm around her waist. "That is not a good idea."

"Okay. We could get your favorite pizza."

She shook her head rapidly again. He thought for a moment, running out of usual suspects. "I could run over to Libera's and pick up something."

"YES!" she said, louder than she intended. "But take my card. You shouldn't have to pay for everything."

"You don't have—" he stopped at the look she was giving him. "Or… that sounds great, thank you."

"Thank you. Should I just text you what I want?"

"This seems like a stupid question after the previous ones, but you don't want what you usually get?"

She stared blankly back at him. "I'm just making sure," he said, standing and kissing her forehead. "I'll be back as soon as I can."

He begrudgingly took her credit card out of her bag and put it with his money clip before putting a fresh shirt on, followed by his gun and jacket. After kissing her and locking the door behind him, he took the stairs to avoid his injuries causing conversation with her neighbors and made the short journey with Joel from her apartment to the restaurant.

As he walked in, he saw that Libera was alone at his table going over the restaurant's numbers. Instead of making his way to the bar to put their order in, he took a deep breath and approached his Patron. "Hello, Don Libera."

"Hey, Simone, what— Jesus. Joel said you took a little bit, didn't say it was this bad."

"It looks worse than it is," Simone said.

"Drink?" Libera asked, motioning for Simone to sit.

"Absolutely."

Libera waved and Marshall came over, finally more relaxed in Simone's presence.

"Yes, Mr. Libera?"

"Usual drinks here, and I'm assuming you're here for a pick up?"

"Yes, sir."

"Standard order?" Marshall asked.

Simone took out his phone. "Christ, I'm glad you said something. Actually, I need..." he trailed off. "Sorry, she's changing her mind again."

Marshall looked to the floor to hide his amusement and Libera said, "Sounds about right."

"Okay," Simone said, "Can I see your pen?"

Marshall obliged, handing Simone his pen and notebook. He wrote down a list of five items and said, "I want you to put my standard and one other on this card." He handed him Estelle's card, ignoring the confounded look from Libera. "The rest I'll pay in cash."

Marshall made no effort to hide his look of surprise, but said "Yes, sir," and took the list to the back.

Trying to avoid the silent question from Libera, Simone said, "It'll be easier to just bring all of them in case she changes her mind again."

As Marshall brought their drinks over, Libera continued to say nothing, but took a patient sip from his glass and waited for Simone to answer the look he was giving.

"She made me promise to use her card, and frankly I'm more afraid of her tonight than I am of you."

Libera laughed. "How'd she take—" he gestured to Simone's bruised face.

"She full named me."

"That's always effective."

Simone's face relaxed into a gentle smile. "Then she asked for my shirt."

"Why?"

He looked embarrassed for a moment, and, looking into his glass, said, "She wanted to get the blood out."

"Didn't bother her?"

"She was just worried."

"Good. Not that she was worried. It's good that she can handle it."

Simone nodded, but looked concerned.

"What is it?"

"I want someone with her. And I want someone watching her building, and the library."

"I thought you'd already paid the security at the library?"

"It's not enough. At least until the baby's here."

"What's got you so worried?"

"I just don't want her to have to worry. I want her to be able to do what she's always done, and focus on herself and the baby, not if someone's pissed off with me. She's already got enough to worry about, I don't need to add to that."

Libera considered him for a moment. "Thirty, and three a week."

"I'll have it for you tomorrow."

"I'll probably call in Marco Portelli and Gianni Fabbri. I take it that's acceptable?"

"Absolutely, sir. Thank you."

Marshall reappeared with the bags for Simone and Estelle's card. "Stephen put some cheesecake in there for her, said to tell her to name the baby Stephen."

Simone laughed, took out two hundreds and handed them to Marshall. "Keep whatever's left." He stood and said, "Thank you, Don Libera."

After an arrogant nod from Libera, Simone decided to leave his car at the restaurant and walked back to Estelle's building. Thankful for an empty elevator, he unlocked her door and said, "Sorry it took so long."

"Hmmm?" she said, jerking awake.

He smiled and set the bags at her side.

"What did you do?" she asked, turning and laughing at the disproportionate amount of food in front of her.

"Well, I got mine and the last one you asked for on your card as requested. I was worried you'd change your mind again, though, so I had them make the others. Figured we could live off what's left for a couple days."

She got up and hugged him on her way to get plates from the kitchen. "I love it when you're right!"

She came back, sat down and started taking the food out of the bags. "Aww, what's this?" she asked, opening the cheesecake.

He laughed as he sat next to her, and picked up his comfortably predictable pasta. "A bribe from Stephen."

"Oh?"

"Yeah, he wants us to name the baby Stephen."

She giggled and set the cheesecake on the table. "I haven't even started thinking about names yet. Is that bad?"

Simone swallowed and said, "Of course, not. Between all of the books between us, we've probably read a thousand names or more. I think it'll take some time before we're even close to sure."

"I love that you say 'we' and not 'you' when you're talking about the baby. I can tell how much you're there for me, and how much you'll be there for us."

"Speaking of," he said, setting his food down. "I talked to Libera while I was there."

"What about?"

He hesitated for a moment, but said, "Protection for you."

"What kind of protection? Like, people following me around?"

"Not people, plural…at once…"

"Simone, is that necessary?"

"I know that you're not crazy about it, but it would be a big peace of mind for me knowing that someone's making sure you're okay when you're at work, or here, and then you'd have somebody to take you from the house to the city, so you wouldn't have to call a cab."

"Why not just talk to the security at work and…" she trailed off as he looked out the window. "You already have, haven't you? How long?"

"About six months ago."

"Are you that worried?"

"It's not about being worried, it's about being proactive."

She looked at the concerned face across from her and sighed. "All right, Mr. Proactive. If it makes you happy. Just out of curiosity, how much is this costing you?"

"About the same as I pay Joel."

"And how much is that?"

"Thirty up front, and then three a week. Which is actually pretty low, if I were anyone else—"

"You don't mean thousand?"

He looked at her, confused. "Yes?"

"And you have that just sitting around?"

"No," he said, standing and retrieving a bottle of Perrier for each of them. "I keep about five hundred on hand, a hundred in the bank here to keep the books in line, and the rest of it's offshore in various locations."

"How do you—?"

He smiled and said, "I'm good at what I do. And with the house paid for, I don't have that much going out, except what I spend on clothes and paying Joel, and Libera's always paid for my cars as bonuses for big accounts. Of course, now I don't feel as strange spoiling you as much as I'd like."

She took another bite and said, "You weren't spoiling me before?"

"Oh, no. I didn't want you to think that I thought I could buy your affection, so I've held back. Quite a bit, actually."

"When does Libera want me to sign the prenup?"

"He hasn't said anything about it, but I also don't think it'll be long before he does. Is that okay?"

"Oh, that's fine. I assumed I'd have to."

He picked his food back up and said, "He'll probably expect us to have a Catholic wedding and baptism."

"You're not Catholic," Estelle said, bemused.

"Technically I'm not a practicing Catholic. I was, however, baptized in a Catholic church, and that's all Libera seems to care about."

"TECHNICALLY, so was I. But…we're not Catholic," she said again, laughing this time.

"I know, but it's REALLY important to him."

"Don't worry, I don't mind, so long as we can still have the small, court house ceremony we talked about."

"Shouldn't be a problem. I'm sure Libera will have someone on the payroll he can call it into."

"On a related note, I did want to talk to you about something. I've asked Carolyn to be the baby's godmother. Is that all right? I probably should have come to you first…"

"No, I think that's a wonderful idea," he said, taking her hand.

"Good. I take it we'll have to ask Libera?"

"I hadn't thought about that," he said, frowning.

"What's wrong?"

"I just realized that I hadn't considered what's expected of me. He's the closest thing I have to a father, and I guess I'd forgotten that he's not the baby's grandfather…"

He looked out the window, eyes suddenly filled unexpected tears that she had never seen before.

"Simone?" she said quietly.

"I know he can be a jerk…"

"No… I know how much he means to you."

"I hadn't even considered that he'd be the logical option…We name him Padrino, he'll expect that the baby will be brought up for… we can't…"

She walked over and sat on his lap, putting her arms around his neck. "That won't happen. That's not his decision to make."

He nodded and laid his head on her shoulder, taking a deep breath.

"You know," she continued, "I was kind of hoping we could ask Joel." Simone looked up at her as she went on, "Like you said, Libera really is like the baby's grandfather, and Joel's been so wonderful, for both of us."

Simone nodded. "I'd like that."

"New subject?" she said, resuming her seat on the couch.

"Absolutely," Simone said, going back to his food, grateful for a new topic.

"Do you think it's a boy or a girl?"

Grinning, he said, "I'll bet it's a girl."

"Why do you say that?" she asked, smiling and taking a bite of the cheesecake.

"Just a feeling I have."

"Is that a feeling or a preference?" she asked, nudging him with her   foot.

"Little bit of both."

"It would be easier to keep a girl out of the business, wouldn't it?"

He smiled. "It would, yes, given that they perfected the word 'patriarchy'."

"That's no kidding."

"It doesn't matter, though. I'll do whatever it takes to give her, or him, as normal a life as possible."

"Are you worried about Libera and his gender role crap?"

"No. If she wants to play with dinosaurs and super heroes, he can deal with it."

"And if it's a boy?"

"You wait and see. It'll be a girl."

"You're very sure of yourself, Mr. Belvedere."

Simone moved closer to her on the couch. "I thought that's what you loved about me?"

He leaned forward and kissed her, wincing again from his wounded lip.

"Wait here." She stood and retrieved a small bag of ice from the freezer. Sitting back down, she said, "I got this ready after you left. Lie down."

He complied, laying his head in her lap. Gently placing the ice on the swelling, she said, "Did you want to stay here tonight and head to your place in the morning?"

"Probably a good idea," he said, closing his eyes. She stroked his hair for a few minutes and soon realized he was nodding off. Keeping one hand lovingly holding the ice in place, she picked up her book with the other and started to read, glancing down occasionally and smiling at her sleeping lover.

Chapter 29

The next morning, Simone walked to retrieve his car from Libera's and came back to pick up Estelle, who was waiting with an overnight bag, irritated that it had taken much longer than his estimated half hour. Once she was comfortably settled in the passenger seat, he sped towards the interstate and said, "Sorry for the delay. I called Libera, he'll be meeting us at the house. I hope that's all right."

"That's fine. Do I need to hang out somewhere else for a little while?"

Merging lanes onto the highway, he shook his head. "It'll   happen sooner or later, and I think he wants to see if you're okay being there when I'm paying him."

"Ah. So, no pressure."

He laughed. "Pretty much."

They continued driving in content silence, but as they pulled off the interstate, Estelle asked, out of nowhere, "Can we stop at that gas station?"

"Ye-yeah. You okay?"

"I'd really like to not throw up in front of you before we're married."

He laughed gently and pulled over, barely coming to a stop as she leapt out of the car and ran inside. Ten minutes later, she came back, carrying a bottle of water. "You okay?"

"I will be. In about seven months."

"I'm sorry, baby," he said, pulling back out onto the street.

"I'd say it's not your fault, but this time, it kind of is."

He laughed and said, "I suppose you're right. Maybe this will make up for it a bit?"

He held up a velvet box and opened it with his right hand, keeping his left on the steering wheel, showing her a diamond pendant to match her engagement ring.

"Simone! What did you do?" she squealed delightfully.

"That's why I took so long this morning. I wanted to make sure it was still there."

Teary eyed, she said, "You know you don't have to spend all your money at once, right?"

"Not even close." Wincing slightly and glancing at her raised eyebrow, he said, "That came out more douchebag than I intended."

"That's okay. You're cute when you're all cocky."

As he pulled into his driveway, waving to Libera and still smiling from Estelle's remark, he asked "You ready for this?"

"Absolutely."

As they got out of the car, Simone shook Libera's hand and said, "Sorry to keep you waiting."

"Not a problem," he said, turning towards Estelle. "Simone sent me a text saying you weren't feeling well. Everything okay?"

"Okay for now, Mr. Libera, thanks."

Simone unlocked the house and held the door open for his Patron and fiancée. As he turned around from closing the door, he said, "You need anything, Estelle?"

She smiled patiently, making herself comfortable on the couch and said, "No, but try again in another ten minutes."

"Sorry," he said, half-smiling. "Shall we, sir?"

Libera nodded and led the way upstairs. As Simone unlocked the door to his office, Libera said, "You look happy, Simone."

"I am, sir, thank you."

Libera laughed and sat down at the mahogany desk as Simone unlocked his safe and began putting cash into an empty cardboard box labeled 'BOOKS'.

"Do you want me to pay ahead a few months?"

"If you'd like. I know you're good for it."

"I'm putting in the thirty plus six months, which would be 108, call it 110?"

"Sure thing."

Simone finished counting the hundred-dollar straps and taped the box closed. "Thank you, sir."

"My pleasure. That all you need from me?"

"Well, no, sir. Not exactly."

"How can I help?"

"Estelle and I were talking last night," Simone started, sitting on the floor and leaning against the now closed safe, "and she asked when you wanted her to sign the prenup."

Libera tilted his head in surprise. "She asked that?"

"She did. She said that she was already assuming she would need to, and wanted to know when she needed to look at it."

"I can have it drawn up next week. Standard terms, though she'd probably be worth more since you are."

"Makes sense."

"How'd she feel about it?"

"Didn't give it a second thought. She just assumed it was how it would be."

"You've got a good woman down there," Libera said. "I think so, too, sir."

"What else?"

Simone didn't show a hint of outward trepidation, but was treading slowly. He knew that what he had to say had equal chances of being welcomed or scoffed, but he knew that he needed to say it for his own peace of mind, if nothing else. "Well, sir, we were talking about asking Joel to be the baby's godfather."

"I thought you might," Libera said, smiling. "He's your right hand."

"She had asked me... if I was planning on asking you," Simone said.

Libera's eyebrows raised for a moment before he softly said, "And what did you say?"

Simone looked down and said, "I told her that I had forgotten that you weren't the baby's grandfather."

The two men sat silent for a moment, unsure of how to acknowledge everything that hadn't been said in the last seventeen years. Simone broke the silence, standing up and saying, "I want you to know, sir, that I appreciate you and your friendship more than you know."

After another long silence, Libera also rose and walked over to Simone. He put his hand on Simone's shoulder and said, "You've been my son for seventeen years, don't you forget that." Simone looked at the floor and nodded. Libera put his other hand on Simone's free shoulder. "Look at me."

When Simone looked up, Libera said, "You're going to be the best father you can be to that child, and I'll be right here behind you. That child's just as lucky to have you as you are to have it."

Simone nodded, unable to speak.

"You and Estelle will not be alone, understand me?"

Simone nodded. "Yes, sir."

Libera briefly pulled him in for the first paternal hug Simone had ever known, before putting a hand back to Simone's shoulder. "Just don't let the kid call me anything stupid, all right? None of that grampy shit."

With a humble laugh, Simone said, "Sì, Nonno."

Libera smiled and looked down. "You're a good kid, Simone."

They looked at each other for a moment, neither speaking, but both understanding. "I should get going," Libera said, breaking the second long silence of the afternoon.

Simone picked up the box and followed his Patron down the stairs after relocking the office door.

"Everything okay?" Estelle asked, looking up from her book.

"Absolutely," Simone said, setting the box on the table.

She looked to his Patron and said, "Would you like to stay for lunch, Mr. Libera?"

"I wish I could, my dear, but I have to meet with Mack and Bronte. Raincheck?"

"Of course!" she chirped, somewhat relieved.

As Libera walked towards the door, he said, "I'll get those papers to you next week. Let me know what Joel says."

Estelle smiled at Simone, who nodded towards the door. "Right back," he said.

She went back to her book, chancing a sip of water. "Nope," she said quickly, scurrying to the bathroom upstairs.

A few minutes later she was splashing some cold water on her face when she heard Simone call out, "Estelle?"

"I'll be right down."

She dried her face and made her way slowly down the stairs, stopping a few steps from the bottom. Simone, unaware of her presence, was sitting on the couch, elbows on his knees and his head in his hands. "You okay?" she asked, coming up slowly behind him and gently rubbing his back.

Without looking up, he said "Yeah. I am. Just dealing with a lot of things I put away a long time ago."

"Do you want to talk about what happened?"

He shook his head. "I don't know." She walked around the couch and sat down next to him, hand still softly rubbing his back. "He said that he assumed we'd ask Joel, and that I'd been his son for a long time."

Estelle's eyes began to fill with tears as she saw one of Simone's fall to the floor.

"He said I'll be a good father, and that he's here for us."

"Come here." She scooted closer, laying his head on her shoulder. "You are going to be a wonderful father, Simone. I've never had any doubts about that."

She stopped as they heard a knock at the door. "That's Dex. Contractor," Simone started, rising to his feet. "Can you let him in? Let him know I'll be right there?"

She nodded, and walked to the door, drying her eyes on her way. As she opened it, the newcomer said, "You're not Belvedere."

"Well, not yet."

"Oh! You must be the fiancée. I'm Dex. Belvedere called me about wanting to recustomize the shelves we put in."

"Of course! He'll just be a minute."

"No, I'm here," Simone said, back to his usual, confident self. "How are you, Dex?" he asked, accepting Dex's outstretched hand.

"Not bad at all. Congratulations to you two, by the way. Set a date yet?"

"Thank you. No, not yet, but soon."

"What did you need from me?"

"I know these shelves are going to need to go floor to ceiling," Simone said, pointing to the living room. And we'll need one of the rooms upstairs completely redone."

"Do you know which one?"

Simone looked to Estelle. "I hate asking you to give up the library," she said.

He shook his head. "It is closer to the bedroom, and it's a little bigger, which would probably be better in the long run."

"Are you sure?" she asked, feeling guilty for taking away his favorite room of the house.

"We could go take a look at it, see what you want to do with it and go from there," Dex suggested.

Simone looked at Estelle. "All right with you?"

She nodded and Simone motioned for them to follow him upstairs. He opened the door to the library and said, "What do you think, Dex?"

"It depends on what you need it for. I think we've gotten as many books in here as we can fit, but if you wanted to sacrifice some of the shelves, I've always thought a big built-in desk would fit great over—"

"No," Simone interrupted. "I'm sorry— I should have been clearer. We need a nursery."

"Get out of here!" Dex said, not thinking, but hurriedly correcting himself. "Sorry, I mean, —"

"That's okay, Dex. We'll probably have to pull the shelves. They won't fit downstairs will, they?"

"No, definitely not."

"That's all right. Just pull them out carefully and send them to a local bookstore? Anonymously of course."

"Sure thing. We can take the walls back to normal, and then build in a better closet to back up against yours?"

"Sounds great. Want to draw something up and get it to us in the next couple weeks? I want to get started as soon as possible, especially downstairs, that's definitely first priority. Is that all right with you, my dear?" he said, turning around.

"It all sounds wonderful to me," she said, putting her hand on his shoulder and looking around at his beloved collection, still feeling guilty.

"Great. I'll try to have something for you next week, week after at the latest," Dex said as Simone led them back downstairs.

"Thanks, again," Simone said, taking out three bills and handing it over.

"Thank you, sir."

After Dex had gone, Estelle sat down on the couch, pulled her feet up and laid her head back. Simone came over and sat next to her, pulling her legs onto his lap and massaging her calf.

"You look tired," he said.

"Mmhmm."

Simone's cell phone started ringing, and as he picked it up and looked at the caller ID, he said, "Damn. Sorry... Hello, sir... Yes, sir, I'll be right there."

He walked over and knelt next to Estelle. "I'm so sorry he said it's important."

"It's okay," she said sleepily. "Mind if I lay down upstairs for a little while?"

"Not a bit," he said, kissing her forehead. "I'll be back as soon as I can."

"'Kay," she mumbled, making her way upstairs.

Once he left, she walked into his bedroom and, even never having stayed there before, felt as though she were already a part of it. She laid down in Simone's bed and nuzzled her face into a pillow that smelled just like him, and pulled another close to her, snuggling it as if he were there, and quickly drifted off to sleep.

Chapter 30

Simone walked into Libera's office, expecting to see Gallo and Mack, but instead just saw Libera looking over figures at his desk. He tapped twice at the door and said, "Hello, sir."

"Hello, again, Simone. Sorry to call you away. Estelle come with you, by chance?"

"No, sir. Morning sickness hit her hard today, and she hasn't quite adjusted yet. I'm hoping she's asleep."

"She'll need all the rest she can get."

"I agree."

"Close the door and sit."

Simone did as he was told, and sat in the chair across from Libera.

"What do you think of March twenty-sixth?"

"For what, sir?"

"Your wedding."

"That— that sounds great, actually. Any reason for that day?"

"March twenty-seventh, I need you in a meeting in Boston to discuss a business venture for the casino. Race track wants to set up off track betting in Olympus and Athena."

"I'll be there, sir. But why—"

"This trip would require you to leave on the twenty-sixth and return on the thirty-first. Knowing you, you'll have the deal signed by the twenty-eighth, leaving you and Estelle some additional time for the New England libraries. Unless, of course, you had a better idea for your honeymoon."

Libera smiled and took a drink from the coffee mug on his desk, waiting for Simone to process everything.

"Sir— that's— that sounds perfect."

"I'd pay for all travel and lodging expenses, of course."

"Don Libera— thank you."

"Run it by Estelle, of course. Try to let me know this week. I need you in Boston in March regardless."

"Absolutely, sir. Thank you."

"That's all I needed from you. You might talk to Sandra on your way out— she had a hell of a first couple months when they were expecting Mya."

Simone smiled. "Thank you."

He shook hands with his Patron and headed out of the office to the bar of the restaurant.

"Hello, Sandra," he said, approaching Joel's wife, who liked to fill in as a bartender on the weekends.

"Hey, Simone! It's so good to see you! Joel told me about the engagement and the baby! We're so happy for you!"

"Thanks," he said, unabashedly grinning. "Is Joel around?"

"He's at home with Mya— said he had the weekend off."

"He does, I just needed to talk to him for a few."

"You're always welcome to stop by the house. I know Mya would like to see you."

He smiled gently. "I'd like that, too. Thanks, Sandra."

"No problem."

He turned and took a few steps towards the door, but turned back around slowly and said, "Can I ask you something?"

"Sure thing."

"Is there something I can do to make it easier on her? She's not feeling very well—"

She gave him a gentle smile and said, "Morning sickness finally kicked in, did it?"

"Yeah, today's been kind of rough on her."

She nodded. "I lived off ginger ale, saltines, and berries off and on for the first two months with Mya, you might see if that helps."

"Thanks, Sandra," he said again. She put a gentle hand on his arm and said, "Let me know if you guys need anything."

Chapter 31

As Simone pulled into the driveway, he waved to Joel, who was wearing a heavy coat and sitting on the porch with his daughter, who was nearing her third birthday and was wrapped in a blanket, holding a picture book. He stepped out of the car, smiling at the loud "Uncle Belvy!" that Mya shrieked.

"Hey, boss," Joel said, setting Mya down, who immediately ran over to Simone.

"Hello, Joel, sorry to just stop by—" Simone stopped at the top of the porch steps and picked up Mya, who had attached herself to his leg. "Hi, Mya," he said softly.

"Daddy's reading book!"

"I see that," he said, smiling. "Is it a good book?"

She squealed, "Yeah! Unicorn!"

"You like unicorns?" he asked, setting her back down.

"Yeah!"

Simone smiled as she ran back over to her grinning father, who said, "Want to come inside where it's warm?"

He nodded, and followed Joel and Mya into the house. "Everything okay?" Joel asked, taking his coat off as Simone sat down on the squishy, blue sofa.

"Of course, yeah," Simone began, watching Mya snap blocks together. "I had a couple things I need to ask of you."

"Sure, thing, boss. What can I do?"

"Can you start taking Estelle to the range and teach her to shoot? Just basic self-defense?"

"Absolutely," he said, puzzled. "I'd have thought you'd want to do it, though. You're a far better marksman."

"Not by much, Joel. Besides, people get all jumpy when I'm at the range now, the distraction it would cause wouldn't be worth it."

"Makes sense. How often?"

"Once a week, maybe, and she can see how comfortable she is with it. It's her call."

Joel nodded and smiled at Simone, not used to seeing him look to anyone else to make a decision. "What was the other thing?"

"Estelle and I were talking last night, and she mentioned that she wanted her friend Carolyn to be the baby's godmother, and we're both very much hoping that you'll stand as godfather for the baby."

Joel was visibly shocked for a moment, and said "You would? Not—"

"I talked to him already, and let him know, and he agreed. You're always there when I need you, and not just when it comes to work. You're a good friend, Joel. It's important that you know that."

"I'd be honored to."

Simone stood, shaking Joel's hand. "Thank you." As he turned to leave, he patted Mya's head and said "Bye, Mya."

"Bye Belvy!"

"See you Monday, Joel. Thanks again."

"Anytime. See ya, Boss."

Chapter 32

Carrying a bag of the items Sandra had suggested, Simone unlocked the front door and, upon not seeing Estelle, set the bag on the table and went upstairs to his bedroom. As he walked in, he saw Estelle, still snuggled up to his pillow, sound asleep. He leaned down and kissed her hair, before walking over to the other side of the bed and sitting; leaning back against the headboard. He picked up the laptop that had been propped against the wall near the head of the bed and opened the online retailer he used to buy gifts for Mya, and started scrolling through giant plush toys. A few minutes later, he heard, "Why are you looking at unicorns?"

Half-smiling, he said, "It's for Mya. Joel's daughter."

"Oh?" she asked, rubbing her eyes and sitting up. "Did you get to talk to him?"

"I did, and he said he'd love to."

"That's wonderful!"

"Sandra was working when I stopped by to see Libera. I picked up a few things she recommended to make you feel better. They're downstairs."

"That's so sweet, thank you," she said, moving closer and leaning her head against him. After a moment, she asked, "You still sore from yesterday?"

"Not much. Looks worse than it is."

"That's good."

"Libera had a very interesting proposition for us," Simone said, confirming his order and closing the computer.

"Us?" she asked.

"He needs me to go to Boston late on the twenty-sixth of March, and I would be away until the thirty-first. He suggested we get married on the morning of the twenty-sixth, and then have you accompany me to Boston. As he pointed out, negotiations won't take more than two days, and he offered for us to take the rest of the time to visit some of the New England libraries."

"Is that his way of offering to pay for part of our honeymoon?"

Simone smiled, "That it is. He said he'd be paying for travel and the hotel. I would have to spend the first couple days working, though."

"What would I be doing while you're working?"

"Whatever you'd like. Sightseeing, reading, sleeping in and ordering room service."

"That does sound pretty amazing, and it would be nice to take a trip together before the baby comes."

"Yes, it would," he replied, putting an arm around her.

"Looks like March twenty-sixth, then!" she said, kissing his cheek. "Should you call and let him know?"

He scooted down the headboard a little and said, "Not just now," as he rested his head against hers and took her left hand into his, looking at the ring he had given her a few days before.

"Is there anything you need? At all?"

"No, I have everything I need right here," she murmured. "What about you?"

He sighed. "What would you think about going with Joel to the range to learn a few things?"

"Probably a good idea," she said. "Especially if I'll be living in the Belvedere Armory."

Simone began to laugh, and pulled her in closer. "It's not that bad. You should see Libera's house."

"I'm good, but thanks." She laughed and shifted to look at Simone. "While you were getting the car earlier I checked my lease, and it doesn't expire until the fifth of May."

"What would you like to do?"

"Well, that depends on how quickly you want me to move in here."

"As soon as you're ready, this is your home."

She kissed his cheek again and said, "Well, why don't I spend this week gathering up the things I absolutely need, and then we can slowly bring the rest over since we have like four and a half months. It'll be cheaper that way."

"Why don't you let me pay for your apartment?"

"Because you pay for everything else. And I know you don't mind," she said, as he opened his mouth to speak. "I mind. I don't want you to have the burden of supporting us on your own, all right?"

"All right," he conceded. "So next week?"

The ardor was still quiet in his voice, but his determined eyes had an excited glint that she rarely got to see.

"Next week." She closed her eyes for a few minutes, before saying, "Have you eaten?"

"No, I was going to wait for you."

"That could be several months," she sighed, sitting up with her feet over the edge of the bed. "Want to sit downstairs, maybe turn on the fireplace and read for a little while?"

"Christ, you're perfect," he said, standing and stretching.

A little while turned into several hours of the two of them sitting on the couch, her legs in his lap, reading in the glow of the electric fireplace. Absentmindedly finishing the Chinese noodles next to him, Simone looked over and saw Estelle nibbling at a cracker and staring into the fireplace.

"You okay?"

She shook her head a little, smiling and saying, "Yeah! Sorry! I was just wondering; do you think we should buy Stephen a present? You know, like a thank you for helping us get together?"

"I wondered that, as well. Have something in mind?"

"Just something that says, 'We appreciate you' without being all weirdly aristocratically sentimental."

"That's very specific… and still exceptionally vague. I'm sure I can find something, though, if you'd like me to take care of it."

"That would be perfect. I'm terrible at picking out gifts, as evidenced by the book I got you for our anniversary..."

He set his book down and looked over at her. "How were you possibly supposed to know that I already had a first edition of The Invisible Man?"

"Because you're you, maybe?"

"Besides," he said, looking back down at his book, "I got mine through a mainstream bookstore. You accidentally came across the one you gave me at an estate sale, which is a lot better. It has a story." He gave her foot a squeeze and smiled. "Get it?"

She broke into giggles and said, "You're such a nerd."

Half-smiling and still not looking up, he said, "Because you're three copies of Pygmalion are SO much better…"

Chapter 33

Over the next week, Estelle spent most of her time that wasn't at the library organizing and packing the clothes, books and other necessities that would be immediately traveling with her to Simone's house, and by the time she got off work Friday night, she walked into Libera's and took her usual seat at the bar, glad that she had everything ready for the next day.

"Hey, Estelle!" Stephen said cheerfully. "Decaf?"

"Can I actually get a ginger ale? Thanks, Stephen," she finished, taking out her book.

As he walked away, she opened her book, but had barely finished the first paragraph when she felt Simone come up behind her and gently kiss under her ear.

"Hello, beautiful," he whispered.

She turned around with a flirtatious simper. "Hello, love." Putting her arms around his neck, she said, "Any luck for Stephen?"

Half-smiling, he said, "Absolutely. Even checked with Libera to make sure it was okay, and he approved, so it's outside."

"What's outside?"

"A 2013 Three-Series BMW."

She blinked at him for a moment. "Are you serious?"

He held the logo emblazoned key up in front of her. "I am. I went ahead and got the newest one instead of the twelve. You should see the beat-up thing from the 90s that he's driving now."

"You know he has to pay taxes on that, right?"

"Cash is already in the car, with a note."

She started to laugh and said, "Is there anything you don't think of?"

"Occasionally," he said, with an arrogant smile. "Here he comes."

Stephen set Estelle's fizzing drink down in front of her and said, "How are you tonight, Mr. Belvedere?"

"Excellent, thank you. Don't you have some time off coming up?"

"Two weeks from now, sir. Flying back to Michigan to see my parents."

"Michigan's not that far— wouldn't it be cheaper to drive there?"

Estelle smiled into her drink, watching Simone casually bluffing his way through the conversation.

"Nah, my car wouldn't make it."

Simone looked at Estelle and tilted his head in mock confusion. "I think it would."

"I really don't think so, sir," Stephen said, confused brows furrowed as he poured a scotch for Simone.

Simone set the key on the bar top and pushed it towards Stephen, who looked wide-eyed at it as if he'd never seen a key before.

"Wh— what?" Stephen stuttered.

Simone put the title for the car next to the key. "Sign this and it's all yours. We wanted to let you know that we appreciate your role in bringing us together."

"Are-are you serious, Mr. Belvedere?" Stephen asked, grinning.

Simone laughed, raised his glass and said, "Grazie." He took a sip before saying, "Oh— and I went through Don Libera's dealer, not Mack's, so we can go Monday and transfer everything into your name. Why don't you have Mandy come watch the bar for a few and go take a look at it?"

"Th-thank you, sir. Both of you!" he said, grinning and shaking Simone's hand.

"No, Stephen, thank you," Simone said, putting a hand on Estelle's shoulder. Stephen sprinted over to Mandy, who made her way back behind the bar.

"I talked to Libera and got her a raise, as well," Simone said.

"You're going to spoil the bejesus out of this baby, aren't you?" Estelle said, smiling at the look of satisfaction on Simone's face.

"Of course, my dear," he replied, taking another sip of his drink. "Though I plan to do the same to you, as well."

"Speaking of, I've got everything ready for tomorrow, if you're still sure. It's about twenty boxes."

"Wonderful. I'm paying Marco Portelli and Paolo Bassi to bring everything over while you're at the gun range with Joel, they should get there around nine."

"Does it have to be Paolo?" she asked. "He's always so squirrelly when I talk to him."

Simone laughed for a moment, until Estelle said, "What?"

"Nothing," Simone said, shifting the ice in his glass. He took another sip and then started to chuckle again.

"What did you do?" Estelle asked, with a suspicious tilt of her head.

"Nothing recently."

"How long ago is not recently?"

"Not long after our first dinner together," he replied with an evasive glance.

Estelle gasped and leaned closer. "Was he the one—?"

"The world will never know," he said, kissing her cheek and setting a twenty on the bar for their drinks.

"Oh! Sandra came by my apartment."

"Did she?" Simone asked, cocking his head. "I didn't realize you two—"

"We'd met a couple times in passing," Estelle replied. "She wanted to see if I wanted some help and company finishing up for tomorrow."

"How did she know?"

"Joel told her. Sandra said he's been keeping her updated— never seen him this happy for someone."

Simone smiled and looked down at his glass.

"Their kid is effing adorable, by the way— Incoming," she said, falling silent and glancing behind him.

"Hello, kids," Libera said, walking up and shaking Simone's hand.

"Hello, sir," Simone said.

"How are you doing today?" Libera asked, looking at Estelle.

"Today's a good day," she said.

"I'm glad. Do you mind if I steal my boy for a little while?"

"Of course not. I should get going anyway and make sure everything's ready for tomorrow." She stood to kiss Simone's cheek and whispered, "I'll be thinking about you."

Simone half-smiled and said, "I'll see you tomorrow."

"Good night, Mr. Libera," she said, before strutting towards the door.

As she walked away, Libera laughed and said, "I'm not sure what she said, but I'd bet good money that you'll be seeing her tonight, rather than tomorrow."

"That's a safe bet," Simone said, chancing a roguish grin at his Patron before saying, "What can I do for you?"

"I need you to stop by Phil's tomorrow, and find out if he's made a decision about his kid. Let him know we can't pay him until we know if Ethan gets anything."

"Yes, sir. Does it matter which decision he makes?"

"No, it's the same amount either way. Phil would get twenty-five percent on his own, or fifteen percent for him, leaving ten percent for Ethan. Those are the only options. Understand?"

"Yes, sir."

"Good," he said, before nodding towards the door with a mischievous smile. "Have a good night."

"Thank you, sir."

As Libera walked away, Simone set out for his Mercedes and began typing out a message on his phone.

Still thinking about me?

He got behind the wheel of his car and as he started the ignition, his phone beeped with her response.

God, yes.

Five minutes.

That better just be an arrival time.

He read the response and set off for her apartment, and already feeling his desire starting to build, he put his phone in his pants pocket, trying to keep his mind off of her until he was in the privacy of her apartment.

Simone unlocked the door and, upon entering, he smiled at the boxes in the living room and had just started to remove his jacket when Estelle appeared in the hallway leading to her bedroom. She was wearing a deep red satin gown that barely came halfway down her thighs, along with the ruby necklace Simone had given her for her birthday.

"Wow," he said, setting his jacket on the couch.

"Why don't you take that off and meet me in the bedroom?" she asked, letting one of the thin straps fall off her bare shoulder.

"Absolutely," he said slowly, following her directions and removing his holster and silk tie, leaving them on the couch before slowly following her.

Halfway down the hall, she turned around and said, "I can't wait for you to see what I'm wearing underneath."

"And what would that be?"

She turned and kept walking towards the bedroom, leaving him only with the seductive word, "Nothing."

When he entered the bedroom, she was lying on her right side, left knee bent to accentuate the short hem.

"You look wonderful," he said, taking off his vest, walking over and kneeling in front of the bed.

She crawled towards him so that they were at the same eye level and said, "I know."

The confidence in her voice pushed his fervor to new heights, and he leaned forward to kiss her, both hands in her hair. She began to inch backwards, leading him back onto the bed with her, his lips still blissfully pressed against hers as she unbuttoned his shirt and turned onto her side, pressing her chest into his. Passion was building quickly, and after a few short, heated minutes, she was fumbling with his zipper as he removed his belt. Estelle's hand had quickly gone to work on him as he pulled his shirt the rest of the way off, and he had just turned her

- 124 -

onto her back and begun kissing her neck when the phone in his pants pocket, now much lower on his thigh, began to ring.

"Dammit!" he snapped, trying to get to it before it kicked to voicemail. "Christ... I'm sorry, baby..." His overzealous hand hit answer before he could see who it was, and without stopping to catch his breath, he let out a loud, raspy, "What?"

His eyes widened for a moment, and he fell onto his back, covering his eyes with his hand.

"You okay?" Estelle whispered.

Simone uncovered his face and turned to look at her, saying, "I am VERY sorry, sir."

She clasped her hand to her mouth, realizing who he was talking to, and who he had just accidentally lost his temper with.

"Yes. I'll be right there, sir."

He double checked to make sure that his phone was off before dropping it onto the floor and covering his eyes again. "He let me go for the night, and he knew I was here, so I didn't even think it would be him when I answered..."

"How pissed is he?"

"Remains to be seen," he said, standing and refastening his belt. As he started to rebutton his shirt, he said, "I am so sorry. The guy I was supposed to meet with in the morning showed up tonight, so Libera wants to seal it tonight."

"No, I understand."

His phone beeped with a text message and he picked it up off the floor, barely reading the full message before throwing his head back.

"Goddammit!"

"What?"

"He wants me to come in through the back of the office. Christ..."

"Is that bad?"

"It's not good," Simone said, before leaning down and kissing her. "It'll be fine," he added quickly, seeing a hint of worry in her eyes. "It just means he wants to talk to me before anyone else does. I'll be back in a few hours." He kissed her again. "I am SO sorry."

"It's okay. Just be careful, all right?"

"Always," he said, kissing her forehead before walking into the living room.

"Can I do anything?" she asked, walking behind him and tying her robe.

"No," he said, hastily knotting his tie and tightening his holster. "It'll all be fine."

He started buttoning his jacket as he walked over to her and kissed her again. "Back soon, I promise."

Picking up his keys on the way out, he ran down the stairs rather than waiting on the elevator, and as he drove towards Libera's, he made his best attempt to fix his hair and finally gave up, rolling the window down to cool the heat still in his face.

Taking a deep breath, he knocked twice on the door to Libera's office and entered. Libera was alone, sitting at his desk; clearly waiting for Simone to arrive. Libera said nothing, but motioned for Simone to sit across from him. Simone obeyed, unbuttoning his jacket and unsure if he should speak or wait to be spoken to.

Libera stood and walked around his desk, standing over Simone. "Would you like to tell me what the hell you were thinking?"

"My sincere apologies, Don Libera. I wasn't thinking."

"Clearly."

"I am very sorry, sir. I didn't see that it was you calling before I answered, and that is entirely my—"

Simone stopped talking as Libera abruptly slapped his face, temper unabated by Simone's words.

Closing his eyes against the pain radiating through the only semi-healed bruises still on his cheek, Simone said, "I am very sorry, sir. It will not happen again."

"Good."

Libera sat back against the front of his desk and said, "Now that you're thinking with your brain again, I'm going to call Phil in, and leave you two alone to discuss. When I come back, I want this over with. Understand?"

"Yes, sir," Simone said, standing and buttoning his jacket as Libera stepped into the dining room of the restaurant.

A few moments later, he returned with Phil, who sat at the requesting gesture of Libera. "I have to take care of something," Libera said. "You boys start without me."

As Libera closed the door behind him, Simone leaned back against the front of the desk and said, "How are you, Phil? I haven't seen you in a while."

"Good, thanks. Look, I'm sorry it's taken so long, but I've been thinking hard about Ethan's share of the profits."

"That's all right, Phil," Simone said, standing upright and putting his hands into his pockets. "We're very interested in this venture, and we want to make sure that it benefits everyone."

"I agree," Phil said, looking hard into Simone's eyes. "That's why I'm taking the twenty-five percent."

"Is that so? May I ask—?"

"Ethan can't handle doing business— especially with you. Hasn't worked a day in his life, and it sure as hell isn't for my lack of trying. Doesn't mind throwing money away, though. Worst gambling instincts I've seen in my life... Putting him into the contract at all would mean he would start trying to weasel his way in further, putting both sides at risk. He can't handle it, and he'll do something stupid, and, even if he is worthless, he's still my kid, and I'd prefer you not having to kill him."

"I completely understand," Simone said, half-smiling as Libera walked back into the room. "Shall we sign the papers now, then?"

"Might as well."

Libera sat down and handed Simone both contracts. Finding the correct one, Simone handed it to Phil saying, "All you need to do is initial next to the monthly cash stipend you'll be receiving, and then sign at the bottom."

Phil obliged, handing the document back to Simone, who set it down on the desk and said, "Don Libera, if you'll be gracious enough to do the same."

As Libera signed the document, Simone said, "Welcome to retirement, Phil," and reached out for a happily accepted handshake.

"Thank you, Mr. Belvedere. And you, Don Libera. Thank you."

"It's my pleasure, Phil," Libera said, standing and shaking Phil's outstretched hand.

Libera saw Phil back out of the office, returning moments later wearing an arrogant smile and walking up to Simone. "Good work," he said, putting his hand on Simone's shoulder. "And," he added, sitting down behind his desk, "I apologize for the...inconvenience."

"No inconvenience at all, sir."

Libera laughed. "You think you're the first guy to answer his phone like that when I call?"

"I'm guessing not."

"Go on. Since we've got this taken care of, I don't need you until the meeting tomorrow afternoon with Gallo."

"Yes, sir," Simone said, turning to leave. "Thank you."

Chapter 34

As Estelle settled into Simone's couch the next evening with her book after spending several hours unpacking and doing her best to calm the organizational chaos that ensued, she heard the front door click as it unlocked. Simone came in and set his keys on the table, before coming over and kissing her. "Hello, Estelle," he said, coming around and sitting down next to her.

"Hey, you," she said, tilting her head as she took in his content smile. "How was your day?"

"Usual," he said, unbuttoning his jacket and putting his arm on the back of the couch so he could turn to look at her. "Better now that I can come home to you."

She smiled and leaned forward to kiss him, slowly bringing her knees up onto the soft cushions so she could crawl towards him. He leaned back against the armrest and put his hands on her hips, which were now pressed close against his own. Estelle brought her arms up to rest around his neck as she continued kissing him, and as she brought her hands down his shoulders, she slid them down to his chest, lifting herself off of him and pulling back.

"We should probably stop now," she said, moving back to the other end of the couch and running her hand through her hair.

"What?" he asked, louder than he intended, still breathing quickly and inching himself back up against the couch.

She tilted her head and looked at him, bemused. "It's the second Saturday of the month. They guys'll be here soon."

"Oh, that," he said, moving forward and kissing her again. "I cancelled the game tonight."

He brought his lips to hers again, but she put her hand on his shoulder and leaned back to look at him. "Why would you cancel? You guys only get together to play once a month—"

Half-smiling, he said, "I'd much rather play with you," and went back to kissing her.

Estelle started to laugh and pulled back again. "And I appreciate that. But I don't want you to blow your friends off for me—"

"They knew you were moving in today— I figured you'd just want to relax and settle in, instead of listening to a bunch of drunk guys playing cards all night."

"See, you say that and hear, 'Oh, I'm Mr. Sensitive and I'm making her so comfortable', but I hear, 'Hey, just so you know, the guys are gonna see you as the bitch that's taking our friend away'."

He dropped his head for a moment before looking back up at her. "I don't think they think that."

"Then they're gonna think I'm not comfortable being here when they are."

Simone gave her a gentle smile and started to say, "You're overthinking—" but stopped at the sight of the look she was giving him.

"Your friends are important to you, and I've already taken away the majority of the time you were spending with them— I don't want to be the reason you put this off. Tonight, it's because I'm moving in. How long before it's because I'm not feeling well, or because I'm tired, or because the baby's sleeping—"

"You want me to call them and see if they're still free?" Simone asked, giving her a calming smile.

She nodded, but as he took out his phone, she said, "Unless you're just doing it to make me feel better— if you had something planned I don't want to mess that up, either—"

He half-smiled and said, "Baby, I promise I was just trying to make sure you had the time you needed to settle in. If you're comfortable with them coming over, then yes, I'd still like to have them over."

Estelle nodded again, smiling. As he started typing the text message, he said, "I'd actually love for you to meet them. I mean, I know you've met them, but I'd like for you to really meet them. Get to know them a little."

"I'd like that, too," she said. "But won't they be irritated that there's a girl at the party?"

"We'll take the no girls allowed sign off the clubhouse tonight," he said, laughing as he stood and walked into the kitchen and took two bottles of Perrier out of the fridge. Handing one to Estelle, he said, "We're not complete dicks, you know."

"News to me," she said, laughing and opening the bottle.

Smiling, he looked up from his phone and said, "Everyone's still free. They'll be over in an hour."

"Who all is they?"

"Joel, Al and Libera. Sometimes Bronte joins in, but there's an event at Olympus he has to attend, so he can't make it."

"So, the angry casino guy isn't coming?"

Simone laughed. "I assume you're talking about Mack, from Athena?"

"Yeah, that one."

"No, he doesn't spend a lot of time socially with me or Al."

"How come?"

He shrugged. "He just doesn't. There're a few guys like that. Jim Duvall, for instance."

"I don't even know who that is."

"He's Libera's friend and advisor…they've known each other for years. We've never really seen eye to eye on anything, so we tend to avoid each other as much as possible. Mack's just a douchebag and doesn't spend a lot of time with anyone in the business outside of the casino unless it's an important event."

Estelle nodded. "Why don't you let me buy dinner tonight for all the confusion?"

"I wouldn't call three group text messages confusion," Simone said, laughing.

"Come on, this is important to me," she said, eyes sad as she prodded him with her foot.

Giving her a soft smile, he nodded and leaned forward to kiss her.

"Thank you," she said, smile returning as she continued kissing him.

This time it was him pulling back, as he half-smiled and said, "You see, last time you got my hopes all high, and then stopped me."

She stood up and took his hand into hers, giving it a gentle pull. "We've got close to a full hour."

Simone stood and followed her, hand still gently holding onto hers as she led him up the stairs. She stopped outside the closed bedroom door and said, "It's still kind of a mess in there."

"I assumed," he said, leaning down and starting to kiss her neck.

She closed her eyes for a moment, focusing only on his lips moving down to her collarbone. He looked up at her and nodded towards the closed door, but she smiled as another thought struck her, and shook her head, giving him a coy smile. She kissed him again, and then took his hand back into hers, seductively pulling her bottom lip under her teeth as she led him to a different door.

His desire began to peak as he realized where Estelle was taking him and he pulled himself closer to her, pressing her up against the door of his library. Reaching down behind her, he put one hand on the small of her back to keep her balance as he opened the door and slowly started to walk her backwards. He closed the door behind them and turned on the light, before putting his arms around her waist and quickly pulling her up against him, his kisses becoming faster and rougher as his hands made their way up into her hair.

Estelle moved her hands along his waist, slipping them up under the jacket he was still wearing, and he felt her fingernails through his shirt as they moved up just below his shoulder blades, before making their way back down. She put one arm around his neck as the other hand started to move up his thigh along his inseam, her right knee slowly moving along his leg until it rested at his waist. Simone put one hand around her waist, the other under the thigh against his hip and lifted her, walking them back so she was leaning against one of the built-in bookshelves.

As he lowered her to the floor, he took one of her hands into his and turned her, pressing his chest into her back as she closed her eyes and leaned her head back, giving a soft moan at the kisses and gentle bites to the back of her neck. Simone's breathing was quick and shallow, his intense passion building faster than ever before. He pulled her shirt off over her head and unhooked her bra, before reaching his hands up to gently massage her breasts as his lips continued to trace their path down her neck to her shoulder.

Estelle began to sway her hips from side to side against him as he quickly reached down and unfastened his belt. As he started to unzip his silk-lined slacks with one hand, the other reached around and started fumbling with the button on Estelle's jeans. Her breathing and excitement just as high as his, her hands quickly came to his aid, and as her jeans hit the floor, she felt his hand lift her left thigh, letting her foot perch on the second shelf from the bottom.

They both gave a loud gasp as he entered her from behind, slowly easing himself in as far as possible. His hips continued to move faster as he opened his eyes, watching as his movements pushed her up against the shelves, her left-hand gripping tightly to the front of a shelf— her right palm pressed flat against several books on the next shelf up. Simone's hands were holding on tightly to Estelle's hips, and as he leaned his head forward to kiss just below her ear, she gave a coy smile and turned her head to say, "How long have you been wanting to do this?"

Flashing an arrogant smile, he stopped the movement of his hips as he pushed himself further into her and nibbled on her ear lobe. "Since the night I met you."

She gave a seductive laugh that turned into a loud gasp as he started to build his pace back up, and after several more minutes she felt his erection start to strengthen. His hips began working faster and his gruff moans in her ear were becoming louder as she reached her left hand around to his waist, pulling him closer against her back. His chest was tight against her as he leaned his head back, his words becoming increasingly incoherent for several moments before she heard her name loud in her ear, and she felt his hands tense around her hips as his climax began to envelop him entirely.

Simone gave her shoulder a long, slow kiss as his body began to relax, and as she turned around, he brought his lips to hers and gave an embarrassed laugh. "Sorry that happened so quickly."

Brushing her nose against his, she smiled and said, "I'm not. It was sexy seeing you that turned on."

Estelle picked up her clothes as he was refastening his belt and she started to redress, but before she could, he put his hands on her waist and pulled her closer. "The score's still a little uneven," he whispered, half-smiling.

"That it is," she replied, putting her free arm around his neck, nestling her fingers in the ends of his hair. "But WE have people coming over soon, and I am perfectly content waiting until tomorrow."

"Makes me feel like I was leading you on—"

"Don't think of it as leading me on— think of it as waiting until you have all of a Sunday morning to wake up in our shared home together for the first time—" she stopped and started to kiss up his neck towards his ear, stopping between her words to give another gentle kiss. "With a nice, slow build up... where you can really... take your time... and indulge both of us... for as long as we'd like..."

He brought his lips back to hers for several moments before smiling and saying, "I'd love that."

"So would I."

After one last kiss, she finished dressing and followed him into the bedroom, where he had stopped and looked around at the piles she had spent the day sorting.

"Sorry it's such a mess— it's taking me a little longer than I thought it would."

"It's fine," he said, not making eye contact with her.

"You don't have to hide your compulsion to keep everything organized."

"I don't have a compulsion," he said, giving her a stubborn smile.

Estelle just crossed her arms and stood looking at him, tapping her index finger against her elbow.

"Fine, maybe a little compulsion. But it's fine..."

"I promise I'll get it done tomorrow. It'll all be back to normal."

Simone looked up at her and tilted his head. "You don't have to explain yourself, Estelle."

"No, you had everything perfect and then I came in—"

He shook his head and put his arms around her waist, pulling her closer. "But it's you being here that makes it perfect."

She smiled and nuzzled her face into his chest, giving a soft sigh as he kissed the top of her head. As he released her and walked over to the bed, he looked over at the boxes labeled CLOTHES stacked next to the closet. "Were you able to get your clothes unpacked?"

Estelle shook her head as he sat and started to remove his shoes. "I didn't want to touch the closet without you being here."

Simone frowned and cocked his head. "Why not?"

She walked over to the bed and sat down next to him, putting her head on his shoulder. "Because I didn't know where you wanted me to put anything, so I wanted to wait until you were here—"

"But why?"

Estelle raised her head and looked at him, neither understanding the other's confusion. "Because it's your house, and you have everything the way that you want it—"

His eyes softened at her words, and he leaned his head forward so that his forehead was resting against hers. "This is your home just as much as it is mine. You can change whatever you need to, live as comfortably as you want to, and take as long as you want to get everything the way you want it to be. All I'm worried about is making sure that you're as happy as you are fully capable of being."

Estelle nodded and laid backwards on the bed, looking up at him. "So, what are you guys up to tonight?"

"Probably poker and massive amounts of alcohol."

"How late do they usually stay?"

"I usually lose somewhere between three and four, Libera usually taps out around four thirty and then we sit and watch Joel get pissed off as he finishes losing around five."

"Why do you guys play if you always lose to Al?"

"Al's ego is almost as entertaining to watch as the actual game itself."

She started to laugh and turned onto her side, watching Simone stand and start to change into more comfortable clothes. "Should I go ahead and order dinner so it's here when they get here?"

"If you'd like. The Chinese place I ordered from last time you were here keeps the usual order on file for us. You just have to call and let them know when to bring it, and of course add whatever you'd like."

As he returned from the closet in Nike running shorts and a Ramones t-shirt, she said, "What should I be doing?"

"Whatever you'd like," he said, cocking his head again. "You do know you don't have to ask permission to do things?"

"I know," she said, resting her foot against his hip.

"Just making sure," he said, still sounding worried.

"Don't worry, I'll relax soon. I've just never done this before."

"Neither have I."

"Yeah, but you already live here," she said, laughing. "It took you a month to unlock the door to my apartment without texting to ask if it was okay as you were coming up the elevator."

"Fair enough," he said with a begrudging smile.

"So, if everyone's drinking tonight, how is everyone getting home?"

"They all just take a cab over and then back again later. Al usually sleeps it off at Joel's, so they come over together since he lives further away."

She nodded and stood, kissing him and walking towards the door. "I'll be downstairs ordering food."

"Thank you," he said, glancing at the piles.

"If you start rearranging I won't be able to find anything."

"Would I do that?" he asked, voice thick with mock sincerity.

She gave him a warning smile before heading downstairs and retaking her spot on the couch. Once the food was ordered, she picked up her book, intending to pick back up where she had left off, but even as she started the first paragraph, there was a sharp knock at the door. Looking out through the peephole, she saw Landini and Joel, each holding a new bottle of liquor. As she opened the door, Landini looked at her for a moment, before saying, "Well that's a first." She cocked her head, questioning his remark, and he laughed and said, "A girl answering his door, that is."

"First time for everything I suppose," she replied, laughing as she held the door open for them to enter.

Joel patted her shoulder as he walked by, saying, "You two know each other?"

"We met at the engagement party, I think," Estelle said, turning to Landini and looking over his Blondie t-shirt, black jeans and Converse sneakers. "Joe Strummer, right?"

He looked down and nodded his head a few times as he laughed, looking up as Simone came down the stairs. "Hey, guys," Simone started, walking over and taking the bottles they were holding. "How's it going?"

"Good," Landini replied. "Just getting to know Yoko over here."

Estelle laughed, before looking to Simone and saying, "Told you."

Simone glared at Landini for a moment, which just caused him to start laughing again. Ignoring him, Simone said, "Yeah, so this is Al."

"Landini, right?" Estelle asked.

Landini nodded his head and said, "You can call me by either, I'll answer to pretty much anything. Kinda like a poorly trained dog."

"That's the most accurate metaphor I've ever heard," Simone said, before rubbing the spot on his arm Landini punched as he walked by.

As they all laughed, Estelle looked over at Joel and said, "How is it that I don't know your last name?"

He smiled and said, "It's Fontaine."

"I can't believe it took me so long to ask that."

"'S'alright. Not many people call me by it."

"Don on his way?" Landini asked, opening the bottle of gin Simone had added to the minibar and starting to make himself a gin and tonic.

"I think so. Said he was running a little late."

Landini sat down across the couch from Estelle, and after a heavy, awkward pause, asked, "How'd the move go?"

"Good," she said, relieved. "Didn't take very long. Paolo was pretty itchy to leave."

"I'll bet he was," Landini said, laughing to himself as he took a sip of his drink.

After a quick, yet ignored, silencing hit to Landini's shoulder, Simone looked up and smiled at Estelle, before saying, "You need anything?"

She shook her head, and then looked up at Joel. "They always like this?"

He laughed and nodded, taking a seat at the round table. "Just wait till they get a little liquored up."

Simone gave an embarrassed laugh and went to answer Libera's knock at the door. "Hello, sir."

"How's it going?" Libera asked, walking in and setting his keys and a bottle of Bowmore on the table.

"Good. Food on its way?" Simone asked, looking at Estelle.

"Probably twenty minutes at the most."

He smiled and put his hand on her shoulder as he walked past, picking up the new deck of cards he had left on the kitchen island. Libera sat down at the table across from Joel as Simone came back and looked over to Estelle. "You joining the game tonight?"

"Oh— no, just hanging out for a bit. I don't want to intrude."

"Don't be silly," Landini said, already standing to refill his drink. "I could always use the money."

"You're very sure of yourself," she said, watching him.

He smiled and nodded, ignoring the laughter of the others. "There's room at the table if you want it."

"What's the buy in?"

"Three grand."

"It's cute that you think I carry that much cash," she said, standing as the delivery driver knocked at the door. Once she had signed the credit card slip, she came back carrying three bags of take-out boxes. "No, that's okay, boys. The pregnant lady can carry everything."

She started to laugh as they all jumped to their feet, and said, "Just kidding. I think I can handle it."

Laughing, they followed her into the kitchen, and Simone appeared at her side, still laughing as he started to help her unpack the bags. As Estelle turned to take plates out of the cabinet, Simone realized that the others were all watching them.

"What?" he asked, tilting his head.

"Nothing," Landini said, patting Simone's shoulder as he walked by. "You're just fucking adorable, that's all."

Simone gave another embarrassed laugh and nodded a few times, before gesturing for Libera to help himself to food. "Ladies first," Libera said, tilting his head towards Estelle.

Landini tapped Simone's shoulder again and said, "Yep. Go ahead, Belv."

Dropping his head back, Simone looked back at Landini and said, "How long have you been waiting to say that?"

"'Bout twenty years."

Simone nodded and leaned against the counter, watching Estelle silently giggle at their banter, relieved that everyone was so comfortable with each other. As the men sat down around the table and watched Joel start to shuffle the new deck of cards, Simone looked up and said, "Seriously, want to join us?"

"No," she replied, narrowed eyes warning him to stop talking.

"I can buy you in," he added, as everyone set their cash in the center of the table.

"It's true," Landini added, leaning forward on the table. "Baby-daddy over here's worth seven figures."

"Come on, it'd be weird."

"Not as weird as you'd think," Libera remarked, taking a sip of his scotch.

"Here," Joel said, taking ten more hundreds out of his pocket. "I'll put in a third of it."

Landini nodded and did the same, before looking up at her and starting to count out chips for everyone. Libera followed suit and said, "See, now he's not putting anything in, so it's not weird anymore."

"Maybe for you," she breathed, giving in and sitting down at the table next to Simone, who smiled and put his arm on the back of her chair.

Libera half-smiled and waited for everyone to ante before he accepted the deck from Joel, dealing everyone five cards. "You know how to play five card?"

"It's been a while, but yes."

He nodded and set the deck down, stopping to take a bite from his plate before picking up his hand. Simone finished arranging his cards and said, "I'll check."

"Shocking," Joel mused, rearranging his cards.

"Check," Estelle agreed.

"Twenty," Joel said, tossing a chip into the center of the table.

After everyone had called the bet, Simone asked for two new cards, and Estelle tilted her head as she looked at her hand. "One for me."

Libera handed her a card as she set her discard on the table in front of her, and looked up at Landini's arrogant laugh. "Problem?" she asked.

"Not for me," he said, not looking up and asking for two cards, after Joel had done the same.

Libera took three for himself, before Simone sighed and tossed his cards on the table. "Fold."

"Again, shocking," Joel added.

"Fifty," Estelle said, adding a chip to the pile.

"What?" she asked, as everyone looked up at her.

They all shook their heads and looked down again, Landini still half-smiling to himself. Joel considered his hand for a moment and dropped his cards. "Fold."

"Hundred," Landini said, dropping two chips onto the pile, keeping eye contact with Estelle.

"Call," Libera added, setting two of his own fifty-dollar chips onto the table.

"Two," Estelle added.

Simone leaned forward against the table, propping his head up on his hand, watching Estelle with a completely unreadable expression. Landini chuckled as he called, but Libera dropped his cards onto the table, picking up his glass and draining it before pouring another.

"Bring it," Estelle said, giving Landini a challenging stare.

He nodded, and set his cards on the table. "Two pair, kings and ace."

"You speak Italian, don't you?"

"I do," he said, laughing. "Do you?"

"Just a few random words and phrases… I just learned a new one recently, though."

"What's that?" he asked, leaning forward.

"Non fare un cazzo." Estelle sat her cards down on the table, showing three sevens and two queens.

Simone, Joel, and Libera all laughed as Landini leaned back, nodding his head and giving the first self-conscious laugh she had heard from him. As Estelle smiled and started to stack up her newly acquired chips, she looked at Simone and said, "Did I say that right?"

"In more ways than one," he replied, laughing as Libera refilled both of their glasses. Landini stood to make himself another drink, and as he walked by, he tapped Estelle's shoulder, but said nothing, laughing to himself.

An hour and a half later, Joel and Libera laughed as Simone lost the last of his money to Estelle and stood to put some ice into his glass. He set down another Perrier for her and kissed the top of her head before sitting back down, leaning back in his chair and resting his arm on the back of Estelle's.

"How come you never do that for me?" Landini asked, laughing.

"This a big problem for you?" Simone asked, standing back up.

"Nah, I'm good," Landini said, holding his hand up.

"Damn, I was kind of interested to see what would have happened," Estelle said, glancing at Libera, who had started to laugh.

Half-smiling, Simone poured himself another drink and watched as Estelle dealt the cards. After everyone checked, she handed Joel the requested three cards, and looked to Landini, who said, "Your streak's gotta break sometime."

"That's what we said to you three years ago," Joel said, looking over at him.

"Yeah, we'll see."

"I think I have to agree," Libera said, taking the two cards Estelle was handing him. She took two for herself, before looking to Joel. He looked down at the dwindling pile in front of him and said, "Fuck it," before putting his last three hundred dollars' worth of chips onto the table and nodding his agreement to Simone shaking his head.

As Landini finished his sixth cocktail, he called, and once Libera and Estelle had done the same, they all set their cards down and Joel poured and downed another shot, before standing and patting Estelle on the shoulder, silently congratulating her win with two pairs. Joel walked into the kitchen and picked up an egg roll, before coming back and sitting next to Estelle, watching as Landini filed away another hit to his wallet and ego. Estelle, also watching this, looked over to Simone and said, "You're right, this is fun."

She dropped her ante casually onto the table, and nodded her thanks to Landini, looking to Libera as she awaited his bet. "Fifty."

"Call."

Once Landini had called and started to dole out the requested amounts of cards, he looked over to Libera's stack of chips and started to make a hurried calculation in his head. Once Libera had dropped another fifty onto the table that was called by Estelle, Landini said, "Eight hundred."

Libera laughed and finished his drink, before saying, "All right then," and putting the rest of his chips into the center of the table.

Estelle clicked her tongue against her teeth before looking at Simone, who tilted his head, expecting her to ask a question. "See, when I learned to play, and I was in this situation, the house rules wouldn't let me raise the bet once someone else had gone all in."

"It's perfectly fine," Simone said, half-smiling at her confidence and finishing his seventh scotch. "Just put it in a different pile."

She nodded and watched Landini shake his head as she replicated his calculation strategy. Libera leaned back against the back of his chair and poured another drink, sipping slowly as he watched Estelle say, "Eleven hundred."

Landini just shook his head. "No, absolutely not."

"No, you don't think I have the cards, or no, you're too much of a pussy to place the bet?"

Simone looked back and forth between Estelle and Landini, before pouring and taking another shot of scotch. Libera and Joel both looked over to Landini, who was sitting with his hand covering his mouth, considering Estelle, rather than the cards in his hand. "No. You're bluffing."

"Then call it."

Landini ran his hand over his jaw, before just saying, "Fine," and pushing each of his stacks into the new pile Estelle had made and holding up his hand, silently asking her to show him her cards.

She looked at him for another moment and said, "You should have listened earlier," before setting her cards down on the table. "Straight flush, ten high."

Everyone looked over to Landini, who continued to sit expressionless for half a minute before starting to laugh and saying, "I have another phrase to add to your collection." He tossed his cards down, showing all four aces and a lonely queen. "Vaffanculo."

Landini stood as the other men at the table sat in shocked laughter, finished his drink and walked around to where Estelle was sitting. He picked up the cash from the center of the table, giving a sigh of defeat as he put the cash in her hand.

"Thanks," she said, confidently watching his embarrassed smile.

He put his hand on Simone's shoulder and said, "I like her."

Simone laughed and said, "Thanks, me, too."

Estelle ruffled his hair and smiled for a moment at his tipsy smile, before counting out thirty of the hundred-dollar bills. After handing a stack of ten to Joel and Libera, she walked over to where Landini was sitting on the couch and held out the thousand he had put in for her.

"I'm gonna go find my sweater, if you wanna tell them you let me win."

He leaned his head back against the couch and started to laugh, taking the cash from her.

As she walked towards the stairs, she heard Landini say, "She's right. I totally let her win."

"Really?" Libera asked, skeptical.

"No," Landini said, starting to laugh again.

She smiled at their laughter as she rummaged for her sweater, and as she came downstairs, wrapping herself in the warm wool, Landini said, "Seriously, though. That was fun."

"You sound a little too surprised, Al," she said, sitting on the couch opposite him.

Simone stopped at the minibar and opened a new bottle before sitting down on the floor in front of Estelle, leaning his head back against her calf. Landini looked at his watch and said, "How is it only nine thirty?"

"I have no idea," Simone said, laughing. "Usually it takes us three or four more hours to start stress-drinking from watching you play."

Libera took the seat between Estelle and Landini as Joel crossed over and leaned against the wall next to the fireplace, sitting on the floor across from Simone and watching as Estelle started stroking Simone's hair. "Gotta admit, Al, I didn't mind losing this time."

Landini laughed and nodded, saying, "Don't worry. I'll be back on top next time."

Simone leaned his head back and looked up at Estelle, saying, "What, are you not playing next time?"

As everyone started to laugh again, Estelle said, "Actually I'll probably be too tired next time."

Simone nodded, before smiling up at her again. Joel, however, laughed and said, "See, Al, he was just planning ahead. He procreated so you could keep winning at poker. That's JUST how nice of a guy he is."

Laughing, Simone said, "Yeah, that's why I did it. Poker."

Estelle continued stroking his hair, and looked down at him, saying, "I don't care why you did it, I'm just glad you did."

Simone half-smiled and looked down, avoiding making eye contact with anyone. After a moment, Landini stood to mix another drink, this time running a hand through his dark, wavy hair. "Christ," he said, looking over at Simone. "You know it just hit me that there's gonna be a tiny version of you running around soon?"

"God save the world," Simone said, holding his glass up towards Landini.

"That's no kidding," Landini said, sitting back down.

"So, who's known you the longest?" Estelle asked, looking down at Simone.

He looked over to Libera, who nodded. "That would be me. Met him when he was three."

"That long?"

Libera nodded. "I'd see him every once in a while, usually sitting in a corner reading a book. Not much has changed," he added, laughing as Simone nodded his agreement. "Didn't get to know him till he was a lot older, though. How long have you been working for me now?"

Simone leaned his head back, attempting to do the math and failing. "Somewhere between seventeen and eighteen years."

"Doesn't seem like that long, does it?"

"No, sir, it doesn't."

"You're both going on fifteen, aren't you?" he asked, looking between Landini and Joel, both of whom nodded.

"We started within a couple months of each other," Joel said, looking over to Landini, who agreed.

"Looks like you've got a good team," Estelle said, putting her hand on Libera's shoulder.

"That I do," he said, looking over at her. "That I do."

Chapter 35

"You're right," Simone said, several weeks later, as he closed a file and looked up at Gallo, before looking to Libera. "Phil's numbers are steady, but there's definitely something that's off."

"I've seen stuff like this before," Gallo said. "It's usually just a poorly paid employee taking some cash to pay a bill, and then putting it back once they get paid."

Libera nodded. "I've seen it happen, too. And being perfectly honest, I just let it happen, so long as it's just a couple times. But you sound like this is happening a lot."

"Semi-regularly, but not daily, or even weekly. And there's no way to tell who it is right now."

"Keep an eye on it. If it gets any more frequent let me know."

"Yes, sir. Thank you, Don Libera."

Simone stood along with Gallo and walked him out, before starting to make his way back to Libera. As he passed the bar, however, Landini was leaning against it, nursing a gin and tonic. He raised his hand, hailing Simone's attention.

"Everything all right?"

"Just odd, that's all. Got a minute?"

"Of course."

He nodded to Stephen, and once his scotch glass was in his hand, he followed Landini out the back door of Libera's office to the parking lot. Setting his glass on the hood of Landini's jeep, he lit a cigarette and handed it to Landini, before lighting one for himself and leaning against the fender.

"So," Landini started, taking a long drag, "I had this guy approach me today. He said he and two of his friends were wanting to see if we're looking for any new hands."

"He came to you?"

"Yeah, I thought that was weird, too. And he specifically said it was for my crew, for all three of them.""Have you EVER had somebody brand new underneath you?"

Landini half-smiled and said, "That's really a different conversation."

Laughing as he exhaled, Simone said, "That's not quite what I meant."

"Seriously, though, no. Starting people with me would be a very, very, VERY bad idea. Even aside from lack of experience when people need to know what the fuck they're doing, patience for explaining what needs to be done is not something I possess, in any quantity."

"I agree," Simone said, half-smiling and picking up his glass. "You think someone sent them?"

"Normally I'd say yes, but I don't know of anyone who'd be making a move like that."

"Nor do I. Want me to run it by Libera, see what he says?"

"I was hoping you would. They want to meet tomorrow."

"That quickly?"

Landini just nodded, taking the last drag from the cigarette and putting it out against the tire of his jeep, putting the filter into his back pocket. He absentmindedly ran his hand over the group of stars tattooed below his right elbow and said, "I haven't met the other two, just the one guy. Seemed pretty sure of himself."

Simone started to drop the end of his cigarette, and then sighed at Landini's exasperated stare, extinguishing the last of the tobacco and handing the filter to Landini, who said, "Three seconds, seriously. It takes you three extra seconds."

"Sorry, Mom." He took a sip from his glass as Landini gave a short laugh, and then asked, "What's your gut tell you?"

"I think they're up to something. I don't think coming to me was their idea, but I honestly don't know who it could have been. I have a bad feeling we'll find out soon, though." He stopped to take a sip from his gin and tonic, and then said, "This is just fucking ballsy, and I don't think it's because he thinks it'll get him a job."

"I agree. Thanks for letting me know— I'm sure one of us will need to talk to you about it again tonight, so you might hang around for a little while."

"Already planning on it. Thanks, Belv."

Simone nodded and then turned to head back in to see Libera. As he resumed his seat, Libera said, "Took you long enough."

"Sorry, sir," Simone started. "Al had a bit of a quandary."

"Oh?"

He began to recount Landini's story, nodding his thanks as Libera poured a little more scotch into their glasses. His eyes continued to stare at the melting ice, mind trying to relay the facts and discover their motive simultaneously. "I don't like it," Simone finished, looking up from his glass at his Patron. Their quiet discussion in Libera's corner booth of the restaurant was several tables away from the nearest customer, but Simone still glanced around to make sure no one was approaching them. "If these guys were serious, they would have waited for an introduction and not just asked for a meeting up front."

"Maybe it's just the younger generation," Libera said, tilting his head to the side in consideration of Simone's words. "Like Bassi. They just don't have the same standards— they all want instant gratification."

"Maybe," Simone responded, unconvinced. "Something just doesn't seem right."

"How many are there?"

"Three, and they all want to join Landini's crew, which isn't where we usually start people. They obviously haven't talked to anyone inside the organization."

"That's true. Do you think someone sent them, or do you think they're just naïve?

"Hard to say for sure, but they were far too specific for me to just think they were overestimating themselves."

Libera nodded. "I can have Landini bring them in…see if they'll tell us anything."

Simone's eyes narrowed and he tilted his head, running his thumb along the rim of his glass. "Or we could let it play out."

"That's a big risk."

Simone leaned forward and lowered his voice. "These guys want to move fast, and they'll probably make a move regardless of what we do. What if we set the meeting down at the Garage, so we're on our territory with our own terms, and then see how it rolls out? I'd rather them try something there than something clumsy around civilians."

"There is truth to that. All right… I'll talk to Al tonight, and have him set it up so the meeting is held at one thirty tomorrow afternoon in bay two. Make sure Joel goes with you, and I'll have Bassi head over with Landini, I don't want anyone one-on-one, got it?"

Simone nodded. "Yes, sir."

"If this is what you think it is, it needs to be nipped in the bud."

"I agree, sir."

Chapter 36

Much later that night, after an exhausting day of unpacking the day's delivery of boxes and continuing her attempt at mimicking Simone's well-honed system with her own belongings, Estelle woke up in Simone's bed, unsure at first as to what had caused her to awaken so abruptly. *It's barely past midnight,* she thought, glancing at the clock. She pulled herself up against Simone's back to kiss his bare shoulder, and just as she was drifting back off to sleep, she again felt the pleasant jolts that had awoken her.

"Simone?" Estelle squealed, shaking her fiancé.

"Simone— wake up!"

"What's wrong?" Simone mumbled, turning over to face her.

"The baby's kicking!" She grabbed his hand and held it over the sporadic movements from within her womb.

"Really?" Simone said, louder than intended, causing an already excited Estelle to jump in surprise. "Sorry!" he said, sitting up and kissing her cheek before leaning his head on her shoulder. He kept his hand pressed to her and kissed her shoulder. "Sometimes I still can't believe this is happening," he said, rubbing his eyes.

"I know. Me, too. It feels so much more real now."

He gave a tired nod, but she could still feel his smile against her arm. Once the movement subsided again, she nuzzled her head against his and said, "Sorry for waking you up, I know you have to be up early."

"Are you kidding? I wouldn't have wanted to miss that for anything. Has it happened before?"

"Not that I've noticed! It must have been what woke me up!"

He laid back down, pulled her in close and kissed her. She brushed her nose against his and said, "You look happy, love."

"I am."

"I'm glad," she said, sleepily nuzzling her face into his bare chest. "You deserve to be happy."

He kissed the top of her head and smiled as he felt her drifting back off to sleep. "You need to know how much I love you," he said, closing his eyes and trying to ignore the hint of worry setting in about the next day's meeting. "Both of you."

Chapter 37

The next afternoon was warmer than usual for early March, as Joel pulled Simone's Mercedes up next to Landini's off-roader outside of the Garage. Landini was standing with his arms crossed and looking irritated next to Paolo Bassi, who was leaning with one foot behind him against the building. Simone and Joel walked up, both shaking hands with Landini, who said, "They should be here any time. Don said you thought there would be trouble, too, so I parked one of the backup cars in the second bay, in case we need cover."

"That was good thinking. Hopefully it won't come to that. I want everybody behind it, though— at least until we know what we're dealing with."

"I agree."

"For fuck's sake, we could use some action," Paolo interjected.

"You want action, Bassi, join the army," Landini snapped, irritation showing through. "We've got a fucking business to run."

Simone heard approaching tires and looked around to see a beat up, pale blue sedan driving towards them. "This them?"

"Yeah," Landini said, opening the door of the garage.

Three men exited the car, none of them older than Paolo. "Hey," one of them said, walking up to Simone. "I'm Johnny. This is Luke and Tommy."

"I know," Simone said, nodding towards the open door. The three newcomers followed Landini and Paolo into the building, followed closely by Joel and Simone, making their way downstairs into the middle, underground bay. The cold, stone room had a cement floor and a workbench stretching the length of the wall with the door, and was currently only home to a few tall tool chests made of red steel and the rusting Dodge Charger from the seventies that Landini had parked in the center of the room earlier that afternoon.

Landini leaned against the workbench, watching the three men take in their surroundings. Simone, knowing that his silence was his most intimidating feature, kept his distance, and was standing with his left hand in his pocket, waiting for one of them to start talking. Joel stood a foot away from Simone, eyes on Bassi, who was the only one of Libera's men standing in front of the carefully placed vehicle with the new arrivals, who were clearly out of their depth. After several moments of silence, Simone finally asked, "So?"

Johnny gave Simone a confused look and said, "So?"

He's the leader, Simone thought. "You requested a meeting, and now we're here. What is it you want?"

"We thought Landini talked to you about it—" Tommy said, sounding nervous.

"I'm asking you."

"We want to help you guys out."

"And what is it you believe you can do to accomplish this?"

They looked around nervously at each other before Johnny said, "Whatever you need us to do."

Bullshit, Simone thought, looking over at Landini, who nodded in silent agreement. Looking back over at the trio with a confident calm, he said, "Who sent you?"

"No-no one," Luke said, taking a step backwards.

Simone said nothing, but continued to wait for someone to answer him.

"Really, we're just looking for work," Johnny said, glancing at Paolo's disbelieving laugh. "Something funny?"

Paolo shook his head and leaned against the wall, looking at Simone. "These guys for real? It took me six months to get in here."

Simone shot him a silencing stare before turning back to Johnny. "So, what is it that you want?"

Johnny looked down at the floor, flashing an arrogant grin and saying, "Just the bounty."

Landini sprang forward, but before he could react, Johnny pulled out his pistol in a single, barely visible motion and fired a single shot at Paolo, who fell to the floor. In the next second, Simone, Joel and Landini ducked down behind the passenger side of the Charger, pulled out their weapons and began to fire at the fledgling hitmen.

Goddammit, Simone thought, firing two shots to break the only remaining window of the car in front of him before ducking back down below the door handle and hearing a bullet ricochet off the window frame above his head. They had the advantage of the largest spans of cover in the room, but their opponents had much more space to move, making it nearly impossible to get a straight shot.

Simone's focus was set on firing at Johnny, who was ducking behind one of the red tool chests back to back with Tommy, as he emerged a few seconds at a time to fire several rounds at Joel. Landini was exchanging fire over the trunk of the car with Luke, who was ducking behind the other tool chest. Joel was kneeling between Landini and Simone, alternating firing at both Tommy and Luke between brief moments of safety.

Realizing he would quickly be nearing the end of his first magazine, Simone ducked back down, back against the steel door and pulled his magazine out just far enough to count the three remaining bullets before reloading and rising again to fire. Joel was firing in tandem with Landini, neither of whom were able to make contact.

After losing two more rounds in the stone wall, Simone crouched back down and took a deep breath to recover from the surprise and reformulate his mental blueprint. *Johnny's clearly in charge. We get him first, it'll throw the others off, and they'll slip up.* He knelt up again, right hand ready to pull the trigger, left hand stabilizing his grip. With both eyes fixated on Johnny, he fired again and heard the tinny ring of the shell hit the floor as the bullet lodged in Johnny's amateurishly exposed chest, rather than the stone wall behind him. As Simone knelt back down, Tommy and Luke hesitated for a moment, taking in the loss of their leader, before firing more rapidly than before. They had started to close in on Landini's end of the car, trying to draw them from their partial sense of safety.

In one well-rehearsed motion, Simone released his empty magazine and pulled the spare from his holster, pushing it into the awaiting weapon. He looked over to see a bullet miss Joel by a matter of centimeters and thought, *I brought them here. This ends now.*

He stood up and turned so that his body faced away from his weapon, trying to make his profile as small as possible. Simone stood in front of the hood of the Charger and watched the bullet he fired hit Luke in the shoulder, before a second bullet entered his chest. He then turned his attention to Tommy, who was running to take cover against the driver's side of the car. Simone took a step towards where Tommy was heading and suddenly felt a searing pain rip into the muscle of his left arm. He felt blood running down his extended arm towards his chest, and he clenched his jaw as he took another step forward and fired a final shot, causing Tommy to drop the gun that had been aimed at Simone's heart and slump down the rusty metal onto the floor.

A ringing silence fell upon the room as all gunfire ceased. Without saying a word, Landini and Joel jumped up and ran over to examine Paolo, who hadn't lived seconds after the first shot was fired, both unaware that their own leader had been hurt. Simone threw his head back and closed his eyes, now fully aware of the pain in his arm that seemed to magnify by the second. He opened his eyes, and with vision blurred both from pain and having his eyes closed so tightly, saw Landini still kneeling over Paolo, now talking on his cell phone.

"Hello, sir. It's over. Belv was right. You might want to come down and— yeah…"

Simone turned and faced the car, trying to regain his composure. Blood was starting to leak out of his cuff and trickle down his hand, and the pain was starting to overwhelm his thoughts. He leaned forward against the hood of the car, slamming the butt of the gun still in his right hand into the rusting metal, trying to gain some kind of psychological relief. Looking up at the loud sound echoing around them, Joel and Landini ran over to Simone. "Hold on, Don Libera, you still there?" Landini added, having already started to hang up.

Joel was trying to get Simone's attention. "Boss— look at me—"

Simone refused to look up and just shook his head, but felt Joel's hands on his shoulders, turning him around.

"Jesus," Joel said, seeing the circular rip in the arm of Simone's jacket that had also started to leak blood. He took the Taurus from Simone's hand and eased him down against the front fender.

"Belv's been hit," Landini relayed, trying to keep his voice level. "Just the arm, but we're gonna need Doc down here now."

No longer having to worry about keeping his balance, Simone began to focus on taking off his jacket, using his teeth to pull his cuff over his right hand. Once his right arm was free, Joel pulled the left side away, exposing a larger rip in the white button up that had rapidly stained as the blood spread across the soft fabric. As Joel loosened and removed Simone's holster, Simone set his pocket watch on the floor and unbuttoned his vest, slipping his arm out and saying, "Mind using that to put pressure on it?"

Nodding, Joel complied as Simone started to loosen his tie. They both looked up as Landini lit a cigarette and started to laugh. "Jesus Christ, you're high maintenance, Belv."

Half-smiling, Simone leaned his head back against the car and said, "You have no idea."

He took the lit cigarette Landini was handing him and closed his eyes as he inhaled. After a few silent minutes of waiting on their trusted, retired army doctor to appear, Simone's phone began to ring. He handed the cigarette back to Landini and shifted, gritting his teeth against the pain, and pulled his phone from his pants pocket.

"Dammit," he said, seeing it was Estelle, and having absolutely no grasp on how to approach the situation. He sent the call to voicemail and bent his right knee, nodding in thanks to Landini, who had returned the cigarette to Simone's hand.

"You gotta tell her sometime," Joel said. "Trust me. You want her to hear it from you, and not from somebody else."

"I will. Just not right now." He reclosed his eyes and took another long drag, only looking up when his phone beeped with a text message.

I know you're working. Doctor was fine, all tests normal. I love you.

He smiled and put his phone next to his watch as Doc and Libera hurried into the room.

"I'd hoped I was done sewing you up, Mr. Belvedere," Doc said, setting down a black, leather bag and taking Joel's place, unbuttoning Simone's shirt enough to get better access to the injured arm.

"You know, I'm not crazy about it, myself," Simone quipped, handing Joel the last of the cigarette.

Libera stood off to the side, talking quietly with Landini and getting updated on all that had happened.

"Well," Doc started, putting on new gloves and sounding resigned, "The bullet didn't go down into the bone, but it's lodged in the muscle. I'm going to give you an injection to tone the pain down, but I'm going to have to take the bullet out now to be able to stitch it back up, and I doubt that injection will do a whole lot for you."

Simone leaned his head back against the fender again, and just said, "Thanks."

"I can never tell if you mean that," Doc joked, taking out a new syringe, along with a vial and a packet of alcohol wipes. As he took the cap off of the syringe and started to draw the fluid into it he glanced up at Joel and Landini and said, "I'm going to have to ask the two of you to step outside."

After they had left, Doc found a suitable spot in Simone's right arm and quickly cleaned the skin before piercing the needle into the vein and injecting the strong pain reliever. After the needle was removed, Doc started to locate the necessary tools and opened their sterile packages, arranging them in the order he would need them. Simone closed his eyes to keep the room from spinning after the strong medication started flooding his system, and heard Doc say, "You ready?"

Simone nodded, and then let out a low, gruff yell as the doctor removed the deformed bullet and handed it to him. "You're lucky it was a nine mil," Doc mused. "Anything bigger probably would have just gone further and broken the bone."

He sat there looking at the bloody bullet in his hand for a moment, feeling lucky to be going home to Estelle at all. "Estelle..." Simone muttered through his fog.

"What's that, son?" Libera asked.

"Estelle... she called... didn't answer..."

Libera smiled. "She'll understand."

Simone nodded in agreement, trying to stay awake. "That's right," Doc said, trying to keep Simone talking as he stitched the wound closed. "I heard you two were expecting. How's she doing?"

"Good... First couple months...hard on her..."

"That's not uncommon. When is she due?"

"July..."

"Do you know the sex yet?"

"No... started kicking... last night..." He smiled in spite of himself and the pain he was in. "Woke her up."

"That's wonderful," Doc said, starting to pack his tools back into his bag. "Right on schedule, it seems." He turned to Libera and said, "Can we take him back to your office so we can watch him for a bit? He's lost a fair bit of blood, I'd like to get a little back in him."

"Of course," Libera said, eyes full of concern.

He called Joel in to help get a still floating Simone ready for transport, before leaving Landini alone in the quiet bay, dialing the phone number of one of his crew members, readying his team for the cleanup.

Chapter 38

Estelle awoke with a start, unsure if the door slamming had actually happened or if it was part of a dream she had already forgotten. Deciding it was just a dream, she looked at the bright red numbers on the clock reading 3:47 a.m. and ran her hand over Simone's vacant pillow. Getting up for a drink of water, she approached the stairs and saw the soft glow of light from the fireplace and could hear ice shifting in a glass. *He's home.*

She tiptoed down the stairs in her oversized 'Hogwarts Alumni' t-shirt, not wanting to startle him. Simone sat facing the fire, shoulders leaning against the back of the couch, left arm gingerly perched on a pillow. *He can't have been home long*, she thought, noticing that he was still wearing his jacket. Her voice, subdued from mingling exhaustion, still echoed in the silent living room she had come down into.

"Simone?"

"Hey," he whispered, turning his head too quickly and wincing. "I'm sorry I woke you, the door—"

"What's wrong?" she asked quickly, seeing the exhaustion and pain in his eyes, even from the backwards glance he had given her.

"It's been a long day," he said, leaning his head back and closing his eyes.

She sat next to him and laid her head on his right shoulder. "Do you want to talk about it?"

He put his right arm around her, taking care not to touch the cold glass in his hand to her arm, and shook his head.

"Why don't you come to bed?"

He shook his head again. "I'm all right. I have to take a shower before coming to bed and I'm not at all feeling it right now."

"You've been up for nearly twenty-three hours. You need some sleep. And I'm guessing you didn't eat again, either."

"Not hungry."

He drank the last sip of scotch left in his glass and shifted the arm on the pillow, wincing again.

"What's wrong?" she asked again, taking his glass and starting to sit up.

He tightened his arm around her shoulders, keeping her pressed against him and kissed her forehead. "It's just been a long day."

Her phone, still set on silent, lit up the end table, alerting her to a text message. "Who the hell is that?"

Wriggling out of his arm, she stood and picked up her phone. "That's weird. It's Libera."

Simone looked up, just as confused as Estelle. "What does it say?"

She looked over at him, her newfound anger palpable, even across the dark room. "He's asking me to make sure you stay in for the next couple days while you heal up, and that he'll stop by tomorrow with your phone and your watch."

Fuck. He let his head drop back against its resting place, trying to find a less dramatic way of explaining what had happened. "It's really not—"

"Simone, I know that there are a lot of things you can't tell me, and I accept that. But you need to not lie to me."

He covered his eyes with his right hand. "You're right. I'm sorry."

"I thought that you'd agreed to be up front with me, about everything. I thought our relationship was built on trust."

He looked up, several levels of guilt stampeding through his mind. "You're right. I was afraid of upsetting you, and I should have been up front with you."

Her eyes softened at his words. "I know you worry about us. But you have to trust that I can decide for myself what I can and can't handle."

Putting his hand back over his eyes, he nodded.

Estelle picked up his glass and poured another few ounces over the melting ice from the still open bottle sitting on the table next to Simone's shoulder rig. "Why is your gun on the table if you're still wearing your jacket?"

Simone knew she was getting closer to figuring it out for herself, and he wanted to be the one to tell her, but he couldn't find the right words to string together. Without looking up, he just said, "I took it off earlier."

She walked back over to the couch and stood in front of him, blocking most of the light from the fireplace. She looked at his tired face for a moment, and whispered, "Here you go."

He looked up at her, and gave her a soft smile. "Thank you, baby," he said, not thinking and leaning forward to take the glass.

With an involuntary, raspy moan he shifted his weight off of his left arm as he took a sip. Her eyes drifted down to the arm he had resting on the pillow, and came to rest on the unmistakable, frayed rip in his jacket, just inches below his shoulder. "Oh my god."

"It's not that bad," he said quickly, realizing where her eyes were focused. "Really—"

Her eyes widened, and in a slight panic she asked, "Were— were you shot today?"

"It's not that bad."

"I swear to god, Simone, if you say that one more time... I want the real answer."

He sighed and said, "Yeah."

Estelle's anger was clearly unabated by his monosyllabic answer, so he went on to say, "It all happened down on the underground level of the Garage, so it was all contained. No one will know. The meeting today was a setup. A poorly conceived setup, but it was nonetheless effective."

"Do you know who set it up?" Her arms were still crossed, but her anger was quickly giving way to anxiety.

He shifted, trying to get more comfortable. "No, not yet. And you know I couldn't tell you even if I did know who sent them."

"I know," she said, waving her hand and sitting down next to him. "The guys that set you up, did you have to—?"

He nodded and finished his drink. "Yeah."

Running her fingers through his abnormally messy hair, she asked, "You going to be okay?"

"Yeah. Takes a few days, but I'll be all right."

"Can you tell me who was helping you?"

He hesitated before he answered. "Joel and Al are both fine. Few cuts and bruises, that's all." He leaned his head back again and, staring up at the ceiling, whispered, "Bassi's dead."

"Oh my god."

"Yeah."

"So, what happens now?"

"Now, we figure out who sent them, and go from there."

"No, I mean...what'll happen to Paolo, and the others..."

"Oh... Honestly, I don't know. Bassi didn't have any family, that's why he came to work for us in the first place. Libera, Al and his crew are the only ones that know. Libera told me a long time ago that I was better off not knowing. Aside from that, if I knew, it would put the casinos at risk because they pay me. If I talked, for whatever reason, it would pull the casinos' books down with me, which would just domino the rest of the organization."

"I guess that makes sense." She put her hand in his, interlocking their fingers. "You sure you're all right?"

"I will be. Doc pulled the round out and stitched me up. It was a smaller round, and it didn't hit the bone, so I was actually pretty lucky. He's going to come by before noon and look at it."

I'm worried about more than that. "Promise you're okay?"

He looked over at her worried eyes, and tucked a stray strand of hair behind her ear. "Lo prometto."

She laid her head back onto his right shoulder, and they sat in silence for a while, watching the electric flames. Just after five, Estelle ran a comforting hand through his hair and said, "Let's get you to bed."

He shook his head. "Let me clean up first."

Standing, she held out her hand. "That's what I'm here for."

Very slowly, he rose to his feet and took her hand. "You   don't have to—"

"Simone, let me be there for you like you are for me."

He gave her a gentle kiss and said, "I love you, and I'm sorry."

"I know, baby. Come on."

She took his right hand into hers and led him upstairs. Once he was sitting on the foot of the bed, she helped him ease his jacket off. "Oh, Simone…"

The left side of his once white shirt was deep red with blood, and the rip in the sleeve was half an inch bigger than the one in his jacket had been.

"You okay?" he asked, giving her a tentative glance.

She gave an exhausted laugh and started to unbutton his shirt. "You're sitting here covered in blood and you're asking me if I'm okay?"

His brief smile quickly turned into a grimace as she eased his left arm out of its sleeve. "Where do you want these?" she asked, holding up his shirt and jacket.

"Just on the dresser. I'll take care of them tomorrow."

Nodding, she removed the bloodstained bandages and said, "I'm going to let this breathe for a minute while I get a towel, okay?"

He nodded, and she went to the bathroom, returning with a wet washcloth, a soft, dry towel, and the first aid kit he kept in the pristinely organized linen closet. The wound was cleanly stitched back together, but the skin surrounding it was badly bruised, and there was a layer of dried blood on the left side of his ribs, shoulder blade and arm, trailing down past his bicep. "Do you want me to start closest to it or furthest away?"

"Closest… best to get it over with…"

She nodded and gently touched the warm cloth to the skin around the wound, taking care not to put any pressure on it. Simone closed his eyes and clenched his jaw, trying to remember to breathe through the searing pain still shooting through his arm, despite the gentility of her hand. As she inched away from the damage, Simone's breathing eased up and his arm relaxed a little, exhaustion finally setting in. She gently dried his skin and began taping the bandages in place, saying, "You probably shouldn't be drinking until this heals up a little bit. You'll bleed more."

"You're probably right," he said, standing and changing into more comfortable pants.

"Did he give you anything for the pain?"

"He gave me an injection before he started, and then again before he left. My car's still at Libera's since Joel drove me home."

He sat down in their bed, his bare back propped up against the headboard. Once the towels were safely in the hamper and her hands free of Simone's blood, Estelle turned the light off and set the alarm for less than four short hours away. "What time do you expect Libera to show?"

"Probably around ten or so."

"All right. I have to be up for work, so I'll be up in time, even if you're not. Try to get some sleep."

"Thank you...For everything."

She walked around to his side of the bed and kissed him. "I love you."

As she climbed into her side of the bed, he said, "I love you, too. So much."

She laid down next to him, taking his hand into hers.

"Estelle?"

"Hmm?"

"It was my fault."

She propped herself up on her elbow and looked up at him. His eyes were still closed, and his head leaned back against the soft velvet. "What was?"

"Bassi... I knew it was a setup. I told Libera to keep the meeting anyway so we could find out who was behind it..."

"Simone that's not—"

"...barely twenty-five fucking years old..."

"Listen to me, this is not—"

"I should have known he wasn't ready... didn't even find out who..."

"You couldn't have known it would happen like it did."

"I should have known." He laid down and rolled onto his right side, trying to get somewhat comfortable.

She pulled herself closer into him and said, "You couldn't have known, Simone."

He said nothing, but shook his head and gave a heavy sigh. She kissed his shoulder and laid watching him sleep for a couple hours before giving up on her own rest, turning on the small lamp by the bed and opening her book, glancing over at him every few minutes.

Just before nine thirty she turned off the alarm to keep it from waking Simone and got dressed for the day before heading downstairs to find the next book that she needed. Already feeling emotionally exhausted from the day, she reentered the bedroom carrying 'The Return of the King,' and was surprised to see Simone sitting up and staring at the wall across from the bed.

"How are you feeling?"

"All right," he said, not looking up at her.

"Can I get you anything?"

He shook his head. "Thanks, though."

"Tell me what's bothering you?"

Shaking his head again he said, "I've already told you too much as it is. I just need to deal with it on my own. I'll be fine."

"I'm worried about you."

"Don't be."

"What?" she whispered.

He closed his eyes. "I didn't mean that."

Her hurt eyes filled with tears as she sat down next to him, looking at her hands.

"Hey," he started, looking over at her. "I'm sorry. I'm just not myself today."

"It's okay."

"No— I can't take work stuff out on you. I'm sorry."

"You're allowed to be human, Simone. You haven't ever had to hide how you're feeling from me—"

"It's just work stuff, I'll be—"

"You'll be fine. I get it," she snapped, leaning back and opening her book.

"I'm not trying to be a jerk, Estelle. I just have to work through it on my own."

"Why?" She leaned forward so she was looking at him, trying to find some understanding in his features as to what had changed in the few hours he had been asleep.

"Because it doesn't fucking change ANYTHING!"

Physical and emotional pain were quickly blending, spurring him to lose his temper completely. "It was MY fucking fault, because I thought I knew better, and even if you COULD fucking understand it, talking to you about it doesn't change ANY of it!"

There was a light tap at the bedroom door. "Sorry for interrupting," Libera said, pocketing his keys and watching Estelle turn to brush away her tears.

"Not at all," she said quietly. "We didn't hear you come in."

"I noticed," he said, not breaking his fierce eye contact with Simone, who was still breathing quickly from his adrenaline-fueled flare.

There was an awkward pause, and all Estelle could think was, *Do I stay or go?* "I can make some coffee," she said.

"That would be great," Libera replied, putting a gentle hand on her shoulder as she walked by. "Thank you, Estelle."

She nodded, closed the door behind her and headed downstairs into the kitchen. Simone slowly rose to his feet, looking nervous. Libera's interruption had broken the stream of his fury, and the weight of his outburst began to set in. He glanced at the door, wanting to rush after Estelle to make things right, but he knew better than to abandon his Patron. "I'm—"

"Oh, I think I should talk first," Libera said, trying to maintain control of his own temper.

"Yes, sir."

Libera stood directly in front of Simone with his hands in his pockets, anger clear in his sharp eyes. "I'm going to pass over the way I just saw you talking to her. Your relationship with her is your business, and if you want to fuck that up, it's your prerogative."

Simone looked down, heart breaking further at the way he had lost his temper with her.

"I'm the one that sent you down there— everything that happened is on me, and not you— understand?"

"Yes, sir."

"Don't lie to me. What the hell did you think would have happened if you hadn't said to keep that meeting underground? You said yourself that it would have happened anywhere, and keeping it there kept civilians from being involved— just like you said two days ago. I know you hate having to make eliminations—"

Simone looked up. "It's not them."

There was a moment of sad understanding in Libera's eyes. "Ah."

Simone sat down on the foot of the bed, looking at the floor.

"It's been a long time since we lost somebody," Libera said, sitting down next to Simone. "Couple years for the organization. Bit longer for you, isn't it?"

Simone nodded, but stared resolutely at the floor.

"Bassi knew what he had signed up for. We all know the risks."

"I know."

"You didn't pull that trigger. That's not on you. Understand?"

"Yes, sir."

"And from what Al was telling me, if you hadn't taken that bullet we would have lost two more, including your child's godfather."

"He's making it sound better than it was."

"Or he's telling it how it is and you're letting yourself get wrapped up in that self-deprecating bullshit that happens when you can't prevent something like this from happening."

Estelle knocked at the door before opening it. "Sorry, Mr. Libera. The doctor just got here, and wants to take a look at him."

"Thank you," he said, standing. He walked to the door and said, "We're not done, here."

"Yes, sir," Simone said, looking at Estelle, who was instead looking at Libera, pointedly trying to avoid returning Simone's gaze.

As the doctor came in and set his bag down, Estelle led Libera back downstairs and into the kitchen. "Coffee should be ready," she said, trying to sound happier than she was. "Black with sugar, right?"

"Thank you, Estelle."

She poured him his coffee and sat down across from him at the sparkling black island. "I'm sorry if he told me too much last night, he wasn't really himself."

He watched her stare into her juice for a moment before responding.

"My dear, I've wanted for a very long time for Simone to find someone who could understand him the way you do. I've watched him put himself through this several times, and killing's never any easier on him, even if he is saving someone else."

She looked up, surprised at how blunt he was being with her. "Is he...?" her voice trailed off, afraid of overstepping her boundaries.

"It's okay," he said, taking a sip of his coffee. "Go ahead."

"Is he afraid I'm judging him?"

Libera shook his head. "He's judging himself." She nodded, and after a moment he continued, "We also haven't taken a loss in a few years, and he's still blaming himself for the first one."

"The first what?"

Libera set his mug down, giving Estelle a confused look. "The first associate he had under him."

"I thought Joel was the first one. Simone said Joel's been with him for a little over five years, back before Joel was promoted. He's never mentioned anyone else."

Libera gave her an awkward glance, surprised that he had accidentally brought up unknown information. "This was about eight years ago. Simone had just been promoted, and a guy that thought he'd be next in line didn't like that someone as young as Simone was being promoted over him...tried to take him out..."

"Oh my god."

"I'm sorry— I thought you knew, or I wouldn't have said..."

"I thought he had told me everything..." she stopped, thoughts clicking into place. "The scar on his hip— he'd never give me a straight answer..."

Libera nodded. "He took a .45 to the hip; almost didn't make it. The kid that had just joined under him— about twenty-two, name of Ren Accardi, wasn't even with us a month— took two to the head before Simone could put a stop to it. He's blamed himself since."

"But that's not his fault."

"I agree. But he puts so much pressure on himself to prevent anything like that from happening again, and he can't control everything. He can't predict everything. But he tries like hell. And that's why he's the best man I have working for me. Men like Al and Pagani— they don't care. But Simone cares. Sometimes too much. He keeps them in line, though."

"I shouldn't have pushed him into talking about it this morning," she said, looking back down.

"No, Estelle. You need to trust your instincts. He was out of line, and he knows it. But it's not you. It's his bullshit that he needs to deal with, and he's not going to be able to deal with it without you— despite what he's telling himself."

"Why didn't he tell me?" she asked, putting her head in her hands.

Libera stood and put a hand on her shoulder. "Like I said. It's not you. It's the guilt."

"Why are you telling me?"

"Because he should have."

She nodded and wiped away the stray tears that escaped. "I'm sorry, I don't usually cry this much..."

"No worries at all, my dear. I heard the baby started kicking."

She gave a teary laugh and said, "Night before last."

Libera laughed. "You should have seen him yesterday after Doc gave him those meds. The man's getting a bullet pulled out of his arm and that's what he wants to talk about."

She smiled for a moment and said, "He's going to be a good father, isn't he?"

"He is."

She looked back down at her glass— Libera's story from Simone's past making her feel suddenly distant and confused. Libera resumed his spot across from her and said, "Good husband, too."

She met his gaze and said, "I just wish he knew it, too."

"As long as I'm pushing my boundaries," Libera said cautiously, "Simone's mother contacted me."

"The hell?"

"That was pretty much my response, as well. She showed up at the restaurant a few weeks ago while Simone was in a meeting somewhere else. She's been trying to contact him for a while now...just before the two of you got together. I'm assuming he didn't tell you."

Estelle shook her head. "No, he didn't."

"I think he just wants to keep that part of the past behind him, and I don't blame him at all. But she wants to make things right with him."

"That's not what he wants."

"I know that. And you don't have to tell him. But I said that I'd pass it along, and now I have. Do with it what you will."

"I'll have to think about it."

Libera nodded and then turned, hearing Doc say, "I want you taking at least two days off. And none of that sneaking back in to work like last time. I don't want to have to re-stitch that."

"Yes, sir," Simone said with a small laugh.

"We'll keep him here," Libera said, walking over to shake the doctor's hand as they walked into the living room.

Libera took out the cash from his pocket, but the doctor said, "Mr. Belvedere has already paid me, Don Libera. Thank you."

Smiling, Libera nodded. "Good. Thanks again."

"Of course. As usual, Mr. Belvedere, hopefully we'll make it a year without seeing each other again."

"Thanks, Doc," Simone said, shaking the doctor's outstretched hand.

"I'll walk you out," Libera said, following his friend's path to the door.

After watching them step out onto the porch, Simone walked over to Estelle in the kitchen, whose hurt eyes were still avoiding his gaze. "Estelle, I am so sorry. I shouldn't have—"

"Not now," she said, standing and walking over to the couch.

"Baby, please—"

"Later. Do you want me to call in today and stay with you?" she asked as Libera walked back in.

"No," he said a little too quickly. "You don't need to disrupt your day for me. It's best for you to go in."

Libera looked over at Simone, understanding what Estelle was missing.

"Yeah, okay. Whatever. I have to go. Gianni's here to drive me in."

Libera nodded and walked over to Estelle and kissed her cheek. "Remember what I said."

She gave him a weak smile and said, "Thank you."

Her smile faded as Libera walked over to the couch to sit down next to Simone, and as she picked up her purse, she said, "Today's my short shift, so I'll be home around seven."

"Okay," he said, silently berating himself for the hurt he had caused in her. He got up and walked over to the door, where she was buttoning her cardigan. "I'm so sorry," he whispered.

She shook her head and turned to leave without another word, and as he locked the door behind her, he leaned forward and rested his forehead against the door, trying to decide if he should text her a better apology so she could read it at her own pace.

Libera spoke up, breaking his concentration. "You think they're watching her?"

"Yes, but only because it's the logical thing for them to do. If she would have called in, it just would have brought attention to what happened yesterday."

"Al said you didn't find out who sent them."

Simone shook his head. "Not even close."

"We'll get this figured out. But it's probably not going to happen today. It's going to take some time, and you need to accept that now."

"Yes, sir."

"Take a couple days, get your head straight."

"Thank you, sir. I will."

"Your phone and watch are on the table. I have to get going— I'm already late to meet with Al."

"Yes, sir. Thank you, again."

"Thank you, Simone. I appreciate what you've done."

After shaking hands, Libera left, leaving Simone alone with his thoughts. He laid down on the empty couch and closed his eyes, but no sooner had he started trying to walk through his emotional labyrinth had he fallen back asleep, breathlessly waking several hours later from the dreamt gunfire invading his repose.

Chapter 39

Running his hand through his hair, he stood and started to head into the kitchen, but stopped as he heard a knock at the door.

"Hey," he said, opening the door for Landini to enter. "What's wrong?"

Landini came in and walked past Simone into the living room, taking off his Cubs hat and pushing his hair out of his face before putting it back on. "Why do you think something's wrong?"

"Because I've known you for over twenty-five years. What's wrong?"

"I'm sorry."

"For what? You didn't do anything—"

"You're right, I didn't, and that's the fucking problem."

"That's not what I meant."

"But it's the truth. I get paid to do one thing, and I didn't. I don't know what the hell was wrong with me yesterday."

"I'm sorry— you drove half an hour to come over and apologize for not being able to hit a moving target at the wrong angle?"

Landini looked at him for a moment, and then turned around. "Yeah."

Simone nodded as he went to sit on the couch, and gestured for Landini to do the same. As he took his seat, leaning against the armrest opposite Simone, Landini said, "I fucking put the car down there, I knew where the best shot would come from, and I wasn't there. Three of those motherfuckers and I couldn't fucking hit one of them."

"I hate to break this to your ego, but you're not perfect."

Landini gave a short laugh, and then leaned forward, covering his face in his hands. "I should have done what you did long before you had to do it."

"And from that angle you would have been killed, nearly instantly."

"That's my job, Belv. Not yours."

"My job is to do what has to be done, and that's all I did."

Simone stood and walked to the minibar, pouring them each a glass of scotch. As he handed one of the highball glasses to Landini, he resumed his seat and said, "You seemed irritated yesterday…"

"Mostly just Bassi. I swear to god, he didn't let up the entire trip over there…"

At the mention of Paolo's name, Simone finished the scotch in his glass in one mouthful and stood to pour another. "Belv?" Landini asked, eyes narrowed as he stared at the back of Simone's head.

"I'm fine."

"Yeah, that's what you said last time, and I still had to talk the fucking gun out of your hand."

"You're right," Simone said, turning around. "I'm not fine. I should have spoken up and told Libera that he wasn't ready. Or that I was completely incapable of keeping him under control. And I should have just—"

"I think we all should have done a lot of things, including searching the bastards before we brought them in. I've been doing this for ten fucking years. I know how these guys work because, honestly, I've had to do it myself and I didn't have the common fucking sense to see if they were armed. It doesn't make a difference now. And we can tell each other this as many times as we want, it's not going to change the fact that we both feel equally responsible for something that should have gone a lot differently. It's not going to make you stop feeling responsible for Bassi getting shot, and it's not going to stop me from feeling responsible for you getting shot, so just cut the bullshit, pour another drink, put on a record, and deal the goddamn cards."

Simone half-smiled for a moment and nodded once, standing and walking over to the stereo. He rifled through his records and pulled 'London Calling' from its faded, shabby cardboard cover and gently placed it on the turntable, easing the needle down onto the vinyl and turning up the volume. Grabbing the scotch bottle as he passed, he sat down at the round table, followed closely by Landini, who pushed aside Simone's gun, watch and cell phone before sitting across from him.

Shuffling the deck of cards in the middle of the table, Simone began to deal them each ten cards as Landini poured more scotch into each glass. He took a moment to check his phone, brow furrowed at the lack of messages from Estelle.

"How'd she handle it?" Landini asked, taking a sip from his glass.

Simone began to sort his cards to delay speaking, before turning over a card and gesturing for Landini to make the first play. "She was mad at first, because I waited too long to tell her and Libera texted her. But then she was just worried. Helped me get cleaned up— I don't even know if she even went back to sleep after I did..."

"But?"

He set his cards down and rested his elbow on the table, right hand covering the bottom half of his face. "But then I took everything out on her this morning."

"How bad was it?"

Simone picked his hand back up and picked up another card, dropping the jack of diamonds onto the discard pile. Picking up his glass, he said, "I just closed myself off. Told her she couldn't understand it and that talking to her wouldn't do anything to help me."

"Jesus…"

"Yeah."

"You work it out?"

Simone closed his eyes and slowly shook his head. "Libera walked in just in time to see me yelling at her and then she had to leave for work… And now she's not talking to me, just like I was stupid enough to ask for."

"She knows you. She'll come around."

"It's not just that… we've never… never mind."

Landini set his hand down and said, "Gin. You've never what?"

Dropping his cards onto the pile in front of him, Simone watched Landini start to shuffle and said, "We've just always been able to talk through anything, and I've been as up front as I can be with her— I don't know why I pushed her away like that."

"Does she…understand…everything that happened yesterday?" Landini asked cautiously.

"She does."

"And you weren't just pussyfooting around it—"

"She knows I'm the one that pulled the trigger, yes."

"Then I'm guessing she's probably more okay with it than you are. I mean, fuck… the first time I met her, I introduced myself, and she just laughed and said, 'He's never mentioned what you do for Libera, so I'm assuming you're the problem solver'," he finished, miming quotation marks with his fingers. "I don't think she's the one with the problem, here."

Simone laughed, finishing his drink. "No, I know it's me," he went on, propping his head up with his hand, elbow casually against the table. He tapped his fingers against his hair, realizing how long it had been since his last cigarette, and immediately craving one. He glanced at the pack on the end table but put the thought aside, picking up the cards Landini put in front of him.

"I just thought I could talk to her about anything, and then all this shit happened, and now it's like I don't even understand how to talk to her anymore."

"You don't know how to talk to HER, or you don't know how to talk to yourself?"

"Meaning?"

"Come on, Belv, I know how you separate yourself from all of it. You can't just keep filing everything away hoping you'll never have to deal with it again. I, of all people, understand how hard it is. And despite popular opinion, I don't actually enjoy having to do it, myself. But I also know that I don't define myself by it, and that I can live with the things I've done. I know that I'm not taking out innocent people,

- 165 -

and I know that I'm not cleaning up after people that do. That's not the kind of organization Don runs. If someone's dying, it's because they've threatened one of ours. People wanna run their mouths, or renege on deals— fine. I won't pretend that we haven't beaten the crap out of someone that thinks they can talk their way out of a contract. But business is never the reason we've pulled a trigger."

Simone nodded and played another card. Neither spoke again for several minutes as they continued the game, and after a while, Simone looked up and watched Landini tapping his thumb against his cards in rhythm with the music. "What did you mean earlier when you said you've had to do it yourself?"

Landini set his cards face up on the table again, causing Simone to give a heavy sigh and toss his own cards back onto the table, before getting up to flip the record. Landini poured himself another half-shot and said, "It was just before I was brought on full time as Soldier. Actually, I'm pretty sure that's why I was... It was that group of cops that were trying to blackmail Don into making the 'Stang girls their own private on-call girls."

Simone sat back down and held up his hand as Landini pushed the bottle towards him. "I wondered what came of that... It was just over one day and he told me not to worry about it... He was actually willing to work with them on a reduced fee until they said that the girls wouldn't have a choice in the matter."

"Those bastards were something else. When I went in, they actually told me that the girls were something— I remember that distinctly— they said some THING and not some ONE— they deserved, and that they would do what they wanted with them, when they wanted it, regardless of what Don told them, and regardless of what the girls wanted. Only time I've ever snapped like that. I mean, it's what I was sent in to do, but I'd never finished a job out of pure anger like that before— I didn't know that I had that in me. And it's worried me since."

Nodding, Simone leaned back, before looking over again at his cigarettes. Landini followed Simone's eyes and said, "Cutting back completely or just a little?"

"Hmm? Oh... No, Estelle's really sensitive to smells right now, trying to avoid making it worse."

"You do realize that she's not here?"

Simone laughed. "I know." He started to shuffle the cards again, but as he started to deal, he said, "Fuck it," and stood, walking over to his cigarettes and picking them up, along with his lighter, nodding for Landini to follow him outside.

Once they were sitting on the steps of the porch, Simone lit his cigarette and closed his eyes as he inhaled, trying to forget about the pain pulsating in his arm.

"You doing all right?" Landini asked, lighting his own cigarette.

"I don't know." Simone leaned forward on his right elbow, running his hand through the back of his hair. "He send you over?"

Landini nodded as he exhaled. "He wanted me to clean your gun, see if you needed a new one. I figured you'd want to do that on your own, and I wanted to see how you were doing...wanted to tell you..." he looked down, and then back over to Simone. "Thanks."

Simone cocked his head, and Landini looked down, staring at the cigarette in his hand. "I knew they were closing in, and I knew there wasn't a damn thing I could do. I had to keep going back and forth between them, and Joel was doing the same thing, and I swear to god, if you hadn't done what you did, we'd both be dead right now."

"I'm sorry it got that far."

"I know, Belv. But what's done is done. Nobody'll know anything."

"Thanks."

"That's what I'm here for."

"Not just for that."

"I know."

Simone nodded. "How're things at home?"

Landini dropped his head and gave a humorless laugh. "We made it two whole days without an argument this week."

"Well, that's an improvement."

"No, it's a sign that I've learned to just keep my mouth shut."

"Al, if you're not happy anymore—"

"That's the thing. When we're not fighting, it's almost fine. But I'm getting the feeling that I'm the only one that wants to be married now...and I'm starting to get paranoid about what's going on when I'm not there... and even when we..." His voice trailed off again, and he took his hat off, setting it on the ground in front of him.

"What?"

"No, it's nothing. Forget it."

"Can I ask you something?"

Landini nodded, but looked hesitant. Simone's eyes softened as he asked, "Why don't you talk to me about sex anymore? I used to be your go to, but the last few months..."

He gave a heavy sigh, but looked directly at Simone and said, "Because Justin accused me of sleeping with you."

Simone nodded once in comprehension, but just sat patiently as Landini looked away and worked through whatever it was that was eating at him. Several silent minutes went by before he finally looked up and said, "And it fucking hurt. Never, in our entire relationship, have I even looked at anyone else. And if he wants to think I'm out screwing around when I say I'm working, fine. But he's destroyed every major friendship I've had out of unfounded jealousy, and he's not taking my fucking brother from me."

"He can't."

Landini nodded, but continued to stare resolutely at his hat.

"I mean it. That's not his call to make. I have seniority."

Laughing softly, Landini accepted the freshly lit cigarette Simone handed him. Simone lit another and said, "Do you think it's because he's..."

"Yeah. But I can't prove it."

"Is that why you think he doesn't want to be married?"

"He ran into an ex a few months ago, they've started hanging out again... And if we do have sex, it's very clear that it's very one-sided, and once he gets me off, he's chatting online again. And even that's barely twice a month anymore. I'm to the point now that just not having sex with him would be less of a rejection than what's happening."

"Do you know what started it?"

"The other night he was out until close to five in the morning. I just laid in our bed in the dark, trying to figure it out. I think part of it is that I still don't want to talk about or even consider having kids. And I think another part of it is that he's just tired of me. I'm not exactly the most exciting person to live with..."

"What did he say when he came in?"

"Nothing. I just acted like I was asleep. Next morning, he told me he came home at two. I didn't think it was worth the fight to push it."

"Why won't you stand up for yourself?"

"Because the fight isn't worth more than our relationship. Once I figure out if it's more than just my pride that hurts, then I'll consider it. But right now, I can't even tell."

"Fair enough."

"I'm sorry he brought you into it."

"Don't be."

"It was...kind of...public..."

"How so?"

"It was at the coffee shop over on Alabama."

"So?"

"So... It was like eight in the morning. The place was packed."

"And?"

"And he was trying to make a point... a very loud point..."

"Look, I can guarantee that this isn't the first time someone's questioned my sexuality, and I can also guarantee that there are far worse things for people to think of me than me being gay. People have just assumed I was for years, and it's never bothered me. I mean personally, I'm more tired of everyone looking at me like I'm gonna start shooting up whatever store or restaurant I go into, but that's just me. I know who I'm attracted to, hopefully Estelle knows it by now, and that's all I'm worried about."

Landini laughed, and put out the end of his cigarette, putting all four of their filters into his back pocket. "All right. I should get back to Libera. If he asks, your gun is clean and switched with the one you keep in the safe."

"Thanks, Al."

"You, too."

"Call if you need to talk, all right? You're not the only one that's had to talk a gun out of one of our hands."

"I will."

Chapter 40

Estelle came in barely past seven that night, looking just as sad and exhausted as when she had left. Simone was sitting at the round table wearing a black, ribbed A-shirt and dark, heather gray Nike shorts. His Taurus was in several pieces laid out in front of him, and he had just finished thoroughly cleaning the barrel. The two magazines from the day before had already been refilled with live bullets and were sitting off to the side, waiting to go back into the newly cleaned steel.

"Hey," he said, setting down the metal piece in his hand.

"Hey. Drinking for both of us this afternoon?" she asked, gesturing to the glasses on the table.

Simone chanced a soft smile and said, "Al came by earlier, needed to talk."

She sat her purse on the table across from him and began to take off her sweater.

"I'm so sorry, Estelle. I can't believe I said what I did. You didn't deserve that."

"Why don't we talk about this when you're feeling better?"

His head drooped a little, and his sad eyes followed her across the living room. "I'm fine. Please talk to me."

She sat down on the couch and shook her head, overwhelmed by the sadness she had for how much emotional pain she knew he was in that was quickly merging with the rebuilding anger from him withholding something so important. "I don't want to argue with you while you're hurt. I'll work it out on my own."

He sat down next to her on the couch, mortified at the damage he had singlehandedly done to their previously undiluted channel of communication. "To hell with me being hurt— we need to fix this. I know how other guys in the business treat their wives...I don't want you to believe that I think I can talk you like that, or that I want to leave you out of this part of my life— baby, you need to know that I'm not that guy— I swear to god, I'm not that guy—"

She looked up at him and said, "You said that you told me everything important."

"What are you—?"

"Ren Accardi."

Simone's eyes narrowed and his head leaned towards her, anxiety fluttering inside his chest. "How do you know that name?"

"See, I think the important question to ask is why you thought telling me that you almost died once wasn't necessary. Or why something that is obviously still gnawing at you wasn't something that I needed to know. Or maybe why you made me believe you had been up front about everything that matters? About something that clearly reshaped part of your soul—"

He leaned forward and rested his right elbow on his knee, hand covering his eyes. "Libera had no right—"

"No. Don't blame him. It was an accident. He only brought it up because he thought you had already told me. He seemed to think that I had the right to know."

It was fear this time, and not anger, controlling his thoughts. Still not ready to confront the beast that he'd been battling for so long, he whispered, "That was not his decision to make."

"No, you're right, it wasn't, and he knows that. But lying to me was the decision you made, and that's not okay, either."

"I wasn't trying to lie to you. Really. I don't know how to begin to talk about it. I haven't even talked to Libera or Al about it since right after it happened."

"I'll be upstairs when you figure out what you want to do."

"No, Estelle, please. Don't walk away."

"Simone, I'm not being passive aggressive. Paul was in a shitty mood all day, I've had one bad surprise after another since you got home last night, and I never got to sleep once we went to bed. I'm tired and sore, and I don't have the energy for this right now."

"Okay. I understand," Simone said, contradicting the anguish that was consuming him.

She sighed and went upstairs, only stopping to change into sweat pants and a t-shirt before lying down. Around nine that night she woke up in the soft light of the bedside lamp, feeling Simone's hand on her shoulder. "You should eat," he said, holding a plate with the turkey sandwich she'd been exclusively craving for the last week.

Estelle took the plate from his hand, comforted by the effort he had put in. "Thanks."

Simone knelt down next to the bed, unsure of how close she wanted him to her. "Look, I didn't tell you about Ren because I still haven't dealt with it."

"Why are you still carrying this around?"

"Because I don't know why I lived and Ren, and now Bassi, didn't."

"Simone—"

"Please, I need to tell you this. Yesterday, Bassi was hit by the first shot fired to catch us off guard, just like I was before. And I was shot yesterday trying to end the fight, just like Ren was. I don't understand why it worked out like it did. I don't want this to sound like I don't feel grateful for being alive, because I do— I am. I just don't understand why I was able to come home to you."

"You don't need to understand it," Estelle said, trying to keep her tears contained. "You can't. And torturing yourself for nearly a decade trying to understand isn't bringing that any closer."

"I know."

"Why…why doesn't it bother you when someone like Al pulls the trigger, if it bothers you so much when you do?"

"It's a weird, unattached double standard that I have. I think that all of us in the organization have to have it. When someone gets involved, either on our end, or people doing business with us, there's always some level of risk, and we all accepted that risk from the beginning. I can't control what happens when I'm not there, and as much as I loathe it, I can't control what the other side does. But when they make the decision to fire at us, that's on them."

"Then why isn't Paolo on them, too?"

"The meeting was too big of a risk. I knew it up front. Even Libera said it was a big risk."

"Why did you keep it, then?"

He sighed and looked down. "Because I figured they would just try something somewhere else, and people outside of the organization would get hurt."

"Then you made the right decision, didn't you?"

"I thought I had. But now…"

"Now you're here with me— and our child. If you'd have made a different decision, it could have been Libera waking me up last night, and not you."

Her tears finally broke free, and she set the still uneaten food on Simone's side of the bed, covering her face in her hands.

"Christ," Simone said, quickly sitting next to her and pulling her tightly into his chest. "No— come here. I'm so sorry. Jesus— I didn't even think about how this was impacting you. I am so sorry."

She nodded but continued to cry for several minutes, face still hidden against his chest. He kept his arms around her and closed his eyes, feeling the burden he had been carrying for so long lifting as though her tears were his own. After a while, she looked up, dried her eyes and started trying to regulate her breathing. "I need to calm down. I think I'm upsetting the baby."

She took his hand and pressed it against the kicks she was feeling. She smiled at the love in his eyes as he looked at his hand, and leaned forward to kiss him. "We have to be able to talk to each other about things like this. If you're hurting, you need to let me be there for you."

He nodded. "I'm sorry I didn't tell you, and I'm sorry I was such a jerk this morning. I had no right to talk to you like that."

"You were just upset—"

"No," he said, shaking his head. "I can't lose my temper with you. Not like that, and especially not right now."

"Why especially not right now?"

He looked nervous for a moment, worried he had accidentally offended her. "I just meant that since you're having our baby, the least I can do is not be the Douchebag King of the Midwest."

As she laid her head onto his shoulder and started to laugh, she felt the light sting of his unshaven face finally move into a smile against her forehead. "You should eat," he said again.

She picked up the sandwich he had made for her and started to realize how hungry she was. As she started eating she asked, "Did you eat yet?"

He nodded. "About an hour ago."

"Good," she said, taking another bite. "How are you feeling?"

"Mostly just sore," he said, stretching his arm a little. Several minutes later, he looked up, eyes filled with anxiety. "Estelle, can I ask you something?"

Mouth full, she nodded.

"I know we've talked about my work before, and I think both of us have implied what goes on, but we've never really talked about...this part... of my job before."

She set the empty plate on the floor and moved closer to him. "No, we haven't. I assumed that you weren't supposed to, so I let it be."

"I probably shouldn't, but I need to know you understand..."

"Understand what?"

"I need to know that you understand what's expected of me. What I have to do...what I've... done..."

"So, tell me."

He hesitated, staring down at the floor. She put her fingers under his chin and turned his face so he was looking at her. "Simone, I know that you've killed people. I know you had to do it yesterday, and I know that you'll probably have to do it again. And I don't love you any less."

Simone said nothing, but continued to look into her eyes, so she kept going. "I can tell how much you hate it. Even Libera told me how much you hate it."

"Christ, I do hate it," he said, turning away from her and running his hand through his hair. "I've always hated it."

"Have you—" she stopped short, wanting to hear his answer, but no longer knowing where his boundaries were.

He looked up, and when he spoke, his voice was soft, like his sad eyes. "Have I what?"

"Have you ever killed someone that didn't attack you first?"

"Once," he said truthfully. "When I moved up to Soldier, and even then, he had tried to kill Libera the day before. Since then it's always been self-defense."

"Have you ever come close again?"

"Several years ago, as a Capo. A guy had threatened Libera's life if I didn't raise his stipend. Not the proudest day of my life... But he's still alive and actually still on Libera's payroll. I see him from time to time in passing, but I don't interact with him. I can't tell you any more than that, though."

"Is that why all those rumors started about your temper?"

He laughed and said, "No, as far as I know, word never got out about that. Those started because I saw a guy slap his wife in Libera's and I kicked the crap out of him."

"Right there in the restaurant?"

"Ask Sandra. She was bartending that night."

"Was Libera angry?"

"No, because he saw it happen. Disrespect is not something Libera tolerates, especially when it comes to women."

"I figured that's where you learned it," she said, smiling.

"Yeah, I guess I don't much, either."

"What happened to the man's wife?"

Simone gave a short laugh and said, "She dropped her wedding ring on his face, bought me a scotch and then walked out. Pretty sure she slept with Libera a couple weeks after, but he wouldn't confirm it..."

He fell silent again, and she watched him continue to stare at the floor for a few minutes, trying to understand where his anxiety was leading him. "What's wrong?"

He closed his eyes, as if afraid of what he was about to ask. "Have you ever been afraid of me?"

"Not even a little."

His eyes opened, and to her surprise, there were tears forming. "Promise?"

Estelle leaned forward and put her forehead against his. "I promise." She put both of his hands on her belly and said, "This should tell you how purely implicit the trust I have with you is. If I thought even for a second that I or this baby were in any danger of being harmed, neglected or unloved by you, I'd have left months ago."

Simone moved his hands around to Estelle's back and hugged her. He laid his head on her shoulder, brushing his forehead against her neck. "I do need to ask something of you, though," Estelle said.

"What's that?"

"This morning, I was sitting in the kitchen with Libera listening to him explain something that was clearly such a big part of who you are, and I felt so isolated—"

He sat up and looked directly into her eyes. "Never again. I swear."

Standing, Simone pulled off the black A-shirt he was wearing and gently lifted her hand, moving her fingers slowly over the scar on his right hip.

"The guy's name was Malachi Salone. Ren and I were at the apartment I was living in at the time, waiting for Libera to come by to go over the numbers for the week like he always did. When we heard the door open, we thought it was Libera, but it wasn't. Never did find out how he got the key… I remember Salone telling me that I took his place as Capo, and that he was taking it back. Then he pulled out a Colt Double Eagle; forty-five caliber. He shot me once before Ren stepped in front of me and started to fire, but only hit his shoulder. Salone fired twice at Ren, but by the time I took him down, Ren was already gone."

Simone took a deep breath to steady himself and sat back down next to Estelle, who was leaning against the headboard, her eyes softly watching his. "Next thing I remember is waking up in the hospital with Libera next to me. I'd never seen him look that way before… He told me that the police put it on record as a standard home invasion, so nothing ever came of it legally. I had a fracture in my pelvic bone, and had already had surgery to remove the bullet, along with a blood transfusion. I spent several weeks in the hospital, and a few months with Doc trying to get it back to normal. It took a couple years before it was fully back to normal, though. The doctor that took the bullet out said that if it had been much longer before Libera found me, I probably wouldn't have made it."

He laid down with his head in Estelle's lap, looking up at her. She ran her fingers through his hair and said, "I can't imagine how you must have felt. Or how you still feel."

"I mostly just put it away so I didn't have to feel it. When I have to 'make an elimination,' as Libera calls it, I do what I have to do, I call Al, and then once he's there I leave, usually have a few drinks alone and sit and think for a while, which is what you saw last night. I replay it in my head a few times, making sure that was the only option, which so far it has been. I spend a few days being irrationally irritable, and then I accept it as a risk of the business and move on. It's different when it's one our guys, though. With our guys, we know each other, sometimes better than our spouses. You can't strip away the human element and replace it with business. You just can't. Even when it's someone you don't get on with, it's still there."

Estelle continued to look down at him, the fingers of her left hand still in his dark hair and her right hand resting on his chest. She had shared countless kisses with him, made love to him, and had even created a new life with him, but never had she felt more intimate with Simone as she felt in that moment.

"I'm sorry you've been through so much," she said. "I want you to know how much it means to me that you've told me."

"I expected to feel overwhelmed and confused, but for the first time in a very long time, I feel free. Exceptionally flawed, but free."

"I've told you before, I love you, flaws and all."

"I love you, too. And you officially know nearly everything I can tell you."

"Nearly everything?"

He smiled. "Yes, nearly everything. All that's left are a few gifts I have planned for you, and two nagging fears I'm not sure if I'm supposed to talk about..."

"What are you afraid of?"

He hesitated, but said, "I'll never be a normal husband. I can't be home at the same time every night, I can't always tell you about my day— I can't even always tell you where I'm going..."

"Sounds pretty normal to me," she said, ruffling his hair.

"Come on, you know what I mean."

"I do. But it's normal for us, and that's all that matters. It's not like I never get to see you, and Libera's pretty good about making sure you have at least one full day off every week. Besides, even when you're swamped for a few days, you still find a way to let me know you're thinking about me, and I love that. I think you're a lot better than you give yourself credit for."

He half-smiled in spite of himself and sat up so his head was on her shoulder, making his wounded arm more comfortable. She shifted a little and sighed, slowly rubbing just below her navel. "Am I hurting you?" he asked, worried he'd been laying on her for too long.

"No, you're fine. Just a little achy still, is all. Doctor said it's from the baby growing, so I don't mind it so much."

He stood up and walked around to her side of the bed and said, "Here, trade me sides."

She gave him a confused look but moved over to his side of the bed. He sat down next to her so that his left arm was resting safely on the outside and replaced her hand with his right one, soothing the aching muscles surrounding their child. "That better?" he asked, putting his head back on her shoulder.

She leaned her head back against the green velvet and murmured, "Mmmhmm."

A few minutes went by, and then Estelle, eyes still closed, said, "What's the other thing you're afraid of?"

Simone whispered, "What if I'm not good at this?"

"What do you mean?"

"I mean, what if I'm not good at the...the dad thing..."

"Not a chance," Estelle said, leaning her head over to kiss his cheek. "You're going to be a wonderful father, Simone. We're barely halfway through the pregnancy and I already know how much you love us. I can see it in your eyes. It's when you get home every night. And every time there's a new first— every time you feel the baby move— there's a gentle love in your eyes that makes me fall even further in love with you. And it's that look that tells me how wonderful of a father you're going to be. Everything else, you'll have to learn along the way, just like me."

He smiled and kissed her cheek. "How are you so calm about it?"

"I have my moments," Estelle said, opening her eyes and giving him a tired smile. "But I know that I'll have you to help me when I need it, and that keeps me grounded. I mostly worry about not being around enough. I don't want to stop working, but I don't want our baby to be raised by a nanny, either."

"What if you went down to part time? Might be a good idea anyway, as sore as you've been."

"I think Paul would just fire me if I asked to take my schedule down. He's already being more of a jerk than usual—"

His eyes narrowed as he looked over at her. "How so?"

"Calm down, Prince Charming. He's just been more stressed out than usual for whatever reason, and he's been a bit passive aggressive since he found out about the engagement. The two mixing are just obnoxious."

"Should I—"

"I can handle it. I promise. I just wish I knew what to do."

"At least think about taking your hours down?"

"I will." She leaned her head back again, wondering when Simone would be ready for bed.

"Anything else you're worried about?" he asked.

"I'm always a little worried about you."

"I'm sorry."

"Oh, don't be. Dad was a career Marine. Worrying is what I do best." She laughed for a moment, and then shook her head, surprised at her forgetfulness. "Remember I told you he came over for coffee last week?"

"Of course."

"He was talking about you."

He looked over, intrigued. "What did he say?"

"He said that Mom's been acting really judgmental about you, and that finally he got pissed off and told her that your work is more honest than some of his was."

He laughed. "That's no kidding."

"Dad also said that he likes you a lot."

He cocked his head with genuine surprise. "He does?"

"Yeah— he'll just never admit it with Mom around."

"She REALLY hates me, doesn't she?"

"She's Catholic. She's not allowed to hate people."

Simone started laughing, but Estelle gave him a sad look and said "I thought she'd ease up on you a little because of the baby, but she hasn't."

"It's okay," he said, still smiling. "There will be no lack of anything for you or our child, including love, and your mother being judgmental won't change that."

Her eyes brightened at his words and she leaned over for a kiss. "I was thinking of taking a shower and getting ready for bed. You think you'll be ready soon?"

"Absolutely. I need to put my gun into the safe and pull the other one, but then I'll be ready."

"You really are set in your routine, aren't you?"

"Very much so. But I'll adapt as needed." He stood up and held out his right hand to help Estelle to her feet. "I wouldn't have it any other way."

Chapter 41

Around eight the next morning, Estelle awoke to the sounds of Simone getting dressed. "I thought you weren't going to be called in today," she mumbled.

He walked over and leaned down to kiss her forehead. "I wasn't. I just need to take care of a couple things. It won't take long. Joel should already be here with my car, so I have to run. Go back to sleep."

"No, I'm okay getting up. Are you sure you should be going out?"

"Joel's already made me agree to let him drive, I'm wearing my hip holster instead of my shoulder, and I double wrapped my arm, just in case. I just have to pick up some paperwork from Libera's, run an errand and then I'll be back. I promise. Honestly, the time off is more for my mental health anyway, which you greatly improved last night." He kissed her and asked, "Today's not your Saturday to work, is it?"

She stood and stretched her arms, shaking her head. "Nope."

"Good," he said, smiling and kissing her again. "I love you."

"Love you, too," she called behind him, yawning and watching him rush down the stairs.

Simone locked the door behind him and came out to see Joel smiling at him from the driver's seat of his Mercedes.

"Good to see you, boss. You're lookin' good," Joel said as Simone got into the vehicle.

"You, too, Joel," Simone said, half-smiling and lighting a cigarette as Joel pulled out of the driveway.

"He know you're coming in?"

"I don't think so. It's better to ask for forgiveness than permission, right?"

Joel laughed, glad to be back in Simone's company, and somewhat back to some semblance of their routine. "Let's hope so."

He pulled the car into the parking lot of a small, local bookstore a few streets away from Libera's. Simone opened his door, put out his cigarette and said, "Need anything?"

"Yeah, make sure this one doesn't have fucking unicorns."

"No promises," Simone said, smiling as he closed the car door.

He walked into the bookstore, which was barely open for the morning, and took a deep, comforting breath, feeling as though he had walked into another part of his own home. He looked up only when he heard, "Hey, Belvedere!" coming from the twenty-something woman sitting on the counter by a vintage cash register. She had short, white-blonde hair, a silver septum ring, and her shiny, black nails were holding on tight to the latte in her hand.

"Hey, Carmen. How are you?"

"Good! It's been a couple months since we've seen you, we were starting to get worried."

He smiled and said, "It's been busy. I still haven't worked through everything I got last time."

"There's a first time for everything, isn't there? It's that girl you got the Shelley for, isn't it?"

"Of course. I'm glad you called. Your timing is impeccable."

"I take it that's who you wanted this for?" She jumped down from the counter and reached under it, pulling out an exceptionally old and tattered book.

"Absolutely," he said slowly, picking it up and caressing the cover.

"Now, I hope you don't mind, but I was actually able to locate two of them in the States, and I know I quoted you thirty-eight hundred, but this one actually cost a bit more. I think you'll find it completely worth it, though."

He didn't look up from the cover, but said, "How much more?"

"Nine grand more."

He laughed and looked up. "That's a big difference."

"I know it is. But that—" she pointed to the book, "Is worth it."

"That's still a big difference—"

"Open it."

He cocked his head, opened the book to the cover page and promptly set it down on the counter, clearly in disbelief of what he was seeing.

"Told you," she said, laughing at the stunned look on his face.

"That's not actually Brontë's signature?"

"I have a COA that says it is."

"Jesus Christ," he said, moving his index finger along each letter of the signature.

"I can still get the other one if you want it instead."

"You kidding? This is amazing. How did you find this?"

"Actually, this one wasn't that hard to get ahold of. Not a lot of people would scoff at twelve grand."

He took an envelope out of the inner pocket in his jacket. "I have four and a half here, I can bring the rest by tomorrow. Do you mind holding it?"

She laughed. "Please. I know you're good for it. We don't have any new unicorn stuff, though."

"That's okay, her dad told me to go with something different, anyway. Have something with a triceratops?"

She laughed and walked him over to the wall of children's books and pulled out a thin book with a pink triceratops on the cover.

"You're the best," he said, smiling and looking over the obnoxiously bright cover.

"I give it less than five minutes before he figures it out," she said with a sly smile, putting the first edition of Wuthering Heights and its certificate of authenticity into a bubble-wrap lined box.

"Thanks, Carmen," he said, returning her smile. He picked up the box and the shiny picture book and tapped his hand twice on the counter. "You're the best. See you tomorrow?"

"I'll be here."

He opened the passenger door and handed Joel the book for Mya before easing himself and the safely guarded box into the car.

Simone looked over to see Joel giving him a look that was halfway between amused and irritated. "Very funny."

"I don't know what you're talking about. It was highly recommended."

"Even Mya's gonna figure out it's a fucking unicorn dinosaur."

Simone just smiled and looked out of the window, laughing to himself. After a few minutes Joel said, "Want me to stop by so you can give it to her?"

"That's okay," Simone said gently. "It'll hurt her feelings if I can't pick her up, and it'll be a few weeks before I can do that."

"That is true," Joel said, pulling into the lot at Libera's. "It's funny. Sandra's brother'll come over and Mya won't even look up. But you walk in the door and she's running over, begging to be picked up. Makes me wish we'd have asked you to stand for her instead of him."

He pulled the key out of the ignition and handed it to Simone, who put his hand on Joel's shoulder. "I'm always there for you guys."

He went to open his door, but Joel said, "The other day, I never said—"

Simone shook his head. "I didn't do anything you wouldn't have done."

Joel nodded, and as they got out of the Mercedes, he said, "You know he's gonna want me to drive you back."

"Yeah, I know."

Simone took a deep breath and knocked twice at the back door to Libera's office before opening the door.

"What are you doing here?" Libera asked, laughing and standing to shake Simone's hand.

"Just needed to pick something up. Sorry to interrupt, guys," he said, turning to face Mack and Gallo, who were finishing their weekly meeting with Libera instead of Simone.

"Not at all," Libera said. "You boys mind giving us a minute?"

"Of course," Gallo said, leading Mack outside with Joel.

"How is everything?" Libera said, motioning to Simone's usual chair across from him.

"Better," Simone said, taking a seat. "Much better."

"Good. How's Estelle?"

Simone nodded in appreciation. "She's great, thank you. We had a long talk last night and got everything sorted out."

"I wanted to apologize for bringing up what I did. I didn't realize you hadn't told her."

"No, sir, you were right. And after talking to her last night, I've finally been able to let it go."

"It's about time."

"I agree, sir," Simone said, glad to finally have that part of his past behind him.

"So, what brings you in?"

"I need to pick up my Will so I can make some changes, assuming that's all right."

"I wondered when you'd do that. Bring it with you Monday and I'll look over it."

"Thank you, sir. Did you need anything from me tomorrow?"

"No, I want you to take that time off like Doc said."

Simone smiled as Libera got up to get the documents out of the locked filing cabinet. "Yes, sir."

"Here it is," Libera said, handing Simone the folder. "Have Joel drive you home, okay?"

"I'm all right—" he stopped at the look Libera was giving him. "Yes, sir," he conceded.

He shook hands with Libera and walked back outside, silently handing Joel his keys and shaking his head.

"Told you," Joel said, starting to laugh.

"It was good to see you, Mr. Belvedere," Mack said. "We should get back to Don Libera, but let us know if there's anything you need."

"Thanks," Simone said, shaking hands with both Mack and Gallo. "Sorry I couldn't be there today."

"You're not so good at taking time off, are you?" Gallo said, laughing.

"That I'm not," Simone said, waving to them as he begrudgingly got into the passenger side of his car.

They drove in silence, Simone's mind on the document in the folder, and as they pulled into Simone's driveway Joel said, "If you want I can have Sandra follow me over later so I can bring your car back."

"That would be fantastic," Simone said, looking up at a smiling Estelle, who had been reading on the porch, but was now standing next to the door. "Thank you."

"Anytime. You know where I'll be," Joel said, before waving to Estelle and pulling out to drive back towards Libera's.

Chapter 42

"Hey, you," she said as he set the file of papers and the box from the bookstore down on the table.

"Hey," he replied, putting his arms around her waist and kissing her.

She nuzzled her face into his chest and sighed. "Either you smell like books or it's been way too long since we've had sex."

He laughed. "Well, I was at the bookstore today, and it has been a couple weeks. But with you being sore, I thought it would be...insensitive... to ask."

He leaned his head forward and kissed her again, the kiss lasting a little longer this time. "Your arm..." she said, as he pulled back again and took her hand, leading her over so they were standing in front of the couch.

"What about it?" he asked, leaning down to kiss her neck.

She closed her eyes, his gentle lips against her neck weakening her resolve. "I can tell it's still hurting you."

"Mmhm," he breathed, moving his lips up the other side of her neck before pulling at her ear lobe with his teeth and whispering, "And it'll be the same, regardless of what we do right now."

She turned around and slowly unbuttoned his jacket so she could run her hands around his waist and up his back. "Are you sure?"

He put his right hand on her hip and brought his lips back to hers, breathing faster. In a slow, hoarse whisper, he said, "I need you," before feeling his words quickly echoed in the strength of her kisses.

Chapter 43

Two hours later, they were both asleep on the couch, Simone still lying on his back, his left arm hanging comfortably off the side, and his right arm tight around Estelle, who was lying just as comfortably on top of him, both under the oversized, leopard spotted blanket she'd fallen in love with online shortly after moving in. Seemingly out of nowhere, Simone awoke with a start, thinking he heard something.

After a few seconds he heard the key in the door, and slowly moved his hand off of Estelle's back, taking care not to wake her. He reached behind him, calm hand closing around the Taurus he had put on the end table after Estelle had begun to remove the clothes that were now scattered around the living room floor. He used his thumb to cock the weapon and put his finger on the trigger, but then relaxed when he saw Joel come through the door, holding up Simone's car key. "Just me, boss," Joel said, quickly realizing where Simone's right hand was before noticing Estelle asleep on top of him.

Simone gave an embarrassed smile and released his grip on his gun, putting his arm back around Estelle, holding the blanket to her and looking around for his nearest piece of clothing. "Sorry, one second."

Joel laughed nervously, turned around to face the door and said, "No, don't wake her up. I was just bringing the car back. I knocked a couple times, but I thought you weren't home... apparently you are... didn't want to leave the key outside... I am so—"

Simone's voice was barely loud enough for Joel to hear, out of fear of startling Estelle. "No, it's okay. Do you, uh, do you mind if I pay you Monday? I can't find..."

"Not at all," Joel said, waving his hand. "Have a good weekend, boss. Sorry I—"

"No, you're fine. You, too. Thanks."

As Joel locked the door behind him, Simone laid his head back and shifted, stretching his shoulders. He reached back behind him again, this time for his book, and tried to one-handedly open the paperback to the turned down page, promptly dropping it on his face.

Estelle awoke at the sound, looking up at Simone's laughing face. "Sorry," he said, picking the book up and putting it back on the table.

"S'okay," she said, sitting up with a sleepy laugh. "I'm just glad it was a paperback this time."

"Me, too."

"Been awake long?"

"No, Joel woke me up. Can't believe it didn't wake you up."

"I was out," she said, laughing and pulling the blanket around her. "Wait— he was here?"

"Yeah, he dropped the car off, and he didn't want to leave the key outside. And since we were asleep we didn't hear him knocking, so he thought we weren't home. Not sure who it was more awkward for…"

She smiled. "So, what did you want to do tonight?"

"Well, I need to go over some papers, but other than that, I'm all yours. Tomorrow, too."

Estelle got up and stretched before looking around for her clothes. "Those DVDs I ordered came today. Want to order some food later and watch with me?"

"Of course." He stood, fastening his pants that he had found pushed partly under the couch and said, "What is it, again?"

"Sherlock."

"Which one? There's so many—"

"Cumberbatch. Also called 'the good one.'"

"I haven't seen that one yet."

She gave him a scandalized look as she finished dressing and said, "How have YOU not seen this?"

"How have YOU not seen Lord of the Rings?"

Estelle looked ready to retort again, but then laughed and said, "We'll be here all day if I don't let you win."

He buttoned the bottom half of his shirt and walked over to kiss her cheek before picking up the file on the table and then rifling through his jacket for his cigarettes. "Want to come out with me?" he asked, picking up a red pen from the end table.

"Sure!"

She picked up her book and followed him out onto the porch, sitting across the small table from his usual spot. He sat down and lit a cigarette before putting a document on top of the file and starting to cross things out, occasionally writing new words in the margins. Looking up from her book, she asked, "Can I ask what you're working on?"

He exhaled, making sure the smoke was floating away from her and said, "You can, but it's not the most pleasant conversation."

"What is it?"

"I'm writing you and the baby into my Will."

"You are?"

He cocked his head at her surprise. "Of course, I am. I had forgotten to do it before now, but I remembered after…" he trailed off, not wanting to upset her again.

"That's…" she stopped, looking for the right way to say what she was feeling.

"I know, it's kind of morbid…"

"No," she said, taking his hand. "It's really sweet of you."

He smiled, relieved that he could talk to her about it. "Libera makes it standard that the organization—"

"In other words, him…"

"Yes," he said, laughing. "Gets twenty percent. I originally had the rest going to charity, but I'm changing it here to say that Mya would get ten percent, you would get thirty-five, and the rest would go to our child, or equally divided should we have more than one child."

"More than one child?" she asked, both touched and overwhelmed by his forethought.

"I know we haven't talked about it…I figured, just in case… NOT a decision we need to make now…"

"I like that you think about things like that."

He inhaled again and half-smiled, before looking back down at the document. "I'm also putting you in charge of the estate and the house, if that's all right."

"Whatever you want, love," she said, trying and failing to comprehend a time in her future without Simone.

"You're welcome to look this over when it's done. The rest of it's fairly standard. Should anyone play any part in my death, they would forfeit any inheritance. Libera covers any of my medical expenses that might come up because of work, things like that. I just want to know you'll be taken care of."

"Makes sense," she said, watching him concentrate on reading the last page. *I didn't realize how deeply what happened unsettled him…*

After several minutes, he realized she was still watching him and he looked up, taking the last drag from his cigarette. He gave her a gentle smile and said, "What are you thinking about?"

"More than one child?" she asked.

He set the papers down on the table, putting the ashtray on the top to keep them from blowing away and leaned back; the afternoon of blissful passion and his new level of openness with Estelle filling him with a sense of serenity he was unaccustomed to. "Just something I've thought about. Mostly that we've never talked about it."

"I've thought about it a few times. Sometimes, when I'm feeling really good about being pregnant, I think I'd like to have another close to this one's age. And then I start to freak myself out about the actual giving birth part of it, and decide that this one is just going to have to learn to apparate or stay where it is."

Simone started to laugh. "I'm not sure apparition is the best plan. You might want to have a backup."

"Yeah, all right."

"Do you know how much I love you for doing this? I can't imagine being strong enough to do what you are."

She took his hand into hers and said, "I do know. But isn't it a little heavy handed to say that after THAT?" she asked, nodding to his injured arm.

"That was outside of my control. YOU are doing this for us because you choose to. And that's incredible."

She smiled and said, "You really are the sweetest."

"Oh!" Simone said, remembering the box inside the house. "Wait here— I have something for you."

"You didn't have to—" she started, as he stood.

"I know," he said, hurrying inside and then returning with the box. "I've been hoping to get this for a few months now, and I got the call early this morning that it came in."

He handed her the box and pulled his chair closer to her. She carefully opened it and gasped at the sight of the cover. "Oh my god. Is this—?"

"First edition," he nodded. "Remember the first time you came over here? And you quoted—"

"Wuthering Heights," she said, running her fingers slowly over the same words on the cover.

"Well," he said, kissing her cheek and resting his chin on her shoulder. "That was the day I realized I wanted to spend the rest of my life with you. So, I thought that this would be the right one to start our collection together."

"Simone," she cooed, leaning her forehead against his and accepting the tears that she felt coming on. "This is the most romantic thing..."

He kissed her for a moment, and then said, "It actually gets better, though I admit that it was my broker that gets the credit for this one."

"You have a book broker?" she asked with a gentle laugh.

"No, I have the best book broker," he said seriously. "I can take you to meet her tomorrow if you want. I have to pay her the difference for this in the morning."

"Her?" she asked, feeling oddly jealous of another woman being involved in Simone's literary endeavors.

Half-smiling, he said, "Yes, her. And it's just business."

"All right," she said, still feeling a small trickle of jealousy, but regaining her excitement about his gesture. "What can possibly make this better?"

He looked into her eyes and opened the cover, showing her the authentic signature within.

"Oh. My. God. Is that—?"

"It is."

"Simone— this is incredible."

"I was pretty impressed with this one, myself," he said, running his fingers over the cursive ink again.

"This must have cost—"

"Don't worry about it," he said. "The look in your eyes is more than worth it."

They sat together looking over the book, occasionally stopping to silently read a favorite passage. "We should get this inside," Estelle finally said, feeling the wind start to pick up a little.

"I agree," he said, picking up his papers and following her in the house. "I can finish this up tomorrow if you'd like."

"Sounds good," she said, crawling back under the blanket. "If you put the disc in, I'll order the food."

"Perfect."

"Pizza okay?"

"Is it ever not?"

"Good point."

Chapter 44

After another episode had ended, Simone looked down at his phone and said, "How the hell is it after midnight already?"

"Bed?"

Simone gave a sleepy nod, and followed her upstairs. As they got into bed, she said, "Can I ask you about something you said last night?"

He leaned against the headboard and said, "Of course."

"Remember when you said that you guys sometimes know each other better than your spouses?"

"I do."

"Why 'spouses' and not 'wives'?"

"That's an odd question," he said, cocking his head.

"Why? You're always very specific, and it was weirdly generalized."

"I'm not being politically correct," he said, still looking confused. "It's accurate."

"Huh?"

"You know you've met Al's husband, right?"

"When?"

"The night I proposed. Justin. He's the guy—"

"Good-looking guy from Puerto Rico?"

"Sure? Stayed about half a foot away from Al all night?"

"Oh! I didn't put that together! They didn't seem—"

"Yeah, they're not big on PDA."

"Such a warm and fuzzy guy like Al, that's shocking," she said, sarcasm ringing in her voice.

"Oh, yeah. Al's Mr. Sensitive." He shrugged and turned out the light. "Honestly, though, most of it's Justin. He likes to keep his distance."

"I guess I just assumed Libera was more conservative than that, and wouldn't hire people based on something like that."

Simone laughed. "He can be a dick, but he's not that much of a dick. He was actually the witness at their wedding. I'm also pretty sure that's why he put Bronte in charge of Mustang. He wanted to find someone that wouldn't get involved with any of the girls working there."

"Sound logic," she said, lying down. "Looks like I underestimated the Patriarchy."

"Only slightly," he said, slowly bending down to kiss her. "I don't know of another organization in the country that shares Libera's views. He's never even given it a second thought. But even if he did have a personal problem with it, Libera hires people based on merit, and that isn't influenced by outside factors like that. He is much more liberal than people give him credit for, though."

"You know, the more I get to know him, the more I'm coming around on him," Estelle said. "He's a lot different once you get to see the human side of him."

"I'm glad. He likes you a lot."

"No, he cares about you a lot, and he likes that you're happy."

He smiled as he settled into his pillow, trying to find a comfortable angle to hold his arm.

"What would you like to do tomorrow?" she asked, voice quiet from exhaustion.

"I need to run by the bookstore to drop off the rest of the cash for that book— I was hoping you'd come with me to do that, and then I was wondering if it would be a good time to pick out our wedding rings."

She kissed his bare shoulder and put her arm around his waist, trying to avoid moving his arm. "I'd love that."

Chapter 45

"Oh, my," Estelle said, walking through the door Simone was holding open.

"I can't believe you've never been in here."

"I go to the other shop across town. And now I'm having trouble remembering why— this place is amazing."

"Thanks," Carmen said, walking around the corner. "Hey, Belvedere."

"Hey, Carmen. This is Estelle."

"Good to finally meet you," Carmen replied, shaking Estelle's hand.

"You, as well, thanks."

Simone took an envelope out of the inner pocket of his jacket. "Here's the rest of it. Sorry I couldn't get it to you yesterday. That, along with yesterday is the twelve plus fifteen percent for you.

"You're the best, Belvedere. Need anything else?"

"I don't think so," he said, looking around at Estelle. "Unless you needed anything?"

She shook her head. "No, best to get me out while you still have some money left."

He smiled and put his arm around his fiancé. "Thanks, again, Carmen. Tell Becky I said hello."

"I would, but we broke up a couple weeks ago."

"Sorry to hear that."

"Why? I'm not," Carmen said, waving a hand. "Thanks, though."

He nodded and led the way out to his car.

A few minutes later, they pulled into the parking lot of Simone's favorite jeweler.

"You like going through local businesses, don't you?"

"I do. We depend on them for a lot of our business, so I try to go to them as often as possible." He held the door open for her and smiled at the way her eyes lit up as she walked past the sparkling display cases.

"Mr. Belvedere!"

"Hello, Charlie."

How does he remember everyone's name? She smiled as the jeweler whose name she had already forgotten came over to Simone, shaking hands and saying, "This must be Estelle."

"Absolutely," Simone said. "Estelle, this is Charlie, I've been coming to him for years."

"That he has!" Charlie said, gently shaking her hand. "Sold him a pair of cufflinks when he was nineteen years old, and he's been coming back ever since."

"They've held up well," Simone said, gesturing towards the emeralds at his wrists.

"They certainly have. Never go out of style, will he?" he asked Estelle, nodding to Simone.

"Never," she agreed, taking in Simone's unabashedly arrogant half-smile.

"What can I do for you today?"

"We were hoping to purchase our wedding rings today, if you have something you think we'd—"

"Come," Charlie said, pointing over to a small table next to the glass case with the cash register. "I'll be right back."

They took a seat at the table, and just as Simone had put his hand on Estelle's shoulder, Charlie came back with two small, black velvet boxes. "I pulled these a while ago," he said, setting them down and opening the smaller of the two boxes. "I was hoping you'd come to me for them."

He pushed it across the table to Estelle and sat down across from them. "Oh, my," she said, picking up the box. "This is beautiful."

She looked over at Simone, who was gently smiling at her, rather than looking at the ring. "It's perfect," she said, handing it to him.

"That's a three-millimeter platinum band," Charlie started. "May I?" he asked, taking the ring out of the box. "The diamonds go halfway around the band, I think any more than that with your engagement ring would be a bit much."

"I agree," Estelle said, watching Simone look over the diamonds.

"About a third of a Carat, all together?" Simone asked.

Charlie nodded. "Yes, sir. Retails around four thousand, thirty-five hundred for you."

"You don't need—"

"It's my pleasure. For yours," he continued, picking up the barely larger box. "I thought you would prefer a smooth band to a rounded one. This one is definitely timeless, you'll never have to worry about it looking dated. Six millimeter, also platinum."

"I agree, you do seem to have hit it, spot on, Charlie. What do you think, love?"

Estelle kissed his cheek and said, "I love it. It suits you well."

Simone looked up into her eyes, his love and gratitude for Estelle overwhelming all of his senses. *This is really happening.*

After a moment, he realized that Charlie was still waiting for an answer, but was watching them with a look of kind patience. "We'll take them," Simone said.

"I'm glad. I had them sized for you when you picked out the engagement ring."

Charlie smiled over at Simone, who half-smiled and said, "How long have you had these set back?"

"I set hers aside when you picked out her engagement ring. I've had yours in the back since you purchased the rubies."

"That long?" Estelle asked.

"Oh, I know the look when I see it," Charlie said. "I was actually surprised that it took him so long to come in for the ring. But I was still right. Three months later, there he was."

She paused, looking over to Simone. "You bought the ring five months before you proposed?"

"I did. I was waiting for the perfect moment. Though you still made it more perfect than I ever could have." He kissed her cheek, and then looked up at Charlie, saying, "Do you mind engraving them for us?"

"Not at all," Charlie said, quietly smiling at the side of Simone that wasn't normally available to public display. He took out a piece of paper and a pen and handed it to Simone. "I'll go write up your receipt."

As Charlie walked away, Estelle asked, "What did you have in mind?"

Simone smiled and took out his money clip. He opened it to the center, and underneath the creased sonogram was a small cocktail napkin, still folded in half. As he unfolded it and handed it to her, tears started to well up in her eyes. "You carry this with you?"

"Every day," he said softly. "What if we had 'no more yielding' in mine, and 'but a dream' in yours?"

"That sounds perfect," she said, pulling her bottom lip under her teeth as Charlie returned. As Simone put his most prized possessions back into his money clip and began to jot down the instructions, Charlie put a large velvet box on the table, along with the receipt. "This," he said, pushing the box towards Simone, "Is a gift."

Simone cocked his head and opened it, before smiling and showing it to Estelle. The top of the lined box was embroidered with the word *famiglia*, and housed a thin, silver, diamond-embellished watch for Estelle, and a matching pocket watch fob for Simone.

"Those are both around eighty years old," Charlie said. "I updated the watch so it'll work, but everything else is all original."

Simone stood, shaking Charlie's hand. "This is wonderful, Charlie, thank you."

"So much," Estelle said, following Simone's lead and standing.

Simone looked over the receipt and took a second envelope out of his inner jacket pocket. He counted out seventy hundred-dollar bills and set them on the counter, putting the rest back into his jacket.

"Want me to call you when they're ready?" Charlie asked, putting the cash into the locked register and shaking Simone's extended hand.

"That'll be great. Thank you, again."

"It's my pleasure. I couldn't be happier for you."

After they had gotten back into the car, Estelle said, "He likes you a lot, doesn't he?"

"He does. It also helps that I go to no one else for big ticket items."

"Should we let Libera know about the gift?"

Simone smiled and looked over at her. "I should. But I'd love to know what made you think that."

"I assumed he was buying protection from Libera, so not telling him would probably look bad."

"Valid point," he said, turning the car out of the parking lot. "You know I can't tell you if you're right."

"I know."

"You've got good instincts, though...Oh— I was supposed to tell you— Libera wants Joel and Al to go with us to Boston. He was telling me that when I was waiting in his office for Doc's okay for me to come home."

"Yeah, I figured someone would have to."

"I know it's not the most romantic scenario. I'm sorry—"

"No, it's fine. I was expecting it."

"You sound disappointed," Simone said, trying to keep his eyes on the road and glance over at her at the same time.

"Not really. Since you have to take those meetings, I figured someone would have to be with you, especially after all that's happened..."

"You can tell me you wanted us to be alone. God knows I did."

"Of course, I did. But that doesn't mean that I'm not okay with it being this way. I'd rather have the people you need around you for your meetings and steal you away at night, than have you by yourself and needing them."

"Thank you for understanding. I am sorry, for what it's worth."

"I know. But we'll have a wonderful time, whether they're in the next room or not."

Chapter 46

The month of March flew past in a flurry of doctor's visits, honeymoon planning and wedding shopping. Carolyn had gone with Estelle to a local designer to have a custom dress made and fitted to allow the dress to still fit as the baby grew. Estelle was also overseeing the renovations with Dex, which were finally allowing her to get some of her books out of their boxes.

Simone spent most of his time with Libera, trying to figure out who organized the attack at the Garage, but they were both coming up empty handed. They finally decided to bring in Gallo, to see if there was an error in the books they hadn't noticed, but this was no small task, as they had to go back through several months of numbers if they had any hope of finding a pattern from within.

In what seemed both like minutes and decades, the day had finally come for Simone's trip to Boston, and his marriage to Estelle. The sun was bright on the morning of March twenty-sixth, and arriving early to avoid as much attention as possible, Estelle and Simone walked hand in hand, meeting Libera on the steps of the city building housing the marriage license office.

Simone took a moment to button the jacket of a new, perfectly tailored Tom Ford suit, as black as his perfectly slicked backed hair, and adjusted a cuff of his crisp, white shirt that stood out sharply against his black silk tie. Estelle was wearing the barely pink, custom sewn tea-length dress she had managed to keep as a surprise to Simone, along with a pair of matching pink Manolo Blahnik pumps that she was already dreaming of slipping out of. She had added loose waves to her now shoulder-length hair, along with the diamond necklace Simone had given her to match her engagement ring that was currently residing on her right hand. As Libera shook Simone's hand, he said, "I've been waiting for this day for a long time, Simone."

"As have I," Simone said, smiling at Estelle.

"I talked to Chuck; he's got a few extra people around to make sure we don't have any issues, and he was able to get you an appointment slot, so you don't have to wait in line all day."

"Thank you, sir."

"Yes," Estelle said, voice straining a little from the cocktail of emotion and hormones racing through her. "Thank you for being here."

"My pleasure, kids."

The office they entered was empty, save for the employees, and a smiling blonde woman, no older than Libera, said, "Hello, Mr. Libera, we've been expecting you."

As Libera walked forward to greet his acquaintance, Simone leaned over to Estelle and whispered, "That's Judge Capra, friend of Libera's. She'll be the one marrying us, since she's the only Catholic judge."

Estelle smiled and kissed Simone's cheek.

"You must be Mr. Belvedere!" Judge Capra said. "It's so nice to finally meet you."

"You as well. And this is my fiancée, Estelle Presswood."

"It's wonderful to meet you both! If you want, we can go ahead and get the paperwork started and get you married."

"Absolutely," Simone replied.

They stood at the desk, filling out their respective forms, and as Simone signed his name to the bottom of the form, Estelle said, "Would you like me to fill out this form, too, changing my last name to Belvedere?"

He turned and smiled at her, saying, "More than you'll ever know," before kissing her cheek and adding, "Assuming, of course, that's what you want."

She pulled her bottom lip under her front teeth, trying to hide her smile as she filled out the form. Minutes later, the four of them were standing in a closed room, Libera next to Simone, who was standing opposite Estelle, less than a foot apart.

Judge Capra smiled at the two lovers, and said, "Simone and Estelle, have you come here freely and without reservation to give yourselves to each other in marriage?"

Speaking in unison, they answered, "We have."

"Will you love and honor each other as man and wife for the rest of your lives?"

Separately this time, with Simone speaking first, they said, "I will."

"Will you accept children lovingly from God and bring them up according to the law of Christ and his Church?"

Again together, they said, "We will."

"Since it is your intention to enter into marriage, join your right hands, and make your solemn vows."

After they had joined hands, Judge Capra said, "Simone, what is your vow?"

He looked into Estelle's eyes, feeling as though he'd unknowingly been waiting his entire life for this moment. He said, "Estelle, I have never, in all my life, known anyone like you. I look back on all the time before I knew you, and wonder how I never realized that such an important piece of myself was missing. I want you to know that I swear to you, my love, that I am going to do everything I know to make sure that you are loved, happy, protected and taken care of. I know that things can be unpredictable, but always know, that even if I'm not with you, I'm there for you, always, just as you've been there for me. No more yielding, but a dream."

"Estelle?"

Brushing a tear away, she said, "Simone, I've spent my entire life reading about great loves, never dreaming that I would find a love greater than any I've ever encountered. We complete each other in a beautiful way that I couldn't dream was possible. No matter what happens, you will always have understanding, safe, loving arms to come home to. My devotion to you is, and will always be, unchangeably steadfast. No more yielding, but a dream."

"You have declared your consent before the Church. May the Lord in his goodness strengthen your consent and fill you both with his blessings. What God has joined, men must not divide."

A soft, "Amen," was spoken by Libera.

"Lord, bless and consecrate Simone and Estelle in their love for each other. May these rings be a symbol of true faith in each other, and always remind them of their love. Through Christ, our Lord."

Libera again responded, "Amen," and handed Estelle's ring to Simone.

"Estelle, take this ring as a sign of my love and fidelity. In the name of the Father, and of the Son, and of the Holy Spirit." He placed the ring on Estelle's finger, gently caressing her hand with his thumb.

Libera handed Simone's ring to Estelle, who said, "Simone, take this ring as a sign of my love and fidelity. In the name of the Father, and of the Son, and of the Holy Spirit."

As the ring slid onto Simone's finger, Estelle felt an all-encompassing sense of calm. They were two halves of a perfect circle, joined together, ready for the life together ahead of them, and ready for the life growing inside of her.

"If none here have any objections, I invite you now, to share your first kiss as husband and wife. Thanks be to God."

Simone stepped forward and placed a long, chaste kiss on her lips, before nuzzling his cheek against hers, closing his eyes and whispering, "I love you."

They stood in each other's arms for a long moment, as Libera shook hands with Judge Capra, thanking her for her time. Simone let go of Estelle and turned to do the same, giving Libera a chance to walk over and hug Estelle. As he kissed her cheek, he whispered, "Watch after him." She nodded, and as he let go of the hug he said, "I've got a surprise for you guys down at the restaurant before you catch your plane."

"Thank you, sir." Simone put his arms back around Estelle's waist and said, "Shall we, Mrs. Belvedere?"

Chapter 47

Libera held the restaurant door open for them, and as they walked in, Simone's arm around Estelle's waist, she put her hand on his chest, happily taken aback by the room of applauding people they had walked into. Carolyn ran over and hugged Estelle, and as Sandra came over to do the same, Carolyn hugged Simone and leaned up to whisper in his ear. He half-smiled and patted her shoulder, and as she walked back over to her seat, she picked up her champagne glass and took a sip, trying to avoid Libera's eye.

"You look wonderful," Estelle's father said, coming over and hugging his daughter, keeping one hand momentarily on his grandchild. He turned to Simone, hand extended, and said, "Congratulations, Simone."

"Thank you, sir."

"So, no Mom?" Estelle asked, already bristling at the expected answer.

"No, she's at home. I'm sorry, sweetheart."

"No, don't be. It's probably best."

"When you get back from your honeymoon, give me a call, and you and I will go together to pick out your gift. That's assuming—"

"Oh, Dad, of course. I'd like that."

He turned and looked at Simone. "I'd like for you to be there as well, if you'd like."

"Thank you, I'd like that very much."

Libera looked around at Stephen, who nodded to him. "If you have time, the boys in the back made brunch."

"Of course, sir, thank you," Simone said, taking Estelle's hand and following his Patron's silent instructions to the long grouping of tables that had been rearranged in the dining room.

The tables were soon full of food and people, all laughing and talking. Joel was holding Sandra's hand atop the white linen, and Carolyn was between Joel and the smiling bride, happily chatting with Estelle's father. Across the table, Landini had his hand on Justin's shoulder, both of whom were laughing along with Mack, Gallo and Bronte, all listening to a funny story Libera was telling about Simone. Even while eating, Simone kept his left arm around Estelle, who would occasionally glance up at him, feeling grateful for the friends around her and the smile on her new husband's face.

After the waiters began to clear the plates away, Libera stood and said, "As you all know, Simone and I have known each other for a long time, and he's been here with me for most of it. Almost eighteen years you've been with me now, isn't it?"

He turned to look at Simone, who was looking up at his Patron, respect and gratitude emanating from him. "Yes, sir, it is."

"You've worked hard, built yourself up from nothing. There isn't anyone in this room today that doesn't know how much I value and respect you."

Heads nodded in agreement around the table, and Simone stood, shaking Libera's outstretched hand. Libera then reached out for Estelle's hand to help her up and said, "You, my dear, have been a much-needed light in this man's life. I am grateful for all that you do for him, and I want you to know that everyone here can see how perfect the two of you are together."

The people surrounding the table began to clap as she put her arms around him. She leaned forward and, making sure only Libera could hear her, she whispered, "He's a good man, and a lot of that is because of you."

As the applause subsided, Libera gave a small nod in acknowledgement and put his hand on Simone's arm. "You've been a good friend, Simone, and it's clear that you are going to be just as good of a husband. And this child," he continued, gesturing to Estelle, "Is lucky to have you. Both of you. I know that, even as excited as you are, this can be an overwhelming time for you both, so I want you to know that I will be paying for this child's education."

There was a collective breath taken around the table. "Oh my god," Estelle said, putting her hand on Simone's chest and looking up at the stunned look he was giving Libera.

Libera looked into Simone's eyes and said, "Preschool, private schools, college, everything. The best you can find."

Simone looked down for a moment and said, "Thank you. I—" he stopped, trying to compose his thoughts. "Thank you." Libera stepped back over to him and gave a brief hug, tapping his hand to Simone's shoulder. As Libera went to hug Estelle, Simone looked up and saw Joel grinning at him with his arm around Sandra, who was happily drying her eyes.

Chapter 48

An hour later, after making sure that Estelle was still in the corner talking to Carolyn and Sandra, Libera approached Simone, who was standing at the bar with Joel and Landini, all of whom were sipping at the scotch in their hands. Simone poured a glass for Libera, who lifted it and said, "You ready for tomorrow?"

"I am."

"Good. Plane's ready whenever you are. These two going with you?"

"They are."

"Good. I want updates every twelve hours until this is done, understand?"

"Yes, sir."

"And Simone?"

"Yes, sir?"

"Try to enjoy yourself, all right?"

Simone half-smiled as he took the last sip from his glass, ignoring the implications of the grinning men surrounding him. He started to lean forward to pour a little more scotch into his glass, but felt a gentle hand on his back. "Carolyn and Sandra offered to take me home to change and pick up our bags for the trip," Estelle said, letting her hand come to rest on his hip. "Though I have a suspicion they have ulterior motives. Will you be terribly upset if I go with them?"

"Of course not," Simone replied. "I have a few things I need to do here before we leave, anyway."

"I figured as much. Meet here in an hour?"

"Absolutely," he said, kissing her cheek.

She leaned forward, but instead of the kiss he expected, she whispered, "I can't wait for tonight."

He said nothing, but she saw the corner of his mouth twitch, and she wished they weren't surrounded by his colleagues, which made it impossible for her to actually kiss him. "I'll be back soon," she simpered, slowly letting go of his hand.

He nodded and watched her walk away, mind wandering far from the business matters standing between him and his amorous night with Estelle.

"Maybe we should get you the paperwork you need?" Libera asked, trying to bring Simone back to the topic at hand.

"Hmm? Yes, sorry, sir." He set his glass down and readjusted his cufflink to avoid making eye contact with anyone.

"Don't worry, Don," Joel said, taking a sip from his own glass. "He'll have his brain back by tomorrow."

Simone and the others started to laugh, and Libera took out a small case with cigars from his inner jacket pocket, handing one to each of them and refilling their glasses. "Files are in my office."

Chapter 49

Estelle unlocked the door and led Carolyn and Sandra, both of whom were carrying several gift bags, into the living room and turned on the fireplace. "Sit, sit!" Sandra said, leading Estelle over to the couch and sitting next to her.

Carolyn sat down on the floor in front of them, arranging the gift bags. "Okay, so we KNOW you hate wedding showers, but we still wanted to do a little something, and now you can't do anything about it!"

Laughing, Estelle said, "You guys are so sweet! You didn't have to do this!"

"We know," Sandra said, "But we have less than an hour until we have to be back, so start opening!"

Carolyn picked up the first bag and handed it to Estelle, who pulled out a silver picture frame that had been engraved with the date of the wedding on the top, and "Amore" along the bottom. "This is beautiful!" Estelle said, looking up at them.

"And," Sandra said, we think this picture would look wonderful inside it."

She took out her cell phone, and showed Estelle the picture she had managed to snap as they entered Libera's, Simone's arm around her, both of them looking at the other with content bliss sparkling in their eyes.

"Oh, my goodness, that's perfect! Thank you!"

"Here, this one next—"

Estelle continued to pull the gifts out of their bags, occasionally stopping to give out hugs or brush away a tear. Twenty minutes later, she sat surrounded by her friends' celebratory offerings. Some, such as the frame and a painting of the covers of several Shakespearian books were for her and Simone, while others were gifts for the baby, including a Hogwarts blanket and a small toy owl.

"Oh, my goodness!" Estelle said, checking the time. "I need to change and make sure we have everything!"

"Want some help?" Carolyn asked.

"No, but I'll never turn down company!"

They followed her up the stairs and sat down on the bed, taking in their surroundings. "In all the times we've been over, I've never actually been in here," Sandra said, admiring the velvet headboard. "Simone's always had excellent taste."

"You know, that was one of the first things she told me about him? Even before she told me who she was seeing," Carolyn said.

"That doesn't make me sound shallow at all," Estelle replied, laughing from within the closet.

"Oh, please. You'd tell me how sweet he was, and how sexy his intelligence was, and then you'd go on and on about how classy and attractive he was."

"I don't blame you," Sandra said, laughing. "He really is a sweetheart, but good god, that man's attractive."

Estelle walked back out of the closet, wearing a white maxi dress and matching ballet flats. Carolyn looked up and said, "You two look amazing together. I can't imagine how beautiful that baby's going to be."

Blushing, Estelle pinned back one side of her hair and said, "He's convinced the baby's a girl. Has been since I told him."

"Joel was the same way," Sandra said, smiling. "He was right, too. Simone trying to say he wants a girl to keep her out of the business?"

"Oh yeah," she said, smiling as she double checked the bags sitting by the door. "But I think he just wants a princess to spoil."

"Know what I like best about him?" Carolyn asked.

Estelle turned around in facetious surprise. "There's actually something you like about him?"

Sandra and Carolyn both started to laugh. "Yes," she went on. "I love how he lights up when he sees you. I can tell he isn't just thinking about you naked— you can see that he really, truly loves you."

"It's true," Sandra agreed. "Though I think he may have been thinking about you naked a little bit ago."
"God, yes," Carolyn said, laughing. "You should have seen him watching you walk away from the bar before we left. I'd NEVER seen him break his poker face around the guys before."

"You know," Sandra said, leaning in a little as Estelle sat on the foot of the bed. "A little part of me has always wondered what he's like in bed. He's so well-spoken and reserved, it makes me wonder what he's like when no one else is around."

Carolyn giggled and said, "Yeah, what's with all this crap where you don't talk about him?"

Estelle blushed again and nudged Carolyn's arm. "Come on, guys. You know how private he likes to keep things."

Carolyn nudged her back. "It's not like we're asking about endowment— though that question's definitely not necessary after whatever you told him earlier... It would just be bragging— just give us something."

"Okay," she said, cheeks reddening again. "He's not a lot different in bed than he is anywhere else. He likes to be the one in charge, but he also doesn't want to push my boundaries, either."

"Aww, that's sweet," Sandra said. "Now tell us something we couldn't figure out on our own."

Estelle laughed at her bluff being called. "All right— I'll tell you one detail in exchange for an equally interesting detail from both of you guys."

"That sounds fair," Sandra said.

"Okay, okay. What do you want to know?" Carolyn asked, pulling her legs underneath her.

"I want to know how many more times you slept with you know who," Estelle said, eyeing Carolyn with a mischievous grin.

"Oh, come on. Do we have to—?"

"It's only fair."

Carolyn hid her face. "Three."

"Seriously?"

"Who are you talking about?" Sandra asked, intrigued.

"I can't even say it!" Carolyn said into her hands.

"Carolyn, it's okay," Estelle started, sounding intentionally over-saccharine. "Who hasn't slept with their friend's new fiancé's BOSS right after the engagement party?"

"You did not!" Sandra said, laughing and prodding Carolyn. "You slept with Libera FOUR times?"

She finally looked up and nodded.

"TECHNICALLY," Estelle said, "You slept with him four and a half times, if you count the morning after the first time when Simone walked in."

"Thanks for that," Carolyn said, flicking Estelle's arm with her fingernail as Sandra doubled over in laughter.

"So, if you hate him so much, why did you go back?" Estelle asked.

"God-DAMN, that man knows what he's doing."

"Really?" Sandra asked. "I'd have thought he'd have been all about him and done."

"That's the crazy part! He didn't NEED to do anything else... By the time he had... you know... I had, too, and more than once. One time he actually thought I was faking because it had happened three times in less than two hours."

"I am having serious trouble comprehending that," Estelle said.

"Good. I think that officially makes it someone else's turn."

"Okay," Sandra said, thinking for a moment. "Mya was conceived in Simone's old Mercedes."

"Oh my god!" Estelle and Carolyn said together.

"It was a night that Simone was working late, and our car was in the shop, so Joel drove me home from Libera's and things got a little... heated... in the driveway."

"Did he ever find out?" Carolyn asked.

"Only because he asked why Joel wanted to have the car detailed the next day. He wasn't mad, though. Thought it was more funny than anything."

"He never told me that!" Estelle said, still giggling.

"That's because Simone's an old-fashioned gentleman about these things," Sandra said, waving her hand. "It would contradict his manners to talk about it."

"Speaking of contradicting his manners," Carolyn said, "WE are running out of time and YOU still owe us some valuable information. And not the thing about Libera walking in on you giving Simone head, I already know about that one."

"So do I," Sandra giggled. "Libera told Joel and Landini that night."

"Seriously? Did he mention it was the first time I, or anyone, had done that for him?" Estelle asked.

"Apparently Libera was exceptionally amused by it. But seriously? Hadn't you been dating for several months by that point?"

"We had. He just never asked for it, and I got tired of waiting for him to ask for it. He was worried I was just doing it because he wanted it, and not because I wanted to."

"I'm sorry— did you say you or ANYONE?" Sandra asked, the rest of Estelle's words clicking into place.

"I did."

"How is that even possible?" Carolyn asked. "He's what, thirty-two?"

"Just turned thirty-three."

Even Sandra looked skeptical. "I know he kept to himself a lot, but I figured he was taking advantage of the employee discount at Mustang."

Estelle shook her head. "Never, for anything."

Carolyn thought for a moment, and said, "So, when the two of you got together, Simone Belvedere— easily the most attractive man working for Libera— was still a virgin?"

"Yeah, I was surprised, too. He just didn't see the point in getting involved with anyone if it wouldn't go anywhere, and he's not the casual hook-up kind of guy."

"Damn, I owe Joel fifty dollars now," Sandra said.

"You guys bet against each other on Simone's virginity?"

"Of course, we did. We also bet that you'd be engaged within a year. Joel said six months, so I guess I'm just giving him his money back," she said, laughing.

"That still doesn't count," Carolyn said, laughing along with Sandra.

"You guys aren't going to give up, are you?"

They both shook their heads and she said, "Well, Simone's personality really is similar to how he is in bed. He's very attentive, notices the small things, and the more confident he is, the better he is."

"Really?" Carolyn asked. "He's so sure of himself all the time—"

"I think he was just so used to women hitting on him for his money so he never quite realized how sexy he is. He puts so much effort into himself because he likes it, not to impress anyone else. It really just never occurred to him. But my god, there are times when it's REALLY good, and then he realizes how good he is, and it makes it SO much better," she finished, closing her eyes and giving an involuntary shiver.

"I hate to admit it," Carolyn started, "But he really is most attractive when he has that arrogant-Clark-Gable-smiling-thing going on.

"I agree," Sandra said. "Except maybe when he was looking at you earlier at the restaurant. He'd just look up and watch you laugh— he looked so happy."

Estelle smiled. "He really is wonderful, isn't he?"

Sandra and Carolyn both smiled back at her, glad to see their friend looking so content.

"Absolutely," Sandra said.

Chapter 50

Surprised that they were only five minutes late, Carolyn pulled the car of laughing women back into the parking lot at Libera's, and Estelle got out and hurried over to Simone, who was leaning with Joel against the hood of his car, finishing a cigarette in the afternoon sun.

"Sorry, baby. We lost track of time."

"It's okay," he said, putting his arms around her waist. "Al's waiting inside, he and Joel are driving over together with Sandra. Is Carolyn still okay driving us?"

"She is," Carolyn said, laughing as she walked up. "Everything's in the trunk of my car."

"Thanks," he said, patting her arm before going over to transfer what he needed from his own car. Once everything was settled in the Carolyn's trunk, Simone said, "I'm going to go let Libera know we're leaving."

"Okay."

As he started to walk away, however, Estelle held tightly onto his hand. He pulled gently on it so she would take a step closer to him, before wrapping his fingers in her hair and kissing her. His right hand began to slide down her shoulder and around to the small of her back, pulling her in closer to him.

"You know I've already paid for the hotel room, right?" Libera said, laughing and coming up behind them.

"Sorry, sir," he said, turning around and looking far from sorry.

Libera leaned in and said, "I've already paid Joel and Al, so don't worry about that. Rooms are under your name. Keep me posted, and have a good time, all right? You've earned this."

"Yes, sir. Thank you," Simone said, shaking his Patron's outstretched hand.

Forty minutes later, they were in Libera's jet on their way to Boston. Simone and Estelle were sitting comfortably across from Joel and Landini, who were playing cards. Estelle was curled up in her seat with her book, and Simone was looking over the notes for the next day's meeting. He kept his left hand entwined in Estelle's hair, and would glance over every few minutes, smiling at how happy she was.

After an hour of being in the air, Simone looked up and said, "So what did the girls want?"

She folded the page of her book down and looked up, saying, "Just some girl talk. And they wanted me to open some gifts they had for us and the baby."

"Sounds like a good time," he said, checking the time on his phone. "Though I've always wondered what exactly you mean when you say 'girl talk'."

Estelle hesitated, not knowing how in-depth to answer, but Joel said, "It means they were talking about what you're like in the sack."

"Oh?" Simone said with a laugh, looking over at his new wife.

She blushed and pulled her bottom lip under her teeth. "In my defense," she said pausing for a moment, "They started it."

The three men chuckled, and Estelle looked at Joel and said, "Hey, your wife is pretty chatty, too, mister..." Laughing at Joel's look of intrigue mixed heavily with apprehension, she said, "Oh, I'm supposed to tell you that you won and she owes you fifty dollars."

Simone laughed and said, "Do I want to know?"

"No," Joel and Estelle said together.

"All right. What WERE the three of you talking about?"

Simone gave her a mischievous smile, implying that she was free to talk about it, but she still didn't think she should bring up something so personal in front of his associates. "We can talk about it later."

Without looking up from the cards in his hand, Landini said, "That friend of yours ever tell you about bangin' the Don?"

They all started to laugh. "She was avoiding him like the plague today, wasn't she?" Simone asked. "I figured it was related to that." He stopped and looked up at Landini. "How did you know about that?"

"He was late to a meeting one morning, and I was waiting for him in the restaurant when she came out for the walk of shame."

"Huh. I didn't see you—"

"It was probably a different morning," Estelle said, cutting him off.

"You have got to be kidding," he said, leaning back and putting his right arm behind his head. "After how pissed off she was— she's not still—?"

"No, just a few times after that, as far as I know."

Simone leaned back again and shook his head, laughing in disbelief. "I thought she hated him."

"Oh, she does. But apparently she was more impressed with his...abilities."

"Remember when I said I wanted to know what you were talking about?"

"Yeah," she said, laughing.

"Yeah, I was wrong."

Estelle laughed and settled back into her book, but was focusing more on how comfortable Simone was, and how happy that made her. Several silent minutes went by, and Simone was using his phone to scroll through the website for the horse track he'd be discussing the next day. Out of nowhere, Simone exclaimed, "Goddammit!"

Realizing he had startled the other three he set his phone on his thigh and looked to Estelle.

"What's wrong?" she asked, looking worried.

"Sorry, nothing really. I just left my book on the table and forgot to ask you to grab it."

Estelle smiled and picked up her purse. "This one?" she asked, pulling out a paperback Hemmingway.

Half-smiling, he said, "Christ, I love you."

Estelle handed him the book and kissed his cheek. As he opened up to where his bookmark was, she said, "I don't know how you can read that."

"Says the woman reading Dickens— after complaining about the last Dickens book she read."

"Yeah, I don't know what the hell I was thinking." She pulled the folded piece of paper she'd been using as a bookmark out of the center of the book and stowed it in her purse. "Trade?"

"Sure," he shrugged, handing her 'The Old Man and the Sea' and taking 'A Tale of Two Cities.'

"Nope, can't do it," Estelle said, ten minutes later. Simone smirked and exchanged books with her again, ignoring Joel and Landini's laughter.

After another two hours in the air and a quick cab ride to the hotel, Simone took Estelle's hand and led her up to the front desk. "Hi, I should have two rooms under Belvedere," he said, discretely setting a fifty down on the desk.

"Absolutely," the young man behind the desk said, pocketing the bill and checking the computer. "It looks like you have the Governor's Suite, as well as the suite next to it."

"Sounds right."

"Wonderful. Would you like us to send a bottle of champagne up to the room? The hotel's compliments, of course, to congratulate you on your wedding."

Simone smiled, and glanced at Estelle, who was looking around with a hand absentmindedly massaging the place the baby had been kicking for the last five minutes. "That won't be necessary, thank you. I would appreciate you sending a bottle of scotch up to the second room, though. Eighteen year, at least, if you can get it. Just add it to my bill. We'll also need a third key for each room."

"Of course," the concierge said, nodding his head and turning around for a moment. As he returned, he said, "Here are your keys, and please do not hesitate to let us know if you need anything else. Would you like someone to show you to your rooms?"

"No, that's all right. Thank you," he said, tapping his hand twice on the counter.

"Thank you, Mr. Belvedere."

"You're so cute when you're talking to people," Estelle whispered as they walked away.

Half-smiling, he nodded to Joel and Landini, who followed them to the elevator with the bags in tow. When they reached the correct floor, Simone opened the door to their room and turned on the light, watching Estelle look around at the beautifully furnished suite. After the door was closed, he handed Joel a key to both rooms and said, "We'll meet in the lobby at nine tomorrow morning. I'll have my phone on if you need me, but try not to?"

"You got it, boss."

Landini and Joel both congratulated the couple again, and then left for their own room next door, leaving Simone and Estelle alone together for the first time as husband and wife. Estelle took off her shoes and said, "Did you want to unpack or get some dinner—"

Before Estelle could finish her question, Simone had crossed over and brought his lips to hers, pulling her in tight against his chest, as he'd been longing to do for hours. Her whole body seemed to melt into the kiss, and he walked her slowly backwards until she was sitting on the foot of the bed.

He unbuttoned his jacket and removed it, still taking it easy on his left arm, and then set his holster underneath it on the dresser. He turned back and stood for a moment taking in all of her features, trying to freeze the moment in his mind.

"What?" she whispered, smiling at his captivation.

He sat down next to her and began to kiss along her neck up to her ear, before whispering, "Do you know how much I love you?"

Simone brought his lips back to hers and after a few moments, she pulled back and said, "I love you, too."

He rested his forehead against hers, and said, "How did I get so lucky?"

Shaking her head, she said, "It wasn't luck. It was you."

Estelle kissed his lips again, both feeling as though the love between them was something tangible in the air around them, building in harmony with the energy of their kisses.

Chapter 51

After two passionate hours and two equally passionate orgasms, Simone was lying on his back, with both arms around Estelle. She was curled up to him with her head resting on his chest, and the fingers of her left hand were tracing a slow path along his hip. Simone only moved when he heard his phone beep with a text message.

Reaching down to the floor, he pulled his phone from his pants pocket and laughed as he read the message. "Joel wants to know if we want them to pick up food since they're on their way back."

"Aww, that's so sweet."

"And a little strange."

"Maybe more than a little," she said, relieved that he felt the same way.

"New message says 'if you don't tell us what you want we're bringing you tacos."

"You should probably stop him, then," Estelle said.

"Agreed. What should I tell him?"

"Just anything else. No seafood."

"I'll let him know."

Simone sent the message and laid back down next to her. "We should probably put some clothes on."

"Yeah, probably. Though I was thinking of taking a shower so I can get all this makeup off, which means that you can organize everything like I know you've been itching to do for the last twenty minutes."

"I love you," he said, smiling and kissing her before standing and finding his clothes.

Estelle smiled and looked into his eyes for a moment before simply saying, "Love you, too, Mr. Compulsive."

She stood up and crossed over to her bag, debating between pulling out the romantic, short-hemmed nightgown she had packed for their wedding night, or the warm, fluffy pajama pants and hoodie that seemed much more appealing.

Simone came up behind her, fastening his belt, and kissed her shoulder. He put his arms around her waist and whispered into her ear, "Comfortable is sexy, too."

She turned around and put her arms around his neck. "You really do notice everything, don't you?"

"I try."

He half-smiled and watched her pull out the warm clothes and her shower bag. As she walked away, he took out the other bags and began to organize them in the hotel room's closet, doing his best to mimic the immaculate organization of his own. By the time Estelle had finished with her shower, all of their bags were unpacked, save for the bag now home to his Taurus, Tomcat, holsters and two spare magazines.

"That was fast!" Estelle said, sitting on the bed and looking impressed with his handiwork.

There was a knock at the door and he looked around for his shirt, not remembering where he had left it. Estelle held up the white shirt, but as he went to take it from her hand, she laughed and held it behind her back. "You'll have to earn this back," she said, giving him a coy smile.

He leaned down and whispered, "I thought I'd done that twice already tonight."

He started to kiss her again and momentarily forgot about the people waiting for him to open the door. As they knocked again, she pulled gently on his bottom lip with her teeth and handed him his shirt back, saying, "That you did."

He quickly buttoned the bottom half of his shirt before opening the door and saying, "Sorry, guys."

"No worries," Joel said, waiting for Simone to nod before entering the room.

"'Evening, Belvederes," Landini said, setting two pizza boxes down on the dresser and looking over to Simone. "I can't believe you managed to find the one other person in America that hates tacos as much as you do."

"It was fate," Estelle said, standing and putting her arms dramatically around Simone's neck.

He kissed her cheek and said, "That it was."

Joel sat a paper bag down next to the boxes and said, "Twenty-one-year Bowmore and chocolate ice cream. Probably best not to mix those up."

"Aww, thanks, guys," Estelle said.

"Yeah— you really didn't have to do this."

"It was on the way," Landini said, waving his hand at Simone, who had started to take out cash to pay them.

"See you tomorrow," Joel said, following Landini out of the room.

Simone set the food on the bed, and then picked up the bag Joel had left on the table. He put Estelle's ice cream in the suite's mini-freezer, and then set the bottle on the table.

"You can open that if you want," she said, starting in on her pizza.

"That's okay, I can wait until you're asleep," he said, sitting next to her.

"That's your favorite brand. And, just so you know, you're not being insensitive. The only thing I really miss is caffeinated coffee."

He opened his own box and said, "You sure? It seems insensitive…"

Estelle stood, walked over to the table, and cracked the seal on the bottle. She poured a few ounces into a glass from the minibar and brought it with her over to the bed.

"Yes, I'm sure," she said, putting the glass into his hand and going back to her food. "You've already cut your smoking way back, and it's not like you've ever been drinking just to be drinking. It's okay to like the things you like, and to keep doing them, even when I can't."

"When did you notice I cut back?"

"About a month ago. Why did you?"

"I guess I just feel like it's all I can do to make sure you're both taken care of."

"You're joking, right?"

He tilted his head and said, "No."

She set her food down and looked at him in exasperation. "First of all, you've never smoked in the house, period, and you've always made sure that you're smoking away from me, and not towards me, even before I was pregnant, because you're not a dick. Second of all, you won't let me pay any of the house bills, you work sixty hours a week— sometimes more than that. You've already paid all of the OB bills, you make sure that I'm eating and resting like I should be, you hold me when I'm crying for half an hour because a house elf died in the book I was reading for the fifth time, and you've given up your favorite place in the world for the baby's room. I think you're all set on the sacrifices you need to make."

"Most of those aren't sacrifices— I'm doing the same thing at work that I've always done, and I'm not going to ask you to pay any of the bills that I'd been paying before I asked you to move in with me. And Dobby emotionally traumatized thousands of readers, that's not just you."

He half-smiled at her giggles and took a sip from his glass. "Stop being cute, I'm trying to be serious," she said, nudging his leg.

"I understand what you're saying," he replied. "But giving up the library wasn't a hard decision to make, nor was cutting back on my cigarettes when I could tell that they had started to make your morning sickness worse."

"You don't have to give up everything you love—"

"Oh, Estelle, I'm not. I know you feel like I've had to involuntarily rearrange my life, but I really haven't." He set his box on the floor and moved closer to her. "You've given my life new meaning, and you have no idea how grateful I am to you for that. I never thought I'd have a chance at a life like this— to have a reason to make these changes."

She shifted closer to him, taking his hand into hers. "What do you mean?"

He looked down into his glass and said, "You've given me so much that I've never known before. And it's not just how much you love me, it's how much you let me love you. You've always accepted me, regardless of everything, and you've loved me, regardless of everything. I have something to live for...someone to come home to...Mi hai cambiato la vita."

Estelle rested her hand on his cheek and waited for him to look up at her. "Tu sei la mia famiglia."

"Famiglia..." He smiled and looked down for a moment, touched both by her words, and the effort it took to learn them. "I always thought that would be something I couldn't have."

"It's something I never thought I would want," Estelle said. "I mean, I'd dated around a little, but was never actively looking for someone. And then you came along...you've changed my life, too."

Simone set his now empty glass on the nightstand and said, "Estelle, you've—" he stopped and cocked his head. "You understood what I said."

She smiled. "Mainly through context."

"And you—"

"I tried to learn a few things. Not anything nearly as impressive as you—"

"Are you kidding? I was raised speaking both— you actually took the time... when did you...?"

"A few weeks ago. I thought it would be a nice surprise..."

He leaned in and kissed her. "Absolutely."

She rested her forehead against his and said, "You are a good man, Simone Belvedere. Don't you forget that."

He closed his eyes, but didn't speak; feeling as though his past, and even the unpredictable part of his future contradicted her words. "Don't think that way," she said, correctly interpreting his silence. "You've always been there when someone's needed you, and I know you're going to be there just as much for me, and our family."

Simone brushed his lips against hers and said, "Everything seems so real now. You...the baby, it's all really happening."

She gently laughed and said, "You're just now realizing that?"

"No. I'm just not afraid of it like I was. I feel like I can do this. That we can do this."

"Me, too."

He looked up at her. "You've been worried?"

This time, it was her looking away. "Only a little. I worry that I've changed too much too fast, and that you're disappointed that we only have the next few months that's just us before the baby comes."

"Hey," he said, trying to get her to look up at him. "Of all the things I've felt since I met you, disappointed has never been one of them."

She nodded and laid down, snuggling up next to his hip. "Promise?"

He laid down next to her and looked into her eyes. "Lo prometto."

Estelle brought her lips within an inch of his and said, "Fai l'amore con me?"

Simone half-smiled and said, "Sì, amore mio," before giving her a soft kiss that gradually built into the next, each one longer than the last.

He pulled the blanket over them before starting to remove Estelle's clothes and pulled himself closer to her. The moment she began to unbutton the lower half of his shirt, his lips were gently moving up her neck towards her ear. Her breathing began to quicken as she felt his hand slide up her waist, and his erection brush against her thigh. He pulled at her bottom lip with his teeth and closed his eyes, trying to pace his desire for her.

Pulling three pillows under her shoulders, she took his hand, guiding him up so he was sitting up on his knees, directly in between hers. His gaze never left hers, and as he started to unfasten the slacks he was still wearing, she propped herself up on one arm and ran her other hand down past his chest, letting it stop momentarily for a few teasing strokes before continuing around and coming to rest on his hip. He reached his hand out to return the tantalizing sensations, but she took his hand into hers and said, "Si prega di fottermi."

He quickly brought his lips back down to hers and muttered, "Cristo, sì," and felt her fingernails close around his hip as he entered her. To compensate for the discomfort stemming from carrying a child, her hand never left his hip, steadily guiding his pace to ensure his movements were the perfect balance of comfort and pleasure.

Spurred on by the decadent sounds she'd been making for the past several minutes, he could tell that he was approaching the edge more quickly than he'd like, so he slowly withdrew himself from her and let his lips leisurely stroll across her thigh, until his tongue's new task caught her off guard and began to evoke a renewed energy in the sounds coming from her. After several blissful minutes of losing himself in what he was doing for her, he began to consider returning to what he had been doing before, when he felt her grip on his hair tighten as her sudden orgasm began to swim through her.

Half-smiling at the surprised tone in the sound of his name coming from her, he continued to softly caress where his tongue had been before burrowing himself again inside her. His hands were holding on tightly to the top of her thighs, and it wasn't long before both his pulse and the motions of his hips began to rev. He threw his head back, trying to pay attention to Estelle's hand still against his abs to keep his quickened movements comfortable, and was only semi-aware of the obscenities streaming from him— few of which were actually in English. Once his body relaxed from his climax, he dropped down next to her and laid on his back for a moment, trying to regain control of his breathing. Estelle turned over onto her side and ran her fingers through his hair.

"I didn't understand half of what you said, but you seemed to enjoy it."

He laughed and put his arm around her. "That, I did."

"You need to get to bed," Estelle pointed out, looking at the clock reading close to midnight.

"I will. But not yet," he said, turning over onto his side to face her so he could pull her in close to his chest.

He took her left hand into his and held it up, looking at the rings on her finger.

"Today was wonderful, wasn't it?" she asked, watching him happily moving the light between the facets of the diamonds.

"Absolutely."

Simone laid their hands back down against him, but didn't let go.

"You worried about tomorrow?"

"No, this is the part I'm good at."

"Promise you'll be careful?"

He closed his eyes and kissed her forehead, trying to push the memory of his last big meeting out of his mind. "I always am."

Chapter 52

Estelle awoke just after eight thirty the next morning to Simone loading his Taurus. "Sorry," he said, fitting it into his holster and coming over to kiss her.

"You're fine," she said. "There's not exactly a quieter way to do that."

Simone laughed. "No, there's really not." He turned around after putting the last button of his jacket through the buttonhole and said, "Speaking of, what are the odds they heard any part of last night?"

"Pretty decent," she said, smiling at the memory. "You were quite enthusiastic."

"Yeah, I didn't think about it until this morning."

"It'll only be awkward if you make it awkward," she said. "Besides, if Joel wants to give you a hard time about it, just ask him if he and Sandra need to borrow your car again."

He sat down next to her, laughing. "When did you find out about that?"

"Yesterday afternoon. They wanted me to tell them what you're like sexually, because I'd never really talked about it before."

"So you did?"

"Yeah, I figured I'd have to sooner or later."

"What does that have to do with—?"

"You don't think I'd give away that kind of information for free, do you?"

"Fucking Christ, I love you," he said, leaning in for another kiss.

She kissed him and then smiled and said, "That's how I found out about Carolyn and Libera, too. Apparently, he's remarkably talented, which is saying something, coming from the queen of being overly critical."

"I should hope so, if she went back more than once."

"Not just more than once— three more times."

"I wonder why she was ignoring him yesterday, then."

"I don't know. She doesn't usually back off until the guy starts to get emotionally involved, but I would think he would be the same way."

"Sounds about right," Simone said, organizing the papers in the file in the order he expected to need them. "Though he also refuses to get emotionally involved with anyone that much younger than he is, so it's just strange all around."

He checked his watch and looked up. "I have to get going. Any idea what you'll be up to today?"

"I'm not sure. I was thinking I'd do some shopping, maybe find a café and read for a little while.

"Oh!" he said, crossing over to the bag with his Tomcat. He took out an envelope and handed it to her. As she opened it, he turned around to zip the bag back up and said, "I thought you might want to wander over to Newbury Street while I was working, and I wanted you to be able to—"

"This is fifteen thousand dollars—"

"It is."

"Are you crazy?"

"No," he laughed. "I just want you to have some fun, treat yourself a little."

"First of all, this," she held up the envelope, "Is not a little. Second of all, you really don't need to spend all your money on our honeymoon."

He walked over to her and knelt down so they were at eye level. "I mean this in the least douchey way possible, but you could spend four times that, and not even come close to putting a dent in what I've brought in this year."

"I'm not—"

"You don't have to spend what you don't want to. Just don't feel like you can't, all right? And if it makes you feel better, I'll be spending at least that, myself, when we get to New York in a couple days. I just don't like travelling with any more cash than that at once."

She shook her head in disbelief of his nonchalance. "All right."

He kissed her and said, "I'll text you when I'm on my way back. Sometimes these things are quick, sometimes they make a whole day of it, there's really no way to tell."

"It's okay. Focus on work, and we'll do something when you're done."

"Thank you for understanding," he said, picking up his keys. "I love you."

"I love you, too."

Chapter 53

Simone got down to the lobby with two minutes to spare, and saw Joel and Landini smoking outside the door. Before heading out to meet them, he stopped at the front desk and waited for the perky morning receptionist to end her phone call.

"Can I help you?" she asked, clearly appreciating his appearance—almost as much as the fifty he had laid on the desk in front of her.

"Hi. I'm staying in the Governor's Suite, there should be a rental car waiting for me."

She looked over the notes in front of her and said, "Belvedere?"

"That's right."

"Wonderful. Does this look right?"

He carefully looked over both sides of the form she handed him and signed the bottom. "It does, thank you," he said, taking the key.

"It's our pleasure. Let us know if you need anything else."

Tapping his hand on the counter, he nodded and walked towards the door. As he stepped outside, Landini handed him the last half of the cigarette he'd been smoking and said, "Haven't heard you speaking Italian in a long time."

Simone laughed as he exhaled and said, "Yeah, sorry about that."

"WE don't really mind, but you'll be in confession for a week if Libera finds out how many times you used the word 'Cristo'."

"It's a good thing he won't find out, then, isn't it?" Simone said, smiling and ignoring their chuckles. He handed Joel the key to the Lexus that was waiting for them and opened the passenger door.

Twenty minutes later, they pulled up to the horse track and as Simone stepped out of the vehicle, he buttoned his jacket and approached the three gentlemen that were patiently awaiting his arrival. Landini and Joel followed behind him, leaving a full foot of space between them and Simone. The man standing in the forefront extended his hand and said, "Mr. Belvedere, we're so glad you could make it."

"Likewise," Simone said, accepting the handshake. "You're Mr. Parrino, I take it?"

"Oliver, please," he said.

Simone nodded politely and said, "These are colleagues of mine, Aldo Landini and Joel Fontaine."

"Pleased to meet you, gentlemen. This is our Director of Operations, Rodney Caraway, and Marty Noel, our Director of Money Room Operations. Shall we head inside?"

Simone nodded, not wanting to talk about anything important until they were in the privacy of Parrino's office.

"Mr. Libera mentioned that you were recently married, Mr. Belvedere."

"That's right," Simone said, the corner of his mouth twitching in spite of himself.

"He also mentioned that she may be travelling with you, so if that is the case we would be happy to cover the room-service expenses of her stay."

"She is, but that won't be necessary, thank you."

Parrino smiled and nodded, acknowledging Simone's refusal to accept any hospitality outside of the business they were commencing.

They entered a large office, the walls of which were scattered with glossy press photographs and framed newspaper clippings. There was a sleek, modern desk topped with glass in front of a window overlooking the nearly eighty-year-old race track, and several chairs were placed around the desk, making it possible for the large office to accommodate everyone.

As Caraway closed the door, Parrino gestured for Simone to take the seat directly across from him, saying, "Please make yourselves comfortable, gentlemen."

Simone unbuttoned his jacket and took the indicated seat, saying, "We appreciate you contacting us; I'm sorry it took us so long to make it out."

"Not at all," Parrino said, waving his hand. "We're just glad that you agreed to see us. We've been interested in opening a location within Mr. Libera's casinos for some time, and we feel that the time is finally right to do that. Casinos, and even the races, are coming back into fashion, and the numbers show that these trends are continuing up over the next decade."

"I saw that as well," Simone said, taking the top paper out of the file in his hand. "It shows that race betting is also up, I take it the trends are related?"

"They are. The younger generation is discovering the forties all over again, and this renaissance is exceptionally good for the gambling industry."

"I agree. How many locations are you looking to add?"

"One in Athena, with additional betting allowed in The Hoop, of course. We'd also like a free-standing location and two kiosks in Olympus."

Simone considered him for a moment. "That's a lot of space— it would require extensive renovations in both casinos."

"That it would, but we would be happy to cover up to seventy-five percent of those costs, as well as the cost of any liquor license updating."

Glad that he was doing business with someone that knew what he was doing, Simone said, "What kind of turn around are we looking at?"

"The Hoop and the kiosk betting could begin soon after you return from Boston, which would turn nearly instant profits for both parties—it's just a matter of weeks. The stand-alones would take close to a year to turn a profit, but they'll get there."

Glad that Parrino's words correlated with the documents he had memorized, Simone said, "Athena and Olympus haven't ventured yet into Off Track, do you think that these locations would see the same trends as something on the coast, where horse betting is more prevalent?"

Parrino nodded towards Noel, who said, "We do. The Midwest is seeing very nearly the same trends of the East Coast. There may be an additional month or two of an adaptive period, but the numbers are trending in the same way."

Simone half-smiled. *They'll be signing this today.* Their eagerness at closing the deal quickly was setting him at ease, and he knew that he could push a little further and still not scare them away. "How many other casinos are you currently doing business with?"

"Three," Parrino said. "One here in Boston, one in Atlantic City and one in Vegas."

Again thankful for the correct answer, Simone said, "Mr. Libera will require a ten percent fee on all wagers placed at all locations and kiosks, twenty-five percent of Pari Mutuel, as well as forty five percent of the revenue from the losses at all locations and kiosks. Food and liquor revenue would be fifty-five percent."

"We're prepared to accept the ten percent, as well as the twenty-five, but we cannot accept higher than forty percent on the losses and fifty percent on food and liquor."

"All right," Simone said, half-smiling and standing. "When should we look over the contract?"

"Would you be free for dinner tonight? Your wife and these gentlemen would be welcome to join us, our compliments, of course."

"That sounds great, thank you."

"L'Espalier, then? Say, seven?"

"Perfect, thank you." Simone shook Parrino's hand and led Joel and Landini back out to the rented Lexus.

As soon as Joel had pulled out of the parking lot, Simone took out his phone, dialing Libera's number. Landini asked, "How's he gonna take the counter offers?"

"It should be fine, considering he wanted thirty-five and forty-five." Simone said, flashing an arrogant smile as he hit the call button. "They were too eager, it seemed stupid not to try...Hello, sir. It's done.

Ten, twenty-five, forty and fifty. That's right. We're meeting for dinner later, we'll have it signed tonight. Yes, sir. Thank you."

He ended the call and texted Estelle.

Heading back now. Mind coming along for a business dinner tonight?

You're very fast in Boston! And I don't mind. It'll give me a chance to wear the dress I just bought.

So are you... And thank you. Take your time, we don't have to leave until six tonight.

Oh, so you're funny in Boston, too?

I'm almost done here, anyway. Want to have lunch together?

More than anything.

See you in an hour?

All my love.

And mine.

As they pulled up to the hotel entrance and handed the key to the valet, Simone gave the file to Landini and said, "I want you guys to look over this so you're ready for tonight. We'll meet back here at six, and head over together. I don't want anyone alone tonight, and all answers must be non-committal."

As he took the file from Simone, Landini nodded and said, "Think she'll mind?"

Simone shook his head. "Worst case scenario I just have to say she's not feeling well."

Joel nodded and pressed the button for the elevator. "That went quicker than I expected."

"I knew they were interested, but I didn't realize they'd be that interested. But if the numbers play out as predicted, it should work out well for everyone. Gallo ran the numbers for us, too, and got the same thing."

As they reached the top floor, they parted ways for their individual rooms. Simone, thankful for the silence of the empty suite, removed his navy jacket and holster before picking up his Hemmingway and stepping out into the light, waterfront breeze of the balcony. He sat down and lit a cigarette, opening up his book to where the page was folded down. He was halfway through his first cigarette before he settled into his book, and completely lost track of time. After what seemed like minutes, he jumped at the gentle hand on his shoulder.

"Sorry," Estelle said, giggling softly at his concentration. "I thought you heard me come in."

"It's okay," Simone said, laughing and putting out his third cigarette.

"How did it go?"

"They want to sign tonight at dinner."

"That's good, right?"

"Absolutely," Simone said, half-smiling.

"Who are we having dinner with?"

"The Chief Operations Officer of the track and a couple other higher-ups. How was your morning?"

"Expensive," Estelle said, smiling at the satisfied look on his face.

"Have a good time?" he asked, standing and leaning against the balcony so she could take his seat.

"I did. I got some breakfast at Thinking Cup, and then I wandered around a little bit. Wound up buying from Dolce and Gabbana, Marc Jacobs, Burberry, DKNY, Valentino, A Pea in the Pod, and Chanel… It's amazing how much money you can spend in such a short period of time…"

"That's Newbury for you. Sounds like a productive morning," he said, appreciating that she was finally willing to be frivolous for herself. "I can't wait to see what you picked out."

"You'll see some of it tonight. I found this amazing Isabella Oliver dress, and it goes perfectly with the shoes from Chanel. I'm actually glad to have a reason to wear them."

"You sure you don't mind? These things can be REALLY dull."

"That's okay. All part of the business, right?"

He stood and put his arms around her. "Thank you."

"It's the least I can do for the man that just bought a thirteen-hundred-dollar diaper bag."

Simone thought for a moment and said, "Burberry?"

In response to the inquiry in her narrowed eyes, he said, "Dolce would have cost more, and all you like from Marc Jacobs are sunglasses."

"Right again, Mr. Belvedere."

Chapter 54

Just before six that night, Simone was leaning against the rail of the balcony and finishing a cigarette when he heard Estelle's heels approaching.

He took her hand into his as he turned around, taking in the beautiful figure before him.

"What do you think?" she asked.

He kissed her hand and said, "You look wonderful." *That's the understatement of the year,* he thought, mesmerized by the smile of his wife.

"This is officially my first actual maternity dress," she said, turning in a circle for him to see.

The burgundy dress was tightly fitted, with carefully placed ruching to accentuate her bump. She wore the ruby necklace he had given her for her birthday, and the black, peep toe Chanel pumps contrasted with the burgundy perfectly, while still managing to compliment the leopard-spotted Dolce and Gabbana bag.

"It's perfect for you, my love," he said, taking off his green, silk tie.

"What are you doing?"

He smiled, but said nothing, walking into the closet of their suite. When he returned, he was looping a perfectly symmetrical Pratt knot with the burgundy tie he had pulled from the closet. "This one matches your dress," he said, smiling at her and rebuttoning his black, Tom Ford jacket.

"You look pretty amazing, yourself," she said, admiring him.

He ran his hand through his hair and said, "You sure about this?"

"Why wouldn't I be?"

"I don't know... I'm just suddenly very aware that everyone will know you're married to someone who... does what I do..."

She stepped forward and put her arms around his neck. "I will always be proud to be Mrs. Belvedere."

She brought her lips to his, and then used her thumb to wipe away the rogue lipstick that lingered on him after her kiss.

With his forehead against hers, he rested his hand for a moment on their child and said, "I have something for you."

"Oh?"

"It's actually a wedding present that I intended to give to you yesterday, but I never found the right moment." He took a black velvet box out of his pocket and opened it for her to see.

"Simone— this is beautiful. Thank you," she cooed, looking over the tiara-shaped ring. The round ruby in the center was offset by five tiny diamonds scattered along the smooth curls of the platinum.

As he placed it on her right pinky, she looked at it for a moment, loving how well he knew her, and then started to laugh. "What is it?"

His eyes narrowed, unsure if he felt more amused or self-conscious at her giggles.

She opened her purse and took out an only somewhat larger velvet box from his trusted jeweler and handed it to him. "I was waiting for the right moment, too."

He opened the box and, half-smiling, took out the emerald cut ruby cufflinks, set in platinum, perfectly matching the ring he had given her.

"Amore mio," Simone said, kissing her cheek. "Thank you." He removed his emerald cufflinks and replaced them with the rubies, safely stowing the beloved emeralds in the new box.

"Perfect," he said, admiring the red stones against the black cuffs stylishly falling just further than the cuffs of his designer jacket.

"That you are," she said, putting her arms around his waist and touching her lips briefly to his again. "We are running a few minutes late, though."

He took her hand and led her to the door, stopping for a moment in front of the threshold. "You're sure?"

"Absolutely."

Chapter 55

As they walked into the lobby, Simone saw Joel nudge Landini, who was looking down at his phone. Both men, dressed in equally expensive suits, smiled as the couple approached them.

"Jesus Christ, you two look good together," Landini said, putting his hands in his pockets.

"Thanks, Al," Estelle said, looking up at a self-conscious Simone.

"One car, or two?" Joel asked, following Simone as they left the hotel.

"One, it'll save time with the valet when we get there."

Twenty minutes later, they were just as early as Simone hoped to arrive, and as Joel pulled up to the valet, he saw Parrino, Caraway and Noel waiting for them. He opened the door of the Lexus and nodded in acknowledgement of them before turning and holding his hand out to help Estelle from the car. He half-smiled at her, taking in how graceful she looked as she rose from the backseat to the curb.

"Good evening, Mr. Belvedere," Parrino said, shaking Simone's hand before gently grasping Estelle's. "And Mrs. Belvedere."

"Thank you for the invitation," Simone said, as Parrino silently greeted Joel and Landini.

"Not at all. The table should be ready for us."

Simone nodded and took Estelle's hand, following their host inside. They were immediately seated in a secluded corner, all surrounding a large, square table covered in a cream tablecloth. An immaculately dressed server came over to Parrino and said, "The chef recommends a white wine to pair with this evening's offerings."

"By all means," he said, looking around the table for nonexistent objections. "For all except the expectant Mrs. Belvedere, I take it?"

"Thank you, yes," she said, giving him a polite smile. "Sparkling water would be perfect, thank you."

The server nodded and hurried away, and Parrino leaned forward, saying, "Mr. Libera didn't mention that additional congratulations were in order, Mr. Belvedere."

"Thank you," Simone said, inclining his head towards Parrino. "He's been leaving that to my discretion."

"He seems like a fair man to work for,"

"That he is," Simone agreed. "Very much so."

The server returned with Estelle's Perrier and a bottle of Chardonnay. As he poured each of the men a glass, additional servers appeared with the first course. After an hour of delicately designed courses and small talk had passed, a chocolate soufflé was being placed in front of each of them, and Parrino was taking a set of tri-folded papers out of his inner jacket pocket to hand across the table to Simone. "I take it you'd like to read over these?"

"Absolutely," he said, taking the papers. "Thank you."

As he started to carefully read each word of the three-page document, Caraway and Noel were discussing the last big race of the previous year with Joel and Landini, leaving Estelle to make awkward conversation with Parrino, who said, "So, Mrs. Belvedere, have you been to Boston before?"

"No, I haven't. It's a beautiful city, from what I've seen so far."

"It certainly is. Perhaps you'll be back for the first race in July?"

"That sounds exciting, but the baby will be due around then— it'll probably keep me close to home this summer."

Simone turned to the next page of the document, still intently focused, but she could have sworn she saw the corner of his mouth twitch as she answered.

"Yes, I imagine, so," Parrino said, laughing gently. "I would like to apologize for cutting into your honeymoon."

"Oh, it's no trouble at all."

"It must be difficult, trying to fit a personal life in around such a busy work schedule."

Estelle tilted her head with an attitude that was imperceptible to anyone but Simone and said, "You know, the library doesn't keep me as busy as you'd expect."

Without looking up, Simone said, "I don't know, they've been completely booked lately."

He's been waiting his whole life to say that. Estelle looked over at him and, completely deadpan, said, "Overbooked, even."

Simone's eyes narrowed ever so slightly, but remained focused on the document. She put her left hand on her husband's shoulder and looked up as Parrino said, "It sounds like a busy time for both of you."

"That it is. It helps that we stay on the same page."

Simone's half-smile was hidden by the wine glass he had started to take a sip from, and Estelle pressed her fingernails gently into his shoulder.

The inside jokes went completely over Parrino's head, and he continued on, completely oblivious to the silent dialogue running between the newlyweds. "So how did the two of you meet?"

"Oh, the usual way. Girl walks up to a bar, boy leaves his Shakespeare, girl picks up the Shakespeare..."

"I assume it was something romantic, like Romeo and Juliet, perhaps?"

Her fingernails pressed further into Simone's shoulder, this time in mild irritation, as she said, "Midsummer, actually. It's much more enjoyable."

"I'll have to give it a look."

Sure, you will.

"How long will you be in Boston?"

"We haven't decided," she said, giving Parrino a confident smile.

"This all looks fine," Simone said, looking up and handing the papers back to Parrino, who took out a pen. "We just need your signatures, and then Mr. Libera will look it over and fax his approval."

"Perfect," Parrino said. "We've been hoping to expand with Mr. Libera for some time— we're very glad that the timing is finally right."

"As is Mr. Libera," Simone said, confidence rising as Noel filled in the last signature line.

Chapter 56

After bidding Joel and Landini good night and heading into their suite, Simone unbuttoned his jacket and began to pour himself a glass of scotch. "How much," Estelle started, slipping out of her shoes, "Would you bet that the second I said the baby was due in July he had started to do the conception math?"

Simone laughed and sat down on the sofa. "I was wondering how long it would take him to getting around to asking the right question."

"Subtlety is NOT his strong suit, is it?"

"Oh, absolutely not. Even in the contract he threw in a clause of assurance that none of them are affiliated with any government agency or undisclosed organizations."

"Seriously?"

He laughed again as Estelle sat down next to him. "He found a much more legal way of saying it, but yes. Happens more than you'd think."

"God, it was like having dinner with Ed Nygma."

"I know," Simone agreed. "I didn't think he was ever going to let up. Five points to Ravenclaw for the 'overbooked' thing, by the way."

"You started it," she said, finally liberating her unspoken laughter from the restaurant.

He leaned his head back against the couch and gave a gentle laugh before looking over at Estelle, his love for her overriding all of his other thoughts.

"So," she started, leaning her head on his shoulder and putting a hand on his chest. "Since they thanked you and told you to have safe travels, does that mean our honeymoon can officially start?"

"It does," he said, taking a moment to kiss her. "I'll send the papers with Al, who's heading home with Joel in the morning."

"Just us, all alone?" she said, simpering up at him.

"Absolutely," he said, kissing her again.

He set his glass on the end table and turned to face her. She smiled at the arrogance glinting in his eyes and started to loosen his tie, using it to pull him in closer to her. He pulled at her ear lobe with his teeth as she slid his tie out from under his collar, opening the first few buttons of his shirt, allowing her hand to slip under it as her lips traveled down his neck. His hand had just started to graze its way up her calf to her thigh when his phone began to ring. "Goddammit,"   he   muttered, struggling to take his phone out of his jacket pocket.

He looked at the number that was calling and said, "I'm sorry."

She patiently shook her head as he answered, but continued her hand's slow movement against his chest.

"Hello, sir." Simone sat listening for a moment, half-smiling at Estelle's hand, still tracing a slow path across his chest. After a moment, though, he threw his head back in frustration, but still managed to keep his voice perfectly even. "Yes, sir."

He looked up at Estelle, who was giving him a look of resigned understanding as he continued to receive what was sure to be last minute instructions.

One more night, she thought.

He ended the call with Libera and said, "I'm sorry, he wants us to look over the contract again, and wants me to go over everything with Al so they can talk tomorrow."

"It's okay."

He leaned his head against hers and said, "It's not, but thank you."

"Do you just want to have them come over here since it's bigger? I'm going to take a bath and then lie down, so I won't be in the way."

"You're never in the way, love," he replied, standing to find the papers he needed.

There was a knock at the door, and Estelle sighed before standing to answer it. "He's all yours, boys," she said, locking the door behind Joel and Landini and stopping to pull her ice cream out of the mini-freezer.

Once the bathroom door was shut behind her, Joel said, "You can't catch a break, can you?"

"It's all right," Simone said, suddenly very aware of the lipstick that he couldn't hide on his collar.

He sat back down with his documents, realizing his tie was still on the floor. He absentmindedly set it on the coffee table as Estelle reappeared, looking for the book that was now next to Simone's tie. "Sorry," she said, picking up her book.

"It's okay."

She returned his gentle smile for a moment, and then went back to her newly drawn bath. As she undressed and settled into the warm water, Estelle started on the pint of ice cream and began thinking about how nervous Simone had been when they first met, and how at ease he now was. He was now just as comfortable with her as she was with him, and despite how intriguing she found the subtle nuances of his personality, there was nothing that she loved more than lying next to him as slept, or feeling his head in her lap as they read together—except only the happy sigh he'd give as he'd come to bed hours after her, pulling himself close and resting his hand on their child as he drifted off to sleep.

She climbed into bed an hour later and reopened her book, but couldn't focus her mind away from Simone, who was still working diligently in the sitting room of their suite. Estelle felt far from neglected, however. She knew that his love for her was never lessened by his loyalty to Libera or the hours he had to put in, and that, had he have had his way, he would have been in bed beside her, feeling just as serene and loved as she did.

Chapter 57

It was nearly three in the morning when Simone finally came to bed, accidentally waking Estelle as he moved the book she was still holding. He finished changing and turned out the light, curling up against her, as always.

"Do you think we should have another?" Estelle asked sleepily.

"Another what, love?"

"Another baby, after this one...you brought it up before, but we never talked about it..."

"I wasn't sure if you were ready to talk about it."

"Neither was I. But I am now."

"What changed?"

"Tonight. I mean, it didn't really change anything. It just let me realize that we're equally a part of the other's world now, and that makes new adventures safe and comforting, instead of overwhelming."

He kissed the soft skin at the base of her neck and said, "Would you like to talk about it?"

Estelle nodded and lifted her head, allowing Simone's arm to rest under it. "But I want you to answer first, so I can hear your real answer— not the thing you do when we're ordering dinner and you just go along with whatever I want."

Simone laughed and said, "That's fair... I would like for us to have a second child, yes, but only if, or when you're ready."

"I'd like that, too. Have you thought about how long you want to wait?"

"Only a little. I'm still not sure, though."

"We probably wouldn't want to wait too long, otherwise they probably wouldn't get along as well as they would closer together."

"I thought about that as well, but it's still ultimately your call. I don't want you to feel as though you're being rushed into it."

"Oh, I don't. I'd probably want to stop at two, though."

"I agree. We'd have to move, for one, and I'm already worried about being around enough for the two of you."

"I think it'll be easier than you think. Just look at Joel with Mya. Hell, look at you with Mya."

"True," he said again, nuzzling the back of her neck, but feeling only somewhat more at ease.

"But yes, I don't want to have to move, either. I think the four of us could be happy at our home for a long time," Estelle finished, closing her eyes again.

"Me, too."

They laid in silence for a few minutes, his warm hand massaging the sore muscle at her hip. After a while, Simone said, "If you're sure, after the second one I can just go in and have them close it down, it'd be easier than—"

She turned over to look at him. "You'd do that?"

"Of course. Why wouldn't I?"

"It's just not a common thing to do…voluntarily…"

"You're willing to carry two children for us, the least I can do is make sure you don't have to worry about birth control on top of everything else…"

She leaned in and gave him a long, slow kiss. Resting her head against his, she said, "I love you, Simone Belvedere."

Simone closed his eyes and said, "I love you, too."

Several minutes went by, and as he laid there holding Estelle, his mind started to wander through their evening. Not only was it their first public appearance together as newlyweds, this was the first time Estelle had witnessed this important of a business transaction, beyond being peripherally aware of meetings at Libera's.

"Thank you for everything you did tonight."

"I didn't do anything."

He cocked his head and said, "Oh, but you did. You let me drag you to a horribly boring work dinner, at which you were amazing at deterring his overly personal questions, and then you were a great deal more understanding than I was that I wound up having to work tonight."

"I actually had a good time tonight. Parrino was a bit of a drag, but I love watching you while you're working, and I could listen to people calling me Mrs. Belvedere all night long."

He looked down and grinned for a moment and said, "That was nice, wasn't it?"

"And just so you know, I don't take you having to work personally. I know what's expected of you, just as I know that you hate having to apologize and hurry away, even if we're just watching a movie together."

"Can I ask you something?"

She propped herself up on her elbow and said, "Of course."

"Why do you like watching me work?"

"Because it's like getting to know another side of you," Estelle said, brushing the hair out of his eyes. "It's the last part of you that I don't fully know. I know that I might never be able to fully see that part of your life, but I like getting glimpses. I love how cocky you get when you've outsmarted someone, and how patient you are with Libera's ego. You always know what to say to get a person to warm up to you, but you don't back down, either… Know what I love the most?"

He tilted his head to the side and half-smiled. "What's that?"

"The way people in the organization look at you when they talk to you."

"Oh?"

"It's different than the look they have when they talk to Libera. They respect you, but not because they have to. It's clear that you don't just intimidate people because you can. They really look up to you."

"I try not to. Until my temper gets the best of me, anyway."

"And I feel like that's really the only part of you that I don't know."

"You've seen me like that before," he said, inwardly cringing at the memory.

"No, I mean that I've only seen you work when things are going well."

"To be honest, I prefer it that way."

"I know you do. I just hate seeing you try to put on a front when I can tell how angry or upset you are. You don't have to hide how you're feeling to keep me separated from the business."

"I just hate having to say that I can't tell you why I'm feeling that way…"

"You don't have to, though. I understand that you have to protect the organization, as well as us. But as much as you have to protect all of us, you don't need to hide that part of yourself. Or any part of yourself."

Simone nodded, feeling as though she really did know him better than he knew himself. After a few moments, he noticed a tinge of the guilt that had been creeping in over the last couple months, and knew that she'd understand how he felt, but feared that he had waited too long to tell her.

"I need to tell you something," he said, sitting up as his anxiety started to peak.

"What is it?" Estelle asked, sitting up next to him.

"I should have told you a long time ago…"

She watched him for a moment, not comprehending what Simone would have kept hidden from her. After a few minutes passed, she recognized the look of combined worry, anger, and sadness in his eyes, and knew that only once before had she seen it— in front of her coffee table and a rapidly emptying scotch bottle. "Your mother's been trying to contact you."

"How did you—?"

"Libera told me— the morning after you were shot. I figured I should wait until you brought it up to tell you…"

"Tell me what?"

"She showed up at Libera's a few weeks before that happened, wanted him to talk to you, and tell you that she wants to make things right. Apparently, she's been trying to contact you for a while…"

"I'm sorry I didn't tell you before. I just hoped that if I ignored it long enough she would take the hint and drop it."

"Oh, Simone, don't be sorry. That's why I didn't bring it up. And that's why I didn't—"

She stopped, starting to feel nervous about her own secret.

"What is it?"

"We got a letter in the mail from her just after that. She overheard Libera talking to Al about the baby—"

"What?"

"It was addressed to both of us. I've been keeping it in my purse book so you wouldn't accidentally find it and get upset…"

"And you have it now?"

"I do. You can read it if you want to, but you don't have to."

He sat for a minute, shock giving way to a feeling of deep gratitude from knowing that Estelle was just as worried about protecting him as he was about protecting her. Even if he did finally have to confront his past, he knew he wouldn't be confronting it alone. "Can I see it?"

Estelle stood and turned on the night stand's lamp, allowing her to rummage through her day purse to find the tightly folded, handwritten letter she had pulled out of her book on the plane. She handed it to him, and as he unfolded it, he asked, "And this is all she's sent since then?"

"She explains it in the letter."

Simone (and Estelle),

Hello, my son. I was hoping to see you recently, but I had just missed you. I heard Ben talking to Aldo, and was surprised to hear that you are happily expecting your first child. I want to wish you both all the luck in the world.

I want you to know that I am proud of the man you've become, and that I am so very sorry for all the unhappiness that I caused you so long ago.

*Please know that I am grateful for the happiness you have found,
and that I have no doubt that your family will grow with the same
strength, pride and courage that you have shown for so long.
From this point on, I will not give up hope that we will again meet
someday, but I have accepted that this needs to be your decision. I'll be
in town for the remainder of the year before heading back overseas. No
matter what you decide, know that I am sorry.
And to the three of you,
Vivere una vita bella. Mangia bene, ridi spesso, ama molto.
Angela*

He read over it several times before looking up at an anxious Estelle, who said, "I'm sorry I didn't—"

Simone put his arms around her and said, "No, sweetheart. Don't be."

She nodded, but didn't want to speak until he had processed everything. After several minutes he said, "What do you think?"

"Honestly?"

"Honestly."

"I think she really is sorry, but I think that she mostly wants you to assuage her guilt."

"I agree." He closed his eyes and put his hands over them for a moment. "Maybe that's the best thing to do…"

"Really?"

"Just for closure. She's never going to have an actual presence in my life, and I doubt that she would ever want one. I don't blame her for wanting out, and I've told her that. But I can't keep dragging this around, and I shouldn't force her to, either."

"If it's really what you want, I'll support you."

"I know that."

Estelle nodded, and then turned the lamp off and laid back down, snuggled up to Simone's chest. He leaned down to kiss her head and asked, "So tomorrow, we can rent a car and head out for Connecticut around eleven, or we can stay here another day and take the jet, and then head straight for New York the same day."

"What would we do here for another day?"

He slid down so he could look into her eyes and said, "Absolutely nothing."

"I'd love that," she said, grinning and giving him a gentle kiss.

After several minutes went by, she said, "I've never heard anyone call him 'Ben' before."

Simone laughed. "Very few people do— and it's usually just people that know him on a personal level, and not a business level.

Relatives and old friends that knew him before he was Don... people he likes that are uncomfortable with the business...that kind of thing. Doesn't happen much anymore."

"How long has he been Don?"

"Jesus..." Simone said, doing the math in his head. "Twenty-five years— twenty-seven... something like that."

"How's he held it so long?"

"People like him. He's charmed who he can, paid off who he can't. He's got good control of the organization— civilians don't get involved, no one's pressured into mergers or contracts they don't initiate themselves. It's a lot less bloody than other organizations, and people respect that."

"You know, he told me that it's you that keeps it that way."

"He did?"

"That morning he came in— he said that's what makes you the best man he has working for him."

Simone half-smiled. "He's really comfortable with you."

"He was just being polite, that's all. Trying to make me feel better."

"No, he's not like that with Sandra, Justin, or anyone else— it's only you he trusts that deeply."

"I wonder why..." she said, more thinking out loud than anything.

"He has good taste," he said, kissing her cheek.

Chapter 58

Two very short hours later, Simone was smoking outside the hotel, leaning against the rented Lexus as he waited for Joel and Landini. They finally appeared, and Simone unlocked the trunk of the car for the luggage they were carrying.

"You two leaving this afternoon?" Joel asked.

Simone shook his head. "I talked to Libera this morning, he cleared it for us to leave tomorrow. Thank you both, for everything."

He took two envelopes out of his pocket and handed one to each of them.

"Don's already paid us," Landini said, giving Simone a confused look.

"For the meetings," Simone said, knowing how Libera's pay schedule worked. "Not for making sure Estelle was taken care of."

He shook hands with both of them, and watched them drive away before heading back into the lobby to change their checkout time to the next day. He stopped in Joel and Landini's room for a moment to ensure nothing was left behind, and then came back into his and Estelle's suite, making sure the 'Do not disturb,' sign was still on the door. Taking a moment to only remove his shoes and jacket, he laid back down next to Estelle, and was quickly asleep again. He didn't awaken for several hours— only when he heard Estelle say, "No, that's okay. He's fine, just asleep. I'll let him know, thank you."

"What was that?" he asked, turning over to face Estelle.

She was standing next to the bed, and tossed her phone into the armchair in the corner of the bedroom. "Libera tried to call a couple times, and you didn't answer, so he got worried."

Simone nodded and then turned onto his back, trying to wake up his brain. "I should call him back."

"He said not to worry about it, just that Joel and Al made it back, and they'd be going over everything today. He said if he needs you, he'll call, and for us to have a good time."

"Good," he said, holding out his hand to her, beckoning her back to bed with him. She smiled and took his hand, lying back down against him so he could put his arm around her.

"He's been checking in a lot more, lately," Estelle said.

"Yeah, he gets that way when something big happens," Simone said, subconsciously stretching his left arm. "He'll relax in a few weeks."

"So, what did Carolyn tell you when we got into Libera's after the wedding?"

Simone laughed. "I'll tell you that if you tell me what Libera said while I was talking to Judge Capra."

"He asked me to watch after you."

"Carolyn said the same thing."

"That's sweet of her—"

"And then said that if I didn't she'd hide the murder weapon in Joel's car."

"Aww, nothing like a little blackmail to sweeten up a tense relationship."

"Always works for me," Simone said, half-smiling at Estelle's poorly concealed giggles.

He took her left hand into his and spent several minutes looking at her wedding rings, and began to think about how wonderfully different his life had become. His thoughts began to trace back through the letter he had read the night before and apprehension began to set in, quickly setting up camp over the serene state his mind had been in.

"You don't—"

"What?" Estelle asked, turning over at the abrupt change in his tone.

"You don't expect me to change, do you?"

"As in your personality? Or as in your job? Or—"

Simone propped himself up and said, "Work."

Estelle sat up, brows furrowed, clearly affronted. "I can't believe you have to ask me that."

"I'm sorry," he replied, quickly trying to understand what he was feeling well enough to explain it.

"Jesus Christ, Simone, what the hell do I need to do for you to trust me?"

"No— oh god, no, I didn't mean—"

"What then? Don't try to tell me it's not that letter—"

"You're right, it is," he said, trying to calm her down. "I shouldn't have said—"

"Don't do this," Estelle said, starting to lose control of the tears she had been holding back. "Don't backtrack just because I'm upset."

"O-okay."

"Why are you so afraid that I'm going to abandon you? What have I done to—?"

"Nothing!" he said, trepidation making his voice louder than he intended. "No, you haven't done anything. I didn't mean that I don't trust you, I just don't know why I'm worth everything that you'll have to put up with."

Estelle sat silent for a moment, watching his worried eyes working to avoid hers. "Simone."

"Hmm?"

He still sat stubbornly avoiding her gaze, so she scooted closer to him and ran her fingers through his hair, continuing down to his cheek, her thumb caressing the underside of his jaw.

"Come on," she said, coaxing his eyes into meeting hers. "I need you to understand that your job bothers you more than it bothers me."

He remained silent, but the skeptical look he was giving her was saying more than enough.

"Really. You said yourself that people getting involved with Libera know what they're doing. And it's not like you guys are taking advantage of everyday people, correct?"

"Of course not."

"You're not terrorizing random people. You're not calling little old ladies for their social security numbers. There are a lot of people with mundane, sometimes federally-funded jobs that do a lot worse than you— and enjoy it."

"That's an extremely optimistic perspective," Simone said, wavering between exasperated and amused.

"No, I'm being realistic, and I'm being honest. When I say that your job doesn't bother me in the slightest, I mean it. Penchant for patriarchy aside, Libera's organization runs smoothly and makes logical sense. There are SO many more dishonest businesses being run than organized crime—"

"Like what, exactly?"

"For starters, the American health care system, designed purely around profit," Estelle retorted, riling herself up. "Or the last three American-fought wars? How about the giant corporations completely overhauling local businesses and outsourcing? Or maybe the student loan industry? Or—"

"I get your point," Simone said, moving his hand along her back in an attempt to calm her now rapid breathing. "I understand."

"Good," she said, not remotely calming down. "Then we can settle this once and for all. I am yours, Simone Belvedere, and I don't care what you have to do at work— I am not going to just walk out on you because it gets gritty. You have to stop waiting for the other shoe to drop and just let yourself be happy."

As her words came to an end, she abruptly leaned forward and kissed him. Caught completely off guard, it took him a moment to return the full strength of her kiss, but even as he did, she pulled back, resting her forehead on his, still breathing quickly. "You are the love of my life, the father of my child, and my best friend. Don't you ever forget that."

Simone nodded against her forehead, his pulse still as fast as Estelle's. "I'm sorry I—"

"No," Estelle said, hand clasping the back of his neck, fingers nestled in his hair. "You needed to hear it."

She brushed her lips against his, wanting both for him to make love to her and to continue looking at her with so much love in his eyes. He slowly swayed his head from side to side, easing into the heat that he felt building between them. Her hand slid down his neck to his chest, starting in on the buttons of the shirt he had been too tired to remove before coming back to bed several hours before. He pulled her shirt slowly over her head, and then pressed his bare chest into hers, feeling her hands sliding his unbuttoned shirt down around his shoulders, his open collar brushing lightly against his back.

Estelle's hands moved down his shoulders, one making its way down his right arm, the other down his chest. Simone swept his lips up her neck, and then brushed her lips with his for a moment before looking into her eyes and saying, "I'm sorry I let it get to me— it's not you."

"I understand," she said, running a hand through his hair.

He kissed the palm of her hand as it rested near his jaw, and said, "I've never not trusted you— I just keep overthinking everything."

"Simone, you spent a really long time not opening up to anyone. I don't expect you to just drop all your boundaries at once, and you shouldn't, either."

He nodded and brought his lips back to hers, lying down onto his right side as to not put all of his weight on top of her. She pulled her knee up so it was resting on his thigh and wrapped her arm around his waist; his slow, loving kisses all she cared about. Half an hour had gone by before Estelle helped as he started to remove his pants, and before his head was back on the pillow next to hers, her soft hand was wrapped tightly around his shaft. Reaching above her head, she put her other hand into his, and felt as though the energy between them was completing a full, passionate circuit.

Simone leaned his head forward to continue kissing her, stopping just for a moment when her hand changed from its long, seductive strokes and started with her favorite way of getting him ready for her— by tracing small circles with her thumb on the hyper-sensitive stretch of skin sheathing the back of the head. His forehead gently rested against hers as he alternated between more slow, deep kisses and moments of intense pleasure where all he could do was close his eyes and give a low, gruff moan.

As time continued to rush past, she was so entranced by his vocal response that she had stopped paying attention to the strength of the erection being teased by her hand. His moans were only a touch louder, but his breathing was picking up quickly. He started to think about asking her to slow down, but the impromptu moment had left as soon as it had entered his mind, and instead he heard himself saying, "Estelle— Io sto ottenendo vicino— Sto circa a— Estelle—"

"Hmm?" she asked, not understanding what he was muttering.

In the next moment, however, her question was quite unnecessary, for his hands were tightly gripping onto her as he involuntarily threw his head back, spurred on further by the seductive laugh she gave as she accidentally pushed him over the edge into the full depth of his orgasm.

Chapter 59

Almost a month had passed since Estelle and Simone returned from their honeymoon, well-rested and with blissful souls from the sensual nights filled with uninterrupted romance and the afternoons of taking in equally romantic, ornate libraries along the East Coast. Both were settling comfortably back into their routines, each returning back to work and readying their home for the birth of their child. Simone was busy relaying information between the Boston track and Libera, as well as making sure Dex was staying on target with the casino renovations.

Estelle had come back to find Carolyn at her wit's end from Paul's increasingly bad moods, and had originally tried to act as a buffer between the two, but that, if anything, just made matters worse. No one seemed to know what was eating at him, but they still tried to avoid being around him as much as possible, especially if he was involved in another heated argument on his cell phone.

On the morning of April twenty-ninth, Estelle had just clocked in for the morning and had finally worked up the nerve to discuss her rapidly approaching maternity leave with an already irritated Paul. As she entered the office, Carolyn walked out and patted Estelle's arm, giving her a nod of confidence. Continuing with her morning check list, Carolyn headed upstairs to start shelving the previous day's returns. After fifteen minutes or so, she heard a loud argument with several obscenities being thrown about echoing its way upstairs, and it was several moments before she realized it was Estelle's voice that she was hearing.

Carolyn sprinted down the stairs and ran into the office, originally intending to calm her friend down, when she saw Estelle slap Paul cleanly across the face. Carolyn clapped her hand to her mouth and said, "Estelle, what's—"

"YOU!" Estelle continued, yelling at her seething boss, "Are a lying coward, and I'm just glad that I'll never have to see your skeezy face again! So, you go fuck yourself on your way to hell, all right?"

Paul stormed out past the small group of employees that had gathered in front of the office, and Estelle put a steadying hand on the desk in front of her, left hand pressed hard into her hip.

Carolyn put her hand on Estelle's shoulder and said, "Estelle, what's wrong? What just happened?"

"I think I'm having contractions," Estelle said, a slight panic in her voice.

"No—" Carolyn said, eyes wide with concern. "It's too early— are you sure?"

The next wave of pain hit just over a minute after the first and Estelle said, "Yes— I'm sure— why the hell is this happening? It's three months early—"

"It's all okay— the baby's fine, I'm going to take you to the hospital, and it'll all be okay, all right?"

Estelle nodded and took Carolyn's outstretched hand. "Liam?" Carolyn asked, turning around and looking at the worried coworkers surrounding them. "Can you tell Paul I'm taking her and that I won't be back until tomorrow?"

"Of course. Keep us updated, okay?"

She nodded, and helped Estelle out to the car, hitting the speed dial for Simone's phone number that Estelle had programmed into her phone. As she closed Estelle's door and got behind the wheel, she hung up, let out a frustrated yell, and took off for the hospital.

Chapter 60

Simone was standing between Joel and Landini, listening to Dex run through the renovations that had been completed, and the budget of what still needed to be done. He looked at his ringing phone, and, not recognizing the number, sent the call to voicemail. He pocketed his phone and returned his attention to Dex, only looking up when Joel's phone started to ring. Simone cocked his head to the side, assuming it was the same person that had tried to call him moments before. "Who is it?"

Confused, Joel just said, "Don't know."

"Answer it," Simone directed, trying to figure out who would be calling both of them.

"Hello?" Joel said, trying to keep his tone both polite and direct. "Yeah, hang on."

He handed the phone to Simone saying, "It's Estelle's friend, she said it's an emergency."

Simone's mind began to race in panic. "Carolyn?" he asked, turning his back to the group of men around him, heart pounding in his ears.

His eyes narrowed, and as Carolyn spoke, he hurried to take out his phone and tossed it to Joel, saying, "I need Libera on the phone now."

Joel nodded and dialed, while Simone said, "Which hospital?"

Landini and Joel both looked up in alarm, but Joel said, "He sent it to voicemail, boss."

"Carolyn, hang on. Call me back on my phone, all right?"

He hung up and quickly switched phones again with Joel, answering Carolyn's call.

"We've got you covered," Landini said. "Go."

Simone nodded and caught the key to his Mercedes that Joel threw to him before leaving the casino, walking as fast as he could without attracting too much attention. "I'm on my way," Simone told her. "I'm leaving from the casino, should be less than fifteen minutes. Tell her I'll be there as soon as I can, all right?"

Chapter 61

It was a little after 10:30 that night, and Libera's had been closed for nearly half an hour. Simone was sitting in Estelle's seat at the bar, elbows on the polished wood. The heels of his palms held his head up at the temples, lit cigarette between the first two fingers of his right hand, face staring down at the last sip of scotch left in his glass, as if it could answer the questions his exhausted brain couldn't.

The only remaining staff in the restaurant were the dishwashers in the back, so it caught Simone by surprise to feel a strong hand gently grasp his shoulder.

"You know this is a non-smoking establishment," Libera said with faux disappointment.

"Sorry, sir," Simone murmured, not looking up. He started to drop the half-smoked cigarette into the mostly melted ice residing in the glass that had briefly housed his first drink, now serving as a surrogate ash tray.

"No, keep it," Libera said, taking a cigar from his inner jacket pocket. He lit the cigar and took a moment to take in Simone's appearance, which was starting to reflect the disheveled state of his mind. His jacket was lying on the chair next to him, the collar of his white shirt was unbuttoned and turned up, tie resting upon his vest, loosened to the point of pointlessness. "I'm sorry I missed your call earlier. I was almost to the casino, but when I came in, you had already gone."

"Sorry," Simone said again.

"Don't be. They told me you got a call and had to run. What's wrong, my friend?"

"Bed rest," Simone said into his drink.

"I don't understand."

"Estelle," Simone paused to take a long drag from his cigarette, "has been put on bed rest for the remainder of the pregnancy."

"That's three months still, isn't it?"

"It is."

"But rest is good for her. She works hard, your Estelle. Maybe some time off will—"

Libera's voice trailed off as Simone began to shake his head. Surprised, Libera said "You don't think she needs a break?"

Simone began to laugh. It was an empty, hollow laugh, filled only with bitterness. "On the contrary, I tried to get her to reduce her hours at the library when her back pain became a nightly occurrence."

He put the end of the cigarette into the now shared glass and immediately took out another. As he lit the new cigarette, he looked at Libera and said, "Estelle was fired today."

"You're not serious," Libera said, brows furrowing at the words.

"Oh, I assure you, I am," Simone said angrily. "And because of me."

Libera nudged Simone's arm. "Come on, I'm sure they didn't actually say—"

Simone gave Libera a furious and bitter glare that answered for him. Libera's eyes narrowed as he leaned his head closer to Simone.

"They actually said that it was because of you? It was that whiny supervisor she was telling us about wasn't it?"

Simone nodded as he exhaled. "Paul. The son of a bitch was promoted to manager while we were gone."

"What exactly happened?" Libera asked, incensed.

"Estelle said she went in to establish her maternity leave and instead, Paul said that her affiliation with people like me— his words— people… like… me— created," Simone's voice became mockingly professional, "An unsafe environment for the rest of the staff." His voice became his own again and he continued, "He said that I make them a target, and if she wanted to devote her life to someone like me, she would be doing it without a job." Simone stood and reached behind the bar for the scotch bottle and two new glasses. He motioned the second glass towards Libera, who nodded.

"And then what happened?" Libera asked, taking his drink.

"I got the call from Carolyn telling me to get to the hospital. Apparently," he smiled in spite of himself, "Estelle slapped Paul and spent fifteen minutes yelling at him. Carolyn said she heard it from the next floor up. Called him a 'lying coward'.

Libera laughed and downed his drink. "I could see her saying that."

"Along with several other words Carolyn didn't feel comfortable using in front of hospital staff."

Simone's smile faded as he said, "Carolyn came into the office to see what was going on and she said that Estelle told Paul to go fuck himself and then she started having contractions."

Libera, genuinely concerned, asked, "Are they all right?"

"They are now. The doctors were able to slow everything down, but they said that she has to keep her stress level at a minimum, and that she needs to limit her activity to just walking around. But yes, they're both fine."

"But that's a relief," Libera pointed out. "Why so down?"

"She is so unhappy," Simone said sadly. "I've been sitting here, trying to find some way to fix it. And I've got nothing. How the hell am I supposed to go back and tell her that I can't fix any of it?"

There was a long pause before Libera spoke again. "I can't believe you haven't put a bullet in that good for nothing bastard."

"BELIEVE ME," Simone started, suddenly fiery, "When I say that NOTHING has taken more of my self-control." He calmed his voice back down and continued, "But it would do more harm than good."

"True," Libera said, smiling with respect for Simone's forethought.

There was a knock at the locked front door, and when they looked up, they saw Joel give a small, embarrassed wave. Libera nodded towards the door and Simone stood and unlocked it to allow Joel to enter.

"Good to see you, Joel," Libera said, shaking Joel's hand. "Join us for a drink?"

"No thanks, Don. Estelle can't reach you," he said looking at Simone. "She said she wanted me to see if you were here, but I think she just wanted to make sure you weren't out in the woods with her boss somewhere."

Simone smiled as he finished his drink, Libera laughing next to him. "Damn, that woman knows you well, Simone." Libera continued to laugh as he poured the pair of them another drink. "She's a good woman, your Estelle."

"You are very right, sir," Simone said, taking another sip. "Joel," he continued, "Can you give her a call and let her know that my phone ran out of power and I'll be home soon?"

"You got it."

"Sure you can't stay for a drink?" Libera asked.

"I'd really like to, but I promised I'd bring her a milkshake from Phil's."

Libera laughed again and said, "Lord knows that's one woman I don't want to piss off tonight."

"That's no lie," Joel said, smiling. "She's sure somethin'. I heard what she said to that Paul guy— I wouldn't want to be on the receiving end, that's for damn sure."

Simone laughed and lit another cigarette before taking a hundred-dollar bill from the pocket of his jacket and handing it to Joel.

"Can you make sure they don't put cherries in the bottom? They've been making her sick lately."

"You got it." Joel said. "Good night, Mr. Libera."

"Thanks, Joel," Libera said with a raise of his glass.

"Christ, I don't pay that man enough," Simone said after Joel had gone.

"Ever think of moving him up?"

"I promised Sandra I wouldn't," Simone said, half-smile returning. "Not until Mya's older."

Libera nodded and started to speak again, but stopped as he saw Mack and Gallo approaching the door. "About damn time," Libera said. "What the hell took so long?"

"Apologies, Don Libera," Gallo said. "We had to double check a couple things before coming over. Are we interrupting?" he finished as he looked at the empty glasses on the bar top between Libera and Simone.

Not usually part of Mack's conversations with Libera, Simone shook his head and stood. "No, I should be going."

"Respectfully, Mr. Belvedere," Mack started, "We think you should stay for this."

Simone looked to Libera, who nodded once and poured drinks for the newcomers before refilling his and Simone's glasses. "Sit," Libera said to Mack and Gallo. "What is it?"

"It's Ethan," Mack replied.

"Maxwell's kid?" Simone asked.

Mack nodded. "Yeah, he's been a regular at The Hoop for months. Never had a problem with him till about a month and a half ago. Started betting triple what he used to. He won a few times before, but never a big winner. Thought it was odd, because he's not a regular winner, but we've seen it before. Never bet or won more than five hundred dollars, always paid the losses the same day. Now, he's comin' in three, four times a week, and he hasn't paid up for this week. Comes in today with a buddy, both completely wasted, and wants us to take a lean on Phil's for collateral."

"That's not Ethan's property," Libera said. "Tell him no and move on."

"That's what I told Ethan," Mack explained. "He said it'll be his soon enough and he can do what he wants. So, I called Gallo to see if we could find out where Ethan's cash was coming from."

"And?" Libera asked, looking at Gallo.

"And, it looks like he's the discrepancy we found a while ago— the numbers correlate identically. He's been skimming off of the profits for about a year. Started out just a few hundred here or there that would reappear in a few weeks. Looks like he's feeling a bit braver now. Not even replacing it. But it's still not enough to make up for the amount he's been betting."

Furious, Libera said, "Does he fucking know who he's stealing from?"

"Actually, sir," Simone said, "I don't know that he does. Phil never allowed him anywhere near our conversations. Said he couldn't handle it."

"Looks like Phil was right," Mack said.

"We wanted to know, Don Libera, how you would like us to proceed," Gallo started. "And we wanted to offer our assistance to Mr. Belvedere, if he needed a contract."

Simone looked questioningly at Libera who said, "Why would that be necessary? Simone's who you all should be coming to."

"No disrespect intended, Mr. Belvedere," Gallo said quickly. "We just thought you might not want to be the one to rectify today's situation with Mrs. Belvedere."

Simone slowly turned his head to look at Gallo, who seemed to recoil under the angry stare. "How did you find out about that?"

Without looking at Simone, Gallo nodded towards Mack, who said, "That kid that was with Ethan... he wouldn't shut up about it. He— he was the one that fired her. I had to kick them both out they were laughing so much about it."

There was a heavy, silent minute that went by before Libera poured another drink for Simone and said, "Still want to let him live?"

Simone said nothing for a moment, instead downing another shot and pouring another before saying, "Yes, sir."

Gallo and Mack exchanged a surprised look. Simone had been fiercely protective of Estelle from the start of their relationship, and he was not known for having patience for anyone. Disloyalty to the organization was never taken lightly, especially in front of Libera. "With all due respect," Gallo started. "We—"

"No," Simone said smoothly. "No. We'll give him a couple days to really think about what's going on, then we'll stop in and see what he knows about Ethan."

Libera nodded and said, "Two birds with one stone."

Gallo relaxed and said, "Thank you, Mr. Belvedere."

Simone nodded and tilted his glass and said, "Now if only helping Estelle was just as simple." He drained his glass and held up a hand politely declining when Libera offered him another.

"I figured she'd be glad to not have to go back," Mack said.

Simone shook his head and said, "She put her soul into that place."

"You just gotta stack the deck. Build it so she comes out on top."

Simone nodded and lit another cigarette. "Does Phil know about Ethan?"

Gallo shook his head and said, "Not as far as we can tell."

"Good. Let's keep it that way."

"You got it."

Libera rose and said, "Is that all you have for me?"

"Yes, sir."

"Good. Just keep it contained. Let Ethan keep betting, but don't take any collateral. We need to see how far this will go."

"Yes, sir," Mack said. He and Gallo shook hands with Libera and Simone before heading out into the night.

"Mack's right," Libera said. "Now you can build it how you want to."

Simone nodded. "Thank you, sir."

"You're gonna have some fun with Paul, aren't you?"

Simone smiled as he stood and put his jacket back on over his holstered weapon. "Oh, you have no idea."

"Have Al drive you home. He's out back."

"Yes, sir."

Chapter 62

Simone left through the back of the restaurant and tapped twice on the driver's window of Landini's Jeep. Landini, who had been reading over a file for Libera, looked up and rolled the window down.

"Everything all right?"

"Fan-fucking-tastic," Simone said, embarrassed at being drunker than he cared to be.

Landini looked him over and said, "Don want me to take you home?"

"Yeah."

Doing his best to hide his amusement at Simone's uncustomary state, he simply nodded towards the passenger seat. As Simone got in, Landini said, "Haven't seen you like this in a long time."

Simone nodded and stared pointedly out the window, not wanting to encourage conversation.

"I never heard why you left earlier. Estelle and the baby all right?"

"They are now. Thanks."

"What happened?"

"Estelle was fired. Stress made her to go into early labor. They're fine now, though."

"What can I do?"

"Nothing. We need to wait it out."

"You sound like it's more serious than Estelle being unemployed."

"It's too soon to tell."

Landini nodded, understanding that the subject needed to be dropped. "So, can I ask you something as your friend, and not as your subordinate?"

"'Course."

"Why were you here getting wasted instead of at home with her?"

Simone leaned his head back and said, "I was trying to think of a way to fix it and make her happy again, and I wasn't paying attention to how much I was drinking."

"How'd that work out?"

"It didn't. But Libera would have just called me back once Mack got there anyway."

"Something wrong?"

Simone just looked over at him, eyes clearly warning Landini that he was too close to his boundaries.

Landini nodded again in acknowledgement and as he pulled into Simone's driveway several minutes later, he said, "Look, if there's anything I can do..."

"I know. Thanks."

As Simone haphazardly stepped from the car, Landini leaned forward against the steering wheel and said, "Also, I'm extremely offended that you didn't call me to drink with you."

Simone half-smiled and said, "I wasn't there yet. But as soon as I enter into the angry, reckless stage where I just need to forget about everything, I'll give you a call."

Landini laughed and nodded, and waited to make sure Simone made it inside before pulling out of the driveway.

Chapter 63

Feeling better after his talks with Libera and Landini, Simone ran his fingers through his hair, pushing it out of his exhausted eyes. It was pushing on two-thirty when he waved his thanks to Landini for dropping him off, and as he unlocked the front door, feeling guilty for leaving Estelle alone so late, he started to say, "Hello, Estelle," but stopped halfway through, surprised when he saw a smiling Joel put a quieting finger to his lips and point towards the sofa. He had been so focused on getting in to see Estelle that he hadn't noticed Joel's car parked on the street in front of the house. Simone's worry began to dissipate, being quickly replaced with affection and gratitude as he followed Joel's gesture and saw Estelle sleeping comfortably, wrapped in her favorite leopard-spotted blanket, one arm under her head, the other cradled against her belly.

Simone smiled gently for a moment at the sight of his resting wife before taking full notice of the room. "Hello, Sandra," he murmured, walking over to the round table and kissing her cheek.

"Looks like you've had a hell of a day, Simone," she whispered.

"We'll be all right," he replied gently. "Thank you for staying with her."

"Not at all. We thought it was best not to leave her alone until you got back. Carolyn left around ten. Poor thing needed some sleep. I think she was more worried than Estelle was by the time we got back. I stopped in to check on her, and she wanted to play some Gin, I think to keep her mind busy. Then we put on her favorite movie and she was asleep before Eliza moved in with Higgins."

"I am so grateful," he continued quietly. "To both of you."

Sandra gave Simone's arm a pat. "Really. It was no trouble."

Simone gave her an appreciative and sleepy smile before he walked over to the round table, removed his jacket and gently placed his chrome-laden holster on top of it. Without making a sound, he walked around the front of the couch and put a gentle hand to Estelle's shoulder before even more gently kissing her forehead. Taking care to not wake her, he moved her blanket and lifted her up into his arms.

Estelle only barely realized she was awake. She felt the softness of Simone's shirt under her cheek and smelled the comforting mix of tobacco, scotch and cologne that meant Simone was home safely from Libera's. As she realized she was being carried upstairs to bed, she sleepily nuzzled Simone's chest and gave a soft sigh. He laid her down gently and brought his lips again to her forehead. "I'll be in soon," he said. "I love you, and I'm going to do everything I can for you. Both of you."

She smiled through her sleepy daze and said simply, "You always do."

She seemed to be drifting off to sleep again, so he made his way back down into the living room, where Joel was helping Sandra with her jacket. "Again," Simone said, "Thank you both."

Simone reached into the pocket of the jacket on the table and started to thumb out ten bills, when he felt Joel's hand on his arm. Joel smiled, shook his head and gave a soft wink before opening the door for Sandra. Sandra kissed Simone on the cheek and said, "You let us know if you need anything." She gave him a long, searching look and said, "Try not to worry."

He nodded and Joel gave him another gentle smile before closing the door behind them. Simone turned off the TV and the lights as he went back up to their bedroom, where he undressed as quietly as possible, not wanting to wake Estelle by ruffling through the organized closet for sleep pants. Scotch, stress and exhaustion were fogging his thoughts, and his body felt heavier than usual as he climbed in bed and snuggled up to his wife, her back against his chest, his hand resting on their growing child.

"Simone?" Estelle asked sleepily.

"Yes, love?"

"Matilda."

"Matilda?"

"That's what we should name her."

He opened his eyes and brushed his cheek against hers. "Her?" he asked.

"Her," Estelle said, snuggling herself closer into his chest. Neither of them said another word before falling asleep, but there was no mistaking the grin she could feel against her.

Chapter 64

"Simone ever come home last night?" Carolyn asked the next morning, handing over a bag of donuts, taking her sweater off and sitting next to Estelle at the round table.

"He did. He's actually still asleep," Estelle said, smiling. "It was very late— I woke up and he was carrying me to bed."

"And I thought the donuts would be what gave me the cavity today." Smiling, Carolyn went on, "I didn't think he was usually home this late in the mornings."

"No, but I'm guessing Libera had twice the scotch Simone did—"

"Sound logic," Simone said with a sleepy laugh, coming down the stairs and wearing only the pants he had taken off the night before. He bent down and kissed Estelle's hair on his way to pour himself a cup of coffee. She smiled up at him as he gave the front page of the newspaper a fast glance for familiar names. "It's good to see you, Carolyn," he said as he sat the paper down and went searching through his jacket for his morning cigarette.

"You— uh— you, too," she blundered, caught off guard.

He gave her an inquisitive look and Estelle, grinning, said, "Sorry, honey, she's a chest girl."

"I'm sure I don't know what you mean," Carolyn said with mock decorum, as she stared intently into her cup, taking an overly drawn out drink of her coffee.

Simone laughed, feeling somewhere between flattered and hyperaware of the scars on his chest, hip and arm, and moved his jacket and gun off of the table. "I see."

Estelle smiled at Simone's amusement, and took a moment to appreciate just how comfortable Simone and Carolyn had gotten with each other. "Did we wake you up?" she asked.

"Not a bit," he said, opening the front door, intending to smoke on the porch before getting ready for the day, hoping it would lessen the throbbing in his head.

"Good. You needed some rest."

"As do you." His voice was stern, but there was a noticeable worry in his eyes.

"He's not wrong," Carolyn said bluntly.

"I know. I was thinking I'd spend the day watching some movies and looking through the job listings online."

She looked up, hoping for support from at least one of them, but Carolyn was just looking at Simone, her fierce eyes trying to silently persuade him to speak. He looked out the screen door for a moment, trying to choose his words carefully before slowly making his way over and kneeling in front of Estelle. "Do you remember what I said the night I proposed? When you asked me about keeping your job?"

"Of course, I do."

"I absolutely do not ever want you to feel as though your working is anyone's choice but your own," he began, hesitating as she gave a loud exhale and rolled her eyes. "However," he continued cautiously, "I think that you should probably think about taking the time off that the doctor recommended."

"It's not like I'm looking for construction work. I'm just going to try to find some local bookstores—"

"It's still hard work, you'd be on your feet all d—" Carolyn stopped at the sight of the look Estelle was giving her.

"Since when did you two agree on anything?" Estelle spat, feeling backed into a corner.

"We're just worried about you," Simone said. "We want—" He stopped and cocked his head to the side as a thought hit him.

Estelle nodded her head a couple times and said "WANT?"

He blinked to regain his train of thought and said, "Sorry, remembering something I need to do later. We want you to be as stress free as possible."

"But then you'd be supporting us on your own," she said, tears glistening in her eyes as she looked into Simone's worried gaze.

He gave her a strained look, trying to avoid saying what he was thinking when Carolyn said, "I'm FAIRLY certain that's not an issue." She threw a tentative glance to Simone, who chanced a relieved smile at her.

"I really, really don't mind, Estelle. And I will do everything I can—"

"Honey, I know you can. But you shouldn't have to."

"I WANT to," Simone said, kissing her hand. "It doesn't have to be forever. Just until we know the stress won't be too much for you and the baby."

"Fine," Estelle said, defeated. She stood up and walked over to the couch and sat down with her back to both of them. Simone dropped his head, standing and picking up his coffee cup. He looked to Carolyn and saw her silently mouth the words, "Thank you," as she walked into the kitchen. He nodded and walked over to where Estelle was sitting. "I've got to go take care of something. Will you be okay by—?"

"Yes, your apparently invalid wife will be just fine."

Carolyn put both of her hands in front of her face in an unseen surrender and refilled her coffee. Simone took a deep breath and said "I'm sorry I've upset you. I want nothing more than to fix this."

"I know." Estelle said, silent tears taking over her.

"Hey," Simone said, putting an arm around her and pulling her close.

"I'm sorry, I'm not mad at you," she said into his shoulder. "I just can't believe my career is over."

"No, I know. But it's not over. We just need to find a way to make it better," he said, looking to Carolyn for support.

"The right opportunity will show itself," Carolyn said. "Just give it some time."

Estelle nodded and got up to dry her eyes in the bathroom. Carolyn came over and sat next to Simone. "Please tell me you can fix this."

Simone nodded. "It won't be an immediate solution, but I think I've got something."

"Thank you, Simone."

As he nodded and stood to go get dressed for the day, Estelle called to Carolyn, "Want me to order some food before you head into work?"

"Absolutely!" Carolyn called back. She turned and whispered to Simone, "How about I go do your mobby stuff and YOU stay here with Mrs. Emotional Rollercoaster over there?"

Simone's half-smile reappeared as he said, "Yeah, you know I'm not sure Libera will go for that."

Chapter 65

An hour later, Joel dropped Simone off at the entrance to Libera's office, still tinged with his hangover, but bearing an idea that he thought would eradicate Estelle's problem. "Good morning, sir," he said, knocking on the open door of the office.

"Hey, Simone, come in. Figure it out, yet?"

"Actually, sir, I may have."

"Sit. And what's that?"

"I'm going to buy her a storefront so she can open a bookstore," he said, unbuttoning his jacket and sitting down with a cavalier smile.

Libera laughed and, taking a drink of coffee, said, "You're stacking the deck."

"Damn straight."

"I love it," Libera said, leaning back in his chair.

"In addition to making sure she's doing what she loves," Simone started with a proud look of triumph, "she'll be able to do most of the work from home until the baby comes, and then she'll be able to take the baby with her, alleviating the fear she had of having to hire a nanny, which she was strongly against."

"I'm assuming you want to keep it out of the organization, since she'll be the one running it?"

"I would, yes, if that's all right."

"Perfectly," he started, appraising Simone's reaction. "You know," he continued, "That OTB that you set up for Olympus and Athena is already a big hit."

"I'm glad it worked out, sir."

"I am, too. In the last three weeks we've pulled in a little under a mil, just from the addition of the new kiosks."

Simone's eyes widened in surprise. "That's fantastic."

"I agree. I'm sure the novelty with the regulars will wear off soon, as it usually does, but it does seem to be just as popular as the numbers suggested. Now, normally, when you pull in an account this big, I upgrade your car, but you seem to like the Mercedes."

"I do, sir, thank you."

"So that's why I'll back seventy five percent of the store."

"Sir, that's— Are you sure, sir?"

Libera leaned forward. "Are you questioning my decision?"

"No, sir, of course not—" Simone said quickly. "I just don't know what it will cost yet."

"We'll work all that out."

"Thank you. I can't tell you how much I appreciate this."

"My pleasure. Do you have anything else for me?"

"I do."

He paused with a mischievous glint in his eyes and then said, "I was wanting your permission for myself to escort Estelle to the library today to pick up the things she has there."

Libera smiled. "This wouldn't happen to be a way to get inside Paul's head, would it?"

"Of course, it is."

Libera laughed. "All right, but we need him breathing for this Ethan mess."

"Of course, sir. Thank you."

"When you're done with that, meet me back here. Gallo's bringing the numbers over in a couple hours, we need to see how deep this thing goes."

"I'll be there, sir."

"I know you will. Go have some fun," Libera said, dark humor in his eyes.

Simone stood and buttoned his jacket. "I think I will."

Chapter 66

When he arrived back home half an hour later, he was glad to see that Carolyn's car was still in the driveway, meaning she wasn't at the library yet. "Hello, Estelle," he said after opening the door.

Estelle and Carolyn were sitting at the table, surrounded by a few empty take out boxes and playing Gin.

"You're back awfully fast," Estelle said.

"I am," he replied, sitting next to her. "I wanted to see if you wanted me to take you to get what you needed from the library."

Estelle looked up at him with a suspicious smile. "And why would you want to do that, when Carolyn can just get it for me when she goes to work today?"

"Come on, where's the fun in that?" he asked, standing up and kissing her hair before walking into the kitchen.

"Is this the normal kind of fun," Carolyn started, "or the pull him into a back-alley kind of fun?"

Simone half-smiled as he took a bottle of sparkling water from the refrigerator. "First of all, nobody does that. It's tacky." He came back over and sat down. "Secondly, it's just a little harmless psychological manipulation."

Carolyn started to laugh. "That really shouldn't be funny, but Paul really needs to be taken down a bit."

"See," he said, gesturing towards Carolyn. "Even she approves. And it won't get out of hand, because my main concern is keeping you stress free."

"Let me go get dressed," she conceded.

"Thank you, baby," he said, before turning to Carolyn. "Do you mind not letting him know we're coming in?"

"So long as you promise to let me know when you'll start to talk to him."

"Oh, you'll know."

Estelle came back downstairs several minutes later, wearing a floral printed maxi dress, Chanel sunglasses, and carrying the Chanel bag she had purchased in New York.

Simone half-smiled. "You look wonderful."

"I should hope so. I want that broke bastard to eat his heart out," she replied, leaning down to kiss him.

"Christ, I love you," he said, pulling her closer.

"Alright, kids, not until after mommy leaves," Carolyn said, standing. "Want to follow me in? If I follow you in it might look like—"

Simone nodded, also standing. "That's fine."

After locking the door behind them, Simone opened Estelle's car door and said, "What did you mean when you said that he's broke?"

"Wait till we're in the car," Estelle whispered, glancing at Carolyn, who was unlocking her car by Simone's door.

Simone nodded and walked around to his side of the car. As he opened his door, Carolyn touched his arm and said, "You're not so bad."

"I try," he replied, smiling as she got into her car. He pulled out of the driveway and waited for Carolyn to back out so he could follow her.

"Why do you want to know?" she asked him.

"Let's call it curiosity," he said, glancing at her.

"He's just always bitching about it. Apparently, he went in on something with a friend that didn't pan out, then about a week ago he was yelling at somebody on his phone in the office about money they owed him. They've been arguing on the phone for a couple months now."

"Interesting."

"Why?"

"Just is, that's all."

She watched him drive for a few minutes before saying, "You know who he loaned the money to."

With an arrogant smile he pulled into the parking lot of the library and said, "You know I can't answer that."

"Promise this won't get out of hand?" she asked, watching Carolyn heading inside.

"If I wanted it to get out of hand, I would have just sent Al over and saved us the trouble."

"All right," she said, checking her hair in the mirror. "Let's go."

As they walked in, they saw Paul at the help desk, berating Carolyn for coming in five minutes late. "He doesn't quit, does he?" Simone whispered.

Estelle shook her head. "Remember, he's related to someone on the board, so don't be too hard on him, or he'll have Carolyn fired, too."

He nodded. "Won't be a problem."

As they walked up to the desk where Paul was sitting next to Carolyn, Simone put his arm around Estelle, who said, "Hey, Paul. We just came by to pick up the things I left."

Paul flinched as Simone extended his hand and said, "I don't think we've met. Who are you?"

"Sorry, honey," Estelle said, as Paul reached out a barely trembling hand to Simone. "This is Paul. He was my supervisor, until yesterday. Paul, you know my husband, right?"

"Yes. S-Simone Bel-Belvedere. It's… it's good to meet you."

"Is it?"

Desperate to look away for a moment, Paul looked over and said, "Carolyn, can— can you grab Estelle's box from the break room?"

Carolyn rolled her eyes and said, "Sure."

As she walked off, Simone leaned on the tall desk and said, "So, I hear you're concerned about the safety of yourself and the staff now that Estelle and I have been married."

"N-no," he stammered. "I mean—"

"Funny," Simone said, standing upright and looking to Estelle, "I thought you said that was why he let you go?"

"It was—" Paul stuttered, trying to backtrack, "I mean— but clearly it's not a prob—"

Simone slammed his hand down hard, palm flat, onto the desk, bringing on an echoing silence in the lobby and causing Paul to jump as though scalded. He leaned down again and whispered, "I can see that you're obviously worried about security. So, rest assured that I will continue to pay the security staff a little extra for a while, just to make sure they're watching after you."

Carolyn walked back up, trying to keep a straight face. "Here you go," she said, handing Estelle her box.

"Thank you," Estelle said, balancing the box on her hip.

Simone tapped his palm twice on the desk before saying, "Take care, Paul."

As they turned to walk away, Simone turned back and said, "I'll see you soon, Carolyn, take care."

"Thanks, you, too, Mr. Belvedere."

As they got back into the Mercedes, Estelle started to laugh. "God, that was gratifying."

"I agree," Simone said, leaning over to kiss her.

"You were unbelievable!"

"You weren't so bad yourself, my dear."

"I mean, did you see the look on his face?"

"That's why Libera sends me," Simone said, picking up Estelle's hand and kissing it.

"You're cute when you're all cocky."

He smiled. "I have to get back to Libera's, you okay being by yourself?"

"I am," she said, smiling away his concern. "It'll give me a chance to look at the paint samples for the nursery Dex dropped off."

"I'm going to try to get out as soon as I can, but I have to meet with Gallo to go over several months of numbers, so it may take a while. I would like to talk to you tonight when I get home, though. I think I found a solution for you."

"That was fast. I take it that's why you were out until three and came home smelling like the scotch factory?"

"I am sorry about that. I got a bit carried away venting to Libera."

"It's okay. You don't have to explain yourself. I'd have been doing the same thing if I weren't pregnant."

He pulled into the driveway and said, "Let me know if you need anything."

"I will." She leaned over and kissed him. "Thanks for being there for me. You really were amazing."

"That's what I'm here for."

After she was safely inside, he set out for Libera's, laughing to himself about how easy it had been to intimidate Paul.

Chapter 67

Just after two, Simone walked into an empty Libera's and saw his Patron sitting with Mack and Gallo at his usual corner table, and an associate by the name of Gianni Fabbri laughing with Landini at the bar. As they looked up to see who entered, Libera started laughing and stood to shake his hand.

"We've already gotten word back about your little chat with Paul," he said gleefully. "From two different security guards. Looks like you made just about everyone's day. Come, have a seat."

Simone unbuttoned his jacket and took a seat next to Gallo. "Thank you, sir. I think I made my point."

"I'll say," Mack said, toasting Simone.

"I also learned something very interesting today," Simone said, looking at Gallo. "Paul's the one Ethan's getting the other part of the cash from."

"You're sure?" Libera asked.

"Fairly. Before we left Estelle came downstairs, and when I complimented her she said something about wanting the "broke bastard" to eat his heart out."

His companions all laughed as Libera said, "Sounds like her."

"That got me thinking about why he was with Ethan at The Hoop, and while we were in the car, I asked what she meant, and she said that he's always complaining about a joint venture that failed, and that he's been yelling at someone on the phone about not returning money that was borrowed."

"Think we should pay him another visit?" Libera asked.

Simone shook his head. "No, I think he'll come to us when it counts."

Libera nodded. "Gallo's traced the missing money back to a month after we took over the diner. It's definitely Ethan."

Simone frowned, tapping his finger on the table.

"What?" Libera asked.

"Something's not right. This is too calculated."

"You think he knows what he's doing?" Libera asked.

"The numbers do seem to imply it," Gallo said, looking towards Simone.

"But is it us or Phil that he's trying to hit?" Simone asked.

"I wondered that, too," Gallo added. "If he was trying to hit us, the numbers would be bigger. Sticking us for less than a grand a hit doesn't make any sense."

"Unless he's smarter than we're giving him credit for," Simone said. "All it would take is a long look through the books to see that his

dad's not running it anymore, and if he thought we were taking what he considers his birthright away, he'd be pretty pissed off with all of us…"
He cocked his head, putting the last piece of the puzzle in place.

"What birthright?" Libera asked. "Phil built that diner himself, created a successful business, worked every day of the week, and came to us when he wanted to retire. Ethan's never worked a day in his life. How'd he think he'd be able to run a business?"

"I'm guessing he didn't think about it," Simone replied slowly. "He's just relied on it for so long without having to do anything, he probably assumed it would always be that way."

"What's wrong?"

Simone looked into Libera's eyes and said, "It was Ethan."

"What was?"

Simone's eyes flitted over to Landini at the bar.

Libera lowered his head and said, "You think Ethan organized the hit?"

He said nothing, but continued to think it through.

"He couldn't have had that kind of money," Libera said. "With or without Paul."

"It's not like these guys were professionals— it would have cost a third of what you'd pay Al for something like that."

"And what would he gain from it?"

"I'm not sure."

"You look pretty sure," Libera said, narrowed eyes far from agreeing with Simone's conclusion.

"That's why Paul needed Estelle out of the way at the library. The risk of her overhearing something—"

"Which she did," Mack pointed out.

"Would mean that it would put their entire venture at risk, whatever it is."

"Again, which is what?" Libera asked, starting to sound irritated.

"I don't know." Simone continued to look at the table and said, "I think we need some more time. Maybe run it by Duvall, see where to go from here. If these guys were behind it, this is far from over."

Libera nodded. "I agree. We should consult Jim before we do anything. I'll give him a call."

Chapter 68

Around nine that night, Simone finally headed home. After holing himself up in Libera's office for several hours comparing Ethan's withdrawals from Phil's with his gambling wins and losses, Joel drove an exhausted Simone home, both men surprised to see Sandra standing on the porch, finishing a cigarette and waving to them.

"Hello, Sandra," Simone said, kissing her cheek. "It's good to see you."

Joel walked onto the porch, and smiled as he kissed his wife. "Hi, babe."

She put a gentle hand on Joel's chest, and smiled at Simone, who looked hopeful and asked, "Is Mya with you?" She nodded towards the door, and Simone walked in, stopping to set his jacket on the table and smiling at the couch. Estelle and Mya had both fallen asleep, Mya cuddled up to Estelle's belly, tiny hand clutching a unicorn picture book.

"When you hadn't come home by six, Estelle called and asked if we wanted to come over for dinner to thank me for last night. They fell asleep around eight thirty."

Simone walked over and kissed Estelle's forehead. She woke up, blinking at Simone for a moment before smiling at the sleeping toddler in her lap. She gently moved Mya to avoid waking her, before standing and stretching. "I'm sorry I'm late," Simone whispered.

She waved a hand at him, yawning. "Don't be." She turned to look at Sandra. "I'm sorry I fell asleep!"

Sandra laughed. "It's that silly unicorn, works every time. And it was good to see you resting. There's food in the fridge for both of you," she said, gesturing to Simone and Joel.

"Want me to reheat it?" Estelle asked.

"No, I can do it," Simone started. "You can relax and—"

"Simone, I love you. But I swear to god, if you try to do everything for me—"

He smiled and held up his hands. "Okay— No damsel in distressing. I swear."

"Food?" she asked again, testing him.

He nodded, and she looked up at Joel, who said, "Sure thing, thanks."

Simone sat down across from an amused looking Joel and looked up at Sandra's hand patting his shoulder. "She's almost as stubborn as you are."

"No kidding," Simone said. He lowered his voice and said, "She okay?"

Sandra nodded and whispered, "Mostly tired, still bouncing between angry and letting it go. Probably best not to ask her."

"Thank you again, for being there yesterday."

"Glad to do it. Mya was disappointed you weren't here, though. She's been asking to see you."

"I'm sorry I didn't get back while she was awake," he said, drooping at disappointing the toddler. "I haven't really been there for anybody—"

"No, that's not what I meant," Sandra said, having thought it would comfort him, rather than upset him. "I just meant that she misses you, that's all."

"I know."

"It's not always this hectic," Joel said. "There's just a lot happening at once. It balances out, one way or another."

Estelle came in and sat a plate of Pad Thai down in front of each of them, before picking up three folders from the end table and sitting down next to Simone. "Dex came by this afternoon," she said, opening the top folder and setting it in front of him. "He sent three different ideas over, wanted us to look at them and let him know as soon as we can so he can start ordering what he needs."

Simone smiled and started to look through the sketches and photographs between hungry mouthfuls of noodles. "Do you have a favorite?" he asked.

"You'll know when you see it."

He closed the first folder full of images of antique circus tents and elephants and passed it to Sandra. "I like that one," he said, "But it seems like something she'd grow out of pretty quickly."

"I agree," Estelle said. "Effing adorable, though."

"Wait," Sandra said, "Did you say she?"

Simone gave Estelle a surprised look, but she smiled and said, "I thought you'd want to be the one to tell them."

He kissed her cheek before looking back at Sandra and nodding.

"When did you find out?" Joel asked, grinning.

"She told me last night."

Simone looked to Estelle, also wondering how long she had known.

"They told me just before you got to the hospital yesterday, I made Carolyn promise not to tell anyone so you didn't accidentally find out from someone else."

"I'm glad you did," he said, glad to see the first truly calm look in her eyes since the previous day's debacle.

After a long pause, he opened the second folder and said, "Not this one, it's too trendy. Six months and it'll be outdated already." He passed the second folder, bearing yellow and gray chevrons to Sandra, who nodded in agreement and passed it to Joel.

Estelle laughed. "I told Dex you wouldn't like that one."

"So that must mean that this—" he opened the folder and slowly said, "Is the one."

She sat watching him for a moment as his excitement grew with each image. "You like it?"

"It's perfect!" he said, taking out the paint color swatches.

"Remember he came over to see what we already had for the baby? He got the idea from the owl and Hogwarts blanket they gave us the day of our wedding."

"This is amazing."

He laid the images out flat so they could see them all together.

"I especially love this one," Estelle said, pointing to a mobile made of winged keys.

Simone nodded. "The doe in the woods would look great on the wall across from the closet, wouldn't it? Then the crib could go on that wall, and it wouldn't be right across from the window, so the sunlight wouldn't fall directly onto it."

"And the closet doors could have Quidditch goal posts, or Diagon Alley."

"Or Platform Nine and Three Quarters—"

"You know what they're talking about?" Joel asked, smiling up at Sandra.

"Only sort of, and that's just because I picked out the blanket," Sandra said, trying to hide the happy tear that had escaped.

"What do you guys think?" Estelle asked, helping Simone to turn the images around so they were facing their friends.

Joel looked at Simone and said, "I think you're happier than I've ever seen you before, so I call that a win."

Sandra nodded in agreement. "Perfect."

Estelle ran her fingers through Simone's hair and stood, saying, "I can let him know tomorrow. You guys want a glass of wine?"

They all nodded as she walked into the kitchen, bringing back a bottle and three glasses. Simone finished refilling the folder, and then closed his eyes and leaned his head back, subconsciously nuzzling his head against Estelle's hip as she poured their guests a glass of Merlot. He leaned forward and looked at Sandra, who had been gently watching him with a gaze reminiscent of a mother watching her child sleep.

Simone's phone started to ring, and he quickly muted the ringer to avoid waking Mya and said, "Sorry, one second."

He quickly made his way upstairs, and before he was halfway up, they heard, "Hello, sir. No, it's okay."

Sandra held up a deck of cards, and upon seeing Estelle and Joel nod, began to shuffle and deal them each ten cards. It was a full twenty minutes before Simone came back downstairs, laughing to himself. Estelle looked up, slightly worried and said, "You have to go?"

"No," he said, sitting and putting his hand on her shoulder. "Just had a question. What's the game?"

"It was Gin, but since we're four now, Hearts will be easier," Sandra said, waiting for a group consensus and then dealing each of them thirteen cards.

It was close to midnight when they left, Mya curled up against Joel's shoulder as he waved good night to them. Estelle sat down next to Simone on the couch and said, "You wanted to talk?"

"I do." He hesitated, not knowing where to start. "Well, I actually have two things to talk to you about now. Do you want the weird part or the proposition first?"

"Weird first, always."

He gave a nervous laugh and said, "Now look, I don't know what this means, and I don't know how you'll feel about it, so you have to promise me that you'll stay calm, all right?"

"Okay..." she replied, starting to feel nervous.

"All right... Well, we've been going through the books for a few days making sure everything's on track, and for the first time in about three years, there's a new high roller at Mustang."

She cocked her head and said, "How can a brothel have a high roller?"

"That's what we call the guys who come in three times in a single week or seven times in a month for three months or more. Sounds better over the phone to just call them a high roller."

"Unless you're telling me that the new guy is you, I'm not seeing why this is weird—"

"No, it's not me," Simone laughed, thoroughly amused by the implication. "No, I've never been in for more than a meeting with Bronte. It's weird because it's... John Presswood."

She sat stunned for a moment, and then said, "My father, John Presswood— or is this just a coincidence—"

"No, Bronte recognized him at the wedding. Libera thought I should tell you before it came up—"

"MY father is having an affair?"

"Several, from what I understand. Most high rollers have one girl they go to—"

"You can stop now," she said, holding her hand up.

"Sorry— I know this is weird."

"I guess it's not really that weird. It's not like my mother is the most affectionate of people— unless he's racking up a huge debt or something—"

"No, Libera said he pays same day, never started a tab. Apparently, he's been a semi-regular for several years, more so in the last year."

"So, do I need to tell him I know, or something?"

"Not unless you want to. Libera just thought it best to have the awkward conversation at home instead of risking an awkward encounter somewhere else."

"Okay, so what's the proposition?"

"What would you say to opening up a bookstore?"

She sat in silent shock, not completely sure if he was being serious. "Libera's offered to finance seventy five percent as a bonus for the Boston deal, and it would be kept completely separate from the organization."

"You're really serious?" she asked, still incredulous at the idea.

"Well yeah, why not? God knows you'd have better product knowledge than most people do when they start a business, and you're really good at making tough decisions and making sure things are moving the way they're supposed to. You'd be great at it."

"You think so?"

"I really do. And a lot of it in the beginning would have to be done from home anyway, so you could still work like you want to, and rest like the doctor wants you to, and then you could even take her with you if you wanted—"

"And we wouldn't need a nanny!" she exclaimed, starting to fully consider it.

"Exactly! You like it?"

"Oh, Simone, it would be wonderful. But I don't want to put either of us in debt—"

"I haven't even started looking at the cost yet— Libera said we'll work it out. I assume he'll want to sit down with both of us and figure it out together— that's what he usually does in a situation like this."

"And there wouldn't be any money laundering, no rackets…Because I'm fairly certain I don't know how to do that."

"None. Libera would simply be an investor, just like me. Except I'll be the only one that gets to sleep with the owner," he added with a mischievous smirk.

"Can we put that in the contract?" Estelle asked, taking his hand into hers.

"Does that mean you want to?"

"I thought you knew I wanted to sleep with you," she teased.

"You know what I meant."

"You really think it's a good idea?"

"Absolutely!"

"Okay, let's do it!"

Simone leaned forward and hugged her, thankful for the light in her eyes and that he was able to unburden her worries.

"You are so good to me," she said, nuzzling her cheek against his.

"That's what I'm here for, love."

Chapter 69

Simone walked into Libera's the next evening and unbuttoned his jacket as he started to sit down for his meeting with Libera and Landini.

"Before you sit," Libera started, causing Simone to pause midair, "Fabbri was wanting a minute of your time. He's at the bar."

"Thank you."

Once Libera nodded his acknowledgement without looking up from the document he was reading, Simone made his way over to the bar, tapping his hand twice on Gianni's shoulder. "What's up?" he asked, nodding to Landini as Gianni turned around and leaned against the bar.

"Estelle wanted me to let you know that she thinks she found the place."

"Already?" he asked, looking at his watch.

"Yeah, she knows what she wants. We looked at three other places, but then we found this one, and she won't even consider a different one."

"I guess that's the one, then. Thanks for taking her out to look for it."

"It's no problem at all. We actually had a pretty good time. Here—" he said, pulling out a piece of paper with Estelle's handwriting.

He smiled at the pink ink on the page and said, "That's not a bad price, either."

"She called the realtor and they said it's been empty for a few months, so you could probably get them down a bit on price, too."

"I would have thought she'd have wanted a stand-alone?"

"Yeah, well, this one is right across from a coffee shop, it's got lot parking instead of meters, it's not even a fifteen-minute walk from here, and it used to be one of those stores wealthy women shopped at in the sixties."

"Yep, that's Estelle," Simone said, laughing as he folded the paper and put it into the breast pocket of his jacket. He took three bills out of his clip and handed them to Gianni. "Thanks, Fabbri."

He nodded for Landini to follow him as he walked away, and as they approached Libera's table, Simone started to take his usual place across from his Patron, but halfway through, Libera again said, "One second—"

"What's—"

"I'm just screwing with you," Libera said, grinning as Landini turned to hide his laughter. "Sit."

Simone half-smiled and said, "Have you spoken with Estelle?"

"Not directly, but Fabbri gave me this," he replied, showing Simone a scrap of paper identical to the one now in his pocket. "I say get Dex over to double check everything, but other than that, it looks perfect for her."

"I agree," Simone said, half-smiling.

"I gotta hand it to her. She knows how to get shit done."

"That she does."

"She also wanted me to talk you into poaching the girl from the other store. Can't remember her name to save my life—"

"Carmen?"

"Yeah— that sounds right."

"Carmen's been working for the same people for eight years—"

"So, pay her more than they are."

"Seems a little underhanded—"

"Of course, it is. But Estelle said she needs the best, and apparently that's this Carmen girl, so…"

Simone started to laugh. "I'll see what I can do."

"Good," Libera said, turning to Landini. "Have anything for me?"

"Not so far. Haven't seen them together at all. Paul pretty much keeps to the library and his apartment. It's been a bit more complicated trying to watch Ethan. He's definitely paranoid that he's going to get caught for something, but so far, we haven't been able to. Just usual, everyday shit that doesn't help any of us."

"Fair enough. Give it another few days and then pull back. I don't want this escalated unless absolutely necessary, for Phil's sake. Is that understood?"

"It is."

Chapter 70

Once Simone had returned home, Estelle looked over from the couch. "Hello, Estelle," he said, setting his phone and keys down on the table.

"Hey, you."

Taking off his jacket and holster, he asked, "How was your day?"

"Stuck here for most of it," she said, frowning.

He walked over to her and as she sat up, he sat down behind her against the arm rest, turned so her back could lean against his chest. As he dropped his shoes to the floor, he put his left leg against the back of the couch, allowing her to come closer. "I'm sorry you were stuck here all day."

"It's all right," she said, nuzzling the top of her head under his chin as he started to massage the back of her hip with his right hand. "You're home now."

He smiled and said, "Do you need anything?" He felt her nod, and said, "What can I do?"

She turned to look up at him and leaned a little closer, beckoning him to come in for a kiss. He smiled softly and leaned in, gently kissing her lips, his left hand resting against her cheek. As she continued to kiss him, he could feel her passion rising quickly, and could feel his own desire starting to flare in return.

Indulging himself in several more intense kisses, he finally pulled back and closed his eyes, resting his chin on her shoulder. "Baby, we can't."

She stopped to kiss him again and said, "Just a little?"

With a gentle laugh, he said, "It could cause early labor again, and I'm not going to put you through that just because..." He broke off as he kissed her again, only barely able to string words together enough to finish his sentence between their kisses. "Because I... want... you..."

Their kisses continued for another full minute before Estelle started to reply, her neck now tilted to the side as his lips traveled along her neck. "I know... we can't... But I can still... for you..."

Simone's breathing was now quick and shallow, making it difficult to stammer, "I'm not going to... if you're not going to."

She turned a little more so she could run her fingers through his hair as she deeply kissed him. "Please, baby," she started. "I just need to be with you. I don't care how— I just need you... in some way." She looked into his eyes before kissing him again and murmuring, "Please, baby."

Simone felt the last of his resolve slipping away and he just started to quickly nod, kissing her several more times. Finally, he let his lips leave hers as he said, "Can we go upstairs so you'll be more comfortable?"

She grinned and started to stand, pausing as Simone stood and helped her the rest of the way to her feet. He put his arms around her and kissed her again, before taking her hand and leading her up the stairs.

Once she was lying comfortably on her side of the bed, Simone loosened his tie and dropped it to the floor— immediately starting on the buttons of his shirt with his right hand as he laid down next to her. Their lips instantly met again as he untucked his now open shirt, and Estelle ran her hands slowly over his chest, feeling as though they hadn't made love in months, even though it had only been two weeks.

Simone, mirroring her desire, pulled himself closer against her and slowly ran his hand down her hip, before letting it drift up her back and into her hair, his breathing now stronger and louder than it was before they made their way into the bedroom. "Oh, Christ," he muttered, watching Estelle fumbling with his belt and zipper. Unable to look away from what she was doing, Simone watched as she took him into her soft hand that was now quickly stroking him.

Finally breaking his gaze from her hand, he brought his lips back to hers, flitting between their passionate kisses and his low, husky moans. After several moments she pulled her head back, letting his forehead rest against her shoulder as she smiled at his rapturous panting.

Switching hands for a moment, she brought her right thumb up, slowly wetting it with her tongue before letting it return to him, her thumb now slowly gliding against his most sensitive spot. His hands were holding on tightly to her back— his head now just above hers as he leaned his head back, brow furrowed.

"Christ, Estelle," he muttered ten minutes later, his hands still gripping onto her.

She nodded and smiled against his neck, before gently nibbling at his skin. She kissed him again and said, "That's it."

His eyes tightly closed, he pulled his arms tighter around her and kissed her lips, barely able to finish a kiss without his moans euphorically interrupting it. She suddenly felt his hips start to sway quickly along with her hand, as though he were moving within her, and instinctively tightened her hand, breathing just as quickly as he was. A moment later, his forehead was pressed hard into her shoulder, his lips breathlessly issuing her name as his orgasm overtook him.

Estelle continued to stroke him for several long, seductive seconds, ensuring he felt every last aftershock of pleasure she could bring him. Once her hand had stopped moving, he gently caressed her cheek with his hand as he continued kissing her, only stopping to whisper, "I love you."

Chapter 71

The evening of June sixth was warm and rainy, and Estelle had taken refuge in the cool air of Libera's office, going over some paperwork for the bookstore. At her request, Libera was double checking her numbers, himself, every week, to ensure they were correct before signing off on the orders.

"Everything looks good. Should be open in no time." He looked up and asked, "You okay?"

She was grimacing, but shook her head, hand to her belly. "Just more Braxton-Hicks, I think. They've been happening all day. Some are just stronger than others, that's all." She breathed and waved her hand. "I'm fine. Dex has most of the shelves in, and I was thinking of trying to find some good tables and old typewriters for budding writers to—" she stopped, breathing deeply again. After a minute she said, "Sorry, anyway…"

"You sure you're all right? You're very pale, my dear."

"I'm fine," she said, standing and adjusting her strapless, pink cotton dress so she could walk around.

He looked at the paperwork for a few minutes and said, "I like your idea about the tables, I think that would be exceptionally good for the community and—"

"Oh, Jesus," she said, breathing through another sharp pain.

"Estelle?"

"I'm fine," she repeated, pacing in a slow circle. After another few minutes went by, she said, "Dex also thought it would be a good idea to add a play area in for Mya and Matilda, that way we could bring them with us."

"That all sounds good to me," Libera said, starting to look worried. "Why don't you sit—?"

"No, I'm okay—" she stopped pacing and took a deep breath of surprise.

"Estelle?" She didn't say anything, but looked into his eyes for a moment, neither able to tell which emotion she was having.

Oh my god. This is not happening now… not here…

"Estelle, what's wrong?"

"Where— where's Simone?"

"Why? What's—?"

"My water just broke."

They both froze, stunned for a moment, both unsure of what to do. As another pain hit her, she clutched onto the desk, and, voice straining said, "I have to find him."

"It's okay," Libera said, standing up quickly and sounding braver than he looked. "I'm going to call Simone, and drive you to the hospital. Come on," he said, taking out his phone with his left hand and offering his right to Estelle. "It's all okay." He led her out the back door attached to his office and over to his parked Cadillac.

Libera dialed as they walked, and as they approached the car he said, "Simone, hold on." He hit the speaker option on his phone and set it on top of the car so he could help Estelle into the back seat. "Simone, where are you?"

Simone's voice, with its standard, casual calm, echoed slightly from the speaker of the phone as he said, "We're headed back from Olympus now, stuck in traffic on the highway."

"You need to get back here now."

"What's—"

"Listen— Estelle's in labor, I'm taking her to the hospital."

"What? She's still several weeks early—"

"Now!" Libera barked.

They could hear muffled instructions being given to Joel, and Joel's voice made a loud obscenity that was only sort of garbled by the speaker, now in the front seat with Libera.

"How far away are you?" Libera pulled up to the exit of the parking lot, fruitlessly trying to break his way into the flow of traffic.

"Joel, take that exit, we'll have to back track but it'll be faster. We're about three miles away from the restaurant, but highway traffic's backed up at least twenty minutes. How long—"

"Talk louder, I've got you on speaker," Libera said. "It looks like she's been having contractions all morning and thought it was Braxton—" his voice dropped off at Estelle's sharp yell.

"All right, we're moving faster now, can you hear me, Estelle?" Simone asked, voice clear with determination.

"Yes!" Estelle yelled, trying to breathe through another contraction.

"Listen to me— I will be there as soon as I can, all right? We're maybe fifteen minutes away now that we're off the highway."

"Please, Simone—"

"Christ!" Libera exclaimed, after being blocked in by another car, the oblivious driver waving absently in apology. "Okay, there's no way I can get through this traffic in time. I'm going to pull around back, and I want you to have Joel call Chuck right now and have them send an ambulance down here on silent."

They heard Simone's muffled voice relay the instructions, and a moment later, Estelle's loud voice was mixed with tears, saying, "No, the baby's coming now! Simone, I can't do this without you!"

Libera parked the car back where it was to begin with and opened the back, driver's side door.

"You listen to me, yes you can," Simone's voice said. "We are not that far away. You're both going to be fine. I'm right here. You can do this."

Estelle looked up at Libera, who was now kneeling in front of her. "He's right, honey. Look at me. We've got this."

She looked up and nodded. There was no longer shocked fear in his eyes, but a calm confidence that assured her everything would be fine.

She took a deep breath, and started to push, letting out a loud, guttural yell. Thirty seconds later, she relaxed her muscles, trying to shift her arms to support her upper body more evenly. She had barely five minutes to breathe before the next contraction started.

"Why aren't you here?" she yelled to Simone, panicked tears starting again.

"I'm sorry, baby. We're trying to get there. You're doing fine."

Holding onto the front seat, she let out another raspy cry and began pushing again as another contraction started.

Simone's voice came through the phone again. "We're almost there, Estelle. You're doing good."

Twenty minutes of pushing and breathing later, she relaxed again against the locked door, next contraction starting only a minute after the last.

"That's it," Libera said. "I can see her head, you're almost there."

"You're doing great, Estelle, you've got this." Simone's voice was louder, but still calm and assuring. She started to push again, weaker this time from exhaustion.

"Nothing's happening! Simone—"

"It's okay— you're doing great. No more yielding, Estelle."

But a dream. As he had intended, the line brought to her mind the image of Simone's face as he made his marriage vows. *Even if I'm not with you, I'm there for you.* She stopped, and, breathing quickly, leaned her head backwards for a moment against the window before bearing down again.

"That's it, Estelle, come on," Libera said.

With one last cry, she felt the baby leave her body, carefully guided into the world by Libera's hands, and heard Simone's joyous laugh as their daughter's cries came through speaker. She leaned her head back, euphoric tears streaming down her face. She looked out the windshield and gently laughed as Simone's Mercedes drove over the curb and into the back parking lot. Joel had barely pulled to a stop when Simone came rushing over, taking off his jacket and handing it to

Libera. He put his arm on his Patron's shoulder and watched as Libera finished wrapping the newborn in the silk-lined wool. Once his daughter was safe and warm, Simone opened the front passenger door and leaned over the seat to kiss his exhausted wife.

"Christ, you're amazing," he said, using his sleeve to dry her forehead.

She gave a weak laugh and leaned her head backwards against the glass. "Now they get here," she said with another weak laugh, watching the ambulance pull into the parking lot.

"She's perfect," Libera said, grinning and doing his best to clean her up with the sleeve of the jacket she was wrapped in. "Dark hair and dark eyes."

"Just like Daddy," Estelle said, with a loving hand to Simone's face.

"I'm sorry I wasn't here," he said, closing his eyes and leaning his head on hers.

"You're always here," she said, nuzzling her nose against his. As she laid back again, he put his arm between the window and her head, trying to make her as comfortable as was possible.

He stayed there, arm around her, even as the paramedics came over to cut the cord binding mother to infant. "Everything looks just fine," the paramedic said, finishing his examination of the baby in Libera's arms, and making sure Estelle was all right. "Do we have a name for her?"

"Matilda," Estelle said.

Libera walked over to Joel, and handed him the baby, saying, "Padrino." Joel took the baby and held her close for a few moments before walking her over to Simone. Estelle gave a teary laugh as Joel put Matilda into Simone's arms, watching Simone close his eyes and gently kiss his baby's forehead. He turned carefully and handed her to Estelle, unwrapping her just enough so that Matilda's soft skin was against her mother's chest.

One of the paramedics took a blanket from the ambulance and put it over mother and child, saying, "I was talking to Mr. Libera, and since she's almost a month early we want to get them both checked out at the hospital as soon as possible."

Simone nodded. "Thank you."

"It's our pleasure, Mr. Belvedere."

"Is it all right for us to drive her over?" Simone asked.

"It is, but you should probably leave that in the car," the paramedic said, nodding towards Simone's exposed weapon.

"Of course," he said, having forgotten about it. He closed the door and said, "Thank you again."

"You are sincerely welcome. Congratulations, Mr. and Mrs. Belvedere."

Libera closed the remaining car doors and pulled behind the ambulance escorting them to the hospital, siren blaring to clear traffic. As they pulled up in front of the hospital, Estelle asked, "How'd they get here so fast?"

Simone looked up and laughed, seeing Landini, Sandra and Carolyn waiting for them outside. Libera answered, "I called Al while the paramedics were looking over the baby, asked him to pick them up."

"Wait here, love," Simone said, taking off his holster, placing it gently on the front seat and walking into the hospital, returning a moment later with a volunteer pushing a wheelchair. Upon his return, Estelle wrapped Matilda tighter in the jacket and handed her to Simone, who walked her over to Carolyn. As he put the baby into Carolyn's arms, he whispered, "Madrina."

She smiled and leaned forward to kiss Simone's cheek. "Congratulations, Dad."

Grinning, he went to help Estelle out of the car, covered her back up with the blanket, and kissed her before allowing the volunteer to wheel her inside.

Chapter 72

After Estelle was comfortably settled in a bed nursing her child, Simone stood, shaking hands with Libera as he knocked and entered the room. "How is everyone?" Libera asked.

"Tired," Estelle said with an exhausted laugh as Simone sat back down on the bed, putting an arm around her. "Thank you, Mr. Libera," she said. "I don't know what I would have done—"

He waved his hand and said, "Not at all, my dear."

"Also," she said, blushing, "I'm sorry about your car."

"Which I will have detailed," Simone said, not looking up.

"I appreciate that," Libera said, laughing. "I was happy to do it."

There was a knock at the door, and a nurse came in. "Sorry to interrupt," she said. "I just wanted to make sure she was latching okay."

"She is!" Estelle chirped.

"Good! Sometimes when they're born early, there are some complications, but everything looks perfectly normal. The doctor wants to keep you both overnight, though, just to be sure."

"Can my husband stay with us?"

"Of course. We'll be moving you to an overnight room in a couple hours."

"I think she's asleep," Estelle said, moving the baby and adjusting her blanket. Should we take care of the paperwork now?"

"Absolutely! Excuse me, sir, can I get behind you for a moment?" she asked Libera, who was blocking the clipboard that she needed.

"Of course," he said, sitting down in the chair next to Estelle's bed and putting a gentle hand on the baby.

"All right. Baby's legal name?"

Estelle looked at Simone and nodded with a gentle smile, and he said, "Matilda Libera Belvedere. If that's all right, sir."

Libera looked up with a softhearted smile Estelle had never seen before, and nodded.

"That's so sweet!" the nurse said, typing it into the computer. "I'll get this printed out and have it sent up to your room once you're transferred so you can check the spelling, and both of you will need to sign it. I'll take her now and get her hand and foot prints, and then we'll bring in a bed for her."

"Thank you," Simone said.

"You are very welcome, sir." She leaned over for Estelle to hand Matilda to her. "I have to say, we've seen a lot of babies come in wearing grown up jackets and sweaters, but I think today was the first time I've ever seen a baby arrive in Armani."

Simone laughed and said, "Only the best for my girls."

As the beaming nurse carried Matilda to the nursery, Libera said, "I've got Landini watching the nursery, Joel will stay outside your room and Pagani's watching the front of the building."

"Thank you, sir."

"Not at all. I have to get back, but you call me if you need me. Both of you."

"Yes, sir," Simone said.

"Thank you so much, Mr. Libera," Estelle said, as he bent down to kiss her cheek.

Simone stood, shaking Libera's hand. Libera pulled him in for a quick hug, and whispered, "I'll put your gun in your car and lock it up."

Simone nodded and looked at his Patron for a moment, unsure of how to express his gratitude for what Libera had done.

Libera just smiled, patted his arm and said, "You're a good kid, Simone."

As Libera left, Simone smiled and turned to his wife. "Carolyn wanted me to let her know when he left."

Estelle laughed and laid her head back. "Thanks. I can't believe she's still so awkward around him..."

He leaned down and rested his forehead against hers. "I love you."

She placed a tired hand on his cheek and said, "I love you, too, Simone." He gently kissed her lips before rising. "I'll be back. Do you need anything?"

Estelle shook her head and said, "I'm okay. Thank you, love."

Simone stepped outside and walked over to the group of anxious people in the waiting room. Carolyn had called Estelle's father, who waved as Simone came over. He was surprised, however, to see that Mr. Presswood was sitting next to their friend and bartender, Stephen, who appeared to be more nervous than excited. Simone put his hand on Carolyn's shoulder and leaned down. "He's gone," he whispered.

"Oh, thank god," she said, standing. "Can we go in now?"

"Sure can."

Carolyn and Sandra both hugged Simone before hurrying off to Estelle's room. Mr. Presswood stood and shook Simone's hand. "Congratulations," he said, looking nearly as happy as Simone was.

"Thank you so much for being here," Simone said, putting his hands in his pockets and trying to give Stephen a calming glance.

"I wouldn't miss it for anything. Estelle's mother sends her regards."

"Regards, of course, starting with an F and ending in an off?"

Mr. Presswood patted Simone's arm and laughed. "You know it."

"You can go see her, if you'd like. Visitor limit is three, and I can step outside to smoke if you'd like to take my place for a little while."

As Estelle's father nodded and hurried off to see his daughter, Simone approached Stephen. "You all right?" he asked, shaking Stephen's hand.

"I am, yes," Stephen said, contradicting his appearance. "I wanted to see if you had a moment."

"Absolutely."

Simone gestured for Stephen to follow him, and he led them to a bench near a quiet patch of trees that was out of earshot from any passersby, but still within Pagani's sight. He lit a cigarette and offered one to Stephen, who declined.

"What can I do for you?"

"Nothing, actually. You— you know I appreciate everything you've done, right?"

"Of course."

"Estelle, too. You guys treat me like I'm an actual person... most people just ignore me until they need something..."

"You've been a good friend," Simone said, trying and failing to anticipate where this was going.

"I overheard something today, and I was going to tell you when you got back, but I didn't think it should wait..."

"Oh?"

"Libera asked me to find a few new cocktails to try out this weekend, so I was at the library where Estelle used to work."

Simone tilted his head in surprise and took another drag from his cigarette, but said nothing, wanting Stephen to set the pace himself, rather than feel rushed into forgetting something important.

"I was looking at the cocktail books, and I heard them a few aisles away. They didn't know I was there... And they were arguing with each other. The first guy was telling the other to 'give up and let it go.' He said that it didn't work the first time they tried it, and it wouldn't work this time. And then the other guy said that it only didn't work because they hired the wrong people, and then said, 'Belvedere's the problem, remember?' Then a couple kids ran past and they left. I only saw one of them, though."

"And that's all they said?"

"While I was there, yes."

"Do you know who it was?"

"I didn't at first, but then I went to check out the books I found, and the first guy was the guy at the help desk. His name's—"

"Paul?"

"Yeah— you know him?"

"Of him. You're absolutely sure?"

"I am."

"And you didn't see the second guy?"

Stephen shook his head. "His voice sounded familiar, but I couldn't place it. I hated bothering you with work today, but I was worried that waiting would be..."

Simone nodded. "You're right. Thank you. Did either of them see you?"

"I don't think so. Even if they did, I doubt they'd know who I am."

"Can I see your phone?"

Stephen obliged, and Simone added his number to the contacts. "Call me if you hear or see anything else, or if you think they suspect you heard anything, all right?"

"Will do. Sorry again, I know work is the last thing you would have wanted on your mind right now."

Simone put out the end of his cigarette and said, "Not at all. You've been a big help. More than you know. Going to stop in to see Estelle? I can call Libera and let him know you'll be a few minutes late."

"Thanks, I'd like that."

Smiling, Simone nodded towards the entrance and waited until Stephen was inside to dial Libera's number. "Hello, sir. Stephen's running late. He stopped by; had an interesting anecdote to share. I'm going to have Joel ride back with him— we need to look into what he said as soon as possible... Thank you, sir."

He walked back into the hospital and approached Joel, who was sitting outside of Estelle's room talking to Sandra. "Hey, sorry to interrupt."

"It's okay, boss."

"Do you mind riding back with Stephen?"

"Sure—"

"Thanks," he said, trying to stem any questions in front of Sandra. Joel stood and kissed his wife's cheek, saying, "Back soon."

She nodded and smiled to Simone before going back into Estelle's room. Simone leaned closer to Joel to avoid being overheard and said, "Once you're in the car, have him tell you what he told me, then pass it along to Libera. Let me know what he wants done."

"Will do."

"I'll send him out to you. Thanks, Joel."

Simone walked back up to Estelle's bed and sat down next to her, kissing her cheek as she rested her head on his shoulder. He looked up at Stephen and said, "Mind giving Joel a lift back?"

"Not at all."

"Thanks. He's out front."

He came forward and shook Simone's hand again. "Thank you. Congratulations, both of you."

As Stephen left, Simone put his arm around Estelle and said, "Sorry I took so long."

"S'okay," she mumbled, closing her eyes and brushing her cheek against him.

The nurse came back in carrying Matilda, with an assistant pulling in a bed for her. "Here you go," she said, handing her to Simone. He gave a gentle smile, looking down at the sleeping child that was changing their lives with every second. He had never felt so complete, or so mortal. Realizing that everyone was watching him, he looked up at Mr. Presswood and nodded towards him. He carefully placed her in her grandfather's arms, and then put his arm back around Estelle.

After an hour of happy chatter between Estelle and her father, Simone looked at her and asked, "You need anything?"

"Water," she said, looking up at him. "And can you find out when I can take a shower?"

"Of course," he said, kissing her again and standing.

"I'll go with you," Carolyn said, walking out with him.

After speaking to the nurse about the things Estelle needed, Carolyn stopped him several feet away from the room and said, "Hey, I'm sorry I was such a jerk in the beginning."

He laughed and said, "That's okay."

"No, it's not. Everybody treats you that way, and I shouldn't have judged you…"

"You're just protective of Estelle— it's nothing I'd want to change."

She came in for a brief hug, and then tapped his shoulder and nodded behind him.

"Thanks," he said, turning to face Libera as she scurried to Estelle's room to relay the instructions and keep her distance from her past lover.

"Everything all right?" he asked, looking at Libera's furrowed brow.

"Yeah," Libera said before leaning in and saying, "Good thinking sending Joel back with him, I want to sit down with you, Al and Jim tomorrow morning so we can get Paul and Ethan straightened out."

He could have called for that… "Of course."

"That's not why I'm here."

"I don't understand."

"I brought Joel back with me, he's out front."

"Okay…"

"I'm not trying to make this decision for you— but it's time you made it yourself."

"Sir, what's—"

"Angela."

Simone's posture stiffened; even his eyes seemed to tense at the mention of his mother's name. His tone was much sharper than he usually used with his Patron, but he had already guessed what Libera was about to say, and his anger at feeling cornered was taking precedence over his normally well-chosen platitudes. "What about her?"

"She's out front with Joel."

"Fuck," Simone breathed, staring down angrily at the taupe tile.

"I know. I'd be pissed, too. But I brought her here under one condition."

"Oh?" Simone snapped, still struggling to keep his manners intact.

"Regardless of which decision you make, I'm putting her on a plane and sending her home tonight. Even if you do agree to see her. If you say no, she's not to contact you, in any capacity, again. If you do, it's your call."

"I need to ask Estelle. It's not just me she wants to see."

Libera nodded. "Call Joel and let him know, one way or the other. I'll stay here until she leaves."

Simone watched him walk towards the pink, plastic chairs in the waiting room before going into see Estelle, taking the moment to go back to his calm, unreadable expression.

"Hey, I wondered where you went off to," Estelle said, looking up at him. "What's wrong?" she asked, narrowing her eyes.

"Nothing, why?"

"You have that look."

"The look?" he asked, laughing as he checked on his daughter sleeping in the bed the orderly had wheeled in.

"Give us a minute?" she asked, looking up at Carolyn.

Carolyn nodded, looked at Sandra and said, "Want to help me track down some coffee?"

Sandra nodded and looked to Mr. Presswood, who said, "Sure thing."

Once they had gone, Estelle looked up at Simone, who still had his back to her.

"Simone?"

"My mother's here."

Estelle scooted up in the bed, wincing. "What?"

He turned and sat down next to her. "Libera brought her. He's sending her back to Italy tonight either way."

"And if you don't want to see her?"

"She's not to contact us again."

"You said in Boston—"

"I know. And I still think it's the right thing to do. It's just a lot harder with her here."

Matilda started to cry, and Simone walked over to her, taking her into his arms.

"She's probably hungry, it's been a while."

He brought her over to Estelle and sat down next to her, gently handing her over to his wife. As Matilda began to nurse, he said, "You need to be okay with this, too."

Smiling at the rapidly calming infant, she said, "I just want what's best for you."

He nodded and took out his phone, taking a deep breath as he dialed Joel's number. After what seemed like the longest twenty seconds of his life, he said, "Wait ten minutes, then send her in."

"Why wait?" Estelle asked as he ended the call.

He kissed her forehead and said, "Because this is the first time I've been alone with the two of you."

Estelle watched Simone gently stroke Matilda's feathery hair for most of the ten minutes he had requested and finally said, "She looks just like you." His dark eyes brightened as he looked up, and she felt warm tears start to run down her cheek. "Sorry," she said, waving her hand. "Hormones."

"Don't be sorry," he said, brushing the stray hair out of her eyes. "I'm the one that should be sorry. I've been much more absent today than I wanted to be."

"You've been wonderful," she said, moving Matilda's sleeping head higher up so she could readjust her gown. She leaned forward and kissed his lips, and as he touched his forehead to hers, they heard a soft tap at the door. He looked into Estelle's reassuring eyes for a moment before looking over at the door and slowly standing, hands in his pockets. He looked up at the woman standing across the room, neither showing any hint of emotion.

"It's good to see you again, Simone."

He nodded and looked away for a moment, and then, unable to honestly reciprocate her words, turned to his wife and said, "Estelle, this is Angela."

"It's so good to meet you," Angela said, coming a few steps closer.

"You as well," Estelle said, taking in the features that were so different from Simone.

Her graying hair was much lighter than Simone's, along with her pale brown eyes. She didn't have Simone's angled jaw or full lips, and she was a little more than half a foot shorter than he was. As different as they looked, they carried themselves in much the same way. Her hands were nervously balled up, clutching tightly to her purse, just as Estelle knew that Simone's were in his pockets. They were both very sure of themselves, and completely unsure of how to handle the circumstances.

"You've done very well for yourself," she said, looking at Simone.

"I have," he tensely agreed. "Mr. Libera's been very good to me, as has Estelle."

"I can see that," she said, looking from Simone to the baby.

"Matilda," he said gently, looking down at his daughter. He looked up and said, "How'd you know to come today?"

"I asked Ben to call me when she was born, and he did. That's when he made his proposal to talk to you."

Simone nodded and looked at her for a moment, determined to not be the one to speak first. He was willing to forgive her, but he wasn't going to coddle her through an apology.

"Last time I saw you," she started, taking another step towards him, "I didn't handle things the way I should have— though that's not anything new..."

"No, it's not," he said, not breaking his fierce eye contact.

"I've been blaming you for a lot of things, and none of them were your fault."

He said nothing, but sat on the edge of Estelle's bed.

"I always seemed to find a way to tell myself that I stayed for you, and that I left because of you. But I didn't. Those were my decisions, all of which were made because I did what I thought was easiest. God knows, if I'd have taken you with me, you wouldn't..."

"I wouldn't be where I am now," he said, finally letting go of his resentment. "And I wouldn't trade this for anything."

Estelle put her hand on Simone's arm, giving him a teary smile that he couldn't see.

"We're just very different people, with very different places to be."

Angela smiled and said, "That we are."

She stepped forward and put her hand on Simone's shoulder. "I am sorry, Simone."

"I know. But it's all worked out for the best."

"I agree. I am so happy for you," she said. "Both of you."

Simone stood, hands back in his pockets and said, "Thank you."

She took a deep breath as she looked into his eyes and said, "Take good care of them."

"Always."

She nodded and then looked at Estelle and said, "Thank you for taking the time to see me."

Estelle nodded and said, "Thanks for coming by."

Angela turned and walked towards the door, stopping at the threshold. "Goodbye, Simone."

Chapter 73

After she had gone, Libera stepped in and said, "Nurse said they want to move you upstairs."

"Thank you," Estelle said, smiling up at him.

"You okay?" he asked, looking at Simone.

He nodded and said, "Thank you, sir."

"Good. Eight, tomorrow morning. Should give you time to get back before she's discharged."

"I'll be there."

He came over to kiss Estelle's cheek and the baby's forehead, and then left the room, sending in those that were still waiting.

Sandra came over and hugged Estelle and said, "I have to go pick up Mya, but we'll come see you tomorrow, if that's all right."

"I'd love that, thank you."

"I have to take off too," Mr. Presswood said, waving his hand. "Let me know when you get home tomorrow, I have a few things for her."

"Thanks, Dad," Estelle said, looking up at him. "Tell Mom I said hi."

Simone chuckled and turned away from Estelle, and her father said, "I'm sure she sends her regards." He laughed and patted Simone's arm and said, "I'll see you tomorrow?"

"Yes, sir," Simone said, avoiding Estelle and Carolyn's inquiring looks.

"Want me to get you guys some food while they're moving you?" Carolyn asked.

"I'm not really hungry," Estelle said, "But you two should go get food, then by the time you get back, I should be moved and cleaned up."

"I'm not leaving you," Simone said, giving her an exasperated look.

She laughed and said, "The third infantry division is surrounding the premises. I think we'll be okay."

"I know you'll be okay, I just don't want you to be alone."

"Not to gang up on you or anything," Carolyn said, "But she's right. You need to take care of you, too."

Defeated, he smiled and nodded. "Text me if you need anything, all right?"

"I will, Prince Charming."

He laughed and followed Carolyn out of the room as two new nurses came in to take them upstairs. There were a few minutes of verifying Estelle's information, followed quickly by several minutes of the nurses cooing over Matilda, before they started to wheel Estelle, holding on tightly to her daughter, in her bed to the elevator. She nodded to Joel so he knew to follow, and as they entered the elevator she said, "Thanks for hanging around, Joel."

"Anytime," he said, patting her shoulder.

As they reached the seventh floor of the hospital, she said, "Do you mind texting him the new room number?"

"Not at all."

"Do you want us to take her to the nursery so you can have some time for a shower?" the nurse asked.

Estelle looked at Joel, who gave a gentle nod.

"He can stay with her."

"Is he family?" the nurse asked, turning into room 729 and pushing the bed into place.

"Of course, he is."

She reached out for Joel's hand and gave it a soft squeeze.

"That's perfectly fine," the nurse said, pulling blankets out of the cabinet. "Try standing and walking around for a few minutes to make sure you're not lightheaded, and call us if you need anything."

"Thank you."

Estelle handed Matilda to Joel, who sat down in the chair next to her bed, and then steadied herself on the nurse's arm as she stood up. "You okay?" The nurse asked, looking for signs of wooziness.

"I'm good," she said, laughing and stretching.

"Good. We'll be out at the desk if you need anything."

She nodded and turned to Joel. "You sure you don't mind?"

"Not a bit, Estelle. Not a bit."

She slowly made her way to the bathroom, turning back and looking at Joel's grin as he looked at the newborn.

Chapter 74

After a slow, but very warm shower, she put on the fresh gown the nurse had laid on the sink for her and came back out to see Simone sitting on her bed, quietly talking with Joel, who was still lovingly rocking Matilda. "You guys better not be talking shop with that baby around," she teased. "You never know what she'll say."

Simone chuckled and walked over to her, putting his arms around her. "How are you feeling?"

"I'm not going to lie, I've felt better," she laughed, kissing his cheek before gingerly climbing back into bed.

"Carolyn said she'd come by tomorrow before heading into work."

Estelle nodded and leaned her head back against her pillow.

"Gianni will be here in the morning when I leave, hopefully I won't be gone very long."

"What's your backup?"

"If I can't be there, Fabbri can take you home, and I'll meet you there, if that's all right."

"That's fine. Do what you need to."

"I'm going to try and get back before they discharge you, though. They guessed around three tomorrow afternoon."

She nodded and closed her eyes, but just as she began to tell Simone she wanted to get some sleep, a nurse came in to check on them.

"Did you want her to stay in the room with you tonight for feedings, or did you want her in the nursery?"

Estelle shook her head, "No, we won't be bottle feeding for some time, still. I want her here."

"Perfect. All of the tests came back fine, so you'll be discharged tomorrow afternoon."

"I was a little concerned about her weight, it seemed low—"

"Just because she was a little early. She's feeding perfectly fine, so the doctor isn't worried."

"Good," Estelle said, glancing over at Simone, whose focus was on Matilda.

"Did you have any questions, Dad?" the nurse asked, pouting her lips and perfecting her posture.

"Not just yet," he said without looking up.

"Hit the button if you need us," the nurse said, still looking at Simone, rather than Estelle.

"Thank you," Estelle said, a tinge of jealousy coming through her voice at the nurse's obvious interest in Simone.

Simone looked over at the change in Estelle's tone, and after the nurse had gone, he asked, "Did I miss something?"

"It's one thing to have women hitting on you while we're out shopping together, I can live with that. But she needs to lay the hell off."

"I don't think—"

"Yeah, she was," Joel said, laughing and setting Matilda in her bed next to Estelle's. "I should get home, see if Sandra needs anything. Portelli's outside the room, and I'll be back to pick you up at seven thirty."

"Thanks, Joel," Simone said, standing.

"Anytime."

Simone took out his clip to pay him, but Joel put his hand on Simone's shoulder and said, "Not for today."

He hugged Simone for a brief moment and said, "Sono felice per te, fratello."

Simone nodded and watched him leave. "You okay?" Estelle asked.

"I am."

"You look worried."

"Just tired," he lied.

There was no way he could tell her about the meeting the next day, and he didn't dream of giving her something else to worry about.

"You suck at lying to me, but you're cute so I'll let it go."

Laughing, he walked over to Matilda, who had started to fuss again.

"Mind handing her to me?" Estelle asked, starting to feel lightheaded from exhaustion.

Simone smiled and went to retrieve Matilda, helping Estelle to position her for nursing again. Estelle moved a touch to the left, giving Simone room to sit beside her. He put his arm back around her, and kissed her forehead as she made herself comfortable against his chest.

After several minutes he realized both mother and daughter were drifting off to sleep, and once he was sure that Matilda had stopped suckling and was just resting, he placed her safely on her back in the smaller bed and covered Estelle up with another blanket. Once he had retaken his place beside her, he started trying to link together Paul's arguments in the library, his gambling with Ethan and the hit at the Garage, as he knew he would have to do in the morning for Libera and Duvall.

Chapter 75

After several hours of sleeping, feedings, and silently giggling at Simone learning to change Matilda's diaper, Estelle awoke the next morning to Sandra's hand on her shoulder.

"Good morning," Estelle whispered, surprised to have a visitor so early.

She looked over at Simone sleeping beside her, only partially on his side with his arm above her head. She nodded towards him and whispered, "That cannot be comfortable."

Sandra laughed and shook her head in agreement. Giving in to Mya's protests at being held, she set her down on the floor, but was too slow to stop the toddler from immediately running over and starting to poke Simone's side. "Uncle Belvy, wake up!"

After the third poke he jerked awake, and once he realized what was going on, he started to laugh. "Sorry!" Sandra said, as he helped Mya in her determination to climb up on him.

"No, it's all right," he said, smiling at Mya's hug. "What time is it?"

"About six thirty. Joel thought you might want to change before your meeting, so I stopped and grabbed something for you. I hope that's okay."

"Of course, thank you." He leaned his head back for a moment before looking over at Matilda, who was still asleep on the other side of Estelle.

Sandra gestured towards the counter at the bag sitting on top of one of the suits he kept ready for travel. "I grabbed a few things for you as well, and something for the baby to wear home."

"Thank you so much!" Estelle said, holding her hand out. Sandra stepped forward and took her hand. "Joel said you didn't eat last night, you feeling like eating something? I can go get you guys something, so you can eat together before they have to leave."

"I am starving," Estelle said, looking over at Simone.

"That'd be great. Thanks, Sandra."

"Oh, honey, it's not a problem. Want anything in particular?"

Estelle shook her head. "Just something warm."

Simone nodded and said, "And caffeinated."

Sandra laughed and tried to pick up Mya, who attached herself to Simone's arm.

"She can stay," he said, surprised that such a small person could have such a tight grip.

"That would be easier. Are you sure?"

"Of course."

Estelle nodded and helped Simone free his arm. "It's the least we can do," she said, smiling at Mya making herself comfortable between them.

Sandra nodded and kissed her daughter's head and said, "Be good, Mya."

As she left, Carolyn came in and said, "They really do grow fast, don't they?"

Simone laughed and said, "This is Mya."

"Joel and Sandra's daughter?"

He nodded and reached a quick arm out to prevent Mya from climbing on Estelle's lap.

"You guys need anything?"

Estelle said, "I don't think so, thanks, though."

"You eaten yet?"

"That's where Sandra's going," Estelle said, smiling at everyone's concern.

She started to stand, but as she did, the nurse from the night before came in with a new nurse and said, "Morning, guys. This is Jen, she's taking over for me."

Jen waved and went over to Matilda to scan her tiny bracelet, along with Estelle's so she could start to take their vitals. The other nurse looked Simone over, pouting her lips again as her mind continued to objectify him and said, "You guys have any questions?"

Trying to hold back a small laugh he said, "No, I don't think so."

She looked at him for another moment and then said, "All right, you guys take care."

Simone nodded and after she had left, Carolyn looked at Estelle and said, "She was subtle."

Estelle gave Simone an angry look and held up her hand towards Carolyn. "See?"

Jen laughed as she handed a fussing Matilda to Estelle. "Happens more than you'd think."

"Really?" Estelle asked. "You'd think this would be the one place you wouldn't have to worry about poachers."

"I know," Jen said, walking to the door. "I don't get it, either."

As Matilda began to nurse, Mya crawled over and leaned against Estelle.

"How come doesn't she eat like me?"

"She doesn't have any teeth yet," Estelle said, smiling down at her.

Sandra knocked and came in, handing a cup of coffee to Simone.

"Thank you," he said, taking a grateful sip and standing.

"All right," Carolyn said. "I've got to head in. Call me if you need anything."

"Thanks!" Estelle chirped.

"I'll walk you out," Simone said, following her.

As they approached the elevator, he said, "Could you wait until she's home to tell people at the library?"

"Yeah— is something wrong?"

"No," he said, only somewhat honestly. "I'd just like to make sure it stays that way."

"Sure thing," Carolyn said, mistaking his concern over Paul for new-dad worries.

"Thanks, Carolyn. For everything."

She nodded and stepped into the elevator, and as he reentered the room, he saw that Mya had taken over his side of the bed, lying flat on her tummy with her feet in the air, gently holding onto Matilda's hand.

"You should eat," Estelle said.

"I can wait for you."

"I can eat once she's asleep. You're going to be late if you don't."

Sandra handed him a breakfast sandwich and said, "Do what she says, and you'll live to see the next one."

He laughed and sat down in the chair next to the bed and started to eat, only then realizing how hungry he was. Once Matilda had fallen asleep, Sandra took the baby into her arms and sat on the edge of the bed, smiling at Mya, who had come over to stare some more at her.

"She looks like Uncle Belvy, doesn't she, Mya?"

"Uh-huh."

Simone looked over at them, and then at Estelle, who was happily smiling at him as she ate. "Dad said so, too."

There was a tap at the door, and Joel smiled and came over to Sandra, kissing her and patting Mya's head.

"Is it time already?" Simone asked.

"Nah, I'm a little early," Joel said.

As Simone headed into the bathroom to change, Joel said, "How ya feeling?"

"Better than last night," Estelle laughed. "Just a little tired, still."

"That nurse ever calm down?" he asked, laughing as he took Simone's seat.

"No," she said, becoming immediately irritated.

"What nurse?" Sandra asked.

Estelle just shook her head and took another bite, so Joel said, "Late shift girl, had the hots for Simone."

Sandra laughed. "You can't be jealous, can you? Simone's never looked at another woman."

"Normally, I don't mind. He doesn't even notice it most of the time. It's just the principle. I clearly just had his baby, maybe wait a few days before hitting on him, that's all I've got to say."

"You have got to let that go," Simone said, chuckling as he came back into the room.

"I will not," she said, looking up at him as he put his pocket watch into place.

Simone looked up at her and said, "I'm sorry I have to leave." His voice kept its normal, pleasant tone, but his eyes were sad and narrowed, as if the thought of leaving them for work was a physical ailment taking hold of him.

"I know, baby. We'll be all right. Won't we?" she cooed, putting a hand on Matilda, who had already fallen back asleep in Sandra's arms.

Simone's sadness immediately dissipated, and was replaced by a comforting feeling of completion at the sight of his wife smiling over at their daughter. As she looked up from Matilda, their eyes met, and after a long moment, he walked over and leaned his forehead against hers, closing his eyes as he said, "I love you, Estelle."

"I love you, too."

He gently kissed her lips before turning and putting his hand on Matilda's chest and leaning down to kiss the top of her head.

"I love you, Simone, but I swear to god, you wake her up and I'll have to get Al in here."

He started to laugh as he said, "Dually noted." He pocketed his money clip, phone and cigarettes, and nodded once to Joel. "Ready?"

"Yep."

Joel started for the door, and as Simone went to follow, he turned again, hating that he was risking missing their baby coming home. Estelle looked into his eyes for a moment, and said, "We'll be fine, baby. Just focus on what you need to do, and we'll be here when you're done."

Simone nodded again, finally turning and following Joel out of the room. He waved in acknowledgment to Gianni, who was sitting outside Estelle's room, and as they got into the elevator, Joel said, "How're you doing?"

He tried for a moment to come up with the words to express how content he was, but failed miserably, only being able to give a soft laugh.

"That's about right," Joel said, putting his hand on Simone's shoulder. "Took me about a week and a half before I could really put any words to it."

Simone lit a cigarette as he got into the passenger seat of his Mercedes, and they were almost to Libera's when he said, "How do you do it?"

"Do what?"

"Find time for everyone."

"I don't."

"Oh, that's very comforting, thank you," Simone said, half-smiling.

Joel started to laugh and said, "No, what I mean is, there just isn't time for everybody. Some nights I know I'm not going to make it home for dinner, and other nights I know I can tell you to fuck off so I can see my wife and kid. It's just about finding the right balance and accepting that something will have to wait for tomorrow."

Simone nodded as they pulled into the lot and said, "I have to get my gun out of the trunk, I'll meet you inside. Mind letting them know I'm on my way?"

Joel handed him the keys and patted Simone's shoulder again before making his way into the restaurant. Simone walked around to the back of the car and unlocked the trunk, standing between the bumper and the tree Joel had parked in front of. He leaned forward and picked up his Taurus and the magazine lying next to it, and as he pushed the magazine into the gun, he heard a twig snap next to him. Without moving his head, he glanced to either side of him, and saw the shadow of someone standing on his right. In one movement he cocked his weapon and stood, aiming at the man standing next to him with his arms raised in surrender, but quickly lowered it.

"What the hell are you doing here?" he asked, inclining his head forward as Paul lowered his arms.

"I need to talk to you."

"Is that so?"

"I have to make this fast— no one can see me talking to you—"

"And who exactly is no one?"

"Look, I'll tell you whatever you want, but you have to promise to let me go."

"I should put a fucking bullet in you right here for what you did to Estelle," Simone said, rage starting to take precedence in his mind.

"I know, but—"

"Oh, is this the part where I pretend like I don't know that it was you that tried to have me and my associates killed?"

Paul said nothing, but nodded and looked down at the ground.

"Yeah, I thought so."

"It— it wasn't my idea."

"But it was your money, wasn't it?"

Paul nodded again, still not looking at Simone.

"I have to ask, what exactly did you think that would accomplish?"

"It shouldn't have happened. He talked me into it— I swear. He knew how pissed off I was that Estelle chose you and he just fed off that until he had me all worked up and I agreed to it— I didn't even think it would happen until I was actually handing him the cash, but by then I couldn't back out. And then he made me go back and check on them while it was happening— once you were shot I ran and told him we needed to back off. He left town for a few days— made me stay so people wouldn't—"

"Am I supposed to feel sorry for you?" Simone asked, taking a step closer.

"No— this just needs to stop. I know I've messed up, but I'm in too far and I just want it to stop. I know I've done some shitty things, but I really do care about Estelle, and I know how important you are to her, and if this keeps going—"

Paul stopped talking and looked around nervously.

"If WHAT keeps going?" Simone asked, picking up his empty holster and slamming the trunk closed.

"I don't know what his plan is, I just know that he's going to try again."

"All right. I'm about to ask you a question, and I think it's important you know that I already know the answer to this question, but I need to hear you say it, understood?"

Paul nodded, and Simone said, "Who have you been working with?"

Paul looked away, not speaking.

"I'm only going to ask one more time," Simone said, taking off his jacket and putting on his holster.

"Ethan," Paul whispered, barely loud enough to for Simone to hear.

Simone started to nod. "Ethan who?"

"Maxwell. Ethan Maxwell."

Simone gave a short laugh and put his gun into his holster, buttoning his jacket over it. "Thank you."

Paul nodded again and turned as if here were about to leave, but Simone put his hands into his pockets and said, "Exactly where do you think you're going?"

Turning on his heels, he backtracked back to Simone, still glancing around, afraid to be caught. "Your phone," Simone ordered.

"What?"

"Hand me your phone."

Paul hesitated for a breath, but obeyed. Simone took it from Paul's trembling hand and said, "I'm adding my number to your contacts, under my initials." After he entered the numbers, he hit call, and held up his own phone. "Now, I'm going to expect that when I call this number," he started, gesturing to the call he was getting from Paul's phone, "That you're going to be the one answering. Understand?"

"I do."

"I also expect that you're going to be fully cooperating and handing me the information I need when I make that call. Understand?"

"I do."

"Good. I don't think I need to explain what Ethan would do if he found out you were talking to me today, do I?"

"N-no, Mr. Belvedere."

"Good. Then I don't need to explain that MY solution would be exactly the same, do I?"

"No."

"Good. I'll be in touch."

Simone watched Paul run to his car and drive away before locking his own Mercedes and making his way into the restaurant, fifteen minutes later than he wanted to be. As he walked up to Libera's table, Duvall gave Simone a glance of disdain before saying, "Mr. Belvedere's decided to grace us with his presence, I see."

"My apologies for the delay, Don Libera," Simone said, ignoring Duvall and looking directly at his Patron.

"What kept you?"

"Long story, but I'm not sure now's the best time for it, respectfully, sir."

Libera nodded in acknowledgement and motioned for Simone to be seated on his left, between himself and Joel, who had pulled up a chair to the edge of the table. Landini nodded across the table at him, and Libera said, "All right. We've all been told what Stephen was kind enough to relay to Simone—"

"Are we sure that this boy can be trusted?" Duvall said, glancing at Simone before making fierce eye contact with Libera.

"Absolutely," Libera said, eyes warning Duvall to watch his tone.

"I simply mean, that if this boy is in a menial service position—"

"Stephen is in the position he wants to be in," Simone interrupted, his loyalty overtaking his manners. "He's been offered a promotion multiple times and declined, because he likes doing what he does. He came to us as a gesture of loyalty, and that should be respected."

"I agree," Libera said, giving Simone the same look he had just given Duvall. "Paul and Ethan are definitely working together."

"And what proof do we have that this is Ethan, beyond coincidental numbers?"

"It's him," Simone said, trying to avoid telling Duvall about his conversation with Paul until the right moment.

"That is a good point," Libera said, looking to Landini. "Have you looked at it?"

"I have, yes, and I don't see how it could be anyone else. I've taken jobs from you before with a lot less to go on, and it's never been wrong yet."

"There's always a first time, isn't there, Mr. Landini?"

Landini took a deep breath and began to tap his thumb on the table in front of him. "I suppose, yes."

"Look," Simone started, turning to face Libera more directly. "We need to get this taken care of before anything else happens."

"You seem very convinced that something is imminent— I'm hoping this is more than burgeoning fatherhood?" Duvall asked.

Landini looked to Joel and mouthed, "Oh, shit," before leaning back against the booth, doing his best to avoid looking at anyone.

"Leave my family out of this," Simone snapped.

"I know that this is a stressful time for the three of you, but you really need to look at this objectively. I'm sure your wife and daughter would also benefit—"

In the next instant Simone was on his feet with Joel next to him, hands tight around Simone's shoulders. Leaning in so only Simone could hear, Joel whispered, "Don't take the bait, boss."

Libera looked up at Simone, and said, "That's enough," before looking to Duvall and finishing, "Both of you."

Duvall nodded politely, but Simone remained standing even after Joel had retaken his seat, glaring at Duvall, who said, "Why, then, Mr. Belvedere, are you so sure?"

"Because Paul just told me himself in the parking lot before I came in here."

Landini started to laugh to himself as he shook his head before looking up at Simone, who said, "I apologize, Don Libera. I assumed this was information you'd like to be given on your own, but clearly my word isn't good enough for everyone here."

Libera nodded and gave him another furious stare, frustrated with the flared pride and tempers surrounding the table. "What else did he say?"

Simone resumed his seat and said, "Paul just flipped on him. At this point, I'm not even sure if he's more scared of us or Ethan. He admitted they arranged the hit at the Garage, and he admitted that he gave Ethan the money. He also said that Ethan's planning to strike again soon, and I think it would be wise to try to nip this now."

"And why is he telling us all of this now?" Libera asked.

"He tried to make it seem like he was doing it because he cared about Estelle, but he just wants out. He can't handle it."

"And speaking of him caring about Estelle," Duvall started, eyes narrowing, "None of this vendetta you seem to be carrying against Paul is related to his attachment to her, correct?"

"If you don't leave her the fuck out of this, I swear to fucking god, Duvall I will—" Simone started, volume rising with every word, before feeling Libera's hand collide hard against his cheekbone. Landini and Joel both looked away, not wanting to instigate Libera's temper or bruise Simone's pride any further.

"That's enough," Libera barked, instantly quelling Simone. "Jim, he's right. Neither Simone's nor Paul's caring for Estelle is relevant anymore. Paul's just a coward, and that's something we can work with."

Libera pointed to Landini. "I want security increased at both casinos and the restaurant, starting now."

"Yes, sir."

He looked back to Simone and asked, "Can you get him to talk again?"

"I believe so, yes."

"Give it a day to see if he comes back to you. If he doesn't, then go to him."

"Yes, sir."

Libera waved his hand, dismissing everyone at the table, and as Simone stood, Duvall said, "My apologies, if I offended you, Mr. Belvedere."

Simone gave a humorless laugh and said, "And mine to you, Mr. Duvall." He turned, eyes still narrowed, and followed Landini and Joel over to the bar, accepting the scotch Landini poured for him. "Thanks."

Landini nodded and took a sip from his own glass before saying, "You have got to stop biting every time he leads it out for you."

Nodding, Simone just said, "I know," and took another sip.

"How's Estelle?"

Simone's expression finally softened and he said, "Mostly tired and sore."

"I should think so," Landini said, laughing. "You guys need anything?"

"I don't even know," Simone said honestly. "It's all been such a blur."

Landini nodded behind Simone, before leading Joel to the other end of the bar as Libera came over.

"I'd like to apologize for losing my temper," Simone said, pouring Libera a glass of scotch.

"You two have always clashed, this is nothing new."

"Even still…"

"Just try to keep it civil next time, all right?"

"Yes, sir," Simone said, momentarily internalizing his anger that Duvall wasn't being chastised as he was.

"You think we'll have any problems from Paul?"

"No, he's too scared to create any problems. It's Ethan we need to be worried about."

"I agree."

Libera reached up to Simone's head, thumb behind his right ear and leaned his head back, looking at the bruise forming. After several seconds, he gently tapped his hand against Simone's cheek and said, "Sorry, Simone," before dropping his hand back down and picking up his glass. As he took a sip, his eyes were sad and narrowed, and he was doing his best to avoid looking at Simone.

Simone looked at him for a moment, confused at the first apology he'd ever received from his Patron after being physically reprimanded. "It's— it's all right, sir."

Libera sighed and nodded as he walked away, still looking angry with himself. Simone leaned against the bar for a moment, finishing the scotch in his glass and setting it down on the polished wood, running his thumb over the rim of the glass.

Everything really is different now.

Chapter 76

An hour later, Simone and Joel were walking back to Estelle's room from the elevator when Simone stopped dead in his tracks. "Boss?" Joel inquired, stopping a few feet ahead of him.

Simone just shook his head and then turned around, heading back towards the elevator. Joel hastened after him, and only barely made it into the elevator with him. "What's wrong?" Joel asked, shooting Simone a nervous glance.

"Just need a cigarette," Simone said, hands balled up in his pockets.

"Okay," Joel said, watching Simone's mental struggle.

The second they were outside the building, Simone was already lighting his cigarette, and as he sat down on the bench where he had talked with Stephen the evening before, he leaned forward, elbows on his knees, head in one of his hands.

"Talk me through it," Joel said, sitting next to him.

"What if I'm like him?"

"Who, Libera?"

Simone shook his head again. "My... biological... father."

Joel sighed and put his hand on Simone's shoulder. "Look, boss. You know I knew Vinny. Not well, but about as well as anybody really cared to. I've seen you at your best, and I've seen you at your worst, and I can tell you, without a doubt in my mind that you are nothing like him."

"My temper—"

"Is nothing like his. You know your triggers, you know your limits, and you know your weaknesses. That man had no limits and only had weaknesses. People were only important to him as long as he could use them to get what he needed, and that included you."

"I've been so caught up with everything happening so quickly— and now that it's slowed down—"

"You panicked."

Simone nodded. "I don't know why."

Joel put his hand back on Simone's shoulder. "Because that's what we do. Fifty percent of parenting is guessing, the other fifty percent is panicking."

Simone laughed and said, "How has Estelle stayed so calm?"

"Because she knows you're there, and she knows that Sandra and I are here, and if you'd stop overanalyzing everything, you'd see that, too."

Smiling and nodding, Simone put out the end of his cigarette and said, "I know you guys are here. It's me being here that has me worried."

"You," Joel started, putting his hand on Simone's shoulder, "Are gonna be great. Really. You're just thinking too much."

"Shocking," Simone said sarcastically, rising to his feet.

"Ready now?"

Simone nodded. "Ready."

Chapter 77

Three hours later, Simone was unlocking the front door of their home, and as he held the door open for Estelle to carry in Matilda, he put a hand on his wife's shoulder, gently kissing her. She smiled and nuzzled her cheek against his, before looking down at their daughter and saying "Welcome home, Matilda."

As she eased herself down onto the couch she said, "Hey, Simone?"

"Yes, love?"

"Where are we going to put her?"

He looked around for a moment as he set the car seat on the round table and said, "That, my dear, is an excellent question."

"Five people, at least, asked us if we needed anything, and neither of us, at any point, thought to say, hey, want to pick up a bassinet before we get home?"

Simone sat down next to her and started to laugh. "Dex still hasn't gotten the rest of the nursery furniture in, has he?"

"No, we thought we still had three weeks! We don't have anything except clothes and diapers!"

"It's all right, calm down," he said, strangely comforted by the panicked edge to her voice that matched his own deafening inner voice from a few hours before. "They finished painting the Quidditch posts on the closet door day before yesterday, which was the last of the reno. Her dresser and changing table came in already, I'm sending a message to Dex now to get an ETA on everything else, and since Joel and Sandra are taking the rest of the day together, I'll see if Al will help me pick up and put together everything else we need right away, all right?"

"Thank you," she said, taking a calming breath.

"It'll all be okay. Want me to order your favorite pizza?"

She smiled and nodded, leaning back and relaxing a little, hugging Matilda closer to her. He looked down at his phone and said, "Dex says furniture should be here in the next few days. Nothing to worry about."

Estelle nodded again and said, "So what all do we need?"

"Well, we definitely need a bassinet, we need to assemble the furniture we have, and we should probably call the diaper service and get that started early, since we don't want to use disposable ones. We still need a couple more blankets and odds and ends... I'm sure we're forgetting a few things that we'll see in the store while we're there."

"I'm curious, do you think all of what you're buying is going to fit in your Mercedes, or is it all supposed to fit in Al's Jeep?"

"Maybe your dad would want to come along and bring his truck?"

"You sure you can handle an afternoon with him?"

"That depends, will your mother be there?"

Estelle gave an irritated laugh and said, "Yeah, she's rearing to go."

"Well, I'll go ahead and call Al and order your pizza if you want to call your dad."

Chapter 78

Around sunset, Estelle heard the key in the door and looked up to see Simone smile and wave to Carolyn, who was holding Matilda next to Estelle, before stepping back for John Presswood and Landini to carry in two large, cardboard boxes that were stacked on top of one another. Once they were safely on the floor in front of the couch, they both went back out to their vehicles, returning several minutes later— all heavily laden with bags as they helped Simone carry in the rest of their purchases.

"Right back," John said, as Simone came over and kissed Estelle. When he returned, he hugged his daughter and said, "This is for the three of you," and handed Estelle a gift bag.

"Thanks, Dad," she said, smiling up at him. She took the tissue paper out of the bag, pulled out a large, leather-bound book with *Baby Belvedere* etched into it, and looked over at Simone and said, "Oh my goodness."

"I had it specially made for the two of you, there isn't another one like it."

"This is wonderful," Simone started. "Thank you— so much."

The cover was a dark, antiqued brown leather, and as they opened it, the pages were made of a heavy parchment made to look centuries older than it was, and had a place for Matilda's hand and foot prints, her baby photo, and every milestone.

Simone stood to shake John's hand, but instead felt himself being pulled into a long, genuine hug. John put a hand on the back of Simone's head and whispered, "Thank you for taking care of my girl."

Simone smiled and nodded, and then walked over to Landini. "So, if someone had told you two years ago that you'd be spending tonight helping me put a bassinet together, what would you have said?"

"For them to pass over whatever it was they'd been smoking," Landini replied, laughing. "All right," he went on, looking around. "Where are we putting it?"

Estelle said, "Is it light enough that we can move it from upstairs to downstairs? Or does it just need—"

"You do remember who you're married to?" Landini asked, laughing again.

She rolled her eyes and looked over at Simone. "You just bought two of them, didn't you?"

"Of course, I did."

"And what about the one Dex ordered?"

"We'll need one to keep in the bookstore anyway, we'll just use one of these."

"And you don't think that's a bit—"

"There's no point in arguing with him," Carolyn said, laughing.

"We should probably get started," Simone said, looking around.

"Have you ever actually physically built anything?" Landini asked, half-smiling.

"No, but it's a bassinet, how hard can it be?"

Estelle laughed and said, "Simone, baby, I love you, but it took you three days to get pissed off enough to call Dex to put my temporary bookshelves back together when I moved in."

"Is that never talking about it again?" Simone asked, half-smiling, as Landini and John started to laugh.

Landini looked at him and said, "Just chill, we can do it."

"You guys don't have to—"

"Fine," Landini said, kneeling in front of the boxes. "You wanna be helpful, go make a beer run."

"Already done," Carolyn said, laughing. "Estelle asked me to pick it up on my way over. There's a six pack of Heineken in the freezer, should be cold by now, and a couple more six packs in the fridge."

"See, it's all done. Just go chill. We've got this."

Simone sighed, defeated, and sat down next to Estelle. He looked over at Carolyn and said, "Mind if I steal my daughter from you?"

"Not at all," she said, standing and handing Matilda to him. He leaned back against the couch as Carolyn gently lowered Matilda into her father's arms. He closed his eyes as he inclined his head forward to kiss her tiny forehead, and as he looked back up, his eyes locked with Landini's, who just smiled and went back to the box he was unpacking. He turned her so she was cuddled up against his shoulder, and as he looked down at her, he smiled at her tiny yawn, and then looked into her eyes as they opened, sleepily looking around, before they closed again as she nodded back off.

Two hours later, Matilda was fast asleep in the first bassinet, and Simone was pulling three more green bottles out of the fridge, handing one to John, and another to Landini, who was leaning against the second bassinet. He opened his own bottle and then tossed the opener to Landini. "You guys really saved us, thank you."

"Glad to do it," John said, taking the bottle opener from Landini, who nodded in agreement.

"Oh!" Landini said, standing. "I'll be right back."

Carolyn and Estelle both looked to Simone for an explanation, but he just shrugged. A moment later, Landini came back in, carrying a smaller cardboard shipping box. "Sorry, giftwrapping isn't really my forte," he said, grinning as he handed Simone the box.

"What's this?"

"Your best friend has a baby, you give them something. That's just how this works."

"Al, you didn't have to—"

"Just fucking open it."

Simone half-smiled and opened the flaps of the box, and then looked up, eyes bright. "THIS— is amazing. Thank you."

He handed the box to Estelle and she started to laugh, pulling out a tiny pair of shoes and a black onesie and looking up at a beaming Landini.

"Where did you find a Ramones onesie?" Simone asked, leaning forward.

"I had to find it online. Joel helped me track down the baby Chuck Taylors."

"Now she just needs some temporary tattoos and she's all ready to hang out with you guys!" Carolyn said, giggling.

"They're in the box," Landini said, half-smiling and taking a drink from his bottle.

As Simone set the box on the floor, they all looked over at Matilda starting to fuss from her bassinette. Estelle started to stand, but Simone said, "Want me to?"

Estelle smiled and said, "She probably needs to be fed. Do you think you can take care of that?"

Simone gave a self-conscious smirk and said, "I highly doubt it." He looked over at Landini and said, "I got nothing."

As they all laughed, Estelle took Matilda into her arms and sat back down on the couch. She looked around and said, "Will it bother anyone if I'm nursing her here?"

"Yes," Landini said, crossing his arms. "How dare you feed your child?"

They all laughed again, and as Matilda began to nurse, John looked down at the sound his phone had made. Once he had rolled his eyes and put it away, Estelle asked, "Everything all right?"

He nodded and said, "Your mother's asking when I'm coming home."

She looked down at Matilda for a moment, and then back up at her father. She started to speak, but then changed her mind, before looking over to Simone, who put his arm around her. John watched her for a moment, and then said, "What is it, dear?"

"You could just tell her you're not."

He tilted his head, not understanding, so she went on, "I know how unhappy you are with her."

He looked down for a moment, and said, "It's complicated."

"I don't want to make you uncomfortable or upset, Dad. I just want you to be happy. And if you promise me that you are, I'll never bring it up again. But I know what it's like to have to live with her, and you deserve to be happy— not just feeling like you're stuck."

He gave her a gentle smile and said, "It was a lot easier to be with her when you were little. And she used to be so different. Sweet, and caring. Then once we were married it was like everything changed. She even told me a few years ago she was just making a show of it so she could land someone she knew would take care of her. And now I can't figure out how to stop wanting to take care of her."

Estelle watched him for a moment, trying to find a delicate way to phrase her words, but before she could, Landini said, "So pay her alimony."

Simone leaned his head backwards against the couch, and Estelle and Carolyn both looked away, trying not to laugh as John looked over at him, eyebrows raised, but smiling nonetheless. "Sorry?"

"Pay her alimony. Then you're still making sure she's taken care of, and you're not torturing yourself living with a crazy bitch all the time. No offense," he finished, looking between John and Estelle.

Estelle laughed and said, "You have no idea how accurate you are."

Landini half-smiled and looked back to John, who said, "You do have a point."

"I know I do. I can always tell because he looks like that," Landini said, pointing to Simone, who was now sitting with his right hand covering his mouth, his eyes wide. Landini looked back to John and said, "I'm the guy he has to explain to people before we meet."

Simone slowly nodded and said, "And I probably should have."

John shook his head and said, "No, he's got a point."

"Look," Landini started, shifting to look at John. "Speaking from experience, it's one thing if you're still in love with the person making your life hell. But if you're not, you might as well just take care of yourself and fulfill your sense of obligation some other way."

He glanced over at Simone, who was now watching him with a much gentler expression. Looking back at John, Landini said, "You've just gotta figure out which one it is."

Estelle looked over at her father and said, "Do you still love her?"

"No," he said honestly. "I'm sorry, but I just don't."

"Don't be sorry," she said honestly. "It's really all right. And I don't blame you."

"I'll always be grateful that she gave me you," he said, standing and kissing the top of Estelle's head. "You're really okay with this?"

"I am," she assured him, smiling as he patted Matilda's head, which was now resting on Estelle's shoulder. "I just want you to be happy."

He smiled and looked between his daughter and his new granddaughter, before looking over to Simone and saying, "So how long have you guys known?"

"Few months," Simone said, gently smiling. "No judgement."

John gave a weak laugh and said, "I appreciate that. Still, bear in mind I ever see you in there for more than work I may have to kill you."

"Understood," Simone said, half-smiling. "I can guarantee it won't be a problem."

With another soft pat to Matilda's head, John said, "All right. I'm heading out. Looks like I have a conversation to get on with."

"You're gonna do it right now?" Estelle asked, looking up at him.

"You want me to wait?"

"No, I'm just surprised, is all. You usually spend a lot of time thinking things over."

"Trust me, I have," John said, helping her to stand.

Estelle handed Matilda to Simone and said, "You want me to go with you?"

"That's all right, dear. I know you're here."

After he had bid everyone farewell, Carolyn stood and said, "I should get going, too. I'm meeting someone."

"Oh, really?" Estelle said, crossing her arms. "And is this the same mystery man you've already seen twice this week?"

"It is."

"Is it getting serious?"

"No," Carolyn replied, laughing. "Just a comfortable friend to have some fun with."

"Up   to   anything   in   particular?   Or   just..."

Carolyn smiled and said, "He knows how much I love Broadway, so he's taking me to see Wicked tonight."

"That's oddly romantic for a comfortable friend."

Carolyn smiled and said, "That's the kind of guy he is. Doesn't want me to feel objectified or anything. And we do have a good time together."

"Then what's the problem?"

"Neither of us are really relationship-y people. We just like having fun together."

Estelle nodded and said, "Well, have fun." As Carolyn hugged her, Estelle went on, "Thank you for everything."

"Anytime." She looked between Estelle and Simone and said, "And thank YOU guys for reminding me about the importance of birth control."

As they all laughed, Carolyn waved good bye before heading out the door.

Estelle resumed her place on the couch, looking Simone over. "What are you thinking about?"

"Libera's had two dates this week, too. And none of us know who she is."

Landini started to laugh and said, "I think we do, now."

Estelle shook her head and said, "I really think it's just a coincidence."

"Maybe," Simone said, unconvinced. "All the same I'm glad I'm not going into the office tomorrow."

Once they had all laughed again, Estelle looked at Landini and said, "Thank you, by the way. For helping Dad, I mean."

"S'all right." He looked between Estelle and Simone for a moment before saying, "Can I ask what he was threatening you over?"

Simone looked to Estelle, who nodded. "Mustang," Simone said, nodding along with Landini's comprehension. "He's a high roller."

"Not surprised," Landini said, shifting his weight and leaning the other way.

"Why's that?" Estelle asked gently.

"Because I've been on the other end of it," Landini said, looking down.

"I'm sorry," Estelle said, watching him. "Are you okay?"

"Fine," Landini replied, forcing a smile.

"Do you mean recently?"

"Nah," Landini said, taking another sip from his bottle. "It's all good."

"Okay," Estelle replied, unconvinced, but dropping it.

Simone looked down at Matilda, before over at Landini. "She's awake," he started, smiling. "You wanna hold her?"

Landini's eyes widened and he said, "Nah, I'd break her or something."

"You're not gonna break her." Simone nodded once and said, "You should meet her."

Landini gave him a nervous smile and said, "All right. But I'm staying on the floor in case I drop her."

Estelle and Simone both smiled, and Simone replied, "You're not gonna drop her."

Simone stood and walked over to where Landini was sitting, before slowly kneeling next to him. As Landini leaned forward to look at her, they both looked over at Estelle as they heard the shutter sound on her phone's camera. Looking away sheepishly, she muttered, "Damn mute thingy didn't click all the way."

Simone gently laughed, but Landini still looked nervous. Looking up at Simone, he said, "Seriously, what if I break her?"

"Relax," he replied, putting his daughter into Landini' arms and sitting beside them. "See? It's all good."

Landini smiled down at her and said, "She's so small." Looking back up at Simone, he said, "She looks like you did when you were little."

They both laughed as she opened her eyes and looked up at Landini. Simone started stroking her hair and said, "This is Uncle Al. You should get used to this guy."

Landini gently smiled as she blinked at him, and then looked over at Simone. "I know we don't really say stuff like this, but I'm really happy for you." He looked down at Matilda and said, "And I'm really happy for you, too." Grinning as he watched her stretch her hands, he finished, "Your dad's gonna take really good care of you. All right? And if he doesn't you just tell Uncle Al and he'll take care of it."

Grinning over at Estelle as Landini leaned down to kiss Matilda's forehead, Simone said, "That may be the cutest way he's ever threatened me."

Estelle laughed, holding her hand over her mouth, trying to keep her emotions under control. Landini looked up at her and, at his inquiring head tilt, she said, "Sorry. I'll stop crying eventually."

He smiled and started to respond, but looked up at the knock they heard at the door. As Simone stood to answer it, Landini said, "Don't leave me—"

"You're not gonna break her," Simone said, laughing as he opened the door. "Don Libera," he started, somewhat surprised to see his Patron.

"Sorry to just drop by," Libera started, his head bowed in unusual insecurity.

"No, you're always welcome."

Libera gave a soft smile and said, "Do you have a moment?"

"Of course—"

"No, he doesn't," Landini chimed in, leaning forward.

"I'll be right back. I promise."

He stepped out onto the porch with Libera, closing the door behind him. Gesturing to the chairs, Simone took his cigarettes out of his pocket and held one up. "I'm all right, thanks. But feel free."

Simone nodded and sat along with Libera, lighting his cigarette and waiting for his Patron to speak. "Al all right?"

Smirking, Simone said, "He'll be fine. He's holding the baby and he's convinced he's gonna break her. Or drop her."

Libera laughed and said, "That man has the steadiest hands I've ever seen. I think he'll be all right."

Simone nodded and chuckled, before saying, "What can I do for you?"

Libera leaned forward with his elbows against his knees, his hands folded in front of him. Finally, he looked up to Simone and said, "I'm sorry, son."

"I don't understand."

"For coming down on you as hard as I did today."

"No, I was out of line."

Libera shook his head and said, "I know the two of you have always repelled each other. And for the life of me I can't understand why. But Jim was the one out of line. I want you to know that I know that, and that I've spoken with him. Believe me, he knows he was out of line."

Simone looked down and said, "Thank you."

Libera nodded for a moment, and then said, "I've told him to keep it civil, and to leave your personal life out of it. I... I'm sorry that it was necessary, and I'm sorry I didn't speak up for you this morning."

"Thank you," Simone repeated before taking another drag from his cigarette and lying it in the ash tray. "But you don't have to speak up for me."

Libera started to speak, but Simone shook his head and said, "I know you're behind me. But I also understand that you're not going to let your personal closeness with me show in a professional setting."

Looking down, Libera said, "No, you deserve to be shown a lot more respect than what I gave you today."

"I appreciate that. But I really was out of line. I deliberately disobeyed your instructions in front of subordinates. You would have done the same with any of them, and I should have held my temper."

Libera gently smiled and said, "You always understand, even when I don't."

Simone returned Libera's smile and said, "That's what I'm here for, Don."

Libera stood and patted Simone's head before saying, "You're a good kid, Simone."

As Libera put his hands in his pockets and looked down at the ground, Simone stood and said, "We'll probably be getting dinner soon, if you want to stay."

Grinning, Libera replied, "I appreciate that, but I have a lady waiting for me."

Simone half-smiled and said, "I'd hate to keep you from that. Big night?"

Libera shrugged and said, "Dinner and theater tickets." He gave an awkward smile and said, "I'm turning into one of those hopeless romantics... Not really sure how I let that happen."

Simone grinned and said, "Bound to happen eventually."

"We'll see," Libera said, starting down the steps. "Raincheck for tomorrow night?"

Nodding once, Simone said, "Of course."

He watched Libera walk back to his car, before turning and walking back into the house. It wasn't until he was relocking the door that he cocked his head, realizing what Libera had said.

"Everything all right?" Estelle asked.

Simone looked over at her, now sitting next to Landini on the floor, who was still holding a sleeping Matilda against him.

"Fine," Simone said, not wanting to go into detail about the morning's meeting. "Just wanted to talk. You mind if he comes over for dinner tomorrow?"

"He's always welcome," Estelle said, smiling up at him. "He could have stayed tonight."

Simone laughed and said, "I offered, but he said he has a date."

He looked between Estelle and Landini, who clearly had opposing opinions of who we was seeing. Landini just laughed to himself and shook his head, but Estelle said, "Still just a coincidence."

"He said they had theater tickets."

Simone and Landini both looked to Estelle, who was still struggling to hold her resolve. Finally, she just shook her head and said, "I'm staying out of it."

"Why's that?"

"Because she stopped seeing him for a while, but every so often she'd mention missing him. So, when I'd suggest just doing what made her happy, she'd get all irritated and say that they were too different."

"They are exceptionally different."

"But they make each other happy."

"Or the sex is just good and it's not any deeper than that," Landini added, looking between them.

Simone slowly nodded, realizing that Libera's feelings weren't anywhere close to being aligned with Carolyn's. "Hopefully it all works out for the best."

Chapter 79

Simone knocked at the restaurant side door of Libera's office and after a moment, the door opened to reveal a surprised Libera. "Simone— something wrong?"

"I'm not entirely sure, do you have a moment?"

"Of course, come in."

Once Libera had stepped aside, Simone saw that Jim Duvall was sitting opposite of Libera at the desk, irritated that his conversation had been interrupted.

"I'm sorry to interrupt," Simone said. Hoping to come back once Duvall had left, he went on, "I can come back later."

"Not necessary," Libera replied, motioning for Simone to take the chair next to his Consigliere and looking back down at the file in front of him.

Great. This'll be useless, Simone thought, taking the seat and waiting for Libera to speak first.

"What's the problem?"

"I got a message from Paul about an hour ago, there's something about it that's been bothering me since."

"What does the message say?" Libera asked, looking up at Simone.

He took out his phone and read, "Spot we agreed on's not safe. I'll be at garage in the A.M."

"And you think he's planning on trying something?"

"No, sir, I think he's dead, or at least will be very soon."

Libera looked shocked for a moment and then looked over to Duvall who said, "And what makes you think that?"

"First of all, because there are two places I've met with Paul, and neither of them are the Garage, nor was the back-up location that had already been agreed upon."

"And you don't think he could have simply forgotten about the back-up?" Duvall asked.

"No, I don't," Simone said flatly, irritated that Libera appeared to be following Duvall's skepticism. "And if he was that worried about safety he would have come to me tonight— he wouldn't feel secure on his own."

"What's the other reason?" Libera asked.

"I don't even think he's the one that sent the message."

At this, Duvall outwardly laughed. "How could you possibly know—?"

"I've been texting with him since the day after he approached me in the parking lot last week. He always uses full words and full sentences. He wouldn't have shortened it."

"Or maybe he was in a hurry, or concerned about tomorrow's meeting."

Shaking his head, Simone said, "I respectfully disagree."

"You're welcome to feel how you'd like," Duvall replied. "But I think it would be unwise to rush anything. If he sensed you were concerned, he would begin to sense weakness, and that would be equally as damaging."

Simone bowed his head and said, "Don Libera, I strongly believe we need to finish with Ethan now."

"Jim says we should wait, we're going to wait," Libera said sharply.

"I mean no disrespect— but Ethan clearly has a lot of accelerating issues with his dad, which means it's not just our lives at stake here—"

"Are you sure you're the best one to be lecturing on father issues, Mr. Belvedere?"

"That's enough!" Libera barked, looking over to Duvall, who was smiling arrogantly and watching Simone's anger race through him.

Simone sat silent for a full minute, chest rising and falling quickly out of fury. When he spoke, however, he kept his voice completely level, but still filled with icy disdain. "We are putting both Paul and Phil in danger by not acting, not to mention making literally everyone in the organization a potential target."

"Taking out his father simply doesn't make sense, Mr. Belvedere, because he's the only one financially supporting him, and so long as your informant maintains his composure and continues to act as your informant, his life is also not in the level of danger you have imagined."

Anger still building, he looked to his Patron for support, but Libera said, "See what Paul has to say in the morning, come back, and then we'll go from there."

Simone had been backed into a corner and knew that he couldn't win against their Consigliere's influence. "Yes, sir," he said, standing and buttoning his jacket. "Is there anything else I can do for you?"

"Tell Estelle I said hello," Libera said, glad that Simone had backed off.

"I will, sir, thank you."

Simone nodded curtly to Duvall and then left through the restaurant to find Joel. Once they were on the highway, Joel glanced over at Simone, who had his elbow resting against the window, thumb braced against his jaw, fingers resting over his lips. He was staring intently out of the window, still seething and trying to figure things out on his own.

"You okay, boss?"

He shook his head, and then ran his fingers through his hair before letting his hand resume its place against his jaw.

"The hell did I ever do to piss off Duvall?"

Joel gave a short, humorless laugh. "Dunno. He's never liked you, that's for damn sure. What'd he do now?"

"Told Libera to hold off on Ethan. Didn't care in the slightest about anything I brought up— I swear to fucking god, if anyone else gets hurt because of this..."

"Libera take his side?"

"Of course, he did."

"You gonna listen to him?"

"What choice do I have?"

Joel nodded and turned the car into Simone's driveway, parking next to Sandra's BMW. Simone sat for a moment long after Joel pulled the key from the ignition, trying to compose himself enough to hide his worry from Estelle.

"There's nothing you can do," Joel said. "You do anything now and Don will just be pissed that you didn't follow orders, no matter how it turns out."

Simone nodded.

"I've been thinking— maybe I should come along tomorrow," Joel said, shooting Simone a tentative glance. "If you think it's already—"

"No, Paul won't meet with me if there's anyone else— assuming he's still able to meet with anyone..."

"I don't like it, boss," Joel said, following Simone out of the car. "I still think I should be close by."

"So long as you're at the restaurant, you will be. Maybe they're right..."

Joel laughed as Simone unlocked the front door. "And maybe we'll just fly home in Estelle's invisible plane when you're done..."

As Simone stepped inside, his laughter quickly stopped at the vehement shushing sound that was made by the very small person running over to him.

"Auntie Stelle is suh-leeping!"

Simone knelt down and said, "Thank you, Mya."

She hugged him for a moment before jumping around her father so he would pick her up. As Joel accommodated her, Simone stood and set his phone and cigarettes on the round table across from Mya's crayons. Looking up, he smiled at Sandra, who was happily holding Matilda and sitting next to a sleeping Estelle on the couch.

"They've both been asleep for about an hour," she said, leaning up as Simone kissed her cheek before taking his daughter into his arms.

Matilda immediately curled herself up against his chest, sleeping head resting on his shoulder.

"Thank you for staying with them," Simone said, smiling at the tiny sigh Matilda gave as she settled into him.

"Oh, honey, it's no problem at all. The first week's the hardest."

He nodded, and said, "I don't know what we would have done without you guys—"

Simone stopped and kissed the back of Matilda's head as she started to fuss. "It's okay, Tilly. Go back to sleep."

He started to pace around the kitchen, gently patting her back, and still softly cooing at her. As she started to fall back asleep, his phone beeped with a new text message.

"Want me to?" Joel asked, nodding towards Simone's phone.

Simone nodded, still focused on Matilda. After a few moments of silence, he looked up at Joel, who was still rereading the message. "What's it say?"

"Nothing important," Joel said quickly, setting the phone back on the table and looking away from Simone.

"Seriously, what's it say?"

Joel shook his head. "It's just Duvall. It can wait."

"Passive aggressive or empty apology?"

"Both."

Simone gave a humorless laugh and said, "I'm surprised it took this long."

Joel nodded and smiled back down at Mya, who was pulling at his sleeve, offended that he was not coloring with her. Simone's phone beeped again, and Joel looked down at it and just said, "Libera."

Simone nodded and put Matilda into the bassinette that had replaced the couch's end table closest to Mya, before picking up his phone and cigarettes. He nodded for Joel to follow him, and as they stepped outside, the sound of the door closing woke Estelle, causing her to sit up poker-straight, looking around to see what had awoken her.

"Just the door," Sandra said, laughing gently.

"Oh!" Estelle said, rubbing her eyes and getting up to check on Matilda. "Simone home?"

Sandra started to reply, but before she could, Mya looked up from her coloring book and said, "He's on the porch with Daddy and a bad decision."

She looked at Sandra who had erupted in laughter. Sandra leaned over and lowered her voice. "About a year ago she asked Simone what his cigarettes were and all he said was, 'a bad decision,' and that's what she's called them since. We all thought it was funny so we never corrected her."

Estelle started to laugh and after a moment said, "I'm so sorry I fell asleep again."

"Don't be. Maybe in a few months you can do the same for me?"

"Of course!" Estelle said, before fully comprehending what Sandra had said. After several long seconds she turned around and said "I'm sorry— are you saying what I think you're saying?"

She glanced over to make sure Mya wasn't paying attention and nodded. Estelle ran over to Sandra and threw her arms around her. "When are you due?" she whispered, sitting back down.

Sandra started counting the months in her head and said, "Well, today's the twelfth of June, so about the first week of December."

"I'm so happy for you!" Estelle said, leaning forward again and hugging her beaming friend. As they heard the door open she whispered, "Does he know yet?"

She shook her head and smiled. "I'm telling him this weekend. I'm putting my notice in with Libera, too. He's been expecting that, though, since you asked me to come on at the bookstore."

Estelle smiled and looked up at Simone, who was still looking irritated and having a whispered conversation with Joel. After a moment he looked up and completely changed his expression when he realized they were watching him.

"Hey, you," she said, as he came over to kiss her.

Joel came over and put his hand on Sandra's shoulder. "We should get going if we're going to make it to your mother's on time," he said, looking as though he wanted nothing more than to stay longer.

"Yeah, you're probably right," she replied, standing and stretching.

"Knew I shouldn't have said anything," he breathed, only being heard by Estelle.

As she giggled, Simone and Sandra gave her an inquiring look, but she shook her head and said, "Just remembering something."

Joel momentarily caught her eye and smiled before looking at Simone and saying, "I'll still be at Libera's tomorrow, all right?"

Simone nodded in appreciation and hugged Sandra again, before going over to help Mya put her crayons back into their box. Estelle watched Simone laughing at the story Mya was telling, and once all the crayons were back in their box, she gave him a tiny high-five and then ran over to her mother.

"You going to come back and see me tomorrow?" Estelle asked the toddler as she was lifted into Sandra's arms.

Mya looked to her mother who nodded before doing the same herself. "Just tell Tilly not to cry so much."

"I'll do what I can," Estelle said, pretending to be as serious as Mya was.

Half-smiling, Simone walked them out, and as their friends drove away, Estelle picked up Matilda, who was crying to be fed, and put a light nursing blanket over her suckling child before stepping out onto the porch with Simone. He was sitting in his usual chair, smoking and scrolling through his phone. He looked up for a moment and smiled as she sat down. When he looked back down, she said, without thinking, "You hungry?"

He half-smiled, but didn't look up and said, "I am, but if it's all the same to you I figured we'd order out tonight."

It took her a moment to realize what he meant before she started to laugh, gently nudging his foot with hers. His quiet laugh soon dissipated and he quickly went back to staring at his phone. "Fuck it!" he said a minute later, locking the screen and sliding it across the table so it was several inches away from him.

"You doing okay?" she asked, becoming irritated with his preoccupation that had been exacerbated in the week since Matilda was born.

"Yeah, I'm sorry," he said. "This...no, I'm all right."

He took a deep breath and looked up at her, realizing she was starting to feel neglected. "It's just been a shitty day, that's all. I'm sorry."

"You've been like this since we brought her home, I'm starting to take it personally..."

"God, no," he said quickly. "Work's just kind of a shit-show right now, and I can't get everything to piece together and it's making me fucking crazy."

"Anything I can do?" she asked gently, watching him run his hand through his hair.

He shook his head. "Thanks, though. How was your day?"

"Good! We finally got the rest of the nursery put away, and finished filling the bedroom bookshelves. Mya had a fit because I was arranging the books wrong. Apparently, SOMEBODY told her that height was better than alphabetical order..."

Simone laughed and leaned forward, resting his elbows on his knees. "It is better if half your books are giant rectangles and the other half are made from paperboard."

"She really looks up to you."

He lit another cigarette and nodded as he inhaled. "Her actual uncles are never around, so she likes it when I take an interest in her."

"Sandra said you were the first one after Joel to hold her when she was born."

"I was. We had been on a job and I rushed him back to the hospital. Thirteen hours, I think, she was in labor, and that was just after we got there."

"Jesus…" Estelle said, grateful for the relative ease of her own delivery.

He nodded and said, "She likes people paying attention to her, I like spoiling her. Works out for everyone."

"Except Joel. I think you're going to wake up one morning with a stuffed unicorn head in bed with you…fluff and glitter all scattered around…"

Simone leaned his head against his palm as he laughed, thumb fidgeting with the cigarette held between his fingers. Estelle adjusted her camisole and moved their now sleeping daughter up to her shoulder, gently rubbing her back. Simone looked up and waved as their elderly neighbor came out into the warm air to watch the sunset and empty her mailbox. She walked over and leaned on the chain-link fence, saying, "How's that baby doing?"

"Wonderful," Simone said, perking up as he always did when someone asked about Matilda. "Thank you for asking."

"Ben get my rent check?"

"He did, thank you."

"Good. Tell him he's late in cashing it again."

"Don't worry, I will."

She smiled and waved again to them before heading back into her house.

"You actually going to tell him?"

Simone closed his eyes and shook his head. "Absolutely not. He only makes deposits on Fridays, and I can personally guarantee that he won't give a damn that he's two days late in cashing a check if it means keeping to Gallo's schedule."

Estelle laughed and said, "Do you mind ordering dinner?"

"Of course not. Usual?"

"Thank you, love. I need to get her changed and put down."

He nodded and picked up his phone, calling to place the order as Estelle saw to Matilda's diaper and put her into warmer, leopard spotted pajamas. As he came back inside, he sat down on the couch, leaning his head back and covering his face with his hands as though he could physically push his worries about Ethan out of his mind. He gave a gentle sigh as Estelle snuggled up against his chest, putting her arm around his waist.

"This still about what happened at the Garage?"

"Yeah," he said, still staring up at the ceiling.

"Maybe you've just thought about it too much."

He shook his head. "No, there's only a finite number of options, and I feel like I've explored them all, but nothing's been plausible enough for Duvall."

"Ugh, I hate that guy."

He looked down at her and said, "Have you met Jim?"

"No, but it seemed like the thing you needed to hear. Did it work?"

Simone chuckled. "It did, thank you." He kissed the top of her head and said, "So what do you need?"

"I'd like a reason to get out of the house for a couple hours," Estelle said. "That new dress I ordered finally came, I'd love a chance to wear it."

"What about dinner tomorrow night?"

"It's more of a day dress."

"Early lunch then? I've got a meeting at the garage in the morning, I could meet you at Libera's place across the street after. I'll have a little time around ten thirty, I can probably give you until twelve. I know it's really early, but it's the best I can do."

"That sounds perfect, love. I thought that place was just for people in the organization, though?"

"I hate to break it to you, but that technically includes you, too, now."

"I feel so fancy," Estelle kidded, nuzzling her head against her husband, who laughed.

She thought for a moment and said, "Why are you meeting someone there if Joel said he would be at Libera's?"

Simone considered her question for a moment and, unsure of how to answer it, he succinctly settled on the word, "Necessity."

Estelle sat up and looked at him, worry glistening in her eyes. He tucked a stray strand of hair behind her ear and said, "It's just a neutrality thing, it's not like last time."

"But you're going there alone?"

"I've got plenty of people close by. It's fine, really."

"Is that why you've been so worried?"

"Estelle—" he stopped, not wanting to push her away, but quickly reaching the limit of what he could tell her.

"Simone?"

"Look, I don't fully know yet. Like I said, nothing's been plausible enough. Duvall says tomorrow will be fine, so hopefully I'll know more tomorrow and I'll be able to get it all added up."

"Okay," she said, laying back down against him.

"So tomorrow, then?" he asked, trying to move the conversation back away from work.

She nodded. "Of course, assuming Sandra will watch the baby."

"Let me know if she can't, and I'll meet you back here."

"I will."

"She looked tired, I wish she'd take a couple weeks off from Libera's."

"Of course, she's tired. Between Mya, helping us with Matilda and the last of the unpacking, and—"

"And what?"

"Nothing!" she said quickly, sitting up and checking the time on her phone. "Food should be here soon."

"You suck at this game," Simone said, smiling and turning to face her. "I don't understand it. You can deter anyone's questions— including Carolyn's— if they're asking about me or Libera, but you hear one piece of gossip..."

"I'm sure I don't know what you mean," she said, holding her hand to her chest and faking modesty.

"You know you want to tell me," he goaded, half-smiling.

"Normally that wouldn't work, but you're cute so I'll let you win."

"You always do."

"You can't tell anyone," Estelle said. "Not even Joel."

"Okay," he said slowly, tilting his head.

"Sometime around December, you're gonna be an uncle again."

"What?" he yelped, before looking over to make sure he didn't wake Matilda. Grinning, he asked, "When did you find that out?"

"While you were out front with Joel. She's telling him this weekend, so don't mention anything, okay?"

"Of course."

"Think he'll be excited?"

"Oh, absolutely. He's been wanting another baby for a while now, but Sandra wanted Mya to be a little older before they started trying again."

"You guys talk about stuff like that?"

"Why, is that weird?"

"Not weird— just surprising. I don't know why, though. I mean, women talk about a lot more personal stuff all the time..."

"Like what, exactly?"

"Like Carolyn badgering me, trying to find out if a certain theory was true."

"Do I want to know?"

"Let's just say she wanted to know if a certain physical attribute was related to being Italian."

"Seriously?"

"Look at me like that if you want to, but we're two for two, here. Pretty sure she's one bad date away from staking out the bar at Libera's to find a third test subject."

He laughed as he stood to answer the knock at the door, and as he came back he handed Estelle her pizza and said, "So you've actually discussed—"

"Not in-depth."

He opened his pizza box and started to laugh again.

"I didn't mean it like that, and you know it."

Simone said nothing, but continued to chuckle as he started in on his pizza.

"But yes, you've been talked about a time or two."

"And by 'you,' you mean...my..."

She nodded, swallowing the bite she had just taken. "All   good things."

"I should hope so."

"If it makes you feel better, you won the race."

"What race?"

"You know, between you and Libera..."

"Why would that make me feel better?" he said— his involuntary, arrogant smile contradicting his words.

"Because it does," she laughed, picking up another slice.

"Is that what you and Joel were talking about on the plane?"

"You mean the bet?"

He nodded.

"No, that was different."

Simone didn't speak, but continued to eat, watching her trying to avoid making eye contact. Giving in to his charming, beckoning eyes, she said, "Sandra bet Joel that you were still a virgin when we met."

"That's not really fair," Simone said, half-smiling and shaking his head. "He asked me that a couple years ago."

"She didn't believe him."

"Who was I supposedly sleeping with?"

"She assumed you were just a regular at Mustang."

"I don't understand why everyone's so surprised that I hadn't been sleeping around."

"Have you seen you?"

"How exactly did all this come up in conversation?" he asked, giving her another arrogant smile.

"I told you on our honeymoon, they wanted to know what you're like in bed, because you're so well composed the rest of the time."

"And what did you say?"

"That your personality in bed is like your personality at work."

- 330 -

"How's that?"

"How attentive you are. You pay attention to the little signals. You follow your instincts, that kind of thing. It's what makes you so wonderful— and not just in the bedroom."

"I'm just following your lead."

She shook her head. "And I'll bet that's what you say to Libera when he's praising you, too, isn't it?"

He looked at her for a moment and said, "Huh. I never thought of it that way."

"Just ask yourself this— how often have you been wrong when you've followed your instincts?"

"Not very," he said truthfully, mind wandering back to his meeting with Duvall earlier in the day.

"See?" she said, unaware that she had just unintentionally affirmed everything he believed about Paul.

Chapter 80

Simone pulled up in front of the Garage the next morning and parked next to Paul's vacant Impala. Seeing Paul's car caused him a moment of self-doubt in his theory, but then he noticed that the rear, passenger window of the Impala was newly cracked down the center, and the Garage's entrance door was propped open— a careless mistake that no one in Libera's organization would make. As he stepped out into the parking lot, he left the driver's door ajar and walked over to open the passenger door, intending to take off his unbuttoned jacket and leave it— along with his tie— on the passenger seat, as well as take the Tomcat from the console in case he needed additional ammunition.

He reached for the door handle, but upon looking into the worn-out car to the right of his polished Mercedes, he threw his head back in frustration, realizing that he had been right all along. "God fucking dammit!"

Paul's body was in the back seat, bruise-covered and still bleeding from a fatal gunshot above his left eye. Trying to determine if this was a struggle or simply torture followed by an execution, he stepped closer and started looking through the window at Paul's body for additional bullet wounds, and only then realized that Paul was lying on the denim-clad legs of another victim. *No— tell me this isn't—* He took another step forward so his eyes could follow the body lying opposite of Paul's, and felt his fury begin to rebuild as he realized it was Phil, not as badly beaten, but shot in exactly the same place, along with two other shots in his chest.

I fucking told them this would happen.

He turned around, drawing and cocking his Taurus before taking out his phone to call for someone to back him up. As he dialed Joel's number, a single shot rang out, missing him by about a foot and shattering the driver's window of Paul's car. Letting go of his phone, he dropped himself down between the two cars, and looked up through the windows of his Mercedes in time to see Ethan running into the open door. He hesitated, knowing it was a trap, but still pursued Ethan into the empty Garage. He briefly considered still calling Joel or Landini for help, but Paolo Bassi's face suddenly flashed through his mind, and he wasn't willing to put their lives in danger for something he felt he should have been able to fix months before.

Once inside, Simone followed the motion-sensitive lights that Ethan had automatically activated, leading him down to the lower, sound-proofed bays. Keeping close against the wall to his left, he slinked along with carefully measured, silent footsteps, gun held ready to fire, making his way down to the first doorway. His ears were searching just as thoroughly as his dark, narrowed eyes, trying to pick up any nonexistent trace of his adversary. He sharply turned his torso as he entered the room, keeping as limited a profile as was possible, but upon seeing that the room was merely an empty stretch of concrete, he turned and went through the side door into the adjoining bay, where he had lost Paolo— and nearly his own life— in early March.

The old, bullet riddled Dodge was still in the same place it had been, but the floor was spotless— much more so than the rest of the building— and the stone wall with the door he had walked through no longer had bullets embedded in it. He slowly approached the Charger, unsure of what he would find behind it, but he was again alone, silence echoing louder than the gunfire that still occasionally invaded his sleep.

He entered the third and largest concrete room with his finger resting anxiously on his trigger, eyes locked on the passenger side of the scrap car Libera kept in the third bay, assuming Ethan would be taking cover behind it. Again coming up empty, his temper was beginning to gain control of his concentration, and as he again came to the other side of a seemingly empty room, he dropped his arms to his side and threw his head back.

"Where are you, you fucking coward?" Simone bellowed.

He slowly approached the driver's side of the defunct '67 Mustang, but was immediately knocked to the ground as Ethan came up behind him, driving a sharp blow to the back of Simone's head with the grip of the pistol that had already taken two lives.

"Right here, bitch—" Ethan said, turning Simone over and hitting him with the pistol grip again, cutting open his forehead. "You think you can take whatever you want from me?"

Simone rose to his feet, mirthlessly laughing and wiping the blood from his forehead out of his right eye with the back of his hand.

"Did really ever think any of that was yours? Jesus Christ. Phil came to us—"

"Only after your Don put the idea in the weak bastard's head," Ethan said, firing a haphazard shot into Simone's left arm. "Déjà vu, eh, Belvedere?"

Simone gave a loud yell in agony as Ethan laughed and took aim at his heart. Faster this time, Simone pulled the barrel down and out of Ethan's hand, before dragging him by his shoulder to the floor. He held his foot against Ethan's throat, and slowly began to shift his weight onto it. "Oh, and just so you know, your dad's the one that cut you out of the contract, not us."

He unloaded the Browning BDM and threw it aside, not wanting to fire the gun that had killed Paul and Phil, but Ethan was unhindered by the slightly blurred vision slowing Simone as he raised his trusted

Taurus. Rage building at Simone's words, Ethan pushed against Simone's foot with all of his might, causing Simone to stumble backwards, dropping his gun. He was able to catch himself on the car behind him, but in doing so, cut his right hand open on a patch of rusted steel.

In the second it took for Simone to chance a glimpse at the deep cut in his palm already oozing blood, Ethan ran forward, pinning him against the rusty driver's side door of the Mustang. Simone drove his knee hard into Ethan's stomach, and his fist was finally able to make contact, breaking Ethan's nose.

Simone lunged forward several feet and picked up his gun, but, filled with endorphins from the force of his fury, Ethan regained his balance quickly and threw Simone's back against the car, before grabbing his shoulders and forcing Simone's head backwards through the thick glass, shattering the driver's door window and knocking his gun again from his hand. Ethan kicked the bloody steel towards the door and pulled Simone forward by the lapels of his jacket, dragging the back of his neck and shoulders across the jagged glass in one swift motion. A moment later, there was an echoing crash as his back was slammed onto the hard concrete, knocking the wind out of him and driving several pieces of glass further into his skin.

Ethan grabbed Simone by his jacket again and twice thrust him face first into the handle of the driver's door, deepening the gash on his forehead and cutting open his cheek and jaw. He grunted in pain as he felt his head being pulled backwards by his hair, and Ethan pulled them back several steps before wrapping his arm tightly around Simone's neck. Unable to regain the upper hand from the ambush, Simone began to frantically reach behind him, grabbing at Ethan's face. His hand was finally able to grab hold of the side of Ethan's jaw with his right hand, but Simone quickly lost his grip thanks to the blood from his palm that was now streaked across Ethan's throat. He tried to regain his hold, but the glass that had fallen inside his collar was slowly sinking below his skin, and the much stronger arm around his own throat was starting to restrict his air flow, making it nearly impossible to even moan in pain, let alone fully fight back.

He continued to try to pull Ethan's arm away, but it was no use. Simone's left arm was weak and bleeding quickly, and his only chrome-plated defense was three feet of cold floor away from him. He was being pulled down to his knees, and there was absolutely nothing he could do about it.

Simone struggled ferociously against the crook of the elbow pulling against him, and looked down to see his own blood from the cuts on his face dripping stains onto the pale arm constricting his breathing.

His struggle slackened for half a second as he tried to again hear what he thought had been familiar footsteps in the empty halls. Whether or not this could lead to Libera's downfall as Ethan imagined, there was a hopeless sense of acceptance beginning to take over Simone's brain when he remembered why he was still fighting. The impossible footsteps of Estelle that he thought he'd heard triggered a momentarily renewed fire in his futile endeavor. It wasn't his life he was fighting for; it was Estelle's and Matilda's.

Within seconds, however, he realized that the exhaustion setting in was from his inability to breathe rather than the exertion from the fight. His thoughts began to prance around his memories of Estelle, and he closed his eyes as his thoughts came to rest on an image of her in pink Chanel. This, even within sight of his quickly approaching demise, struck him as strange, as she had never worn a dress matching the one he could so vividly see. He felt as though he could count his remaining attempts at breathing backwards, and as his arms began to lose their ability to fight back, he heard, in a loud, clear voice as steady as the hand pointing the gun, "No more yielding, but a dream." A single gunshot rang out through the surprised second of silence, and Simone began gasping for air as Ethan's lifeless arm fell to the floor. Simone looked up for a moment and gave a weak smile as Estelle's arm lowered her carefully aimed weapon.

After Ethan had fallen to the ground, Simone felt himself fall forward, his right arm all that was holding up his shoulders. Out of pure fatigue, he dropped down to his side and turned onto his back, instantly regretting his decision as he felt several pieces of glass drive further below the surface. As he laid there, one knee in the air and the other on the ground, all he longed for was Estelle's embrace. Estelle pulled the silk twill scarf from under her collar and rushed to Simone's side.

"Simone?" Estelle asked, quiet at first.

He tried to respond, but couldn't put the words together. He attempted to reach his right hand to hers, but lost strength half way through. His eyes felt heavy, and the pounding in his head was becoming stronger. "Simone?" Estelle said again, louder this time. He still didn't answer, and his eyes were beginning to blink slowly. "Simone? SIMONE? No— stay with me, baby."

Moments after Simone lost consciousness, Estelle leaned her head onto his chest, breathing a high-pitched sigh of relief at the sound of his heart still beating. Even though she was fully expecting his arrival, she still jumped when she heard Joel's loud voice behind her.

"Fucking hell."

She looked around and said "Joel! We have to get him help!"

He nodded, but as he came closer he became aware that the three of them weren't actually the only people in the room. Ethan had been hidden from view by Estelle leaning over Simone, removing his already loosened tie and using her scarf to clean some of the blood off of his face. Joel took a moment to look around and saw Simone's gun lying across the room and the second one lying next to Simone's arm.

"Jesus…Did— did you— was this you or Simone?"

Joel's calm confusion was struggling to accept the magnitude of what was going on, and he looked up at Estelle as she struggled to remain calm, replying, "I did. But right now, we need to worry about Simone."

"On it," he said quickly, taking out his phone and dialing. After a few seconds he said, "Sorry for the interruption, Don Libera, but it's important." Joel waited, rolling his eyes at being put on hold.

For the first time, Estelle felt nervous about Ethan. She was in a highly restricted area of Don Libera's territory, and had just killed someone involved in Libera's business.

What if I can't prove that I was protecting Simone? Surely, he'll know that I was…

She started to examine the rest of Simone, quickly pulling his left arm out of his sleeve and using her scarf to put pressure on the bullet lodged barely an inch lower than the scar from the last time he was attacked in the same building. "Joel— look at this—"

He looked down, fear intensifying in his eyes. "How's his breathing?"

Estelle put her fingers to Simone's pulse, saying, "It's slower than it usually is, but it's there."

Joel nodded, but she only looked up when he began speaking again. "With all due respect, sir, you're not gonna fucking believe this."

Estelle could hear Libera's loud laugh come through the phone before Joel continued, "Estelle's got a flat down at the Garage. We need to get Simone a lift back NOW."

There was silence on both ends for a moment, and Estelle stroked Simone's hair with her free hand, still hoping he would awaken. She could tell Libera was talking again, but couldn't make out the words. Joel responded, "That's right, sir. I REALLY think you should get down here as soon as possible, Doc, too… two more should do it… No, she's okay."

Estelle looked up at Joel in worry, but he just nodded, reassuring her. "Yeah. Lower level. Uh huh. Three. Got it." Joel pocketed his phone, took off his navy jacket and put it under Simone's head. Simone moaned a little at the movement, but didn't awaken.

"Come on, Simone," Estelle implored.

"He'll be fine," Joel said, trying to soothe her.

He walked over and picked up Simone's gun, looking for a moment at the bloody palm print on the grip. He pulled the magazine out briefly to count the seventeen unfired bullets, and then pushed it back in before setting it next to the one Estelle had fired.

"Can I?" he asked, pointing to the scarf.

"Of course," she said, moving her hand but not leaving Simone's side. Joel briefly moved the bloody scarf, trying to feel around the bullet to make sure it was still inside the muscle, rather than having ripped all the way through. Simone's forehead had stopped bleeding for the most part, but his face and neck were bruising spectacularly. His hands had a dozen or more cuts and scrapes, and the left knee of his pants was ripped and wet with blood.

"Looks like he put up a helluva fight," Joel said.

"Mmmhmm." she confirmed, tears threatening her eyes for the first time.

"Estelle?" Joel asked quietly. He hesitated for a moment then, firmly this time, said, "Estelle, look at me." She looked up, unable to speak. "It's gonna be fine."

She nodded, took a deep breath as an attempt to regain her composure, and looked back at her unconscious husband. Joel put a steadying hand to her shoulder. "Really," he went on, "He's just bled a lot. He needs Doc and a little rest and he'll be good as new."

As she gave a weak smile in acknowledgement, they heard a door slam.

"JOEL?" Libera's loud voice echoed down the stairs and into the bay.

"On my way!" he yelled back, jumping to his feet and handing Estelle the scarf, which she immediately returned to the arm still weeping blood. She heard loud, confident footsteps approaching, and then Libera walked into the room, followed closely by Joel, as well as Landini, Gianni— both of whom had their pistols drawn— and a man Estelle had seen once or twice, but never met. She had never seen Libera look this way. Anger seemed to radiate out from him, but a genuine look of pure, human fear took over his features as he saw Simone lying next to Estelle's knees.

"How is he?" Libera asked, making eye contact with Estelle.

"I— I think he's okay. He's just knocked out. He was shot in the arm again, though, and he's pretty banged up."

Libera breathed a sigh of relief and said, "Okay. Doc's already on his way, we'll make sure he's taken care of." He turned to the unrecognized man and said, "Jim, this is Simone's wife."

She started to feel anger build at the name, remembering how frustrated Simone had been in the past several days, as well as who he had told her assured him that this meeting would be safe. Glancing up at Joel, she saw that he was glaring at Duvall, looking just as angry as she felt. For the first time since she had knelt down, Estelle slowly stood and said, "Jim Duvall, right?"

"That's right," Duvall said, giving her a pretentious nod. "I take it Simone's mentioned my name?"

"Just in passing," she said, looking into the only eyes in the room free of concern for Simone. Fury still building just below the surface, she looked at him for another moment, and then, with one smooth motion, slapped him across the face.

"Estelle!" Libera barked, more out of shock than anger.

"You knew this would happen!" she yelled, pointing at Duvall.

Even as fury began to show in Landini's gaze, matching that of Joel and Estelle, Duvall's calm eyes showed no change in emotion whatsoever. "Honestly, how could I have known?"

Joel pulled out his well-polished Beretta and stepped sideways so it was aimed directly at Duvall.

"Fontaine— back off—" Libera directed.

To Estelle's surprise, Joel completely disregarded Libera's order, but instead stepped between his Don and Consigliere, standing directly in front of Libera and a mere foot in front of Duvall, and cocked his pistol.

"Because he came to you for HELP, and you fucking ignored him. He knew this would happen, and you did NOTHING!"

"He brought me nothing with substantial evidence—"

"That's bullshit!" Joel yelled. "You've NEVER been behind him."

"It is not my responsibility that Mr. Belvedere puts himself into reckless situations in an attempt to play the hero. Clearly, some men just aren't cut out to handle the responsibility of holding an elite position in the organization."

At his last words, Landini and Gianni raised their weapons and pointed them at Duvall. Estelle looked at Libera with pride in their loyalty, and saw a new level of cold anger in his eyes as he said, "I swear to god, Jim, if you thought this was going to happen—"

Duvall's eyes were starting to show self-centered concern, but his voice stayed steady, saying, "Are you really implying that I would intentionally put Mr. Belvedere's life in danger?"

"Yes," Estelle snapped.

"These are matters you know nothing of, child," Duvall spat. "Do us all a favor and leave this to the men that know what they're doing."

Joel took another step forward, but it was Libera that said, "You're out of line, Jim."

Duvall looked up, surprised. "You don't honestly think her place is here?"

Estelle looked at him, expecting to be told to leave, but Libera just said, "Considerably more than yours."

He walked around Joel, pulling out his Desert Eagle and putting himself between Estelle and Duvall, who had started to glance nervously at the holster on his hip. "How long?"

"What?" Duvall said, taking a step backwards, but feeling Gianni and Landini's hands, now free of the burden of their weapons, close around his shoulders.

"How many times have you said that Simone was imagining a problem and known that he wasn't? You expect me to believe that it's pure coincidence that every time Simone's been this badly hurt, you've been the one that said there would be no problem?"

"Again, it's not my fault he takes it upon himself—"

"You're right— all of that is Simone— and everyone in the organization knows that him doing JUST THAT is why we're all still here." He looked hard into Duvall's eyes, connecting the pieces in his mind. "It was you, wasn't it?"

Duvall said nothing, but continued to sink lower into his fear.

"You gave Malachi Salone the key."

"Wh— what?"

"I'm not going to ask you again."

"Never— I would never—"

"You sure as hell spent months trying to tell me not to move him up."

"Only because he was too young. There were men with considerably more seniority—"

Libera fired a shot over Duvall's head and said, "How many times have you sided against him because of it?"

Duvall jumped and said, "I only wanted what was best for the organization, and no— I've never felt that was him. S-Salone came to me, and I was looking out for the bottom line of the company—"

Libera nodded, his icy calm more intimidating than his temper. "Bottom line of the company..." He turned to Joel and Estelle, saying, "All right. Who wants to tell me what happened?"

Joel gave Estelle another reassuring nod and, surprised that her nervousness had dissolved, she looked directly at Libera and calmly explained, "I could tell something was wrong when he left this morning. There was something that didn't add up to him, but he wouldn't say what it was— he's always kept me out of it. He said he had to stop by here and then he would meet me for lunch, only he didn't show up, and he didn't send me a message like he always does when plans change. I started to get worried, so I walked over to see if he was still here, and both cars were out front.

"The door to Simone's car was still open, and his phone was on the ground between the cars, so I picked it up and called Joel, which I think is what Simone was trying to do when he dropped it, since the number was already dialed. I looked over and saw that Paul and somebody else were dead in the backseat of the other car. I couldn't see far enough to tell who it was. After Joel told me to leave and that he was on his way, I found Simone's other Taurus under the front seat of his car— it was faster than taking my .25 out of my bag— and came in to look for him."

"He was right," Libera said, looking around at Duvall, who said nothing but continued to stare at the .50 caliber weapon in Libera's hand. "Remember, Jim?"

Anger had fully encompassed his demeanor, and his casual, conversational tone somehow made it inescapably clear that Libera was far from forgiveness. "Simone said Ethan would do exactly what happened, but you said no... it was all an overreaction. So, I'm guessing that this bastard snuck up on him on our own land and caught him off guard."

"That's the only way anyone could attack Simone," Joel said angrily.

Gianni nodded in agreement. "Son of a bitch knew he couldn't lose at a fair fight."

Libera held up his hand in silencing agreement, turning back to Estelle. "So, what was happening when you came in?"

"They were both on their knees. Ethan had his arm around Simone's throat and was pulling him down."

"From the looks of it," Landini said, sounding both angry and proud, "Belv was fighting back pretty hard." Estelle nodded in confirmation.

Libera turned and gestured to Ethan's bleeding body behind them. "And this?"

"I knew I had to do something, but they were moving so much I didn't think I could get a clean shot without hitting Simone." She furrowed her brow as she realized that she didn't feel anything resembling penitence towards Ethan, and that it was coming across in her voice. "They didn't notice me come in at all. Simone was fading fast, so I aimed and said something to get their attention, hoping they'd stop moving for a second. It worked, so I pulled the trigger," she finished succinctly, kneeling back down at Simone's side and looking back up at Libera.

"You mean to tell me," Libera said in poorly veiled disbelief, "that you got this guy with one shot?"

Bemused, Estelle looked up and nodded twice. "Joel's been teaching me for the last seven months or so."

"Damn," Gianni said, exchanging a surprised look with Landini. She wasn't sure if she felt flattered or insulted, and had a sudden stroke of understanding about Simone describing Libera giving him the same feeling.

Libera walked over to her and put a hand on her shoulder. "You did good. Doc'll be here soon. Al—"

"Yes, sir?"

"Pull Paul's car in, get your boys over."

He took out his phone and said, "Yes, sir."

Libera walked up to Duvall, standing an inch away from his terrified face. "Tell me, Jim. If anyone else had betrayed me the way you have, what would you advise me to do?"

"I— I…"

"I thought so, too."

Gianni tightened his grip on Duvall's shoulder and kicked the back of his calf, forcing him down to his knees. Joel stood behind Estelle, keeping a hand on her shoulder to prevent her from turning around. Libera pressed the barrel against the center of Duvall's forehead and said, "You've been a brother to me, Jim. I've trusted you above anyone else, including Simone. I didn't think you'd ever—"

"No— No, I wouldn't—"

"You already have."

"I've always—"

"Goddammit, Jim— you've always hated Simone, just like you always hated Vinny."

"He was—"

"You're right," Libera said, voice becoming gradually louder. "Vinny got what he had coming. But Simone—" he gestured behind him, "That boy might as well be my own son, and I've never had anyone who's worked or fought harder for me— you've seen every step of that. You were there when I brought him on, you were there every time I moved him up and I also seem to remember you being there when he saved your ass RIGHT HERE FOUR YEARS AGO."

"Don Libera— please—"

"You have deliberately put his life in danger, but my loyalty to you didn't let me see that."

"I've been loyal, Don—"

Libera laughed for a moment and then leaned down so that his eyes were level with Duvall's. "No, Jim, you haven't."

Drawing himself back up to his full height, Libera held his finger against the trigger, looking down at the closed eyes of the man before him, before dropping his arm and kicking Duvall hard in the stomach, who tried to double over in pain, but was held firmly in place by Gianni's hand. Libera knelt down in front of him, putting his hand tight around Duvall's throat. "Get the hell out of here."

"Wh- What?"

"WHAT?" Joel echoed, letting go of Estelle.

Libera released his grip on Duvall with a jerk and said, "It's what Simone would do."

"Don—"

"QUIET, FONTAINE."

Standing over the man he thought had been his most trusted advisor, he again raised his gun and said, "But you listen to me. You come back, you won't live to see the next hour— understand?"

Duvall nodded frantically, still in shock that he was being released. Libera looked to Gianni and said, "Let him go."

Obeying his Don's command, he pushed forward before letting go, causing Duvall to fall forward onto his hands. Libera kicked hard into his shoulder, knocking him onto his back. The Don's finger twitched against the trigger, as though his entire being was still wrestling with the decision he had made. "Go."

Duvall hurried to his feet, and then sprinted out of the building. Libera walked over to Estelle and said, "I'm sorry you had to see that."

She shook her head and said, "You're right, you know."

He tilted his head and looked down at her, but she smiled up at him. "It's what he would have done."

He nodded, and then watched her as she went back to stroking Simone's hair, worry increasing with each of the seven additional minutes it took for the doctor to arrive. He finally came in and took a quick look around at what he was dealing with. "There's nothing I can do for that one," Doc said flatly, gesturing towards Ethan and kneeling next to Simone.

"Good," Libera spat.

Doc began to unbutton Simone's vest and shirt, leaving them lying open under him and taking out his left arm. "How long has he been unconscious?"

"About twenty minutes," Estelle said, moving the scarf to allow Doc to feel around the wound as Joel did before. "He was awake when I got to him, but not for long."

Doc nodded and shined a light into each of Simone's eyes. "I'm guessing by the bruising and the cut on his forehead that he's got a concussion, and by the look of everything he's lost a lot of blood. His pulse is a little low, but nothing to be concerned about considering."

He pulled a new syringe out of his bag and unwrapped it, drawing a large dose of pain killer and finding a place to inject it into Simone's arm. "Hold this," he said, handing Estelle the used syringe and vial.

Reaching back into his bag, he handed Estelle a pair of gloves and then took back the vial, saying, "Mind holding a few things for me?"

She shook her head and put on the gloves so she could take the tools the doctor was unwrapping and handing her. He gave Estelle a calming look and then went to work to remove the bullet. This one had lodged at an inconvenient angle, and Doc had to make several additional incisions to be able to properly pull it from Simone's bicep. The bullet made a light echo as it hit the floor, and Doc handed Estelle the forceps so he could begin sewing up the wound. "He may have some nerve damage from this one, we'll need to keep an eye on it."

Joel's eyes were filled with worry, watching the doctor stitch his brother's arm closed, and Landini was still across the room making the calls to assemble his cleanup crew. Gianni was having a whispered conversation about Ethan with Libera, who was still watching Estelle intently focusing on Simone's closed eyes, praying for him to blink awake at any moment.

Once the bullet hole was closed, Doc started adding a few stitches to the cuts on Simone's forehead and cheek before examining the other abrasions, making sure everything else would heal properly on its own. He took another syringe and vial out of his bag and found a new spot for the second injection. "This is just to make him sleep for a while," he added, looking at Estelle's worried face. "I'm also going to give him a Tetanus shot and I'll bring some antibiotics by tomorrow, just in case."

She nodded and then looked up at Joel. "Oh my god! I didn't call Sandra— she's still at the house with the baby—"

"She'll understand," Joel said, not looking away from Simone.

"Ben, help me turn him," Doc said abruptly, after noticing the blood on the back of Simone's neck. "I was so focused on his arm, I didn't even think to—"

Libera knelt down next to Estelle, helping to delicately turn Simone onto his right side and looking at the now exposed neck and shoulders.

"Jesus Christ, how the hell did this happen?" Libera asked, staring aghast at the wounds.

Simone was covered in blood from the ends of his hair to his shoulder blades, and there were several pieces of glass barely under an inch in width protruding from his skin just below his neck.

"Just when I think he can't outdo himself..." Doc said, gingerly touching a shard of glass nearly three-quarters of an inch wide that was embedded halfway between Simone's neck and right shoulder, before shining a light on the other deep cuts and scratches, trying to see how much more glass there was to reflect.

Joel walked over to the Mustang and started to look over the broken driver's window. There were bloody, jagged pieces of glass still jutting up from the door, and there was bloody glass both on the seat of the car and the garage floor. "Looks like his head went through the window...He's lucky it fucking missed his spine..."

Seven times Doc ran a hand through the back of Simone's hair, pulling away the tiny glass fragments he found, and then handed Estelle the tiny flashlight and looked in his bag for smaller forceps. He pulled several glass splinters from behind Simone's ears, and then eased out the biggest piece, which was mercifully shorter than it was wide. He sewed the cut closed, and then restarted the process, pulling out more shards only barely smaller than the largest. By the time he was finished, there were three more glass pieces from his shoulders and two from the left of his neck lying next to the bullet at Doc's knees.

"He's going to need blood," Doc said, snipping the excess suture away from the last stitch, "And we can't wait until dark. We've got to get him home now."

"Boys," Libera started. "Let's get Simone home to his wife."

Once she had handed everything back to the doctor and eased Simone back into his shirt and jacket, Libera helped Estelle to her feet and hugged her. As he did, he whispered in her ear, "Thank you for all you've done here today. This will not go unnoticed."

He kissed her cheek before gesturing for her to follow Landini and Gianni as they carried Simone to his car. Once Simone was safely in the backseat, Landini put Paul's car into neutral and started to push it through the open door of the garage's ramped access tunnel. Libera approached Joel and glanced around at Estelle, who was simultaneously trying to get ahold of Sandra and overhear what her husband's Patron was saying.

"Can you get him home and inside?"

"'Course I can."

"Good. These guys will take care of everything here. I'll send Doc over to meet you there. I want Simone conscious before you leave." He grasped Joel's hand and leaned in to say, "Clean their guns. Make sure she's all right with what happened."

Joel nodded. "She knows how this works. She'll be fine."

"I know she will." He laughed and then checked to make sure Estelle couldn't hear what he was about to say. "We've never had a Made woman before."

Joel laughed. "Good luck getting her to do it. That would really be somethin', though."

"That it would." Libera said, as Joel got in the car with Estelle and Simone. "That it would."

Chapter 81

It was after midnight when Simone awoke. As he slowly regained awareness, he realized he was no longer on the concrete floor of the garage, but rather at home in his and Estelle's bed. He put a hand to his aching head and gently rubbed at his temples before slowly raising himself up onto his right elbow. He looked around to see Joel dozing across the room, his hand on Matilda's bassinette.

Simone's left hand felt heavy, and he looked down to see that Estelle's hand was holding tightly onto his, even though she was sound asleep. He smiled, moved her hand and carefully leaned down to kiss her forehead, causing her to jump at his touch.

"You're awake!" she yelled, accidentally waking Joel.

"I am," Simone replied, voice straining from the aggressive arm that had attempted to take his life.

"How are you feeling?"

"Still spinning a little...Sore... Happy to see you," he finished. He pushed himself up a little higher so he was almost sitting up, and leaned his head back against the emerald headboard, closing his eyes to ease the dizziness overcoming him. "The hell happened, Estelle?"

She hesitated, unsure of how he would feel about her taking Ethan's life. "How much do you remember?"

He put his hands over his eyes, trying to bring back the hazy memories. "I remember fighting with Ethan, and I remember him being behind me—"

"And— and then what?"

"No," he said, shaking his head, but instantly regretting the quick movement. He had just remembered a glimpse of her pointing his gun at them, and her running over to him as Ethan fell. "No, that couldn't have—"

"What?"

"What happened to Ethan?"

She didn't look up at him, afraid that he was judging her as much as he judged himself when he had to make the same decision.

"Estelle?"

She finally looked up, but couldn't bring herself to say it. After a long pause, it was Joel who finally spoke up.

"It was Estelle, Simone."

"Estelle? You—?"

"I'm sorry. I know you wanted to keep me out of this part of your life, but I—" Estelle sat up and kissed him gently before lying her head on his shoulder. "I was afraid I was going to lose you today."

The room was silent for several minutes, and then the tears she'd been fighting all night finally broke free.

"Hey," he said, putting his hand on hers, which was as far as the strength in his right arm could let him reach.

"Do you hate me?"

"What?" he said, turning a little too quickly and wincing in pain. "No— of course I don't. Why would I?"

"Told you," Joel said, nodding at her. "You did what you had to do."

"He's right," Simone said, trying to make sense of everything. "I couldn't do anything. I think I cut my back up—"

"You did— well, he did," Estelle said, becoming angry again.

"What all happened after I passed out?"

"Well…Doc said you have a concussion, pulled out the bullet and all the glass, gave you some meds and sewed up everything that needed it. Then we brought you here, and Sandra offered to take the kids to their house until we got you upstairs and hooked up for the transfusion. She took Mya home a few hours ago. Doc left around ten, he'll be back tomorrow."

Joel turned on another light and said, "Should I call him?"

Simone nodded, then rubbed his throbbing head again. Joel dialed and after several long seconds said, "Sorry to bother you, sir. He's awake and talking… yep… Got it." Joel hung up and looked at Simone. "He says you're taking a week off and you're to take it easy. He's on his way."

"Thanks, Joel," Simone said, wincing as he shifted again.

Joel looked up and said, "Oh, Al stopped by just after eight, said everything's taken care of. Libera's going to have a meeting with Gallo tomorrow to figure out what to do about Phil's books."

"Later," Simone said, angry at Joel's indiscretion.

"Oh, I think we're way past that," Joel said, nodding towards Estelle, who looked away from Simone's quick stare.

"What the hell's going on?"

Estelle continued to avoid looking into his eyes, knowing that she'd never been able to say no to them.

"Estelle?"

She shook her head and looked to Joel, who said, "Don will explain when he gets here."

Simone looked at Estelle, wanting to speak, but then closed his eyes again.

"You need to lie back down," she said. "Come on."

She helped him back down onto his pillow, barely turned onto his right side to alleviate the pressure in his back.

"Someone needs to tell me what's going on."

Just as the last words left his lips, they heard the front door close, Libera's keys hitting the table and rushed footsteps on the stairs.

"I'm fucking serious— one of you needs to—"

"Simone, I can't," Estelle said, looking into his frustrated eyes.

"Why the hell not?"

"Because I told her not to," Libera said, walking into the room.

"Sir—"

"The hell do you think you're doing?" Libera asked, watching Simone trying to sit back up. "Stay where you are. That's an order."

Simone nodded and watched Libera pull the chair that Joel had vacated for him over next to Simone.

"I'm sorry I couldn't—"

"No— I should have listened, and I didn't. That's on me. Everything that's happened to you— that's on me."

"Sir—"

"Just listen."

Simone stopped talking and looked over at his Patron, trying to make sense of what was happening.

"Do you remember me asking if you wanted to be my successor?"

"I remember," Simone replied, looking over at Joel's proud eyes and trying to ignore the anxiety starting to gnaw at his chest.

"Has your answer changed?"

"It has not, sir, I'm sorry. The last thing I want to do is disappoint you—"

Libera shook his head. "Not at all, son. But there is something I need from you."

"Of course—"

"I understand how…different… things are now. Working for me has always been a full-time responsibility, and now you've added husband and father onto the list of things to make time for. But you're the only one that can do this."

"You know I'll do whatever I can, sir," Simone said, voice still raw and raspy from the swelling in his throat.

"Should I go?" Estelle asked, looking at Libera.

"No, my dear. I want you here for this."

Simone looked at Libera and said, "May I ask—?"

"Jim Duvall is no longer with the organization."

"I'm sorry, what?"

He looked at Libera, and then over at Joel, who nodded.

"Duvall's fled the city. I was given confirmation three hours ago that he boarded a flight for the west coast."

"How did— I mean, why did—"

"As I said before, Simone, I should have listened to you. Jim Duvall's loyalty was compromised by his dislike of your father, and consequently by his hatred for you. I spent a lot of years pushing your words aside and we both paid the consequences for it— you much more so than me. For that, I apologize."

"With all due respect, sir, you've done what you thought was best."

"I have. But that doesn't mean that what seemed like what was best is what was right for the organization. Duvall intentionally put you at risk many times, including being the missing link with Salone, but I wasn't able to see that until this afternoon, thanks to Estelle."

"Oh?" Simone said, locking eyes with her as Libera went on.

"She's got a hell of a quick hand, let me tell you. But she and Joel called him out, and I am humbly grateful that they did. If there's one good thing that came from today, it was the display of loyalty, not just that you showed for me, but the people that stepped forward for you, including Al and Fabbri."

Simone sat in silence, starting to feel overwhelmed by everything that was being said.

"I need you to understand that what I'm about to ask of you is in addition to what you're already doing. You're the best, and I need to know that you'll stay that way."

"What can I do for you?" Simone asked, pain quickly thinning his patience.

"I want you to take Jim's place."

Shock was clearly etched on Simone's face, and he looked over to Estelle, who was giving him a proud smile that perfectly matched that of Joel.

"Don Libera, I'm honored, sir. But you need someone more qualified, someone with legal experience—"

"I don't need a lawyer, Simone. Gallo can find us a new lawyer. No, I need someone I trust at my side. And that's you. You'd still have your current responsibilities, but you'd have considerably more delegation power, should you choose to use it, and I'll bump up your salary up by twenty grand a year, in addition to another ten for Estelle."

Estelle looked to Simone, but his expression was just as confused as hers. "Why me?"

"Estelle, you watched me hold a Desert Eagle to someone's head today. We're well beyond the point of pretending that you don't know what goes on, but I need to assure your silence on things like this, and I'm not going to expect you to do that for free. I do need to keep it out of the books, however."

"That's kind of you, but—"

"Good." He passed over her attempt to stop him and said, "What do you say, Simone?"

"I'm honored, sir. Thank you."

Libera grinned and said, "Thank you. Get some rest. I'll be by tomorrow evening to check in after I've spoken with Gallo. We've got to move quickly to make sure Phil's absence doesn't fall back on us."

"Yes, sir."

Libera stood and put a hand to Simone's shoulder. "Enjoy your week off, Consigliere."

"Thank you, sir."

As Libera hugged Estelle and shook hands with Joel, Simone closed his eyes, still trying to absorb everything that had happened. Everything was suddenly so very different, and he wasn't close to comprehending how he felt about any of it. Once Libera had left, Simone reached out his hand for Estelle and gently pulled so he could whisper in her ear. She kissed his cheek before walking over to Simone's bloody jacket on the dresser and took out his clip, counting out the ten bills Simone had asked of her and putting it into Joel's hand, before taking Matilda from the bassinette. With a laugh, Joel said, "You know, if Libera has his way, you'll be doing this more often."

Estelle laughed and looked at Simone, who was looking back at her with unsurprised resignation. "I imagine so."

She laughed again, lying down on the bed with Matilda between them, their daughter's happy eyes looking up at Simone. Estelle took his hand into hers and said, "Let me know how that works out for him."

Made in the USA
Monee, IL
24 December 2021

86905730R00204